Back to Africa

by

Hugh Chare

Publication data

Book and Cover design by Hugh B. Chare.
ISBN: 978-1-940012-58-2

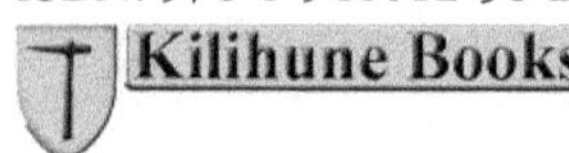

The James Martin series
African Encounter
Across the Zambezi
Just off the Great North Road
Well, there you go!
Back to Africa
The Sagitta Mishap
Carbon Copy
Flight 5 to Johannesburg

Marieke Englebrecht mysteries
Death in the Mopane
Revenge after twenty years
Death in a Bush Camp

Other books
The journal of Jan Englebrecht
British Spy in the Bushveld
Federica
First to the Cape

Preface

This is a work of fiction. Names, characters, businesses and incidents are fictional except for obvious references to historical figures, companies or events. Any resemblance in the featured characters to actual persons, living or dead, is purely coincidental.

The company James & Brown, which is featured in this work, is wholly fictional. It has no relationship with the automobile maker James & Browne, which produced cars in England in the early 1900s. There is no relationship between the fictional character, James Martin, who appears in this book and in four earlier novels, and James Martin of Martin Consultants, author of *Surface Mining Equipment*.

Namibia and Zimbabwe were still known in the period of this novel as South West Africa and Rhodesia. No conclusion should be drawn from the use of those names, other than that it was common usage in South Africa at that time. Also, since the era of this novel, many place names have been changed, as have road numbers; common usage of the 1970s has been maintained.

Contents

A new opportunity

"James, could you come down and see me?" Hank Miller asked. As Hank Miller was the Chairman and Chief Executive Officer of James & Brown, a builder of mining and construction machines, the company that James worked for, he could hardly say no. So, James dutifully descended the stairs that led to the inner sanctum that was mahogany row.

"You wanted to see me?" James asked when he arrived.

"Take a seat," Hank invited. "We'll be joined by John Williams and Fred Johnson, coffee?"

"Thank you, Sir," James replied.

"Lou, would you get some coffee for Mr Martin, what is it, James, milk, no sugar?" Hank asked.

"That would be fine, thank you," James replied. Lou was back in short order with coffee for James and another cup for Hank.

"Sorry to keep you waiting," John Williams said as he joined them, and about a minute later, Fred Johnson followed. John Williams was the Vice President of Sales for the company, and an executive director and Fred Johnson was the International Sales Manager.

"So, James, I'm sure you're wondering," Hank said. "Let's review here. You joined us at the end of February 1975, worked as an application engineer, we put you on the management training program and the Executive MBA program, that about right?"

"It is," James replied, thinking that Hank knew full well it was right.

"So, here we are now, two years later," Hank said. "You've got your MBA, you're doing well in the management development program, and now we have an opening, Fred, will you do the honours?"

"We need to replace Ben Lindstrom at J&B Africa," Fred said. "Ben has decided that he wants to go back to Stockholm and has given us notice."

"What is entailed?" James asked.

"We have the sales rep for southern Africa there, George Murphy; we also have service people based there and a parts depot," Fred replied. "We lease the land and buildings and everyone, bar George, is employed by J&B Africa. We need someone to take charge of the place, interface with customers, new and existing, schedule service calls, manage the parts inventory and keep us front and centre with the mining industry down there and work with our dealer for construction machines."

"You think you could do all that?" Hank asked.

"I'm sure I could," James said. "If I were to go, how long would it be for, who do I report to, when do I go, and of course, how much?"

"That's pretty direct," Hank laughed. "Well, how long, two years, then we'd pull you out and send someone else, unless you tell us that there is someone there who could do the job. Administratively, you report to John, who has the title VP J&B International, that covers all the subs, day-to-day, keep Fred up to date and the various product managers. When, well, Ben has given us a month's notice, we'd need to know pretty quickly if we're going to get you a visa to work there. As soon as you have a visa, we'd expect you to go and spend some time with Ben. Compensation, you're at $1,850 a month now, right?"

"That's right," James confirmed.

"Okay, so we'd bump that to $3,500 a month, plus participation in the Sales Bonus scheme, and we'd also put you into the stock option plan," Hank added.

"There is, of course, the expatriate package that helps with local housing, car, annual leave back to the US, local leave and assistance with relocation," John added.

"What about pension service?" James asked.

"No interruption," John said. "You'd still be employed by the parent, not by J&B Africa, so no worries there."

"How does the stock option plan work?" James asked.

"Essentially, we grant you the option to buy 5,000 shares of stock in the future at today's price," Hank said. "So, if the price goes up, you basically could cash in your option and pocket the difference, less tax. Of course, if the price goes down, then you would be wise to do nothing. The options mature at the rate of 20% per year, beginning on the first anniversary of the award, so next year you can exercise and realise on 1,000 shares, if the price of the stock is higher than it is today. So, we're trading now at $25.50. If a year from now we're trading at $26.50, then you could get $1,000 less tax, but you could hold onto the 1,000 shares and trade at a later date, if you think the price will go up more."

"I see," James said.

"So, what do you think?" Hank asked.

"Could I discuss this with my wife?" James asked.

"You should," Hank said. "We know that she's also employed here, so if you go off to South Africa, then you'd lose that income. We don't think it would be a good idea for her to work for you in Africa, can't have that kind of work, marital conflict possibility."

"When do you need to know?" James asked.

"As soon as possible," Hank said. "If you go, we need to start the visa process right away; if you decide not to go, then we need to find someone else."

"I understand," James said.

"If you have any further questions, then talk to Fred or John," Hank suggested. "Okay, anything else right now?"

"No, it's a lot to think about," James said. "I will have an answer for you tomorrow."

"Good, let John know," Hank said. "Okay, James, would you excuse us?"

James returned to the office he shared with Tony Whitaker, the manager of application engineering at James & Brown.

"So, what did Hank want?" Tony asked.

"Asked me if I wanted to go to J&B Africa," James replied. "I need to talk to Katrina about it, they want to know tomorrow, apparently Ben Lindstrom has handed in his notice and leaves in a month."

"You'd better call her," Tony advised. James did that and gave her the bare bones and said that they would talk about it that evening. John Williams poked his head around the door and asked Tony if he could have a minute with James. Tony left, and John closed the door.

"Come to dinner with me and Bobby," he said. "Then we can talk about this."

"Thank you," James said. "That would be a good idea."

"Good, just come straight to the house after work and we can hash through all that it means," John said. He then left and waved to Tony to go with him. James thought about it and agreed that it would be a good idea to talk to John and Roberta. They had essentially adopted James and Katrina when they had moved to Wisconsin and had become friends, the sort of friends that you take holidays with and share confidences with, particularly when it came to Katrina and Roberta. They had grown close and spent time together when James and John were away on business, as Katrina once remarked to James, misery loves company, and both she and Roberta knew what it was like to be alone and miserable when their husbands were away.

Katrina picked James up outside the office at five, and she told him that Roberta had called her and suggested that they go and have dinner with them.

"What do you think?" Katrina asked James.

"It's another big move," he said. "It's more money for me, actually, even for us it's more, they're talking about $3,500 a month, and between us now we make $3,350, and, we get a housing allowance, a car, moving expenses, a paid holiday back to the US each year, plus bonuses and I go onto the stock option plan. What happens to the degree course that you're working on?"

"I'll need to check that," she said. "But here I gather that everything is by credits and the credits might carry over."

"I'm sorry that this may interfere with that," he said.

"It doesn't matter, this is a great opportunity for you, and I think we should go. What happens to our Green Cards if we're gone that long?" she asked.

"I'll need to check to be certain," James said. "But, Ray Pierce says that what we would need to do is get a re-entry permit, and even then come back every six months, keep a bank account here, file taxes here and essentially show that we intend to live here long term."

"So, keep the house here?" she asked.

"That might not be a bad idea," he said. They were talking about the little house they had purchased earlier that year in Oak Creek. "I think, given that we probably should come back every six months, then we get the company to fund two trips a year."

"Good idea," she said. "I'll miss Bobby, that's a negative, but it's not that far to Calitzdorp to see my folks and Will and Bridget live in Jo'burg."

"Come in, come in," Roberta said when they reached her house that afternoon.

"Thanks for having us over," James said.

"You need to talk about this," Roberta said. "That's what John and I are here for."

"I don't like the idea of going away and leaving you," Katrina said.

"We'll stay friends," Roberta said. "I can come and see you, you can come back here and see us. Ah, there's John now. What can I get you to drink?"

"Just a white wine, please," Katrina said. James nodded his agreement.

"So," John said as he joined them. "Are you ready for your next big adventure?"

"I want to say yes, but what am I missing?" James asked.

"You'll be fine," John assured him. "It's only two years, and we've got some ideas about what you can do when you come back. From a money point of view, you'll do well, particularly if Katrina gets a job there as well. From an experience point of view, it's P&L experience, I know you had some of that in Zambia, but this is the whole company of J&B Africa, not just a cost centre. We'll miss having you here, but we can visit, you can visit, we don't want to lose touch."

"If I look at people's careers, does being off in Africa take me out of the possibilities that might arise?" James asked. "It happened to me at Kasalia Copper. We got back from long leave, and I was asked if I would take over the pit project because the last manager had just been killed by a hippo. So, we moved to Mkushi and ran the open pit, but when it came to review time, I was dismissed as having no real experience, and by that, they meant underground experience. It caused quite a row at the time. So now we're here again, James, we have a problem. Can you go and fix it for us? Will the same thing happen again? Your experience is not mainstream, so won't count."

"I wondered that when we went to England," John said. "The trick is to make sure we don't forget, send in reports, send in sales leads, let us know what's going on, don't be a pain in the arse, but make sure we know you're alive, but most importantly, we don't think that running one of the subs is out of the mainstream."

"What do you think, Bobby?" Katrina asked.

"As much as I don't want you to go away, you should go," Roberta replied. "It's the kind of opportunity that you don't get offered twice."

"So, if I turned it down, then I'd be looked at less favourably?" James asked.

"Sadly, yes," John confirmed.

"George Murphy was the one who first recommended me," James said. "Will it bother George that I'll be in charge, not him?"

"I don't think so," John said. "George likes being a salesman; he doesn't want to deal with accounting, parts, service, all the other stuff that goes with running the sub."

"Why does Lindstrom want to leave?" James asked.

"I think he's having a difficult time dealing with the racism that's there, he doesn't like the politics, and he's had enough," John said. "It's not an easy job; the mining companies would all like us to think that they're very progressive, but they have to work within the system, and that's not always that easy. It would be better if we could get a local guy to take over."

"There's no one?" James asked.

"You'd have to tell us," John said. "Ben hasn't told us too much."

"Where do your parents live, Katrina?" Roberta asked.

"Near a small town called Calitzdorp," Katrina replied. "It's in the Cape, about 190 miles from Cape Town, or 750 miles from Jo'burg."

"And your brother, James," Roberta asked.

"Will and Bridget live in Bedfordview, a Jo'burg suburb, it's almost halfway between Modderfontein, where the explosives factory is, and Alberton, where the paint factory is," James replied.

"Remind me, which one works in which?" Roberta asked.

"Bridget used to work at Modderfontein, and Will works at the paint plant in Alberton," James replied.

"We have to go, James," Katrina said. "It's only for two years, then we can come back here."

"She's right," Roberta agreed. "You have to go, it's a good career move."

"It is," John confirmed. "We won't forget you, isolated away there in the wilds of Africa."

"Jo'burg is hardly the wilds," James laughed. "Where's the office and the parts warehouse?"

"Germiston," John replied.

"So, not too far from Jan Smuts," James thought. "Who's our dealer for construction equipment in South Africa?"

"Consolidated Mechanical Industries, CMI for short," John replied. "They handle us plus a whole raft of other smaller companies; they handle things like concrete plants, road rollers, excavators, scaffolding, anything and everything to do with construction. Their place is not too far from ours in Germiston. They've also got branches in most of the bigger cities down there."

"Do you know if Lindstrom rented a house or if he bought one?" James asked.

"He rented," John said. "I'd do the same if I were you, get a lease on a place for two years."

"Have you spent much time in South Africa, Katrina?" Roberta asked.

"Not really," Katrina replied. "We visited a few times when I was growing up, but we never spent a lot of time there. My folks moved to Zambia when I was a baby, so all my early memories are of Zambia. We did visit my folks at their place in Calitzdorp, once when we went on long leave between contracts and last year when we left Zambia."

"We were thinking we'd keep our house here," James said.

"I'd do that," John said. "I know a property management company that will keep the place up for you if you don't want to rent it out."

"Is renting it out a good idea?" James asked.

"You can get caught by squatter laws," John said. "But if you have a good, legally binding lease agreement, then at least there's somebody in the house and you won't get vagrants and others camping out there."

"There is one other thing," Katrina said. "I've been working on a degree after hours. What happens to that?"

"Your credits will still be there, and if you start back when you come back, you can essentially pick up where you leave off," Roberta said.

"I'll check with the college and see what I have to do," Katrina said. "If I took some classes in South Africa, could I get credit for those?"

"You'd have to ask the registrar here," Roberta said.

"I'm sure you'd get credit for them," John said. "But I'd check to make sure."

"We should get something to eat," Roberta announced. "Katrina, James, you're staying for dinner and for the night?"

"That would be super, thanks," Katrina replied.

"John, you and James set the table while Katrina and I get busy in the kitchen," Roberta said.

They ate, they talked, they discussed the move, the possible future after J&B Africa, and James and Katrina agreed that they should go. John suggested that they make appointments at the South African Embassy in Washington for their work visa and with the INS, the Immigration and Naturalization Service, to get a re-entry permit. He suggested that the company call and set those interviews up for him. Both James and Katrina would need to go to Washington, as the embassy would want to see them in person. By the time they all went to bed, plans were made for a property management company to see to the house in Oak Creek, plans were made to go to Washington, and plans were discussed for the move itself. Their personal effects would go by sea, and that would take a while. Whether to fly direct from New York or to go via London was also discussed. It was all a little more complex than when they had first moved to the US from England. Then they had had no house to deal with, and their effects had been minimal.

James told Tony the next day that he had decided to take the job in Johannesburg and that he needed to go to Washington to get his work visa. Tony then fell to musing about whether or not to replace him with another application engineer. The challenge there would be finding one. Mining engineers were still in high demand, and the schools that graduated mining engineers had no bigger classes than they had had five years earlier. James called John's office and asked the secretary to pass on the message that he had accepted the position. She called back two hours later with appointment times at the embassy and with the INS, and with airline bookings for that afternoon and a hotel for that night. James called Katrina to let her know what time their flight was, and she told Fred Brock, the manager of the Parts Department, that she was going to leave the company because James was taking a position in Africa, and that she also needed to leave early that day to fly to Washington. Fred was sorry to hear that she was leaving. She had done a good job for him, but he wished her well in Africa. Before they left for Washington, James was given an appointment letter that he could show the embassy people, which named him as the putative managing director of J&B Africa, to take over the position on the 1st of May, 1977. The appointment letter included details of compensation so that the embassy officials would be happy.

The visa formalities the next day were quite straightforward. The company was sending James to run the local subsidiary, and they were going to pay him, so he would be no burden upon the state. They got work visas good for five years, and the embassy official pointed out that Katrina did not actually need a visa as she had been born in South Africa and was entitled to citizenship. The INS was, for a government agency, quite helpful, and they got their re-entry permits after explaining why they would be gone for extended periods. They disclosed that they were keeping their house, their bank accounts and would be filing tax returns in the US. James called the office and told them that he was set, so they arranged for just him to go to meet with Ben Lindstrom and start the handover process.

"How long will you be gone?" Katrina asked James as they flew back to Milwaukee.

"About a week," he replied. "Then, I'll come back and spend a week here, then we can both go, and I'll get to spend another week with Ben before he leaves."
"It all seems rather rushed," she commented.
"I think it is," he agreed. "I suppose when someone like Ben gives you a month's notice, then you have to scramble to get a replacement."
"And there's no one local?" she asked.
"I've no idea," he admitted. "Maybe that's one of the first things I should do, pick someone out and develop them for the job, to take over in two years."
"I'll take care of the property manager while you're gone," she said. "I'll get George to arrange for our stuff to be shipped, and I'll also put the car up for sale. When we come back, we'll be able to afford a new one. I'll also talk to the bank manager about arranging for our mortgage payments to be made automatically."
"Thanks," he said. "I should let Will and Bridget know that we're coming, and we should also tell your folks."
"I'll call them tomorrow," she said. "You should call Will and maybe your folks as well."
"I'll do that," he said. "Let's go out and eat tonight."
"Good idea," she agreed. "It's been a bitty day, and I don't feel like cooking."

"Hi guys, I haven't seen you in a while," said Vittoria, the waitress at the Italian restaurant that they went to.
"We moved," James explained. "We bought a house in Oak Creek."
"Well, good for you," she said. "So, what'll it be tonight?"
"What do you suggest?" Katrina asked.
"Sausage and broccoli frittata," Vittoria said. "Have that with a glass of Prosecco."
"That sounds nice," Katrina said. "Let's do that."
"I'll be back with the wine," Vittoria said. She left and was back with glasses and a bottle that she opened at the table. She poured and waited while they tasted and approved, then left the bottle with them.

"Well, here's to the next adventure," James said, raising his glass to Katrina.
"I wonder what living in South Africa will be like, where the folks are, is not like Jo'burg, it's unlikely to get bombed or have any incidents, but what about Jo'burg?" she pondered. "Maybe I should carry a gun when we're there. Do you know where Lindstrom lives?"
"No idea," he admitted. "I'll ask him when I see him. I'll also find out who he rented from."
"Will and Bridget bought, but then they were both working and they're there for the long term," she said. "I wonder how much longer they'll stay?"
"Francesca is what, two now?" he asked.
"She is, I gather from Bridget that they're planning another at some time, she told me that since she quit Modderfontein, she's been doing some freelance work," Katrina replied.
"I wonder what my folks will think of us moving to Jo'burg?" he asked.
"Probably be happy enough, because then if they visit, they can kill two birds with one stone," Katrina thought.
"Here you go, guys," Vittoria said as she brought out two plates of the frittata. "Get you anything else?"
"No, thank you, Vittoria," James said. They ate in comparative silence, enjoying the food and wine and then asked for coffee and thought more about the impending move.
"At least we'll be able to go out into the bush," Katrina said. "Kruger is close enough to Jo'burg that if there's a long weekend, then we could drive out there."
"I've never been there," James said. "Have you?"
"Once when I was small," she replied. "But, I don't remember much about it."
"We should ask Will and Bridget, I'm sure they've been out a few times, and if not them, we know your folks took mine there a couple of years ago," James said. "Are we done? Should we go home?"
"I'm ready," she said. James waved to Vittoria, who came and collected money, then they left.

James packed his bag, and Katrina took him to the airport to catch his early flight to New York. He would have a short layover in New York and then on to Johannesburg. That was a long flight, some fourteen and a half hours, all over water except the last leg over South West Africa and Botswana. In New York, he found the South African Airways counter and checked in and got his seat. The wait was not too long, and then they boarded the Boeing 747 Jumbo. He had a seatmate, a woman he guessed to be in her forties. She nodded hello and then buried her head in a guidebook of South Africa. The doors closed up and they taxied out onto the longest runway that the Kennedy airport boasted, all 14,511 feet of it. With a full fuel and passenger load, they would need the long runway to get off the ground safely and into the air. They were flying into the afternoon and night and would arrive in Johannesburg early the next afternoon. It seemed to James as they lumbered down the runway that they would never take off, but they finally did and climbed out over New York, turning to head east. Once they had levelled off, the crew set about their duties, and one came to the seat where James was.

"*Goeie môre, Mevrou, Meneer, wil jy iets hê om te drink*, good morning, Madame, Sir, would you like something to drink?" she asked.

"Scotch and soda, please," the woman next to James said.

"Net bietjie tee asseblief," James replied. "How long is the flight today?"

"Captain Cillie told us fourteen hours and twenty-five minutes," the stewardess replied.

"You speak the lingo?" the lady next to James asked.

"Only some," James admitted. "Is this your first trip to South Africa?"

"It is," she confirmed. "Claudine Williams, I'm a wine buyer so I'm going on a tour of wineries in the Cape Province, and you?"

"James Martin, I've been before a couple of times," James replied. "I work for a company that builds mining machines."

"Like in diamond mines?" she asked.

"Some are used in surface diamond mines," James confirmed. "Others in iron and coal mines."

"Here we are, Madame, Scotch and soda, and Sir, tea, milk and sugar with that?" the stewardess asked.

"Just milk, please," James asked.

"My name is Maryke. If I can get you anything, please let me know," the stewardess said.

"So this is a long flight," Claudine said. "Hopefully, I'll be able to sleep a bit. I guess I have to take another flight when we get there, to Cape Town."

"That would make sense," James said. "The major wine districts are in the Cape and start not far from Cape Town. Will you be met in Cape Town?"

"The guy who put the tour together is going to meet me and drive me around for the next three weeks," she replied. "It looks like a packed schedule."

"My in-laws run a small winery not far from Oudtshoorn," James said. "They make a dessert wine."

"What grape?" she asked.

"The hanepoot grape, it's a variety of Muscat grapes," James replied.

"That's not on my list," she said. "Should it be?"

"Only if you're in the market for dessert wines," James said. "I doubt if there's any on this flight, so you won't be able to try any before you get there."

"Let's find out," Claudine suggested. She pressed the call button, and Maryke came over.

"Madame?" she asked.

"Say, do you have any, what's it called again, James?" Claudine asked.

"Hanepoot," James said.

"That's it, hanepoot, you have any on this flight?" Claudine asked.

"I'm sorry, Madame, we don't have many requests for hanepoot, so we don't carry it," Maryke replied. "I'm sure you will be able to find some when we get to Johannesburg."

"Maybe I'll go to this place of your in-laws, James, where it is again?" Claudine asked.

"Calitzdorp, it's a small town west of Oudtshoorn," James explained.

"Oh, I'm from Oudtshoorn," Maryke said. "Calitzdorp is a pretty little town in the mountains, Madame. If you can fit it into your schedule, then it's worth a visit."

"What else is around there?" Claudine asked.

"Oudtshoorn is famous for ostrich farms," Maryke replied.

"Can I get ostrich handbags and things?" Claudine asked.

"You can indeed, Madame," Maryke confirmed. "May I offer you the menu for dinner tonight, please look it over, and we'll be by later to serve you with your preferences."

"She's nice," Claudine said, as Maryke went to see to other passengers. "Have you lived in South Africa, James?"

"No," he said. "We lived in Zambia, two countries north over the Limpopo and Zambezi rivers."

"Zambia, what was that?" she asked.

"Northern Rhodesia until independence in 1964," he replied.

"Worth a visit?" she asked.

"For wine, no, for safaris and game viewing, yes," he replied. They were interrupted by Maryke, who came by with a food trolley and served them from her cart, carving meat and serving vegetables from tureens.

"This is service," Claudine commented as they ate.

"It beats North Central," James agreed.

"The Blue Goose, I used to fly them before I moved to LA," she said. "You're right, this beats the Blue Goose."

After dinner, Maryke cleared everything away and then offered blankets and pillows. James put his seat back as far as he could and tried to get some sleep. He must have succeeded because he was awakened by Maryke tapping him lightly on the shoulder.

"We have about ninety minutes before we land. Would you care for some breakfast?" she asked.

"Thank you," James said. He excused himself to Claudine and climbed past her to visit the bathroom. Refreshed, he came back to find a breakfast setting already there and Maryke poised with tea and coffee pots. He opted for coffee.

"It looks pretty dry out there," Claudine commented.

"It is," James confirmed. "We cross the Kalahari Desert before going into Johannesburg."

"What's the weather going to be like?" she asked.

"We're going into winter," he replied. "So, the days will be a little cooler and dryer. The cold months are May and June. You may see some snow on the mountains in the Cape."

"May I take everything?" Maryke asked. "We need to prepare the cabin for landing."

The plane descended and made some turns, and James could see the buildings and yellow dumps that bespoke Johannesburg. The yellow dumps being from the gold mines, the reason Johannesburg existed. On the ground and at the gate, people wasted no time in leaving the plane.

"Enjoy your trip," James said to Claudine.

"Thanks," she replied. James left the plane and walked quickly into the terminal, and the line at immigration quickly grew. James passed through easily enough, then had only a short wait before his bag appeared. Outside, he saw a man with a J&B sign.

"Ben?" he asked.

"James, welcome to Jo'burg," Ben replied. Ben led the way to the car park and opened the doors and the boot. James deposited his bag, then climbed in the front. Ben drove out, paid their way, then took off for Germiston, making small talk as they went, about the flight, the weather and the traffic. At the facility, there was a gate guarded by a uniformed man.

"Security service," Ben commented. "Never quite sure whether they protect us or tip off the villains. Anyway, thanks for coming, let's take a coffee and I'll fill you in." After they had got coffee, they sat in Ben's office and went through the organisation, the people, the customers and the financials. At least at a high level, James would delve further in the coming days. Ben suggested that they bring in George Murphy to talk about the sales potential for mining machines.

"James, hi," George said. "Didn't expect to see you so soon."

"You know each other?" Ben asked.

"James was never a customer, but I did call on him a few times when he was in Zambia," George explained.

"Oh, so you know Africa?" Ben asked James.

"I wouldn't go that far," James said. "I worked in Zambia and then went to the States to J&B."

"So, give James an idea of the current customers and the potential," Ben said to George. George did just that, he gave a quick synopsis of the markets, the players and their participation. It largely followed what James had expected: iron, coal, copper and diamonds in South Africa, diamonds in Botswana, Angola and South West Africa, copper in Zambia and various and sundry small operations in Rhodesia. Coal was the growth market, but there were still opportunities with iron and diamonds. Copper was always there, but was in the doldrums with a depressed market. George enumerated those sales that they had lost lately, draglines, drills and shovels and gave his assessment as to why they had lost the sales. Ben added his comments, but added little to what George had said.

James then asked about parts and service, and Ben went through the situation quickly. They had a warehouse full of parts, some of which had not moved in ten years, and they had a backlog of parts orders waiting to be filled. Service was a little different; they had some service engineers and technicians, but they relied heavily on people coming from Didcot, the British subsidiary headquarters, or Oak Creek. Accounting and administration were in the hands of a relative newcomer, but both George and Ben seemed to think that he was competent. Ben then gave James a tour and introduced him as the new Managing Director of J&B Africa, a grandiose title James thought for running a place with thirty people. They took a break for a short lunch, then returned to talk about parts and service for the rest of the afternoon.

Ben offered to take James to dinner, but James declined and told Ben that he was going to have dinner with his brother. That led to more discussion about what his brother did. James set things up to spend time with each department the next day, starting with Ben to talk about housing, cars, personnel and other issues, then George, then rotating through parts, service and accounting. He could already see that he would have his hands full. At five, Will stopped by the facility and collected James.

"So, how are you?" he asked. "How's Katrina? When do you actually move here?"

"I'm fine," James said. "Katrina's doing well, what about you and Bridget and Francesca?"

"We're all fine, delighted that you'll be here. I've moved up a bit in paints, so we're comfortable even though Bridget doesn't have her regular salary any more," Will said. "So, where are you going to live?"

"Don't know yet," James said. "We get a housing allowance, so we're looking to rent for two years, then we'll go back to the States."

"Sounds as if J&B is pretty generous," Will commented.

"Only because I'm coming out to run the office here, if I were just an engineer, then they'd give me the minimum necessary, but not the package I'm on," James said. "I'm supposed to take over officially on May the 1st, so we'll be out a week or so before that."

"If you want to stay with us until you find a house, that'd be fine," Will offered. "We've got plenty of room."

"Thanks, how did the company deal with Bridget when she told them she was pregnant?" James asked.

"Not well," Will said. "When she finally told them she was pregnant the senior managers and personnel wanted to fire her then and there, saying what you'd expect, this is what you get for hiring women and so on, but the operations management rallied and told the senior blokes that if she went, they went, so an accommodation was reached, and she worked until she was eight months, then she quit."

"I suppose it will be a while before women are treated as equals in the workplace," James lamented. "J&B is a little better, but I'm not so sure sometimes."

"Okay, here we are," Will said as they pulled up to a gate, topped with barbed wire and spikes.

"Sad to have to live like this," James said.

"It's not too bad," Will said. "But, it will get worse. The government shows no sign of changing, so the anti-government actions will get more aggressive as time goes on. Anyway, come on in."

"James," Bridget said. "Lovely to see you, how's Katrina?"

"She's fine," James replied. "We're getting organised to move here. How's Francesca?"

"Growing like anything," Bridget said. "I'm busy with her and the odd piece of work I get in as a freelancer."

"We should introduce you to our friend, Bobby, she's a polymer chemist and consults and charges an arm and a leg for her time," James said. "Most of her work is in textiles; you'd like her, Katrina does."

"I'm looking forward to getting to know both of you a little better," Bridget said. "It struck me when you called and told us that you were moving here, that I'd met you both briefly in England before we got married, and then again briefly when you left Zambia and came south to get the boat to Southampton, so now that you'll be here for two years I can actually get to know you."

"You're right, you can help us in the short term by telling us where the shops are, who your doctor and dentist are, all those mundane things that we just went through in the States," James said.

"Does Katrina plan to work when you're here?" Bridget asked.

"She may," James said. "She's been working for J&B in Parts, but they told us that she couldn't work for J&B Africa, as she'd be working for me, so she may look for something; she has a work permit, so she can if she wants."

"Will, start dinner while I take care of Francesca, please," Bridget said.

After she had left the room, Will got a couple of beers from the fridge and gave one to James, then set about cooking dinner.

"How long do you think you'll stay with the paint chaps?" James asked.

"For a while yet," Will replied. "We've been toying with the idea of moving to Botswana and going into the safari business. We're thinking maybe 80 or 81, so three or four more years here. We've been putting everything we can aside so that we'll have enough to do it. Bridget has been researching the business and who's currently there and who's the market."

"It's a risk," James said. "You've got a family now, so think about it carefully."

"Don't worry, we will," Will said. "Now, get me another beer, would you, while I work the stove here?"

"I should call Katrina," James said after dinner.

"Go ahead," Will said.

"James, you made it. How are Will, Bridget and Francesca?" Katrina asked.

"They're doing fine," he replied. "They're even thinking of another baby."

"Your folks will be happy, another grandchild, keep them off our backs," Katrina laughed.

"It will," he agreed.

"So, how is J&B Africa?" she asked.

"I'm not sure," he said. "I get this undercurrent of dissatisfaction that I can't quite put my finger on yet. We'll see what tomorrow brings. It's a quiet place, no chit-chat or laughter, there's something not quite right."

"How is Jo'burg?" she asked.

"Getting cooler," he said. "It's really rather nice outside just now, it hasn't got cold yet."

"Could I talk to Bridget for a minute?" she asked. James handed the telephone to Bridget, and he and Will listened to one side of the conversation. It seemed to dwell mostly on houses and where to live and how much one might expect to pay for what and where. Bridget handed the telephone back to James.

"I should let you get to bed, you're probably jet-lagged," Katrina said.

"I am a bit," he admitted. "I love you, Sweetie."

"Love you too, sleep well," she replied.

Problems

Will dropped James at the J&B offices the next morning at seven. The security guard let him in after James showed him his business card that clearly showed J&B. That bothered James a little; anyone could print up cards with a name and logo on them. He thought that admittance after or before regular hours should be with a badge, not totally secure, he admitted to himself, but a little more so than just a card. There were people in the parts warehouse, and James introduced himself. The parts manager, Kevin Bennet, arrived and introduced himself, so James took the opportunity to ask about parts sales, inventories, slow and fast-moving parts and obsolete parts. Kevin took him to a back corner of the warehouse and showed him parts that had been stocked when the company had been first created, and that were still there, not having moved in over ten years. James asked how much value was tied up in those parts and was horrified to learn the amount. He put that on his list of things to address. At eight, James went to the office part of the facility and waited for Ben to arrive. While he was waiting for Ben, he met Charlize van Deventer, who worked for Ben and also fielded calls that came in. Ben showed up at about eight-thirty.

"Good morning," Ben said. "Sleep well in spite of the jet lag?"

"I did, thank you," James replied. "But I was up early this morning, so got my brother to drop me off."

"So, let's take a coffee each and get started," Ben said. "What do you need to know?"

"I think I'd break it up into two items," James said. "First, living here, houses, doctors, insurance, driving licence, all that sort of thing, and second, who's on the payroll, what do they do, what kind of revenues do we generate, and what kind of assets do we have tied up here?"

"Okay, living here, I leased a house for a year, then renewed it. The owner has no interest in continuing the lease," Ben started. "So, you'd have to find your own place. I can give you a list of doctors and such, but Leon, who is our accountant and office manager, can probably give you a better list. Leon can also help you with insurance companies and banking. You can get a South African Driving Licence easily enough; there's an office here in Germiston. Go early, when they open; they tend to get a bit backlogged by the middle of the day. For payroll and the accounting items, it would be better if we had Leon here."

"That's fine," James agreed. He waited while Ben went to Leon's office and brought him back.

"Leon, this is James Martin; he's the man Oak Creek sent to replace me," Ben said. "James, I have some shipping issues to attend to moving my effects back to Stockholm. Can I leave you with Leon?"

"Of course," James said. They watched Ben leave, then Leon commented that Ben had already left, in his mind at least. James was afraid of that and realised that he needed to be there as soon as possible.

"So, what can I tell you?" Leon asked.

"Where did you work before joining us?" James asked.

"I was the general accountant for one of our competitors in the construction machinery business," Leon replied.

"So, you know that side of the business," James said. "Did they sell much into the mining industry?"

"A few top-end machines," Leon said. "But they weren't really a major player."

"But at least you know what a backhoe is and a crane," James said.

"I do," Leon laughed. "Now, what can I tell you about us here?"

"Let's go through the payroll, and you can tell me who we have, what they do, how long they've been here and if you think they're likely to leave in the next month or so?" James suggested.

"George," Leon said. "George is talking about retiring, so we'll need to replace him now now."

"George is not on our payroll, is he?" James asked.

"No, he's employed by J&B International, but I think we could do as well with someone from here," Leon said. "We get back charged for George from Oak Creek, and that's not cheap. There's another issue: the lease on this place is up on the 1st of July, and we either have to renew, at a much higher rate, or move. I've been looking around and there's a nice place in Isando that's got more yard space, more space under roof, it's got workshops, with cranes, everything that we would need, and it's the same as we're paying now, they do want a ten-year commitment."

"Can we take a look tomorrow?" James asked. "If it's the same price for more space, why hasn't Ben moved?"

"He's checked out," Leon said, in disgust.

"So, if we take the new place, we'll have two months to plan and execute a move, which shouldn't be too difficult," James thought. "How would a move affect everyone here? Would they have further to travel?"

"Some yes, some no," Leon said. "Isando is easy enough to get to, and it's close to Jan Smuts. I don't think there'd be a big issue."

"Do we have a solicitor here that we use for leases and such?" James asked.

"*Ja*, Koot Oesthuizen, he's not bad, reasonably priced and gets on with it," Leon said.

"Okay, I'll call Oak Creek as soon as they open and talk to John Williams. What do our funds look like? Does the lessor of this place in Isando want money up front?" James asked.

"I'm sure that's up for negotiation," Leon said. "I think with a ten-year commitment, then they won't push for much."

"What about here? Do we have to return it to the original condition?" James asked.

"No, but any tenant improvements become the property of the lessor," Leon explained. "I think he has plans for here and pushed the rates up to get us to leave."

"So, if we moved to Isando, where should I live?" James asked.

"Edenvale, or somewhere around there," Leon said. "You could go high-priced and go to Houghton or one of the northern suburbs, but if you're not going to buy, why do that? I've been looking at what's available to lease and have a list here, properties in Kempton Park, Eastleigh, Edenvale, and a few other places."

"Thanks, Leon," James said.

"Are you married?" Leon asked.

"I am, Katrina Englebrecht, folks live in Calitzdorp, but she grew up in Zambia," James replied.

"Ag, n Boere meisie," Leon joked.

"Ja, regte,Boere meisie," James replied.

"Kan jy Afrikaans praat?" Leon asked.

"N bietjie," James said.

"What did she do in Zambia?" Leon asked, switching back to English.

"Her folks had a transport business; they moved mining equipment and other heavy stuff," James explained.

"And they sold up, left and moved to Calitzdorp," Leon mused.

"Do you have copies of P&L statements and balance sheets?" James asked.

"I do," Leon said. "This is the last annual, this is last month's. We're in the black, but we've got assets on the books that have been sitting there forever."

"I saw some of that," James said. "I talked to Kevin this morning and he showed me."

"We need a plan," Leon said.

"That's apparent," James said. "I see Ben's back, give me a few minutes with him, would you?"

"How did things go with Leon?" Ben asked.

"Fine," James said. "Ben, would you object if I asked the managers here to work on some projects for me?"

"Go ahead," Ben said. "I've got plenty to do with my move."

"Would you be prepared to let me take over now?" James asked.

"That would be fine," Ben said. "I've no interest in working out my notice here."

"Okay, if you'll give me your keys and badge, I'll take over as of now, and you can spend your time attending to your move," James said. "Is the car the company's?"

"It is," Ben confirmed.

"When you've cleaned out your desk, I'll have someone drive you home," James said.

"Thank you, you know this is a relief, there are things coming up that I know I should have been dealing with, but I've just got no interest," Ben admitted. "I don't need much from this office, give me a box and five minutes and I'll be ready to go." James watched as Ben packed the few items that he wanted, then asked Charlize to drive Ben home and come back immediately, as there were items to review. She took off with Ben, and James noted that she really did take off; she was an aggressive driver and sped out of the car park as though she were being pursued. James hoped that Ben survived the journey.

James then called together the managers of the various departments and told them that as of that day, he had taken over. He told them that the first task was to find a new facility. He told them that he would be looking at the site in Isando and asked them to put together a plan to move everything by mid-June. He also asked Kevin to give him a list of those parts that had lingered for over seven years and what machines they were for and who had those machines, and where they were. Charlize returned partway through the meeting, and James gave her the task of getting new business cards and stationery, should they decide on the move. By lunchtime, there was chatter and laughter, something that James had noted was absent when he had first arrived. At two in the afternoon, he called Oak Creek to talk to John Williams.
"James, what's up?" John asked.
"I've taken over," James said. "I walked Ben out; he'd retired in place, and there are things that need attending to. Are you aware that the lease on our site is up in a couple of months and the renew rate is considerably higher than the current rate?"
"No, I wasn't aware of that," John said.
"I'm going to take a look at a place in Isando tomorrow that's bigger, got more yard space and more under-roof space and is the same price that we're paying now. The only drawback, if it is one, is that they want a ten-year commitment," James said.
"I think you should do what you think is best for the company," John said.

"Okay, then if the site is as advertised, we'll be moving in mid-June," James said. "There's also an issue with slow-moving and obsolete parts; we've got quite a bit on the books that I think should be cleaned up."
"Let me know what the damage is," John said.
"There may be a P&L hit," James said. "I'll try and unload them at a discount to the machine users, so the hit could be the difference in the realised sale to the initial acquisition cost, if we sell at below cost. We'll talk about it before I do anything."
"Apparently, we needed to keep a closer eye on what was happening there," John commented. "Perhaps it's time to take a look at Brazil and Australia."
"That's your problem," James laughed. "I'll have my hands full here."
"Keep me in the loop," John said. "You've got carte blanche, just don't go out a buy a plane or anything wild."

James drove himself to Will and Bridget's house and pulled up to the gate, and hooted. Will came out to see who it was and let James in.
"They let you take the car?" Will asked.
"I took over today," James explained. "The chap who's here had resigned all responsibility in his mind and was doing nothing of value, so I suggested that I could take over if he wanted, and he jumped at the chance."
"Will you still go back to the States?" Will asked.
"I will," James said. "I'm going to give the managers here projects to work on for the next week or two, so they'll have plenty to do and some direction, which may be even more important."
When James called Katrina that night, he gave her all the news and told her what he had done. She was not surprised; she could not see him waiting in the wings for Ben to go.
"Are you still coming home at the end of the week?" she asked.
"I am," he confirmed. "The next couple of days will be busy, but I'll leave all the managers here with specific things that need doing."
"I've got the house sorted out," she said. "I've also sold the car and hired us a cheap one until we leave. I made arrangements with the bank to have our mortgage payments made automatically. George sent

chaps in to pack our stuff to ship it, and I checked into the hotel until we leave. I don't think there was anything else pressing, was there?"

"Not that I can think of," he said. "I'll call tomorrow, I love you."

"Love you, sleep well," she replied.

James and Leon drove to Isando and met with the leasing agent. They toured the site and agreed that it was suitable. It had office space, more than enough for the people they had; it had warehouse space and workshop space, and there was quite a bit of open space, or there would be if all the junk and scrap were gone. It had plenty of power, with a 6.6 kV supply and a small substation to reduce that to 480 and 240 volts. It had water and sewer, and looking at the site, it looked as if it would drain well, so no issues with flooding in the rains. James told the agent that they would be signing the ten-year lease and that Leon would be the company representative. When they left, James suggested to Leon that he go with the solicitor they used and negotiate the final terms of the lease, and then hire a lorry and a crane with a cactus grab and remove and sell all the scrap and junk that was on the site. The agent had given them a site map, so back at the office, James called in the managers and asked them how they would lay everything out. That started some discussion, but agreement was reached to the satisfaction of all. He then gave them the bad news: all of them would be spending time at the new site, cleaning the place up, painting, and generally getting things ready to move in. He told Kevin to start packing the parts that they had and to record how many of each number, and to decide how he would shelve them in the new warehouse.

James asked Leon to contact the local IBM people and get a System 370 computer leased, and he would bring data from Oak Creek on parts usage by machine. He asked the team to put together a comprehensive list of machines sold into southern Africa, and whether those machines were still operating, and if so, where. Although there seemed like a lot to do, the team were excited about it. They had a new lease on life, as it were, and looked forward to the move and a new way of looking at things. Little bits started to come out in dribs and drabs about Ben, he had not liked the job from the outset, and provided little direction, but seemed more interested in wining and dining his favourite customers. James thought that he would spend a couple of days just spending time with the managers and finding out more about them and the way that they managed things.

On Thursday, James asked George to go to lunch with him; he wanted to find out if Leon's views were well-founded.

"So, George, how are you?" James asked.

"Well enough," George replied. "I'm getting tired, James. I've put my years in, I'm thinking of calling it quits soon."

"When?" James asked.

"I was thinking of the end of June," George said. "I'd like to move to Durban and get away from the cold winters here."

"Who do I replace you with?" James asked.

"That depends," George said. "If you have a free hand, then I'd put Piet Kruger in the job. He's fairly new, but he knows the industry, he knows most of the customers, unlike me; he speaks Afrikaans, which helps at times. If it's up to Oak Creek, then your guess is as good as mine."

"What's Piet's background?" James asked.

"He was in the Northern Rhodesian Army, up until Independence," George said. "Then he came back south, worked for a couple of companies selling machines, construction and mining. He's got a head on his shoulders and can think, oh, and I think he told me that he's got a Brit passport, makes travel easier."

"What happened with Ben?" James asked.

"I was never quite sure," George admitted. "He seemed happy enough to take the job here, but then he seemed to distance himself from everyone, lost interest in the job and just coasted along for the last year. He probably should have left sooner."

"So, if I put Piet in, will you help him?" James asked.

"Be happy to," George assured him.

"We've had a few losses in sales lately. What happened?" James asked.
"I think a combination of things," George replied. "I've looked at all the sales we've lost over the past five years, and it's not price or even delivery, it's the parts and service relationship with the customers. They don't get the impression that we're going to be there to support them. I lay that mostly at Ben's door; he just wanted to wine and dine his mates and never took the time to set any clear direction."
"So, some fence-mending to do?" James asked.
"Some," George agreed. "And we need a clear direction as to where the company, and I mean J&B Africa, not James & Brown, is going."
"Bigger question," James said. "If I leave here in two years, who here can I put in charge?"
"Leon," George said. "The others all look up to Leon. He knows the numbers, he's picked up a lot of the business, you coach him over the next two years and he'll do a good job for you."
"Not Kevin, Piet, Hansie or Frank?" James asked.
"They'd all do an adequate job, but for a good job, I'd pick Leon," George replied. "He might be fairly new to the company, but he's a smart chap; he picks things up easily and quickly."
"Thanks, George," James said. "I'll keep that in mind."

Back at the office, James met with each of the managers in turn to learn a little about them and what their aspirations might be. He also gave them each some projects to do, not all to do with their area of responsibility. He explained this by telling them that he wanted them to understand the business that they had, in all its aspects. Finally, he had Charlize drive him to collect his bag from Will and Bridget's house and then had her drop him at the airport. He had plenty of time to wait as the plane did not leave until after nine that night. While he waited, he read through the past monthly reports that Ben had sent in to Oak Creek. Six months earlier, there had been a very brief mention of the impending lease renewal issue, but it was never mentioned again. Ben focused on the market and talked about the customers, most of which James concurred with. It seemed to James that Ben had seen himself as more of a salesman than the manager of a subsidiary.

When they finally boarded, James was greeted by Maryke, who had been on the flight on his way to Johannesburg.
"Mr Martin, lovely to see you again," she said.
"Nice to see you, Maryke," he echoed.
"Did you have a good visit?" she asked.
"Busy," he said. "I'll be back in about a week."
"There's no one next to you tonight," she said. "So, take your pick of the seats."
"Thank you," he said. "What do you do in New York, turn around and come back the same day, or layover until the next day?"
"We layover," she said. "It's a little much to come back so soon after the long flight there. Excuse me, I have to get things set up in the galley."
James looked around the cabin, and it was about half full. He was surprised; he would have thought that the plane would be full. They closed up and took off, and he returned to his reading of the monthly reports.
"You seem engrossed," Maryke commented as she came to his seat.
"Just some reports that I need to read," he said.
"What may I bring you to drink?" she asked.
"I was thinking of a Sauvignon Blanc," he said.
"We have an excellent one from Stellenbosch," she said. "I'll bring you some." She did, and James tasted it and agreed, it was excellent. She made the rounds of the other passengers and came back to James.
"Another?" she asked.
"Not just yet," he said. "Perhaps with dinner."

Dinner was served from the cart, and he picked another wine to have with dinner, a Nederburg Cabernet Sauvignon. After dinner, Maryke cleared away all the dishes and glasses and brought blankets and pillows. James was grateful for that and settled down to try and sleep. Sleep was interrupted by the plane landing, not in New York but on Sal Island, a speck of rock in the Cape Verde Islands in the middle of the Atlantic, where westbound South African Airways planes would stop for fuel. Passengers were not allowed off the plane and had to remain in their seats. Refuelling done, they were off again, next stop New York. James must have dropped back off to sleep because he was awakened by Maryke telling him that they were ninety minutes out and asking him if he wanted breakfast. That sounded like a good idea, so James ate, drank tea and gazed out of the window at the dawn. When they landed, it was light, but early, and the Kennedy airport had yet to get busy, so clearing immigration and customs was quite quick. James checked his bag back in with North Central, then went looking for his gate. He had about an hour to wait, so he found some coffee and sat and watched people. It was always fascinating to imagine what they did and why they were flying. His flight boarded, and they took off, then headed west towards Milwaukee. The weather was awful: rain, wind, and probably even hail. But eventually they climbed above it, and the plane settled down, and James could look down on most of the clouds, but once in a while they flew through columns of clouds that went up to thunderheads that probably reached 40,000 feet or higher. The weather improved over Detroit, and by the time they crossed Lake Michigan, the clouds disappeared and the sun shone. Katrina met James at the gate, and he had her drop him at the office, with the promise to pick him up early at four.

"So, how was the trip?" Tony asked.

"Busy, enlightening, troubling," James replied. "We should have been paying closer attention to what Lindstrom was saying and doing."

"John asked for you to go down and see him as soon as you got in," Tony said.

"I'd better go then," James said. He went downstairs to the executive offices and had to wait a few minutes until John was done with a meeting.

"So, James, tell me about J&B Africa," John said.

"Lindstrom had checked out already," James said. "He was giving no guidance to the managers there, so I asked him if he minded if I took over from him, and he jumped at the suggestion."

"Is that why we've been missing sales down there?" John asked.

"That and the fact that he gave no clear direction to his parts and service people, so the customers didn't give us much of a weight when it came to evaluating bids, we were on the money for price and delivery, but came up short on after-sales support," James explained.

"What other problems do we have down there?" John asked.

"As I told you when I called, we need to move. The new rates on the lease we had are absurd, and the new place is bigger for the same price as the previous rates," James explained. "We're putting together a plan now to have everything moved by mid-June, and we vacate the Germiston site on the 30th of June."

"Okay, sounds good," John said. "Anything else?"

"George Murphy wants to retire at the end of June as well," James replied.

"Who do we put in there?" John asked.

"The people there think that a young chap we have by the name of Piet Kruger would do a good job for us," James replied. "I met him and talked to him, and I'd agree. Whose decision is that?"

"Good question," John said. "Let's get Fred and talk about it."

John called Fred and asked him if he would join them. While they waited for Fred, John got coffee for both him and James, then they sat and waited.

"John, you called?" Fred asked as he came into the office.

"Hi Fred, coffee?" John offered.

"No thanks, had my ration for the day, hi James, how was Africa?" Fred asked.

"Interesting," James replied. "I took over from Ben while I was there; he'd essentially resigned in place and wasn't providing any direction for the people there."

"But, you weren't supposed to take over until the first of the month," Fred protested.

"I did what I thought necessary," James said. "There were a couple of issues that came up while I was there. We're moving locations, and we have to talk about a replacement for George Murphy."

"Why, what's wrong with George?" Fred asked belligerently.

"He wants to retire to Durban at the end of June," James replied. "I had lunch with him and he told me that he's retiring. So, the question is, who do we replace George with?"

"Why are we moving?" Fred asked.

"The lease is up for renewal on the 1st of July, and the lessor has given us a new rate that is considerably higher than the current rate," James explained. "We can get a new site in Isando that's bigger than our current site for the same money we're paying now."

"Why didn't Ben warn us of that?" Fred asked.

"With the benefit of hindsight, he did, after a fashion," James said. "I read through his monthly reports for the past year, and last September he made an off-hand comment that the landlord is proposing a new base lease rate of two Rand per square foot, which doesn't mean much until you compare it to the rate we're actually paying now, which is one Rand five."

"How did I miss that?" Fred asked.

"As I said, it was just a comment buried in a lot of other administrative things," James said. "I only found it because I was looking for it."

"Well, I hope you keep us better informed," Fred said.

"I intend to," James assured him. "Now, about replacing George?"

"I haven't got anyone in mind that I'd move there just now," Fred said.

"Perhaps we could look at someone local?" James asked.

"We could, who do you have in mind?" Fred asked.

"Piet Kruger," James replied. "He's fairly new to the company, but he knows the market, he knows the customers, George suggested him, and when I talked to him, I was impressed."

"We should have him here for an interview," Fred said.

"We could fly him over next week," James suggested.

"Do that," Fred said. "We'll run him past everyone here. Anything else come up?"

"I'm going to recommend selling off obsolete and slow-moving parts at discounts," James said. "We've got parts in the warehouse that have been there since we opened, and we've got other parts that haven't moved in over ten years. I'm having an analysis run now of what machines would be affected, if they're in fact still in use and where they are."

"What will it mean to us for the bottom line?" Fred asked.

"We need to make up the list of the parts involved, then get from our old records what we paid for them, which will tell us what the hit to earnings would be, if we sell below cost. I think the issue has come up before, and it's always been pushed off into the future," James replied. "I was wondering what you'd think about a part sales incentive program that paid the salesmen ten cents on the dollar of every dollar over the part cost to us, but just for the parts on the obsolete and slow-moving list."

"We'll think about that and let you know. Is there anything else?" John asked.

"Not for now," James said.

"Well, then, would you excuse us?" John asked. James took the hint and left. He did not know whether Fred was going to get a raking over the coals or commiseration, and he had no intention of finding out. Back upstairs, he asked Marlys to send a telex to the Africa office telling Piet to get a flight to New York on Monday night to be in Oak Creek on Tuesday.

Katrina picked James up at four.

"So, how was your day?" she asked.

"I'm not sure if I made an enemy or not," he said. "I pointed out some issues at J&B Africa that Fred should have known about, so don't know whether or not he's mad at me."

"You'll survive," she said. "Once we're in Jo'burg you can try and make the place work well, and then give the credit, or some of it, to Fred."

"Maybe," he said. "Anyway, we've got this *ou* Piet Kruger coming for an interview next week. I like him, George likes him, so we'll see."

"Roberta asked us over tomorrow," she said. "I think she wants to spend time with us before we flit off into the sunrise."

"Where should we eat tonight?" he asked.

"Let's go to the Mexican place," she suggested. "We'll eat early, then come back to the hotel, bath and bed, and we can make up for the days we missed while you were gone."

"Do you miss working?" he asked.

"Yes, and no," she said. "I liked the job, but I've been busy organising the house, selling the car and getting our stuff packed to be shipped."

"It seems strange," James said. "We bought the house not long ago, and now we're leaving it. Should we have bought?"

"We didn't know at the time that this move was even a remote possibility," she said. "So, we made the right decision at the time. It will still be here when we get back, and we'll have somewhere to come back to."

"I asked Will and the accountant at J&B Africa where we should live, and they both suggested Edenvale," he said.

"I've no idea where that is," she said.

"It's not too far from Bedfordview," he explained. "It's sort of between there and Jan Smuts."

"What about aircraft noise?" she asked.

"I looked at a map and it's not in the approach paths of the main runways," he said. "So, I doubt that there'd be any real noise."

"When we stopped to see Will and Bridget that one time, it looked like a fortress. Are all the houses like that?" she asked.

"Those that I saw," he confirmed. "It seems that tall fences or walls with barbed wire, broken glass and steel spikes are common, as are fancy gates, even lockable gates inside the house."

"I suppose we'll get used to it," she said. "Okay, do I need to change before we go and eat?"

"No," he said. "Let's go, then we can come back and take a leisurely bath and then make up for lost time in bed."

"When did Roberta say to come?" James asked Katrina the next day.

"Any time after lunch," she replied.

"So, I've got time to mow the grass at the house?" he asked.

"Lots," she assured him. "You go and mow, and then we'll think about lunch."

James drove to their house, got out the mower, filled it with petrol, then started the back and forth of mowing the grass. He presumed that the management company would do that when they were gone, and not let the place become overgrown. As he marched up and down, he thought more and more about the riding mowers he had seen. It might be good exercise to walk up and down behind the mower, but it did take a long time to mow the acre that they had. It took him two hours to mow it all, and he had to fill the tank seven times, but there was a degree of satisfaction in getting the job done. There were also a few other little jobs to do, trimming a hedge and cutting back the lower branches of a couple of trees that he had bashed his head on as he mowed. Satisfied with his work, James put away the mower and closed up the garage and the house and went back to the hotel.

"All done?" Katrina asked.

"All done," he confirmed. "The property managers can keep the grass mowed from now on. It does look pretty, great green swaths of grass, all nicely mown, and the place smells of freshly mown grass."

"So, let's go downstairs and get some lunch, then we can drive over to Bobby's house," Katrina suggested.

"Katrina, James, come in, come in," Roberta said when they arrived at her house. "How are you? Excited to be off?"

"Excited, apprehensive," Katrina said. "Excited to be going, concerned a little about how we'll fit in over there, concerned about leaving our house, disappointed that I won't see you that often."

"The time will pass quickly enough," Roberta assured her. "James, John is in the garage working on something." James took that as a hint and went out to find John, busy with something that looked to James like a still.

"James, how are you? What do you think of my latest creation?" John asked.

"It looks like a still," James said.

"It is," John said, gleefully. "Don't go telling the Feds about me. I was going to try using the apples that we have in the fall and making some calvados."

"How many apples do you need for that?" James asked.

"The numbers I have are that 16 lbs of apples gets me 1 gallon of cider, which I can then distil down to 1 pint of booze," John explained. "I found a press, over there, that I'll use to crush the apples, then I've got that fermentation vat to make the cider, then I'll see what that's like and take some of it to make booze."

"Sounds interesting," James said. "I would like to see that, pity we won't be here when the apples come."

"I'll keep you informed," John said.

"Sorry to bring this up," James said. "But did I make an enemy of Fred yesterday?"

"No, he was annoyed at first, then we both looked at things and realised that as a company we've not been rigorous enough with our reporting, so we agreed on some changes," John said. "You'll have to live with that reporting now. Anyway, Fred is happier now, and we're taking a look at the other subs to see what we might have missed. We rely on the local guys telling us what we need to know; if they don't, it's only when something goes wrong that we find out."

"Thanks," James said. "Sorry to be a pain, but it bothered me. So, what kind of apples do you have?"

"Gold Rush," John said. "No idea why the guy planted them as they're not the best-eating apples."

"How many pounds of apples do you think you'll get?" James asked.

"About 6 to 8 bushels per tree, that's 280 to 380 pounds of apples per tree, and I've got ten trees, so 2,800 to 3,800 pounds."

"So, that will give you somewhere around 200 gallons of cider, or 25 gallons of booze," James calculated. "What are you going to do with either the cider or the booze?"

"Probably just give it away," John said. "I won't be selling it, too much red tape involved."

"Keep some for me, would you?" James asked. "I'd like to try it when we can."

"I will, I'm going to enlist Roberta to talk me through the chemistry of methanol versus ethanol and how to make sure my booze is high quality and won't send me blind. Of course, I could always add it to the gas tank of my garden tractor if it's not good to drink," John said.

“That would be expensive fuel,” James laughed.
“It would, wouldn’t it?” John agreed. “Anyway, let’s go and see what the girls are up to.”

“So, what do you think of John’s latest enterprise?” Roberta asked when James and John went back into the house.
“I don’t think I’d advertise it too much,” James replied. “But I would like to sample the product.”
“John’s going to try his hand at making cider,” Roberta explained to Katrina. “Then he’s going to take some of the cider and distil it into calvados.”
“James is right, I wouldn’t advertise that too much,” Katrina said.
“We won’t,” John assured her. “So, are you ready to go?”
“As ready as I’ll ever be,” she replied.
“James has already stirred things up,” John laughed. “Maybe we should send new people out to these places more frequently.”
“Why, what has he done?” Roberta asked.
“Well, he went there this last week, then we got the announcement that we’re going to move premises, then he’s going to replace the senior sales guy, then he’s going to fire sale slow-moving parts,” John explained.
“That’s my boy,” Roberta said. “Keep these guys on their toes.”
“What I’m afraid of is what he’ll do next,” John laughed. “Probably buy out one of our competitors.”
“Well, if he does, I’m sure there’ll be a good reason for it,” Roberta said with some finality.
“Do you think you’ll work while you’re there, Katrina?” John asked.
“I’ve no idea,” she said. “I might, just to keep myself busy, and I’m going to check on external university courses, I’ve got a copy of the curriculum, so know what courses would best fit.”
“I don’t have any homemade cider to offer you, but what about a drink?” Roberta said.
“Surprise us,” John suggested.
“I’ll do that,” she said. “If you’ll all go out onto the patio, I’ll bring drinks and snacks.”

"Cheers," John said as the glasses were passed around.

"Cheers," the others echoed.

"Have you decided where you'll live yet?" Roberta asked.

"Not yet," James replied. "We'll start looking as soon as we get there, and we'll stay with my brother until we find a place. I don't think that will take too long; the accountant already gave me a list of possible places."

"Far from your brother?" Roberta asked.

"About two to three miles," James replied. "About the same to the new location and a little farther to the airport."

"What was the flight like on South African?" Roberta asked.

"Very nice," James said. "They used to fly 707s stopping in Sal Island, but that ended last year, and now it's 747s direct, a long trip, but comfortable."

"Would you recommend them?" Roberta asked.

"Well, it's either them or go via Europe and pick up the European carriers," James replied. "I think I'd rather go direct."

"Can anyone fly South African, I mean, if you're a black African, can you fly them?" Roberta asked.

"If they can afford the ticket, there are no restrictions, but very few black South Africans could afford a ticket," James replied. "My guess is that you're more likely to find black South Africans on the various flights to Europe; there's more competition, so the fares are a little more reasonable."

"Are the South African game parks worth visiting?" Roberta asked.

"We'll let you know," James said. "I've never been to one, and the only time Katrina went, she was small and doesn't remember much about it. My guess is that they're a bit more structured than the Zambian parks, but I would think still worth a trip."

"Maybe we'll come out later in the year, and we can take a trip," Roberta suggested.

"That would be lovely," Katrina said. "I'll do some research and send you information."

"When do you think there'll be a change in government in South Africa?" John asked.

"Not for a few years yet," James said. "The current government is fairly entrenched and they have the army with them, but my guess is that over the next few years, we'll see an increase in anti-government actions, possible bombings and shootings."

"Is it dangerous for us to send you there?" John asked.

"Not at this time," James said. "I talked to my brother about it, and he gives the government another fifteen to twenty years, with increasing difficulties to be sure, but in the end, the majority will win out."

"If things start to look untenable, let us know," John said. "Business may be business, but I don't like the idea of employees in danger, be they white or black."

"I think the danger comes a lot from attitude," James said. "I never had any issues in Zambia, but there were chaps that I worked with who did, and it all came down to their approach to the workers."

"That's true," Katrina echoed. "We had good relations with all our drivers; if we had to fire one, it was because he was a bad driver and all the others knew it. I would travel on my own with them and never felt at all threatened."

"That's because they were all afraid of you, like I was," James laughed.

"What do you mean, you were afraid of me?" she asked.

"I suppose I was more afraid that I'd lose you," he admitted. "I had a hard time understanding why you stuck with me."

"Because I loved you, you idiot," she said.

"I know," he said.

"When you two lovebirds are done, maybe we could get back to talking about Africa," Roberta said. "Now, what's the weather like?"

"Now they're going into winter," James replied. "So, temperatures overnight will drop a lot, particularly in places like Johannesburg, which is high up, there could be snow on some of the mountains."

"When's the best time to go for a safari?" Roberta asked.

"Probably September," Katrina replied. "The grass is down after the dry season, it's not too hot, not too cold, animals are closer to water holes."

"So, find out, if you would, a good place to visit?" Roberta asked.

"I will," Katrina promised.

"So, James, tell me about this guy Piet Kruger," John said.

"He's a South African, but for reasons I haven't yet got answers to, he served in the Northern Rhodesian Army until independence in 1964. Then he went south and worked for a couple of equipment companies until he joined us," James replied. "He knows the market, knows the customers, is good with people, got a good head on his shoulders, he'll do well for us."

"You'd hire him?" John asked.

"If he didn't already work for us, I would," James replied. "George Murphy recommended him and said that he'd work with him until he retires."

"Okay, well, we'll run him by Fred next week and see what he says," John said. "So, enough of the office, what temperatures pull off the methanol and ethanol in my still, Honey?"

"As you bring the still up, you'll get chemicals like acetaldehyde and acetone first, but they'll come off at fairly low temperatures of 20.8 and 56.2, then you'll get the methanol at 64.7 and finally ethanol at 78.2," Roberta replied.

"So, what's that in Fahrenheit?" John asked.

"For methanol, 148 and ethanol 174," Roberta said. "Temperature control is really important, you don't want methanol if you can avoid it, 10 millilitres will blind you, 30 will kill you, but 4 to 5 parts per million is acceptable, and is, in fact, common in most commercial spirits."

"So, I should install some good devices to measure temperature?" John asked.

"I would," Roberta said. "And you will."

"That's telling you," James laughed.

"I was thinking of putting in thermocouples and tying them to the heat source, so that I could set my temperatures. The engineer in me sees the challenge," John said. "That shouldn't be too difficult."

"This sounds more like an industrial still than a moonshiner," Katrina commented.

"If you're going to do it, then you should do it right," John said.
"So, is it time for dinner?" Roberta asked.

James went to the airport on Tuesday morning and met the North Central flight that came in from New York. He saw Piet Kruger and waved.

"Piet, thanks for coming," he said.

"No problem," Piet said. "What's the rush?"

"George is retiring at the end of June, and we have to replace him," James explained.

"You think I could do the job?" Piet asked.

"I think so, George thinks so," James replied. "We're going to have you meet the people here; they'll probably want to know what you did before you joined us, how well you know our customers, and can you sell our products to them."

"I can manage that," Piet said. "There's my bag, I'm ready when you are." James drove to the office and took Piet upstairs to the sales offices. He introduced Piet and then stopped at Fred's office.

"Fred, this is Piet Kruger," James said, making the introduction. "I'll leave him with you for a while."

"I'll find you when we're done," Fred promised. James left them to it and went to do some of the things that he wanted to finish before he went back to Johannesburg. He had bought another Texas Instruments SR-52 programmable calculator, like the one that he had set up before and that Tony was now using. It had programs for machine selection that meant that given conditions could be entered and a possible solution calculated then and there. He made copies of all the programs he had written and put them with the new TI. He would explain to Piet how it worked and go through the programs with him. He also met with Herb, the computer programmer that Katrina had worked with to examine parts usage and demand and got copies of all the output that had been generated. They would help him decide what to stock in Johannesburg and which of the old parts he could safely dispose of. He also got a record of all machines shipped into southern and central Africa over the past twenty years.

Fred brought Piet back after lunch, apparently happy enough as he and Piet were chatting about potential sales of machines. James passed Piet on to Bill Evans in manufacturing for a plant tour. James and Bill worked together a lot as they were mentored in the Management Development Program by Hank Miller. That was something else that James had to collect information for and work on, the latest task that Hank had set them, the viability of entering into the bucket wheel excavator market. Bucket wheels were used extensively in Germany and Australia in the soft coal mines, and had been used in odd US mines and in other places around the world. The question was, was it an economic proposition to enter the market in competition with the big German manufacturers. That consideration had to include the potential market for machines, the engineering it would take to design a machine and the manufacturing costs, and the likelihood of beating out the big German companies for a job. Hank was not looking for an immediate answer, but wanted one within a couple of months, so James and Bill had work to do. While Piet was out with Bill, Fred came by to talk to James.

"He's a keeper," Fred said. "I've got no problems with replacing George with Piet. I've given him some things I'd like to see, so he'll be busy when he gets back."

"Should I tell him, or will you?" James asked.

"I told him," Fred said. "I told him that when George retires at the end of June, he's the mining machine sales manager for southern Africa. I'll leave compensation details up to you."

"I'll take care of that as soon as I'm back in Johannesburg," James said. He was a little surprised that Fred had not talked to him first, but then perhaps this was Fred's way of reacting to the issues that James had raised.

Bill brought Piet back at about four in the afternoon, and James let Piet go and re-introduce himself to the product managers on the floor, so that he knew who to contact if he had a viable enquiry. At five,

James collected Piet, then delivered him to the hotel with the promise that they would meet in the hotel lobby at six-thirty to go for dinner.

"So, where are we going to take this *ou* for dinner?" Katrina asked.

"I thought the Packing House," James replied.

"I'm ready," she said. They went downstairs and found Piet already in the lobby.

"Piet, my wife Katrina, Suikerbossie, this is Piet Kruger," he said by way of introduction.

"Aangename kennis," Piet said.

"Bly te kenne," Katrina said. "I gather from James that you're in the office in Johannesburg; this is a lightning trip for you."

"*Ja*, it is," he said. "But, so far it's been great. I get a new job at the end of June when George retires.

"I gather Fred told you," James commented.

"Ja," Piet said. "So, Katrina, where are you from?"

"I was raised in Kitwe," she replied.

"I was in the Northern Rhodesian Army in the Ndola Barracks until 1964," Piet said. "Then I left and went south. Do your folks still live in Kitwe?"

"No, they sold up and moved to Calitzdorp," she replied. "Now they make hanepoot, and yours?"

"My folks live in Koedoespoort," he replied. "My pa is with the railways, he's in the Mechanical Department there."

"Are you married?" Katrina asked.

"I am, Cheryl, one son, David," Piet replied. "We live in Benoni."

"We're here," James announced as they pulled up to the Packing House. He led the way, and they got a table quickly enough. Dinner was eaten over conversation about Zambia, Kitwe, Ndola, and lately Benoni. Piet was fun, and James saw that he would do well with their customers; he had the natural ability to make people feel comfortable.

"I'd like to leave at seven-thirty in the morning," James told Piet when they got back to the hotel that evening.

"I'll be ready," Piet promised.

"He seems nice," Katrina said as they went to their room.

"I think he'll do a good job for us," James said. "He knows his way around, and George promised to pass on everything he can."

"How much more do we have to do before we leave?" she asked.

"I've done everything that I need to do," he said.

"So, have I," she said. "All we need to do now is drop the keys off with the property manager, and we can go. I would like to go and say goodbye to Bobby before we go, maybe we could do that tomorrow?"

"We can," James agreed.

"When's Piet going back?" she asked.

"Tomorrow," he replied. "I'll take him to the airport and we'll see him in Jo'burg."

The move

Roberta took James and Katrina to the airport to see them off on their journey back to Africa.

"Safe travels," she said as she hugged and kissed them both. "I'll look into coming out and seeing you in September. If John can't get away and James is too busy, then perhaps you and I could take a trip, Katrina?"

"That would be fun," Katrina said. "I'll miss you, Bobby."

"I'll miss you too, both of you," Roberta said. "You should board, bye!"

"Bye, love you," Katrina said. She and James then boarded their flight to New York. They flew east into bad weather. It seemed to James that the bad weather he had encountered on his way back from South Africa was still lingering on the eastern seaboard; hopefully, it would not impact their take-off time. In New York, they checked their bags in with South African Airlines and settled down to wait for boarding.

"Mr Martin, how nice to see you again," Maryke said as he and Katrina found their seats.

"Nice to see you again, Maryke, this is my wife, Katrina," James said, making the introductions.

"I hope you enjoy your flight with us, Mrs Martin," Maryke said. "Let me know if there is anything I can do for you."

"You've seen her before?" Katrina asked.

"The flight I took over to Jo'burg and the one back," he explained. "She must fly this route a lot."

"So, what's the service like?" Katrina asked.

"I think better than TWA from London to Chicago," he replied. "It's a long flight, but at least it's direct. When they were flying 707s, it was through Rio, and then they dropped Rio, and it was stopping at Sal Island."

The service was good, lunch was served at a leisurely pace, then Maryke handed out blankets and pillows, and James and Katrina settled down to try and get some sleep. James was awake just before they crossed the coastline of Angola, and a little later, he saw the Etosha Pan out of the window. Then Maryke came around and roused the sleepers and started the breakfast service. They started their descent over Botswana and actually flew over Gaborone. They landed at Jan Smuts about half an hour early, but the ground crew was waiting for them, so there were no delays in getting a gate.

"Thank you for a lovely flight," Katrina said to Maryke as they left the plane.

"We hope you'll fly with us again soon," Maryke replied. James and Katrina joined the throng that was in the arrivals hall and wended their way slowly to the immigration desk. The man there just glanced a them, glanced at the passports, looked at the work permit stamps, then added his own stamp and waved them through. There was a bit of a wait until the bags appeared, but finally they all came, and James loaded them onto a trolley, and they went through the customs check. That was also a wave through and outside. James saw Charlize waiting for them.

"Charlize," he said. "Thanks for coming to pick us up. This is my wife, Katrina, Suikerbossie. This is Charlize van Deventer, she works for us here."

"Nice to meet you," both women said.

"You have all your luggage?" Charlize asked.

"We do," James confirmed. "I was thinking it might be an idea to stop by my brother's house first."

"That was the house we went to before?" Charlize asked.

"It is," James confirmed. Charlize led the way to the car and they loaded the bags into the boot, well, most of them, James had to sit in the back with one, while Katrina sat in the front with Charlize and chatted to her in Afrikaans. James left Katrina at Will and Bridget's house and had Charlize drive him to the office.

"Welcome back," Leon said when James went to the office. "How did things go last week?"

"No issues came up," Leon said. "As you know, Piet went to Oak Creek and is back and is huddled with George. Kevin and his *ouks* have been busy and tasking me to dig out old records for landed part costs from way back. I have here a list of possible houses you might want to look at in Edenvale and Eastleigh."

"Thanks, Leon, would you get Kevin, George, Piet and Frank for me?" James asked. The managers trooped in shortly afterwards, and James asked for an update from each of them. That took a couple of hours, but they were thorough.

"So, Kevin, I've got Oak Creek to agree to a program, all those parts we have on the list that haven't moved in over seven years, you can tell your parts sales chaps that they'll get ten cents on the Rand of every Rand we sell those parts over cost."

"So, we don't have to sell them for list?" Kevin asked.

"They haven't moved in seven years at list, let's see if we can move them at a discount," James said.

"And that's only for the parts that we've not moved in seven years?" Kevin asked.

"For now, yes," James confirmed. "If we're left with some that we just can't sell, no matter what we offer them at, let me know, anything below cost or that we have to write off will be hit for us. I've brought some data on parts sales by machine, so we can get an idea of what moves elsewhere. I've also brought a list of all machines that have been shipped here in the past twenty years. I've no doubt that some of them may have been scrapped, but I would like to know which ones are still running and where. Perhaps, Kevin, you and Frank could look through the list and tell me what's running?"

"We'll compare that to our list," Frank said. "See if we missed any."

"Oh, that reminds me, Frank, I also brought a listing of all service calls in the US for the past five years, give you some idea of what issues arise there and maybe what we could look at here for opportunities," James said.

"I'll take a look," Frank promised.

"Leon, how are we doing with the new site?" James asked.

"We signed the lease, we've been shipping scrap out as fast as we can, we've already made enough money to cover the cost of the move, cover the cost of gutting out the buildings and repainting them, and we're also looking at what we have lying around in the yard here," Leon replied. "Charlize has new stationery ready, new business cards, and we've talked to Escom and the Post Office about switching our power and telephone services. The last one is water, which is the city, but as the water is still on there, I don't think the city ever turned it off; we just need to tell them that we've moved in and arrange for the billing."

"Thanks, Leon," James said. "Is the security service here provided by us or the landlord?"

"We contract with them," Leon replied. "They'll also do the service in Isando. I've got new badges made for everyone, and we'll have badge readers for the doors that are not manned."

"Fencing and gates?" James asked.

"The fencing looks good, it's a bit more robust than the fencing here, and a little taller. The main gate could use some work, oh, and we discovered a weigh bridge by one of the buildings, I'm having that checked out."

"Thanks, Leon," James repeated. "George, Piet, what's new with sales?"

"We've got a few prospects in coal and iron," George replied. "We also got a diamond enquiry for a dragline, and another for a couple of shovels in Botswana. Some of the coal guys have asked to meet you."

"Where do we need to go?" James asked.

"To Middelburg," George said. "Most of the coal mines around Witbank are underground, but the new ones near Middelburg are all open pits. I'll set up a date and time, and we can drive out there."

"Is there anything else I should know about?" James asked. He got head shakes all around, so suggested that they meet at the same time a week hence to review things, but to see him immediately if there was something that needed his attention. That done, he confessed to jet lag and said that he was leaving for the day.

"How was your day?" Katrina asked when James arrived at Will and Bridget's house.

"Busy," he replied. "And you?"

"Lazy," she said. "Bridget and I just spent the time talking about things."

"Leon gave me a list of possible houses," he said.

"I'll start tomorrow, taking a look at them," she said. "Do you want to come with me, Bridget?"

"I might just do that," Bridget said. "Give me a chance to explore new places. Where are they?"

"Most are in Edenvale," James replied. "With a few in Eastleigh."

"Not far from here then," Bridget commented.

"I should probably also look at buying a car," Katrina said. "I can't rely on you forever to run me around."

"Have you anything in mind?" Bridget asked.

"Not really," Katrina said. "Something reliable."

"We should ask Will when he gets home," Bridget said. "He knows what's for sale. Do you want new or second-hand?"

"That depends on the price," Katrina said. "Before we do anything like that, James, we need to go and open a bank account. Bridget, who do you bank with?"

"Standard Bank," Bridget replied. "The local branch here is friendly and helpful."

"So, Katrina, James, couldn't stay away," Will commented as he joined them.

"It's only for two years," Katrina said. "Then we'll be back to the States, unless they come up with a crisis somewhere else."

"You shouldn't be so good at fixing problems, James," Will joked. "You need to be careful that you don't become Mr Fix It and get sent in wherever there's a problem."

"I don't see that as likely," James said.

"So, what are we cooking tonight?" Will asked.

"I thought we could have a *braai*," Bridget said. "You and James can cook, and we'll put some salads together and come out and join you soon."

They cooked, they ate, they talked, they laughed until finally James and Katrina both had to admit that they were asleep on their feet. They went to bed and slept the sleep of the innocents, or at least that of the jet-lagged. The following day, James went to the office briefly, then left to go with Katrina to the bank. They picked the Standard Bank branch that was in Edenvale and used Will and Bridget's address as a stop-gap measure until such time as they had their own house. Then James went back to machines and parts, and Katrina went with Bridget to look at houses. James stopped at Leon's office to talk to him.

"Leon, I need to meet with Piet and talk about compensation. Do you have any information on what other companies pay their sales managers?" James asked.

"No, but I know where I can get it," Leon said.

"Would you please?" James asked. "How do you think preparations for the move are going?"

"As far as I can see, well," Leon replied. "Kevin has done a good job with the parts, and we're busy entering everything into the IBM. I've already got the accounts entered, and the next task is to get the machine population entered. I heard a rumour the other day that CMI has got problems."

"What, financial or other?" James asked.

"Financial," Leon replied. "I belong to an accounting group, and there were odd comments the last time we had lunch together."

"Great, that's all we need," James said. "If CMI goes under, then who do we get to be our distributor here in South Africa?"

"There aren't many options," Leon conceded.

"How many machines do you think CMI has on hand, and how many do they move in a year?" James asked.

"No idea," Leon admitted. "I do know the controller there, I could ask."

"Perhaps I should go and introduce myself to them as the new J&B chap here?" James thought.

"Might be an idea," Leon agreed.

"How much space do we have in Isando?" James asked.

"In all about 16 hectares," Leon replied. "That is the total area of the site; some is under roof, but a good portion is open. Are you thinking of taking on the CMI business?"

"Not all of it," James said. "But, what if we just took the J&B part of it?"

"It's a little different to the mining machine business," Leon said. "I'm sure CMI finances sales of machines, maybe even rents them out, if we were to take on that as well we would need a credit line, or a

relationship with a bank, we'd need more people, credit checkers, financing people, sale people, our own transport trucks, more repair people, plus where does CMI have depots apart from here, do we need to be in just the major cities, or some of them smaller ones as well?"
"Good points, maybe the first thing I should do is go and meet the head of CMI and just see how things are?" James suggested. "You know we should talk to Didcot, they have their own depots around Britain, they don't sell through distributors, they could probably tell us how it's all structured there, and my guess is that most of the machines that CMI sells are sourced from Didcot."
"I'll leave that to you," Leon said.
"Any sense of how long CMI had before they go under?" James asked.
"My information is six months or so," Leon replied.
"I suppose I'd better include something in my reports back to Oak Creek," James said. "Maybe I'll talk to CMI, then report."

James contacted Jan Hofmeyr, the chairman of Consolidated Mechanical Industries and arranged to meet for lunch the next day in the centre of Johannesburg at the Three Ships Restaurant in the Carlton Hotel. He asked in the office for directions, and they all deferred to Charlize, who gave him precise directions on how to get there and back, noting those streets that were one-way and in which direction. She also told him that there was parking under the hotel. The last thing that James really wanted to do was take on the construction machinery side of the business as well as the mining machines, but unless there was a viable alternative to CMI, then if the company wanted to maintain a presence in South Africa, he might have to. George and Piet came to see James about an enquiry for a machine for a diamond operation in the Western Cape, in the desert, hot and dry, but a great source of diamonds. They wanted to fly to Cape Town, then drive the 350 miles to Springbok and then on to the diamond mine. While they were there, they would also stop at the copper mine near Springbok and see how that was doing. James told them to make their arrangements, and in the future, just to let him know who they were going to see and when.

"How was the house hunting?" James asked Katrina that evening.
"Two possibles," she replied. "We're going to look at another three tomorrow, but I'm already favouring one of the possibles."
"Where is it?" he asked.
"It's in Edenvale, belongs to a banker who's been seconded to Singapore for three years," she explained. "It's a nice house, four bedrooms, nice yard, looks like a fortress from the outside, but inside, it's really nice, a rambling place built around an interior courtyard, that's grass-covered. It has a safe room that looks like it would withstand an assault by a tank. It's on a private street, gates at each end. I peaked over the back wall, had to get a ladder to do so. The place behind is another fortress. Is it really that bad, Bridget?"
"Not yet," Bridget replied. "There are crimes of opportunity, but for the most part, fences and gates mean work, and why do that when there may be something easier down the road."
"Can we afford the house?" James asked.
"We can," Katrina confirmed. "Apparently, the price to them is not a big issue; it's who's in the house that's important. The agent seemed to like the idea that we're from the States, seconded here. He wanted to know who you worked for, so I told him J&B he can do his own checking. I looked at cars too today, I can't make up my mind, so I'm still looking."
"There's no hurry," Bridget assured her. "I can run you anywhere you need to go."
"Thanks, Bridget, but I don't want to impose any longer than I have to." Katrina said.
"It's no imposition," Bridget assured her.
"Howzit everyone?" Will said when he joined them. "Good day?"
"Yes and no," James replied. "Katrina may have found a house, and I may have found another problem."
"What?" Will asked.
"Our distributor for construction may be going under," James replied.
"So, what does that mean for you?" Will asked.
"No idea," James said. "I'm having lunch with the distributor chap tomorrow, I'll see what he says."

"James Martin, nice to meet you," Jan Hofmeyr said when James joined him at the Three Ships for lunch.

"Nice to meet you, Mr Hofmeyr," James responded.

"This your first time in Africa?" Jan asked.

"No, I worked in Zambia for Kasalia Copper before we went to the States," James replied. "I've driven through South Africa northbound to Zambia and southbound to Cape Town, and my in-laws live just outside Calitzdorp."

"Well, I'm sure you'll fit in well enough here," Jan said.

"And you, Sir," James asked.

"I'm a Jozi boy," he replied. "I grew up in Berea, went to school there, went to Wits, then did my stint in the army, ran a few companies, then was bought by CMI, came in and took over as Chairman late last year."

"How is CMI doing?" James asked.

"We've got some issues," Jan admitted. "Unfortunately, my predecessor took on far more debt than we can handle to acquire a couple of companies, and that's coming back to haunt us."

"Is there any way we can help?" James asked.

"Not that I can see," Jan said. "I'm struggling with what to do right now. We may have to drop some lines, we may try and divest ourselves of a couple of the subs that are drains, or failing all that, we may just go into receivership and then rebuild after that."

"That doesn't sound like much fun," James commiserated.

"It isn't," Jan agreed. "When they bought out my company, I guessed there were issues, but I had no idea how bad it was. They played fast and loose with the reporting, so I've had to clean things up a lot there. Sadly, Blake, that's the old chair before me, left the country when he retired, or I'd be paying him a visit, and I'm sure the tax *ouks* would as well."

"Is the company salvable?" James asked.

"Tell you that in about three months," Jan said. "What about you? Any issues with J&B Africa?"

"Only some slow-moving and obsolete parts," James replied. "I'm going through it all now to see if I will have to write anything down or off."

"I suppose that's business," Jan said, a little sadly. "There's always some item that will upset things. Anyway, what do you fancy to eat?"

James drove back to his office after lunch and contemplated his good fortune. He did not have to deal with the disaster that it looked like Hofmeyr was having to contend with. J&B Africa was profitable, and apart from the parts issues, there were no real problems. There was no debt hanging over the company like the sword of Damocles. The move to the new location looked as if it would go well; certainly, all the staff were keen to go and make a fresh start. There were potential new sales of machines in the offing, which would mean a revenue boost in parts and service, as well as the two per cent of the purchase price that the company awarded the local subsidiary. A couple of large dragline sales would boost their profit and loss statement considerably. He wondered if Kevin and his salesmen would be able to sell any of the slow-moving parts, but even more importantly, he wondered what value of parts would be found to be unsaleable and therefore have to be written off as a charge against earnings. That decision would take the concurrence of Oak Creek, so he needed to make sure that they were properly informed so that they could plan for the possibility of book loss.

"How was lunch?" Leon asked James when he returned.

"Interesting," James said. "Hofmeyr says that he'll know in about three months if he can rescue CMI. So, I'd better start warning Oak Creek that things may change here. There's no one else who could take over the distributorship?"

"From what I gather, all the likely suspects already represent someone else," Leon replied. "I suppose one might be persuaded to drop their current line and take us on, but I don't see that as likely."

"I wonder what sells here?" James thought.

"At a guess, I would say hydraulic backhoes and loader backhoes, hydraulic cranes, some rope cranes and draglines, and water well drills," Leon suggested. "I think the days of the small rope shovels are over."

"Maybe I'll drive by the CMI yard one day and see what they have there," James thought. "I wonder if Hofmeyr would tell me what they actually sold in the last year?"

"You could always ask," Leon suggested.

"Perhaps I will," James said. "I was also thinking, what parts that we sell for mining machines could we source here in South Africa?"

"You'd have to ask Kevin that, and I'm sure Oak Creek would want a say in who and what," Leon said. "It strikes me that once you start subbing parts out, you're giving away your technology."

"You're right," James agreed. "But, let's suppose we're just talking about things like bronze bushings and bearings, that technology is well known, all we're disclosing are the dimensions and tolerances. Who are the steel and brass foundries?"

"I'm sure we can find a list somewhere," Leon said. "I'll look into it."

"Thanks, Leon," James said. "When were George and Piet due back?"

"The day after tomorrow," Leon replied.

"I should go and see Kevin and see if we've had any luck with moving parts," James thought.

Kevin was full of news when James talked to him. He had completed the inventory of parts and the movements and knew exactly what had not turned in over seven years. His salesmen already had interest in some of those parts; all that remained there was to negotiate the price, and as the salesmen were getting ten cents on every Rand above the landed cost, he thought he could rely on them to get the best price. Kevin also had a list of parts for machines that were either scrapped or sold out of the country. That meant that there was no market for them. James took a copy of the list and thought that he would send it to Oak Creek and ask them if anyone around the world had a need for those parts. If not, he now had an amount that would have to be written off. Fortunately, it was not too high, but high enough, 35,325 Rand in all. He wondered how they even got into that situation and concluded that it was probably the age-old story, defer the issue until the next manager and let him deal with it. His report to Oak Creek that week would make interesting reading. He went back to his office and sat down, and wrote his first report. He kept it brief, but included all the salient points. Then he asked Charlize to type it into the Telex machine, so that it could be sent to Oak Creek. By the time John Williams got to work, it would be on his desk.

"How did the house hunting go?" James asked Katrina that evening.

"I think I'm settled on the one from yesterday," she replied. "I've seen nothing that I like better. I talked to the agent again today and arranged for us to go and see it tomorrow."

"What time?" he asked.

"Noon," she said. "I thought we could take a look, then grab some lunch quickly so that you can get back to your office."

"What should I do, pick you up here at eleven-thirty?" he asked.

"That's more than enough time," she said. "I also decided on a car, well, not actually a car, a *bakkie*, A Toyota Land Cruiser. A Japanese *ou* has been called back to Tokyo and wants to sell his Land Cruiser; it's only two years old, and he hardly put any miles on it. It's a good price, so I'll pick that up tomorrow afternoon. Bridget's going to run me out to his place in Sandton."

"The house we're going to see is it furnished?" he asked.

"It is," she replied. "I'm going to get our own linens and some crockery, but all the basic furniture is there. Do you have somewhere you can store ours when it arrives?"

"We do," he said. "That reminds me, I need to contact the shipping company and find out where our stuff is. I can just see them trying to deliver it to Germiston when we've already moved to Isando. What out of our crates do we really want?"

"Not much," she said. "I wondered if we might get a furnished place, so everything I thought we might really want is in crate one. If we get that shipped to the house, then everything else could be stored."

"Bridget, we've been eating you out of house and home. We should take you and Will out to dinner," James said. "We'll need to find somewhere where we can easily take Francesca, any suggestions?"

"There's a nice place in South Kensington," she suggested. "Will and I have been there before, and it's the kind of place we can take Francesca."

"Do we need to call them?" he asked.
"I'll do that, if you like, what time?" she asked.
"Let's say six-thirty," he thought. "I think I hear Will coming now, so we won't have to wait for him."

"There's a long Telex for you," Charlize told James the next day. "It looks like we're getting visitors."
"Oh, who?" James asked.
"You can read it all, but John Williams, Fred Johnson and Tom Brooks," she replied. "They arrive next Wednesday and have asked you to set up a meeting with Jan Hofmeyr of CMI. They've also asked us to get them hotel rooms, where shall I put them?"
"Southern Sun by the airport," James joked. "Better not, put them in the Carlton."
"I thought that might be the place," she said. "So, I called a negotiated a bit and got three nice rooms at a really good rate."
"Thanks, Charlize," James said. "I should make sure I have all the numbers for here up to date. I'd better get with Leon and confirm the write-off numbers. Oh, and I'm going to be out at lunchtime looking at a house. I should be back one-thirty to two." James called Hofmeyr and made the appointment for the following Thursday, then closeted himself with Leon, and they were busy until James had to leave to pick up Katrina. She directed him to the house, or at least the street it was on, and they met the agent at the gate. He opened it and waved them through, and they drove down the private road to the house. The agent opened that gate, and he drove in, cautioning James not to try and follow. James saw why. As soon as the agent's car was past the gate, it shot across and closed; any car following would have been smashed by the gate. The agent entered a code on the pad inside the gate and opened it for James and Katrina to drive in. Again, as soon as they were past the gate, it shot across and closed off the driveway.
"Sorry about that," the agent said. "It's a little unusual, but it does mean that no one can follow you in unless you want them to. I'm Gareth Morgan, the agent for this house. You must be James Martin, good to see you again, Mrs Martin."

"Thanks for meeting us," James said.

"Let me show you around," Gareth said. He led the way to the front door and opened it, and waved them inside. Once past the front door, James saw that it opened up onto a courtyard, surrounded essentially by a covered walkway, behind which were rooms, all with windows looking inward to the courtyard. That triggered a thought he had had when they had arrived, that there were no windows facing the street. There was a panel by the front door, and it had a television screen with a clear view of the driveway, but no actual window.

"This chap is very security conscious," James commented to Gareth.

"He is a high-profile banker and worried about kidnapping and other issues, so he installed the best systems he could find," Gareth replied.

"It's really nice here," James said. "Could we take a look at the rooms?"

"Follow me," Gareth said. He led the way and they walked through the kitchen, dining and living rooms, then the bedrooms. He also showed them the garage for two cars that was attached that led off the kitchen.

"It really is nice," James repeated himself. "I'm sold. What do you think, Katrina?"

"I like it," she said.

"What's the next step?" James asked Gareth.

"I've been in touch with the owner," he replied. "He's happy to have you as tenants for the next two years until you go back to the States. I have a lease agreement for you to review. Perhaps you could take it and we could meet again on Monday?"

"We can do that," James agreed. "I have some of the corporate staff coming in next week, but they won't be here until Wednesday."

"When can we move in?" Katrina asked.

"As soon as we have a signed lease," Gareth said.

"Do you have banking information where the lease payments would need to go?" James asked.

"I do," Gareth said. "It's here appended to the lease itself."

"Thank you," James said. "Well, when shall we meet on Monday?"

"We could meet here at four," Gareth suggested. "Then I can give you the gate openers and codes, and the keys to the door and the alarm codes. I'll also get the telephone turned back on, so it will be working on Monday. I get the bills from the telephone company along with

those for electricity and water. I'll just forward them all to you for payment."
"That sounds fine," James said. "We'll see you on Monday."

James had time to drop Katrina back at Bridget's house, then call on Koot Oesthuizen to ask him to review the lease, before returning to the office for the Friday afternoon wrap-up session. There was nothing of consequence that could not wait until Monday, so they shut up shop for the weekend.
"Busy week?" Will asked James when they arrived at the gate almost simultaneously.
"Busy," James confirmed. "Let me go and open the gate, I see Bridget's car and Katrina's new *bakkie*." James opened the gate and stood back while they both drove in, then he closed the gates and locked them. It was going to take some time to get used to gates, fences and all the other security measures that were in place. When they had lived in Zambia, the windows had had burglar bars on them, but there were no high fences topped with barbed wire or locking gates. In Oak Creek, there was not even a fence around their house, just some hedges in places. There was certainly no necessity for bars on the windows; it was a new reality, and as Will had commented, it was likely to get worse, driven by the huge income disparity that existed between the whites of South Africa and the black population.

"Do you like it?" Katrina asked James, showing him around her new vehicle.
"It's nice," he said. "I like the colour, what would it take to fit a winch on the front?"
"Not much, I shouldn't think," she said. "I'll look into that next week."
"So, what shall we do this weekend?" he asked.
"Don't know, any ideas, Bridget?" Katrina asked.
"We have a friend who has a place in the Magaliesberg that he lets us use," Bridget said. "We were thinking we could drive out there this afternoon and come back Sunday."

"That sounds wonderful," Katrina said. "What do we need to take?"
"We'll take enough food and drink for the two days, take clothes for hiking in the bush," Bridget suggested. "Binoculars, if you have them."
"When do we leave?" James asked.
"As soon as we're packed," Bridget said. "Will, you and James get the food and drink together, I'll pack our clothes and get what we need for Francesca."
"Okay, James, I'll pack some clothes for you," Katrina said. James and Will then packed up food into boxes and added wine and beer. Will suggested that they take James's car, which was a little bigger than his and would be more comfortable for the drive.
"How far is it?" James asked.
"About ninety-minutes drive," Will said. "We go north to Randjespark, then take off towards Hartebeestpoort, then into the Magaliesberg. Bridget and I have taken up birds as well as animals, so we've been educating ourselves on weekends. The *ou* that lets us use his place has an old Landie there that we can use."
"Are you two ready?" Katrina asked as she came through with two small holdalls.
"We're waiting for you," James laughed.
"Shall we go?" Bridget said, coming through with Francesca.

It was dark fairly soon after they left the house, so James relied on Will to warn him of the roads they would need to take. Will had been right; it took just over ninety minutes to get to the cottage perched high up on the hills. It was isolated and had the minimum of facilities, which included a generator for lights and a solid fuel stove, for which there was an adequate supply of coal. It did have running water, fed, Will told them, from a header tank a few hundred feet from the house. Will knew the routine and started the generator, then got the stove going, as it would heat water for baths. Will told James that at some time on Sunday, they would need to take the old Land Rover into Buffelspoort, refill its tank and also fill the cans for the generator. Katrina volunteered to cook dinner, so let Bridget see to Francesca while she cooked. James watched Francesca wander around the place, quite at home; she clearly had been before and remembered it. James's experience with two-year-olds was limited, so this was all new to him. Francesca was fed first, then bathed and put to bed, and then it was the turn of the adults. Will killed the generator early and they sat outside in the chill of the evening looking at the stars, which shone in their myriads, and listening to the African night noises Will had remembered to bring torches out with him when he had shut off the generator, so that when it was time for bed, they did not have to stumble around in the darkness.

In the morning, the beauty of the place was obvious; they could hear the barking of the baboons that hid away overnight on the ledges and ravines of the mountains as they roused themselves for the day. A short walk from the cottage, they could look down over the Magaliesberg to the lower lands beyond. The scenery was spectacular, and James wondered how long it would be before intensive commercialisation set in. Will and Bridget, armed with binoculars and bird books, set about spotting, debating and arguing about what they had seen. Katrina took Francesca for a short walk along the ridge, then had to carry her back. A two-year-old has apparent boundless energy, but it transpired that it was not so boundless, and there were limits. Katrina and James made a late breakfast, then called in the birdwatchers to eat.

"I didn't know you were that interested in birds," James commented to Will as they ate.

"I wasn't until we came to South Africa," Will replied. "But there are so many different species here, it's been fun to learn at least some of them. Bridget's better than I am, but I'm improving."

"Are you ready to move in?" Bridget asked Katrina.

"I think so," Katrina replied. "We'll sign the lease on Monday and get the keys, so I suppose we can move any time after that."

"Do you know where your things are?" Bridget asked.

"Somewhere between Houston and Cape Town," Katrina replied. "We did get a notification from the shipper that our crates were on a boat that was due to leave Houston two weeks ago. So, I would have thought that it would be approaching Cape Town by now."

"I think you're underestimating the time," Bridget said. "I would think the time will be more like a month, so you'll have to make do for a little while longer."

"Well, as you saw, the place is furnished, so all I really want is sheets and pillowcases," Katrina said. "I thought I'd buy some on Tuesday, then we could move in then and be there when James's bwanas arrive on Wednesday."

"I'll help you with the shopping," Bridget promised. "So, after breakfast, do you fancy a walk?"

"Let's do that," James said. "Fresh air and all that."

"Are you ready for things here?" Will asked James as they hiked along a trail.

"I suppose as ready as I'll ever be," James replied. "I've got parts people, service people and the accountants, and then the machine sales *ouks*. Fortunately, we don't build anything here, or I'd have manufacturing as well. How are you doing with paints?"

"I run the production plant now," Will said. "A chem eng chap's dream, pipes, mixers, solvents, you name it. I find the biggest challenge to be the tint additives, how to get the right colours and make sure they look like the colour sample pages we send out to the retailers."

"Any issues with whites and blacks working in the plant?" James asked.

"We have our share of whites who feel threatened by the very idea that someone black can actually do the same job, but I've been slowly weeding them out. What's your mix look like?"

"I've only got four black storemen, plus some helpers for the service engineers," James replied. "If I want any black service engineers, I'm going to have to put in an education and training program, parts sales, that means going to the mines, and I've not been to any of them yet to get a sense of how they would react."

"You must have found in Zambia that the black population has just as many smart chaps as the white," Will commented.

"I did," James confirmed. "In Zambia, the number of engineers and managers was small, but until independence, the companies had really done nothing to educate the black workforce, so it was really the post-independence graduates that I was seeing, only a year or two out of college."

"Your secondment is for two years, then what?" Will asked.

"They say they have an idea," James replied. "We'll see, I think my main task, or one of them, for the next two years, is pick my successor from the local chaps and make sure he can take over from me."

"Any candidates?" Will asked.

"I'm leaning towards the accountant," James replied. "He's probably the smartest one there. I just need to educate him about mining, methods and machines, and help him understand the parts and service aspects."

"Any political unrest at your place?" Will asked.

"Not that I've found yet," James said. "But, it's early days yet, and I doubt that any of them feel comfortable talking politics with me yet."

"I know I got some ANC supporters," Will said. "But I think that I've also have a couple of AWB loonies, I'm keeping a close eye on them. I don't need some ultra-white nationalist coming in one day with a gun and shooting up the black workers."

"I suppose it will take some time for things to change," James said.

"It will," Will agreed. "It's a shame, the country is amazing, they've got mineral resources, they can grow most things, there is an industrial base, it's just this chasm of opportunity driven by politics, fear of losing a lifestyle that is comfortable and an odd need to feel superior to anyone that's black or brown."

"It's odd," James commented. "I thought the US had moved beyond the racial issues that they had, but I've been to places in Kentucky and Alabama where if you were black, you just wouldn't want to go."

"Are you two solving the problems of the world?" Katrina asked as she dropped back on the trail to see where they were.

"Not really," James replied. "Just comparing notes on a few things."

"Well, there are trees, birds, snakes and animals to look at," she said.

"I know," James said, a little shamefaced.

The hike along the trail and back put everyone in the mood for food, so back at the cottage, Will and James were instructed to get the *braai* going while Bridget and Katrina made the rest of lunch. Francesca was excited; she had seen her first snake, a cobra. They had watched it from a safe distance, and it had eventually slithered off into the brush, and they could track its progress by the noise the birds made. When it had gone a safe distance away, they had resumed their walk, with Bridget fielding all kinds of questions about venom. She tried to emphasise to Francesca the need to watch where she was walking and not to get too close to any snakes. Left alone, they would probably just go off on their own, on whatever missions snakes had. James asked Will if they had ever seen any around their house.

"We've not had any," Will replied. "But they're around, just have to be careful. You need to keep the place clean so that you don't attract rats and mice, get rats and mice, and you'll get snakes. So, I'm extra careful with the *braai* and make sure that it's clean before I close it up. We also take the rubbish out ourselves to a skip that is close to the factory."

"Over there," James interrupted Will, pointing.

"Wow, go and tell the girls," Will suggested.

"There's a big sable just come up one of the gullies," James told Katrina and Bridget. They all crowded outside to look, and the sable looked at them, as if assessing the risk, then turned and trotted off into the thicker bush.

"That's the first one I've seen here," Will said. "I knew that they were found here, but we've not seen one until now. Francesca, did you see it, the big black antelope?"

"Yes, Daddy," she said.

"That was a sable," he told her.

"Why a sable?" she asked.

"It's an old word that means black," he explained. "You saw how black he was?"

"Yes, Daddy, will he come back?" she asked.

"I don't know," Will admitted. "Anyway, he's gone now. Are you ready for lunch?"

"Yes," Francesca said.

They ate, they watched birds, they watched a mountain reedbuck wander by and listened to the alarm calls of the baboons in the gullies below, then heard the cough of a leopard, which explained why the baboons were making such a racket. It was a welcome break from the city, from work and from the hustle and bustle of daily life. James thought about the upbringing that Francesca was getting, trips into the bush at regular intervals, exposure to a multitude of languages, nothing at all like his own upbringing. Francesca's life was much more like Katrina's early life, as she had been raised in Zambia, in similar circumstances. He wondered where her life might go, what her schooling might be like and what opportunities might come her way. His musings were interrupted by Katrina, who told him that he was the washing-up detail of the day. He remembered Will's comments about mice and rats and made sure that he cleaned up well and left nothing for them to take. Then he rejoined the rest as they sat and just watched the world go by, or at least the birds and occasional animal go by. It was a beautiful place, with the quiet only broken by the sounds of the birds and the baboons.

Consolidated Mechanical Industries

James and Will took the old Land Rover and filled it with petrol, and also filled the cans for the generator, and while they were at it, dumped the rubbish from the weekend. Then it was just the drive home, back into the city and the traffic noise and the people. James could see why Will and Bridget liked to go out to the Magaliesberg; it was a refuge from the city. On Monday, James collected the lease from Koot Oesthuizen, who had a few comments but who assured James that the lease was fair and held no hidden pitfalls or traps. That assured, James and Katrina met with Gareth at four, signed the lease, got the keys and the codes and prepared to move into their new house, which they did on Tuesday afternoon.

On Wednesday morning, James was at Jan Smuts, waiting for the South African Airways flight from New York. He saw it land and then waited, for what seemed like an eternity, until John, Fred, and Tom came out of the customs hall, pushing their trolley, laden down with suitcases. James did wonder how long they planned to stay; it looked to him as though they had brought clothes enough for a month.

"James, good to see you," John said. "That's a long flight."

"It's even longer going back," James commented. "They typically have to stop for fuel at Sal Island, which adds to the time."

"So, to the office, then later the hotel?" John asked.

"Whatever you wish," James said.

"Office," John said. "We'll meet and greet, then we can go and check in. When's our appointment with CMI?"

"Tomorrow at ten," James replied. "It's at their corporate office, which is on Fox Street. You're meeting with Jan Hofmeyr, he's the Chairman."

"You mean we're meeting with Hofmeyr, you're coming with us, James," John said.

"I wondered if you would rather meet with him alone," James said.

"You're our Johnny on the spot, so you come with us," John said. "If anything comes up in the future, you're going to be the one who has to deal with it, so better that you are in on things from the start."

James drove them to the J&B offices and warehouse and introduced them to all. He was reminded of visits by corporate bigwigs when he had worked in Zambia, and the edict had been to paint the rocks outside the offices white, not that they had noticed. He then sat down with John, Fred and Tom and told them what he knew about CMI, what the rumours were and what Hofmeyr had told him. Fred knew Bob Blake, the previous Chairman of CMI, and commented that he found it hard to believe that Blake had left the company in any kind of mess. James told them that he was merely passing on what Hofmeyr had told him and what the local business community was saying.

"So, at your last meeting, Hofmeyr said that he'd know within about three months whether he can pull them out of the fire or not?" John asked.

"That's what he said," James confirmed.

"They're short of cash, right, can't pay the debt service?" John asked.

"I understand that that's the fundamental problem," James confirmed.

"How many sites do they operate in?" John asked.

"Most of the major cities," James replied. "Those sites that include our machines are in Cape Town, East London, Durban, Bloemfontein and here in Germiston. Sales leads from other cities are funnelled through those few sites."

"Surely they've got more outlets?" Fred protested.

"They do, in about twenty other towns," James confirmed. "But the only ones that have our machines in their yards are the ones I listed."

"How much yard space is at each location?" John asked.

"That I don't know," James admitted. "I haven't asked Hofmeyr that, and I haven't been to have a look, so I also don't know how many machines are sitting unsold in their yards."

"Well, we know that we've sold 12 machines to them from Oak Creek and 80 from Didcot in the past twelve months, so it will be interesting to see how many of them are still in their yards," Fred commented.

"Do they have much of a rental business, Fred?" John asked.
"No idea," Fred admitted. "I never gave much thought to what they did with the machines after they left our yard."
"I know they do rent out," James said. "We rented a crane with a cactus grab to remove scrap metal from the new site in Isando."
"We should take a look at that," John said. "Why don't we drive out there, take a look, then get some lunch and check in to the hotel, then I could do with a nap. You free for dinner tonight, James?"
"I am," James confirmed.
"Let's go and take a look at this new place then," John suggested. James led them out to the car and drove to Isando and the new facility. There were contractors there busy painting the interiors of the buildings, which had been stripped of everything and in which had been reinstalled electricity, water, sprinklers and in two of the buildings, airlines, and in the one building that had the offices, they were busy building them out.
"Looks nice," Fred said. "Plenty of room, useful buildings for parts, when do you move?"
"We plan to have everything done by the middle of June," James said. "The lease on the Germiston site expires on the 30th of June."
"Plenty of room here for machines," Fred commented. "I need to look again at the mix of machines that CMI bought from us."
"I asked the folks at Didcot what they had shipped here in the past ten years, then looked for trends in machine mix," James said.
"And, what does that show?" Fred asked.
"There's been a steady decline in small rope shovels, replaced by backhoes and hydraulic loaders; cranes have stayed steady, both with lattice boom and squirt boom," James explained.
"Well drills?" Fred asked.
"Steady, not a particularly big market, but consistent, 6 to 8 machines a year," James replied.
"You've been busy," Fred commented.
"Okay, let's go and check into the hotel and get some lunch," John said.

The drive into Johannesburg was quick enough, being almost lunchtime, they did not have to contend with the early morning traffic that plagued all big cities. The Carlton was ready for them, and James offered to wait in the lobby while John, Tom and Fred took their bags up to their rooms. They were down quickly enough, and James suggested that they eat at the Three Ships.

"So, James, settling in?" John asked.

"We are, thank you," James replied. "We've taken a lease on a house for two years, and it's not far from Isando or Germiston."

"Maybe on Friday we can meet with the folks at Germiston again," John said. "Do you have any numbers yet on obsolete parts?"

"We've been through all the parts and the machines that are in South Africa, Lesotho, Swaziland, Botswana, Rhodesia, Zambia and South West Africa, and have six parts on hand that we will never be able to sell," James explained. "I contacted the Parts Department in Oak Creek and asked them if they had any demand for those parts anywhere in the world, and they came back with no. So, we should write them off; the aggregate landed freight and duty costs to us are 35,325 Rand. We need guidance from corporate as to when to write them off, but my accountant tells me that now we've identified the issue, accounting rules dictate that we do it now, and he assures me that our auditors will push for that."

"What are those parts that are so expensive?" Fred asked.

"A bull gear and hoist drum for a dragline shipped here in 1949, two smaller pinions for a shovel shipped here in 1950 and two obsolete control panels for drills," James replied.

"What do you figure the company will make this year?" John asked.

"Before the write-down charge, we're projecting 40,000 Rand or so, unless we get some additional earnings from our parts sales efforts where we're offering those parts that haven't moved in seven years as a discount to possible users," James replied.

"So, we won't have a book loss?" John asked.

"We shouldn't," James confirmed. "I don't like the idea of earnings that low, but we should clean up the books; it has been deferred long enough."

"You seem to have this knack for uncovering issues?" Fred commented. "Why is it that Ben never told us about this?"

"He may not have known," James replied, being generous. "It's only because we're moving that we did a complete review of the inventory and looked at turns."

"Maybe," Fred said. "That makes sense, and I suppose if the guy before Ben hadn't looked at things in terms of turns, then he wouldn't have passed it on to Ben." James did wonder why Fred was so keen to avert any problems from Ben; what was it about Ben that Fred was not telling them?

"Anyway, I'll talk to Stuart this afternoon, let him know what's going on with the finances," John said, referring to Stuart Palmer, the corporate controller. "So, let's eat, would you believe I'm hungry again after all the stuff they fed us on the flight?"

James had time after lunch to attend to some things in his office before going home briefly, then leaving again for his dinner engagement with the bigwigs from Oak Creek.

"I talked to Stuart, and he says go ahead and write off the parts; the lower-than-expected earnings are not material, so no need for any footnotes in the annual report. In fact, Stuart said that this year is a good year to clean up odd things," John said. "There's nothing else likely to come up?"

"Not that I've found," James replied. "The sale of all the scrap we took out of the Isando property is covering the building refurbishment costs and the move costs. I'm not aware of any other stray assets on the books that have no value, and we have no outstanding claims against us for anything, no warranty items or anything like that."

"So, tell us about Hofmeyr," John said.

"He's from Johannesburg, mechanical engineer with a degree from the Witwatersrand University, did his time in the army, then started up as a road contractor, then a drain and sewer contractor, then ran a business dealing in road construction machinery. It was the acquisition of that company last year that brought him into CMI," James explained. "CMI went on an acquisition binge over the past five years, buying up all sorts of equipment dealers and manufacturers, few of which have done as well as they could or should, so there's not enough cash coming in to cover the debt service."

"Age-old problem," John said, nodding in understanding. "Any idea what Hofmeyr proposes to do about it?"

"Not really," James said. "All he said was that he'd know if he could pull things together in about three months."

"He must be going to try and sell something to get a cash infusion, or float a new share issue to get cash that way," John mused. "Well, we'll find out tomorrow. So, what about mining machine sales here, what's the word?" James went through all of the prospects and gave his views as to the likelihood that the project would go, and who he thought would be the bidders for equipment. There was activity, and it all pointed to a good next few years. After dinner, Fred and Tom excused themselves and went off to bed, leaving James and John.

"So, how are things?" John asked.

"Well enough," James replied. "We're just waiting for our stuff to arrive. The people at J&B Africa all look pretty good so far, I may even have stumbled across my successor."

"Who?" John asked.

"Leon Schumann, the accountant," James replied. "He understands the business, has a good head on his shoulders, with some coaching about mining and machine applications, he'll do well."

"Keep me informed," John said. "I'll see you here at what, nine-thirty tomorrow?"

"I'll be here," James said. "We can walk to the CMI office from here."

"Is it safe?" John asked.

"Safe enough," James said.

"Do you think you'll be busy in September?" John asked.

"I've no idea," James replied.

"Bobby wants to come out and go on a safari," John said. "I can't come, but maybe you and Katrina could take her somewhere?"

"I'm sure Katrina would be delighted to do that," James said. "How long is she coming out for?"

"Three weeks," John said. "I'll get you dates, flights and so on. Now, I need to get some sleep, or I'll be nodding off when we're talking to Hofmeyr. I'll see you tomorrow, James."

"How was John?" Katrina asked James when he got home.
"He's doing well, he told me that Bobby's coming out in September, she wants to go on a safari, I probably won't be able to come, could you look into it and set something up?" he asked.
"Love to," she said. "I'll find something nice, do you know how long?"
"John said that she's coming for three weeks, so maybe a day or two here, then two weeks out in the bush, then another day or two here," James suggested.
"Do you want anything else to eat or drink?" she asked.
"Maybe a glass of wine, how cold is it out? Could we sit out in the courtyard?" he asked.
"We can sit out if we put a jersey on," she said. "I was thinking that in the summer it would be nice to have the courtyard, we could sit out a lot."
"I was thinking of something else," he said.
"I'll bet you were, well, it's too bloody cold for shenanigans outside tonight, so it's going to have to be in the bath and in bed," she laughed.
"That sounds great," he said. "Anyway, here's to the new house."
"Cheers," she said. "Are you eating out again tomorrow?"
"Don't know," he said. "I'll call and let you know as soon as I can."
"Well, drink up, bath and bed are calling," she said.

James was at the Carlton at nine-thirty, and he waited in the lobby for the others to come down. He had been and looked at the building on Fox Street where the CMI offices were, and it was just a three-minute walk from the Carlton. At nine-forty, John came down, and five minutes later, Tom and Fred came down and joined them, and together they walked the short distance to the CMI offices. Inside the building, there was a directory that pointed them to the third floor. There was a lift, so they rode up. On the third floor, there was a receptionist immediately outside the lift, and she took their coats and showed them to the boardroom and offered tea or coffee. She had barely begun to pour when Jan Hofmeyr joined them.

"Howzit, James?" he said.

"Baie goed, dankie," James replied. "Mr Hofmeyr, this is John Williams, the Vice President of Sales for J&B, Fred Johnson, Vice President International for J&B and Tom Brooks, Vice President Legal for J&B."

"Nice to meet you," Jan said. "Please, sit, good flight over?"

"It was," John said. "I've never flown South African before, but they did a good job."

"Well, I wish I could welcome you with a little better news," Jan said. "I'm sure that James told you that we're going through a difficult time just now with cash flow, and I don't see that getting any better."

"James told us that previous management probably overdid the mergers and acquisitions and has left you with a problem," John said.

"True, true," Jan said. "Our debts are eating up all the cash we can generate, and I don't see that improving soon."

"So, the likelihood that you'll be looking to buy machines for stock is low?" John asked.

"Low to remote possibility," Jan agreed. "We just don't have the cash to buy any machines. Normally, I'd ask if you would extend terms, but I'm not even sure that would help. I think I'm about a month away from going into receivership. It got worse, James. I thought I had three months, then I uncovered some more items, and the three months shrank to one."

"So, what if you gave our lineup and disposed of all the machines you have in stock?" John asked.

"Depending on what we could get for them in a sale, then that would give me enough cash to restructure," Jan said.

"How many of our machines do you currently have unsold?" Fred asked.

"Sixty-three," Jan replied. "Most here, eight in Cape Town, six in East London, six in Durban and five in Bloemfontein."

"What if we took them all back?" John asked.

"That would help," Jan agreed. "The only question would be how much?"

"Well, I'm sure you agree that we would need to offer a price that would allow us to cover our costs here," John said.
"I expected that," Jan said. "What do you propose?"
"Well, suppose we take on the staff that you have that are dedicated to our machines, we take the parts stock you have, at an agreed price, you rent us some space in Cape Town, East London, Durban and Bloemfontein, we buy all the machines back from you, at an agreed price, then we run our own outlet here in South Africa, those machines that you sold that are financed, we novate over the contracts with the bank or financial institution" John suggested.
"Do you have someone to run the business?" Jan asked.
"We do," John said.
"In principle, I could agree to that," Jan said.
"Do you rent out many machines?" Fred asked.
"We've got twelve out on rental right now, one to you," Jan replied.
"We'd have to novate the rental agreements," John thought. "Do you have any machines on the water now?"
"Four, all from England," Jan said.
"So, let's summarise," John said. "We'll buy all the machines off you and all the parts you are carrying, either here or on the water, for a price to be negotiated, we'll take on the staff you have that are dedicated to J&B machines, with the caveat that we get to interview them first and if we deem someone unsuitable, then we won't take them, we'll rent space from you in the four towns and the machines that are there can stay there, those that are here we'll move to our new site in Isando, we'll novate over the rental agreements you have and pay you a negotiated price for those agreements, we'll novate over the agreements with the banks for machines that are financed, we'll terminate our distributor agreement with you and sell the machines through J&B Africa."
"That's quite a lot to take in," Jan said. "But in principle, I agree."
"Do you have a list of machines that are in your yards and the price you paid us for them?" John asked.
"I anticipated that, and yes, I have the list here as well as the list of parts and values," Jan replied. "As for people dedicated to J&B, I'll need to pull that together. Why don't we get some lunch while I have someone do that?"

"Good idea," John said.

Jan took them to a restaurant that was about a fifteen-minute walk from his office. James let Jan and John go ahead, and he lagged back with Fred and Tom. Conversation over lunch was about anything and everything except the proposal that John had made. Jan and John talked about military service; Jan had done his in South West Africa, and John had done his in the Korean War. They also talked about safaris, and Jan told them about a lodge that had just opened in the Timbavati Reserve, which was adjacent to the Kruger National Park. Apart from the lodge, there was a smaller tented camp. That sounded interesting to James, and he thought that he would suggest that to Katrina for her trip with Bobby. They talked about the situation in South Africa, and based on his statements, James put Hofmeyr in the ranks of the reformers who saw an inevitable end to the current system of government. It might take a few years, but in time, it would have to change; one simply could not suppress the majority population indefinitely.

Back at the office, Jan had a list of people and his prepared lists of machines and parts. John took a quick look at the totals, then made his opening gambit. "Based on our earlier conversation, we're prepared to offer you 1,000,000 Rand in cash tomorrow for the machines and parts."

"That's well below our landed freight and duty," Jan protested.

"That's true," John admitted. "But, if we just wait a month and you go into receivership, we can make an offer to the receiver for probably 200,000 Rand or even less. That's not in our interests or yours."

"I'd die at 1,000,000 Rand," Jan said. "The total cost of machines and parts is 3,250,000 Rand. I'd be willing to come down to 2,750,000. That would give me enough cash to clear much of the debt."

"I could probably squeeze the treasury folks in the company and come up with 1,500,000 Rand," John said. "But we have cash needs too, we need to invest in new machine tools, raw materials and such."

"2,250,000," Jan countered.

"Done," John said.

"I'll get my solicitors working on an agreement," Jan said. "Do you want to just work with them, Tom?"

"That would be fine," Tom said. "James, who's the guy who does work for us here?"

"Koot Oesthuizen," James said.

"Why don't we get him to join us here tomorrow morning so that we can start working on the agreement?" Tom suggested.

"That's a good idea," John said. "But, so that we're all reading from the same script, could you call in your secretary, Jan and have her take down some notes and type up the heads of agreement for us?"

"*Ja*, good idea," Jan said. He got up and opened the door, and asked his secretary to come in with her pad. She sat and took down what John dictated. James was impressed; it was almost as though John had an agreement memorised. He just reeled it off with all the salient points, the price to be paid, after the machines and parts had been inventoried, and all the caveats that go with a good agreement. Done, the secretary left the room, and they heard her typing away. She was back in what James thought was a remarkably short time with five copies of the agreement. John read it through aloud, and changes were noted on Jan's copy. The secretary then took all the copies back, went out and retyped them with the noted changes. She came back with five new copies, and they repeated the process. They did that four times until no one could find any typographical errors or anything to quibble with. Then John and Jan signed the five copies, and they each got one with the caution to James to keep it confidential until the final agreement had been reached. It was by now five in the afternoon, so they agreed to leave it for the day and reconvene in the morning to work out details of inventory checks, space rental in the four cities, and the transfer of personnel to J&B Africa. Neither John nor Jan suggested dinner, so James assumed that each side wanted time apart to reflect upon what they had agreed to.

Back at the Carlton, James asked the others if they had dinner plans. Fred did, he had an old friend who was visiting South Africa and was passing through Johannesburg that day, so Fred was going to have dinner with him. James asked John and Tom if they wanted to get dinner in town or go with him to their house. John opted for home cooking, so James used a public telephone and called Katrina to let her know that he was bringing John and Tom for dinner. As they drove out to Edenvale, James asked John who was going to run the construction machinery business.

"Hans Strydom," John said. "You didn't meet him when you were in Didcot. He's been running the depot in Glasgow and wants to come home. He knows the machines, he has been running the sales office there, the parts warehouse we have there and local service and rentals. The operation here will be a little bigger, but he can handle it. He'll report to you."

"I'll need some funds to put in more offices and warehouse space in Isando," James said.

"Get me an estimate by next week, and you can start work straight away and be ready for machines, parts and people to start moving in a couple of weeks," John said. "Can your accountant handle the extra work?"

"We may need another junior accountant, but otherwise, I'm sure we can manage," James said. "The same is true of parts; we'd need another one or two warehousemen, but not the full complement that CMI has."

"I thought there might be some common functions," John said. "Just looking over Hofmeyr's list, I get the sense of too many people."

"We will need a banking relationship for extending terms to buyers of machines," James said. "We don't sell mining machines on tick, but I'm sure that many of the contractors who buy machines will want to finance the purchase; they can either do that themselves, or we can set them up with a bank that we work with."

"I noticed that they use Barclays, so I'd just stick with them," John said. "There will be existing terms and conditions with the bank that suit machine purchases, so why invent something new. Tom, did you see anything today that causes you concern?"

"No, it looks pretty straightforward," Tom said. "I'm sure we'll find odd little things tomorrow, but I doubt that it would change the basic agreement. For the rental of space in those four cities, how much space do you want, James?"

"I think an office with space enough for one is enough, plus enough yard space to park up to twelve machines on each site," James replied. "If they want too much money, then we'll pull all the machines back here, rent a local office just for the sales rep, but I think it would be good to have at least some machines on display."

"If someone sells a machine in Cape Town and you have to supply it from here, how long does it take to drive there?" Tom asked.

"Well, it's just under 900 miles from here to Cape Town, so two days, unless it's a permitted load with time of day and speed limit travel restrictions," James replied.

"Do you have any low loaders?" Tom asked.

"No, but I think it would be prudent to buy some," James said. "We can always contract with a haulier, but I think having our own would give us more flexibility."

"Do you have anything in mind?" John asked.

"Yes, the local Cat people also represent Oshkosh. We had some in Zambia, I like them, they're good, reliable trucks, couple them with Henred trailers and we could haul anything we're likely to sell," James replied.

"Put them in your budget request as well," John said. "Do you have drivers?"

"I'll have to check who has a heavy goods vehicle licence," James said. "I may have to take on a driver or two, I'll see."

"Is this your house?" John asked as they pulled up to the gate.

"It is," James confirmed. "We moved in yesterday, so forgive us if we're not that organised."

"We don't want to put you to any inconvenience," John said. "We could always go out somewhere."

"Katrina said it was fine," James said.

"Hello, John," Katrina said as they went into the house.

"Hi, Katrina, nice to see you again. I don't think you've ever met Tom Brooks; he's our legal eagle, keeps us from making poor choices," John said.

"Nice to meet Mr Brooks," Katrina said. "Please come in, make yourselves comfortable, what may I offer you to drink?"
"A beer would be fine, thanks," Tom replied.
"Same for me," John said. Katrina handed around beers and then some small things to munch on while they waited for dinner to be ready.
"This is an unusual house," Tom commented, looking around. "From the outside, you would never guess that it's such an open and airy place. I like the way everything is built around this courtyard."
"We like it," Katrina said. "It belongs to a banker who's currently on an assignment in Singapore."
"Oh, Lovey, Jan Hofmeyr was telling us about a new lodge and a tented camp that has just opened up in the Timbavati Reserve next to Kruger," James said. "You might want to take a look at it, the Motswari Lodge and M'Bali camp."
"That sounds like fun," she said. "I will. I forgot if you ever told us, have you been to South Africa before, John?"
"I came here a couple of times when I was in Didcot, easier to travel from there, just about twelve hours overnight on BA, no real jet lag. Tom, have you been before?" John asked.
"Once, a few years ago, when we first set up J&B Africa," Tom said. "I did manage to add a week and spent that in the Kruger National Park. I have to say that that was an amazing experience, and I understand that you grew up with all that, Katrina?"
"I did," she confirmed. "When my folks first moved to Zambia, it was not as developed as it is now, and if we travelled to Ndola, the next town to us, we would see all kinds of game on the road, especially at dusk."
"Can I get you another beer?" James asked. Both Tom and John took another, then Katrina called them to the dinner table. She had cooked beef, and it went well with the beer, so no wine was called for. James abstained; he had to drive John and Tom back into town after dinner, so wanted to stay clear-headed.

The J&B team reconvened at the offices of CMI at eight the next morning and was joined by Koot Oesthuizen and Charles Bristol, the solicitor for CMI. Tom handed copies of the heads of agreement to Koot and Charles and suggested that they start on the definitive agreement. It seemed to James that he was superfluous to this process, and he made a side comment to John, remarking on that. John looked to Jan and suggested that they leave the lawyers to it and repair to another office to talk about markets, trends in the marketplace, changes in the demand for different machine types, in short, what would sell and what would not. James listened while Jan talked about what he had seen in terms of the types of machines that were selling, and why. He thought it was a shame that Jan had inherited a poor situation, because he was clearly someone who knew what he was doing and, under other circumstances, would have made a real success of CMI. By lunchtime, the agreement was ready, and Tom went through it line by line with John and Jan, with the two solicitors looking on, nodding agreement. All the basic conditions were laid out along with remedies should either party renege or otherwise breach the agreement. John and Jan signed, and that was that. Now all that remained was to do the work of counting the machines and parts, then moving everything to Isando. The sooner machines and parts were counted, the sooner Jan would get the money, so he was keen to get started and suggested to James that he take someone on Monday to the Germiston yard who could get started on the task.

They had a celebratory lunch at the Three Ships. After lunch, Jan excused himself, telling them that he was going to meet with his major creditor with the news that he would shortly have an influx of cash. That would make the creditor happy, and the discussion would probably centre around whether or not to pay down the debt significantly or use the cash to continue making interest payments. Privately, James thought that the best course of action was to pay down the debt as much as possible, then streamline the company to reduce expenses, then there would be a good chance that the smaller company would thrive.

"So, James, shall we go back to your office and meet some of the folks again?" John asked.

"Of course," James said. He drove them all to the office and introduced them around again, and let them ask questions and spend whatever time they wanted with whoever they wanted. John used the telephone and called Didcot and talked to Richard West, the Managing Director, and told him that he needed Hans Strydom on a plane to Johannesburg as soon as possible. James concluded that John must have talked to Richard before he came to Johannesburg, because the call had not been unexpected. Richard told John that Hans would be on the Saturday night flight from London and would be at the offices of J&B Africa on Monday morning.

That all done, John asked James to take them all to the airport to get the flight back to New York. He told James that Hans could manage the transfer of all the plant from CMI to J&B Africa, and interview all the people to see who he wanted to keep. What John wanted James to do was to make sure that the business was run properly and that both the mining and construction parts of it had the people best suited to make a success of the venture, and to watch the numbers carefully. He expected that earnings would rocket as they sold machines that all had an artificially low-cost basis, but that that would not last, so to create reserves for possible and probable contingencies that might arise. He explained to James to make sure that the reserves were well documented and agreed upon with the auditors, but create them somehow to drop the spike in earnings. James said goodbye to them all and went home, tired, glad it was over and apprehensive about taking on another part of the business that was new to him. Still, he had adapted to new situations before, and he was sure he would be able to again.

"The bigwigs have all gone?" Katrina asked him when he got home.
"They've gone," he confirmed. "Now the work begins, but we will have help, John got us an *ou* from Glasgow who's been running the depot there and he'll know what to do."
"Who is he?" she asked.
"Some *ou* by the name of Hans Strydom," James replied.

"Sounds like a *Boerjie*," she laughed.

"He might be, apparently, he wanted to come home, so he's from here," James explained.

"So, what do we do this weekend?" she asked.

"Depends on the weather," he said.

"What's the weather got to do with anything?" she asked.

"Well, if the sun shines tomorrow and it gets nice and warm in the courtyard, I thought we could get together outside in the sun," he said.

"I like the sound of that," she said. "It should be, it's been nice and warm the last couple of days."

"Did Will or Bridget mention anything about coming to see us?" he asked.

"No, so we shouldn't expect any visitors to interrupt," she said.

"Good, pity it's cold outside now," he said.

"We'll have to make do with inside," she laughed. "Are you hungry?"

"For you, yes," he said. "Food can wait."

"Oh, randy are we?" she said. "So, what do you plan to do about it?"

"I'm sure I can think of something," he said, running his hands up underneath her dress.

"What do you think you're doing?" she asked.

"Undressing you," he said.

"Well, if you're going to do that, I'd better help," she said. Help, she did, and her dress fell to the floor, followed by bra and panties, then it was his turn and shirt, trousers, and underpants followed. They wrapped arms around each other and kissed, then the kissing led to more, and soon they were on the floor on the zebra skin rug that was there.

"I love you," he said, and they lay together in the quiet period that follows intense lovemaking.

"I love you," she echoed. "That's the one big disadvantage of staying with Will and Bridget, we couldn't do this, nor think of it could they, so I really don't expect them to come over this weekend."

"I wonder if Will's friend would let us use his cottage in the mountains? It would be nice to go there, just the two of us," he mused.

"You just want to screw around outside," she said.

"Anywhere we can," he agreed.

"Well, are you ready for more?" she asked.
"I am," he said.

The weather cooperated, the temperature was only in the 70s, but with the sun beating down from overhead into the courtyard, and with no wind, the temperatures in the courtyard climbed almost to the 80s, so making love on the grass in the courtyard was not only feasible, but highly pleasurable.
"I wonder if the owner of this house planned with this in mind?" James asked Katrina.
"I wonder, but not everyone has a one-track mind like you," she said.
"My mind's not one track," he protested. "I'm currently thinking of at least three things."
"And, I'm sure they all have a common theme," she said. "I'm not complaining, just wondering why you're talking and not making wild passionate love to me?"
They did make love, wildly and passionately, then later on slowly and tenderly, enjoying the moment, the quiet of the courtyard and the fresh air and sunshine.
"Maybe I'll work on an all-over sun tan," she said later as they moved inside as the sun moved over and the shadows lengthened, and it cooled down.
"Well, there's no one here to peek," he said.
"You could do the same," she suggested. "Get some colour into that white body of yours, but carefully, I don't want you to burn and be out of action. Oh, by the way, I checked on that Motswari Lodge and M'bali camp and made a booking at the M'Bali camp for two weeks in September for Bobby and me. I'll send off the details to her on Monday."
"What will you do, just drive out there?" he asked.
"It's not that far," she said. "Drive to Phalaborwa, then it's about two hours from there."
"Might be an idea to stay overnight in Phalaborwa and then on to M'Bali," he suggested.
"We might just do that," she thought.

"I just had a thought," he said. "How do we keep the grass mowed?"
"I found a push mower in the garage, one with a collector thing on the front that catches the grass, there's also hedge clippers and other tools," she said. "I think we're going to have to keep things up ourselves. I wouldn't want someone coming in and doing it, especially inside here."
"No," he agreed. "Tomorrow I'll spend some time in the garden, what little there is of it and see if there's any mowing or trimming to do. I wonder if Gareth has been doing the gardening or if he had someone do it. If he did, did they have some way to open the gate, or did he let them in?"
"Call him on Monday and ask," she suggested.

When James arrived at the office on Monday, Hans Strydom was there waiting. He had introduced himself to those who were there, all of them curious as to what he was doing there. When all the managers had arrived, James called them all in and explained what was happening. He introduced Hans as the one who was going to manage the construction machine side of the business and told Kevin that they were going to get an influx of other parts and probably another storeman or two. He suggested to Hans that everything and everyone get moved directly to the Isando location, then told him that the first task was to verify the machines that were at the CMI site and then to get a parts count done. He would also have to interview all the people that Jan had indicated were dedicated to the J&B business. If he needed help with that, James was there, and the others would pitch in where necessary. James then drove Hans and Leon to the CMI site in Germiston, and they met Jan there, who had just been giving the people there the news. Not everyone was happy, but they all saw the logic of things, and the new arrangement was better than everyone being on the street in a month. James and Jan had a quick conversation about how things would be done and agreed that Hans would come back after lunch and start.

Next on the docket was a visit to the new Isando site. James had a site plan with him, so when they arrived, he explained to Hans how they had planned the use of the buildings for the mining parts and offices. Now they had to add more offices, more parts racks, workshops and machine storage. Hans had brought with him a site plan of the Glasgow depot, and that made things easier, as they had a blueprint to work from. They wandered the buildings and assigned space as needed, marking up the site plan as they went. Leon made notes and said that he would get a quote from the contractor who was doing the current work. James also broached the subject of low loaders, and Hans agreed that it would be advisable to have their own. There was a lot to do, so James suggested that they return to their offices in Germiston and draw up a plan with a schedule.

Isando

The move to Isando was planned out to the day. A day to move parts from rack A, a day to move parts from rack B and so on. As soon as the first parts were to be moved, two of the storemen and one of the parts salesmen would also move to keep an eye on the place. Hans checked off all the machines on the CMI list and reported them all there, which included those in Cape Town, East London, Durban and Bloemfontein. That had taken a couple of air tickets to get Hans there and back. Kevin and two of the storemen went and counted parts at CMI, and as soon as that was done, funds were released, and CMI had a new lease on life. The transaction was reported in the press, and J&B Africa started to get enquiries about machines. For the time being, James and Hans agreed that one of the parts salesmen for the mining side would handle those calls until they could transfer over the people from CMI. Hans interviewed all of them and took those who he felt knew the business and would contribute to its success. Those they did not take stayed with CMI, at least for the moment. James talked to the Barlows people and purchased four Oshkosh tractors and the trailers to go with them, and had the J&B Africa logo painted on the sides. He discovered that they had four drivers licensed to drive the heavy trucks, two of the storemen and two of the parts salesmen. He could not afford to have the parts salesmen driving the trucks around, so they had to recruit.

It took until the 15th of June, but by then the Germiston site was stripped of all J&B parts, part racks, office furniture, files and all the other items that could be moved. The telephones were switched over, keeping the same numbers, which made life immensely easier. They all had new stationery and business cards, and employee badges. It had been a busy month or so, but James was happy that they had moved and that things were beginning to function normally again. They had finally taken on twenty-three people from CMI, five in sales, one for each city in which they had a presence, one in parts, one accountant and eight mechanics and their helpers who worked to service the machines. By the time they had completed the move, four machines had been sold, to be replaced by those that had been on the water, and they had active enquiries for eight more. Not to be outdone, George and Piet secured an order for a shovel and two blast hole drills, so J&B Africa was going to exceed its profit forecast nicely. That forecast had already been amended to reflect the change in organisation and the addition of the construction machine line.

James had lunch with Jan Hofmeyr and learned that with the debt paid down and a reduction in staff, CMI was now doing quite well and Jan was looking to consolidate a bit further, then acquire another company.
"How are things working out for you?" Jan asked him.
"Well enough," James replied. "We had a few hiccups as we moved, but we didn't lose any time, so got our move done by the 15th."
"If ever you want a job, just let me know," Jan said. "I'm amazed that you got all that done in such a short time."
"I think it was working on the open pit in Zambia that prepared me for doing this kind of thing," James said. "We had to transport our whole fleet of equipment from Malawi when the border was closed. We took a whole convoy of low loaders and support vehicles and either drove or carried our whole fleet back."
"I'll bet that was quite an enterprise," Jan said.
"We had a lot of help from the Zambia Police," James said. "The only real concern we had was the integrity of the bridge over the Luangwa. So, who are you looking at as an acquisition?"
"There's a small roller company that builds road rollers here. I think we can get it quite cheaply, and it adds to our current line of rollers with no real overlap. I like the idea of manufacture, rather than being a distributor for someone else's equipment," Jan replied. "In fact, we're probably going to terminate the other two distribution agreements that we have and look to local builders, and if there are none, go it alone. I think we'll have a better chance of success as a manufacturer."
"I've wondered if it would make sense to build some of our machines here," James said. "But I concluded that we don't sell enough to warrant the investment in a manufacturing facility."

"I'd agree with that," Jan said. "How's Hans Strydom working out?"

"He's doing well," James said. "I think happy to be back in South Africa, I got the feeling that Glasgow was a little cold and damp for him."

"I heard that your man George Murphy retired," Jan said. "Where's he gone to?"

"He's moved to Durban, Amanzimtoti actually," James said. "Doesn't like the cold of the Highveld."

"And your new chap, Piet Kruger?" Jan asked.

"I like him," James said. "Young, ambitious, keen to learn, knows the mines and the customers, he'll do well."

"What does your wife do?" Jan asked.

"At the moment she's thinking about getting a job," James said.

"Did she work when you lived in Zambia?" Jan asked.

"Her folks had a transport business, and they used to move machines for the mines and other heavy loads," James replied. "Then they sold up and moved to Calitzdorp, and we moved to a small mine away from town, when we were there she sold industrial minerals."

"That sounds fascinating," Jan said. "And in the States?"

"She joined the company in the traffic department, then they moved her to parts where she was working before we came here," James explained.

"I'd like to meet her at some time," Jan said.

"I'm sure that can be easily arranged," James said.

"Well, stay in touch, we may be able to help each other along the way, you never know," Jan said. "You know, I've got a cottage not far from Rooiberg, in a private game reserve, if ever you and your wife want to use it, just give me a call, we haven't been going out there lately, too many calls for our time here."

"Thank you," James said. "We may just do that."

James instituted a weekly meeting, held on Friday afternoons, where they went through the events of the week, the prospects that had surfaced, the issues and problems of the week and anything else people wanted to bring up. With Piet and Hans talking, they had been able to sell cranes to a couple of the mines, simply because Piet had been there, seen a need and had alerted Hans. Kevin and his people had reduced the inventory of really slow-moving parts to a relative few by offering the old parts at discounts. There remained only about a dozen parts that had been sitting for ten years, but for which sales were conceivable, as the machines they were used in were still operating, so it made sense to hang on to them. James did consult with Oak Creek and wrote down the value of those parts as essentially nil. There was a possibility of a sale, but the probability was not high. Leon made sure everyone was aware of their financial situation and pointed out cost items that needed to be watched. They might be doing well, but that was no excuse for undue extravagance. They discussed many times the age-old issue of expense accounts and what was reasonable to charge for lunches and dinners with potential customers. James had also started to make his rounds of the major customers, most of which were the mining companies, but three of which were actually a crane hire company and two sand and gravel companies.

In early August, James happened to be on-site early in the morning and wandered around looking to see who was there. He went into the parts warehouse and heard voices coming from behind one of the racks. As he put his head around the corner, conversation stopped.

"Mr Martin," Kagiso Dube, one of the storemen, said.

"Mr Dube, good morning," James replied. "How are you all this morning?" The group looked at each other, then it seemed by default that Kagiso was elected spokesman.

"We are well," Kagiso said. "Tell us, Mr Martin, you worked in Zambia, how was it there?"

"I enjoyed it," James replied. "I left because the price of copper dropped and they shut down my mine."

"Ah, I see," Kagiso said. "How was the government?"

"They had their problems," James said. "There were issues between UNIP and the ANC, and the UPP was never really a factor."

"There was ANC in Zambia?" Kagiso asked.

"Yes," James replied. "It started as the Northern Rhodesia Congress in 1948, then changed a few times until in 1964 they won 23 seats in the National Assembly as the Zambian African National Congress and were the opposition party until they were banned along with UPP in 1973. The ZANC was linked to the ANC here."

"Why was the party banned in Zambia?" Kagiso asked.

"Good question," James replied. "I'm not really sure, it may be that Kaunda wanted power for himself and UNIP, or he may he felt that there was too much opposition to his party."

"He wanted the power," Kagiso said. "So, Zambia is now a one-party state?"

"It is," James confirmed.

"How was the time up until 1964?" Kagiso asked.

"There were some problems, but I understand that it was on the whole peaceful. After Independence, there were changes, but some things stayed the same. Names of towns and streets were changed, and in time, the money was changed," James commented.

"And taxes?" Kagiso asked.

"There were taxes," James said. "The government had to pay for the roads and all the other things that we use every day. The mines paid royalties on the copper they mined, so the government had money coming in, but they needed more, so there were income taxes."

"Were there Zambians in the companies?" Kagiso asked.

"Some," James said. "During the colonial period, there wasn't much effort made to educate the Zambians, so after 1964, they sent people off to universities around the world, and when I started, they were just joining the management of the companies."

"Can we ever be more than storemen?" Kagiso asked.

"You could," James said. "The problem I see is that the government here doesn't make it easy for you to get an education and for the jobs like Kevin's we really need at least a matriculation, for the service engineers jobs, we need an apprenticeship or a degree, and the government reserves skilled jobs for whites."

"And if I matriculate?" Kagiso asked.

"I have no issues with who gets the jobs," James said. "All I worry about is, can they do the job, but we'd still have to work around the rules."

"How can we improve our chances here?" Kagiso asked.

"You're the storemen, can you tell me what turns we have on parts?" James asked.

"Sorry, what do you mean turns?" Kagiso asked.

"Take a part, like this one here. How many did we sell in a year? If we have 10 in stock and we sell 20, then we turn it two times in the year," James explained. "Another way to look at it is, we have about 100,000 Rands worth of parts. If we sell 200,000 Rands worth in a year, then the Parts Department turns the inventory twice in the year. I'm looking for people who will ask questions like why does this part sell, why does this part not sell? Are there mines that use a part more than other mines that might tell us something about how they operate?"

"Can we get classes here to help us understand what we do?" Kagiso asked.

"That's a good idea," James said. "Let me see what I can put together. Tell me, how do you like it here?"

"The company gives us a job," Kagiso said, looking around to see who might be listening. "We have some concerns that the company may wish to dictate politics to us."

"I don't care what political party you belong to as long as you do a good job here," James said. "In Zambia, I had mostly UNIP, but I know I had a few UPP, and they had problems after the government banned the UPP in 1973."

"You had no ANC?" Kagiso asked.

"No, they seemed to be mainly in the Livingstone area, not on the Copperbelt," James replied.

"Do other countries have problems with political separation?" Kagiso asked.

"The British have a problem in Northern Ireland between the Catholics and the Protestants, it may seem to be religious differences, but it is political and social. Over time, the Protestants got all the opportunities, and the Catholics have been left behind. In India, when the British left, there was a divide between Hindu and Muslim, which led to the partition of India into India and Pakistan. The Americans have problems in the south with the treatment of black Americans by the whites, there are problems around the world," James replied.

"Tell us, Mr Martin, how many machines will we sell this year?" Kagiso asked, a little louder than he had been speaking. James was surprised by this sudden change in the conversation, but then he saw the door open and Kevin come in.

"Well, we have sold a shovel and two drills and expect a couple more this year, with the construction machines, we expect to sell about 70 to 80 machines," James replied.

"Morning, James, morning Kagiso, morning chaps," Kevin said as he joined them.

"Good morning, Kevin," James replied.

"Good to hear about machine sales," Kevin said. "We're going to be busy now that we have the construction machines as well as mining."

"We are," James confirmed. "Do we have all the parts entered into the computer?"

"We do," Kevin confirmed. "Seems to be working well, the computer spits out re-orders when we sell parts, and we can see at any time what has sold and what has just sat, we shouldn't have the problem of parts that haven't moved in ten years again."

"Good to hear," James said. "Well, I should go and see who else is here, go well, all of you."

"Stay well, Mr Martin," Kagiso said.

James did his rounds and tarried long enough to watch a backhoe being put onto a low loader. Hans came out and joined him.

"Where's this one going?" James asked Hans.

"Kimberley," Hans replied. "There's a construction company there that has a big contract to redo the sewers."

"Are you glad you came back?" James asked.

"I am," Hans replied. "We're both back closer to our families, there's plenty to do here, it's a challenge sometimes dealing with the financing aspect of the machine sales, but Leon's great and the Barclays folks know that they're doing."

"I told the parts people that I expected 70 to 80 machine sales this year. Is that accurate?" James asked.

"We might do better than that," Hans said. "I'm not sure how aggressive the CMI *ouks* were, but since we took things over, the enquiry rate is up, and the order rate is up."

"What do you think about the *ouks* you have in Cape Town and the rest?" James asked.

"I might change out Dirk in East London, I get the sense that he spends too much time socialising with the CMI *ouks*, I'm looking at do we even want to have those sites, I know it's nice to have machines on display, but if I look at the orders for the past five years, we've had ten from Cape Town, six from East London, six from Durban and eight from Bloem," Hans replied. "The parts support in those towns is more important than the machines, so I'm wondering if we shouldn't scrap the idea of renting space for machines at the CMI locations, rent some space for ourselves and move some parts out, with a parts rep."

"Do we know what parts sold in those places?" James asked.

"I'm looking at that now," Hans said. "It's a little hard to try and work out from the CMI documents that they gave us, and what went where and when, but based on what we sold in Glasgow and what machines we think are in those towns, we can get an idea."

"If we did just parts, should we put parts and reps out in more places?" James asked.

"I think that might be a good idea," Hans said. "I was thinking of PE and Kimberley for now."

"Do we have the right kind of people as parts reps?" James asked

"We'll need six, I'm thinking that three we picked up from CMI would work, but we'd need three more, and better to get them from those places," Hans suggested.

"Do we have parts manuals for all the machines in our line?" James asked.

"We need to get more; we'd need seven copies of each, so that's quite a few. We have some, but not enough," Hans replied.

"Go ahead and order them from Oak Creek and Didcot," James said. "Let me know when you want to pull the machines out of Cape Town and the other sites, and what renting some parts warehouse space would cost us. What would you do, put a parts rep and an assistant in each place?"

"That's what I was thinking," Hans said.
"Put some numbers together and let's meet with Leon to look at the overall financial picture; each part's outlet may not be profitable, but it may be a cost of doing business to support machine sales," James said.
"I'll do that," Hans said.

James called together his managers and told them that he wanted to start some classes to improve the understanding of the business for anyone who wanted to attend.
"You mean anyone?" Kevin asked.
"Anyone," James repeated. "I'd rather everyone here knew how the business ran, what is important to us and how we can improve."
"Does that include the blacks?" Kevin asked.
"They're part of the company," James said. "So, yes, I mean everyone."
"But if they get educated, then they'll want more money," Kevin protested. "Once you start educating them, then they'll get ideas and then they'll want to start running the country."
"*Ag man*, Kevin," Piet said. "The better educated your storemen are, the easier your job is."
"I still don't think it's a good idea," Kevin said. "I don't like it, I think it will mean problems for us."
"We're going to do it," James said. "If you can't live with it, you have to make a choice."
"Well, I'm not having any part of this," Kevin said. "You've got my notice."
"Leon, would you pay Kevin his two weeks' notice and see him out?" James instructed. Leon walked Kevin out of the room and was back in a fairly short time with Kevin's badge and keys.
"So, is there anyone else who disagrees with the education program?" James asked.
"I think it's a good idea," Hans said. "I agree with Piet, it will make our lives easier if we have better people."
"Will these sessions be open to my accountants as well?" Leon asked.
"Anyone in the company," James repeated. "I'm thinking of classes dealing with parts management, machine applications and uses, basic

accounting, mining methods, and even in time how to analyse parts sales data."

"Who's going to conduct these classes?" Leon asked.

"We are," James said. "I'll take mining methods and mining machine applications, Piet, you can help with that, Hans, you need to put together something that covers cranes, backhoes and such, Leon, I'd like an introduction to accounting, and we also need someone to do parts sales, including a new Parts Department manager, suggestions?"

"Danie," Piet suggested.

"*Ja*, Danie," Hans agreed.

"How's Danie going to do these classes?" Piet asked.

"I can get him help," James said. "Before we came here, my wife worked for the Parts Department in Oak Creek, and she did a lot of analysis of the parts shipments that had gone out and to whom."

"Oh, so the Katrina Martin that we got messages from was your wife?" Leon asked.

"It was," James confirmed. "The company felt that it wouldn't be best if she worked for us here, but she can teach a class for us."

"What about service classes?" Frank Cronje, the Service Manager, asked.

"That's a little more specialised," James commented. "It might be useful to go through what fails and why, rather than the process of repairs. If we know what fails and why, we can make better decisions about parts stocking levels."

"I can do that," Frank said.

"If you have ideas and suggestions, let me know," James said.

"When are we going to start these classes?" Piet asked.

"I was thinking that we need a good month to prepare, so what about the first week of October?" James suggested.

"That sounds fine," Hans said, and the others nodded their agreement.

"Okay, well, we'll hold an all-employee meeting on Friday afternoon and tell everyone what we're going to do," James said. "We'll use the big conference room and pick days for the various classes. Leon, if you'd get us a large calendar, we'll mark it up with classes. I'd keep the classes to an hour and allow another half an hour for questions."

"If *ouks* go to the classes, will they get paid for their time?" Frank asked.

"No," James said. "These classes are not required, but provided for the benefit of the staff. If they choose not to attend, then they don't; if they do, then they may learn something that will help them and us. Leon, would you round up Danie for me? I think that's all for now. Let me know if you have any ideas."

"You wanted to see me. Mr Martin," Danie Botha said as he came to James's office.

"Kevin decided that he wanted to leave," James replied. "So, now we have a vacancy for a manager, and you were recommended to me by the others."

"Well, I won't let you down," Danie said.

"There is one issue that I need to understand how you feel," James said. "We're going to start some classes to teach our people about the business, about how machines are used, how parts are sold, and basic accounting, and by our people, we mean all of our people, including Kagiso Dube and the other storemen. Do you have any thoughts about that?"

"I think it's a good idea," Danie said. "Kagiso is a jacked-up *ou,* and he knows a lot about parts, the others not quite so much, but with some help, they'll learn, it'll make my life easier. Kevin was like a lot of *Rooineks,* more *verkrampt* than most *Boerjies,* afraid he'd lose his job if the blacks ever got educated."

"Okay," James said. "Then I'm prepared to offer you the job of parts manager, starting today."

"Thanks, Mr Martin," Danie said. "What does that all mean?"

James went through what he was looking for in a parts manager. He also told Danie what his new salary would be and asked him for suggestions for his replacement. That led to quite a long discussion about whether or not someone like Kagiso could be successful selling parts to the mining companies. Sadly, Danie felt that Kagiso would be treated as an errand boy and not taken seriously, which would make it difficult, to say the least, to do the job. Danie saw it as a circle that built upon itself, and it was going to take something quite dramatic to break that circle. He did suggest that they use Kagiso to sell parts in Botswana and Zambia; there, at least, he would not face the systemic racism that underpinned every aspect of life in South Africa. For his own replacement in South Africa, he had the name of a man whom he thought would do well. James asked him if a woman might be possible, and Danie went through the same scenario as he had with Kagiso; the fundamentals of the society would have to change before a woman could be successful in the job.

James called Jan Hofmeyr and asked if the offer for the cottage at Rooiberg was still good.

"Of course, James, any time," Jan said.

"Would this weekend be inconvenient?" James asked.

"Not at all, I'll tell the people at the lodge to expect you. When do you think you'll arrive?" Jan asked.

"Between eight and nine on Saturday morning," James said. "We thought we'd make an early start from here. How do I get there?"

"You have pencil and paper handy?" Jan asked. James confirmed that he was ready, then Jan gave him general directions to Rooiberg, then precise directions to the lodge and the cottage.

"Thanks, Jan," James said. "How are things?"

"Looking up," Jan replied. "We bought the roller company for a song, and now we're looking at wheelbarrows, you've no idea how many get sold in a year. In fact, the company makes a whole range of hand tools, barrows, and similar items, all made here, so we'll pick up more manufacturing and broaden our offering."

"Can you do that without getting into the hole you were in before?" James asked.

"We can," Jan said. "We're going to buy them with shares of CMI. It should hit the press and the exchange on Monday morning."

"I'll stay quiet," James promised.

"I know you will," Jan said. "I hear Kevin left."

"I want to start a program to educate the people here, and for me, that means all of them. Kevin had a problem with that, so he gave his notice," James explained.

"So, if I took him on, it should be in something where his interaction with black South Africans is limited?" Jan asked.
"Not necessarily," James said. "He got on well enough with our black storemen; he just didn't like the idea of educating them, he felt that if we did, they would ask for more money. As one of my people put it, for a *Rooinek,* he was more *verkrampt* than most *Boerjies*. And I trust that this is between us only."
"Absolutely," Jan said. "You know, I think it would benefit both of us if we had lunch a couple of times a month, just to talk about the economy, our businesses and what's going on generally."
"That sounds like a good idea," James agreed.
"What about next Wednesday?" Jan suggested.
"Looks good," James said, after a quick look at the calendar he had.
"My office, eleven-thirty," Jan said. "Bring your wife with you."
"I'll do that," James promised. "See you then."

The all-employee meeting was held on Friday, and James did a quick review of where the company stood, what the sales goals for the year were, and where they were at that time. He then talked about the classes that they were going to institute. That led to questions and more questions, all of which, fortunately, James could answer. The idea that a company would actually do something to help its employees gain a better understanding of the business they were in was rather a novel one, but one which was applauded by all. Now all James and his managers had to do was deliver. For James, it was not a particularly tall order, as he had given a couple of classes at the Zambia Institute of Technology and still had his notes. For the others, they had a bit more work to do, but he offered to help them in any way he could.

At home that night, James and Katrina packed what they needed for the trip to Rooiberg. It would be a short trip, out on Saturday morning early and back on Sunday afternoon, but for all that, a trip they were looking forward to. They needed little outside a change of clothes and enough food and drink for Saturday lunch and dinner, and Sunday breakfast and lunch. They had decided to take Katrina's Land Cruiser, and she had already filled the tanks, of which it had two; the previous owner had had a second tank installed for long trips. They set out the next morning at five-thirty, in the dark and cold. There was a little traffic, but nothing to speak of and the greatest risk was speeding and being caught for doing so. They went north past Pretoria to Warmbaths, then turned west toward Leeupoort, during which time the sun came up, shining in the mirrors of their Land Cruiser and making it difficult for a while to see what was behind them. At Leeupoort, they turned north to Rooiberg, then started looking for the gate to the reserve. It did have a signpost, so they followed the road that was signed and came to a gate that was manned. The gatekeeper consulted a list and waved them through. As the reserve was private, admission was to owners and guests only, so for visitors like James and Katrina, advanced notice was required. At the lodge, they were given directions to the cottage and were told the rules of the reserve, which were pretty liberal; the only real caution being to not go on a walk without a gun, and then to use the gun only if there was real danger to their persons. James rather thought that anything shot would require a lot of paperwork. From the lodge to the cottage was about five miles, along a twisting dirt road that was not used that often, judging by the grass growth in the road. As they neared the cottage, they passed an avenue of trees, then some candelabra trees and then there it was, a thatched cottage, with wooden poles supporting the roof, looking for all the world like a set from a film about Africa.

It was a delightful place. They let themselves in and looked around. It was fairly basic, two bedrooms, a kitchen cum dining cum living room, a bathroom and a spectacular view of the rolling hills from a patio outside the main room. There was an ice box, into which they unloaded their boxes of perishables. There was no generator, so no electric lights, but there were numerous oil lamps about the place. To cook, there was a fireplace with a steel slab on one side that would obviously get hot when the fire was lit. Outside, there was a fire pit, and to sit around it, they found some director's chairs in an attached shed.

"This is super," James said as they finished exploring their new domain for the weekend.

"I like it," Katrina said."It's basic, but we're not here for luxury or for very long."

"I'm thinking that this would not be the place to bring Bobby when she comes in September. I don't suppose they have elephant or rhino here. If she's coming for the first time, then she'll want to see as much as possible," James said.

"She will," Katrina agreed. "It's definitely the M'Bali camp. There is plenty of game here, though, look over there, there's impala, hartebeest, bushbuck and a few others. It says here in the pamphlet that the lodge gave us that we can drive anywhere in the reserve; there's even a map, and it also says we can go off the roads, but they ask that we keep that to a minimum. I suppose they don't want too much *bundu* bashing."

"Probably not," he said. "Shall we take a drive?"

"Let's," she agreed. "First, we need to close the window there. I saw monkeys as we came in and some baboons, we don't want them rooting through our food while we're gone."

"We don't have to close the windows," he pointed out. "Just the mesh shutters, that'll keep them out."

"Okay, so which way?" she asked. They picked left and drove around aimlessly for two hours, stopping when they saw something, stopping to see if they would see something and stopping to just listen.

Over a late lunch, James and Katrina talked about what they had seen to date in South Africa and the differences to Zambia. That brought up politics.

"I think I may have some ANC activists," James told her. "The *ouks* that work in the parts warehouse get there early and huddle off in a corner."

"Perhaps they're talking about what needs to be done that day," she suggested.

"I don't think so," he said. "They tend to clam up as soon as I walk in, and I noticed before when Kevin was there, that they changed the subject just before he walked in."

"Is that a risk for you?" she asked.

"I don't think so," he said. "I've tried to be fair with everyone, and with the classes that we're going to start, it will give them all an opportunity to better themselves."

"Is there any resistance in the company?" she asked.

"There may be," he admitted. "The only one that was vocal was Kevin, and he left. The others have all played along, and so far, I've seen nothing else that points to serious resistance."

"Is Isando a hotbed of political activity?" she asked.

"I don't know," he admitted. "It's very much an industrial area, so everyone is working, it's not like going down to Soweto, where the unemployment rate is high and where I would expect discontent."

"Well, just keep your eyes and ears open," she said.

"I will," he promised. "Jan Hofmeyr of CMI suggested that you come with me when we have lunch next week."

"What's he like?" she asked.

"Older, maybe mid-fifties, done well for himself, I quite like him," James replied.

"So, what do we do now?" she asked. "The sun is shining, the skies are blue, there's no people around, just the birds and the bees."

"Are you hinting at something?" he asked.

"I was wondering why I'm the one who's making the advances," she said. "Normally, I would be fending you off."

"So, what did you have in mind?" he asked.

"Well, I noticed a hammock in the shed where the chairs were," she said. "We've never done it in a hammock. I wonder how difficult it is?"

"There's only one way to find out," he said. "I'll string the hammock between those two trees over there, where it looks like it's been strung before. I'm sure that's what those hooks are for."

"Will it take two?" she asked.

"Only one way to find out," he said. He went out to the shed and found the hammock, and strung it. As far as he could see, the ropes were still in good condition, as was the canvas of the hammock itself. Then came the tricky bit: first James shed all his clothes and climbed into the hammock, then Katrina followed. She perched on the edge,

then swung her legs up and over and landed up in a heap on top of James. Nothing broke, so they did not end up on the floor in a heap, but the ropes did creak a little. They experimented and finally found a position that was comfortable for both of them. It was a little disconcerting at first to have the hammock swing back and forth as they moved, but they soon got used to that and just enjoyed the intimacy.
"We've got an audience," she said, as they lay together afterwards, just enjoying the moment.
"Who?" he asked.
"There's a whole troop of vervet monkeys in that tree over there, and they're watching us," she explained.
"Well, if anyone happened to come to this part of the reserve, they'd let us know," he said.
"That was nice, but I think I prefer the bed," she said. "Shall we go inside and try again?"
"Race you there," he laughed. Getting out of the hammock was easier than getting in, but only just, both of them saw that they could easily tip it over and end up being unceremoniously dumped onto the ground below. James gathered up their clothes and followed Katrina into the cottage and the bedroom.

They took another drive through the reserve, just before sundown, arriving back just in time to light some lamps before the sun dipped below the horizon and darkness started to fall.
"So, what did we see this afternoon?" he asked.
"Let's see, giraffe, zebra, buffalo, kudu, sable, grey duiker, tsessebe, warthog, jackal, impala, steenbok, baboon, wildebeest, vervets, did I forget any?" she asked.
"What was the cat we saw?" he asked.
"A caracal," she replied. "I forgot him."
"They've got all sorts here, I wonder how many were here already and how many they brought in?" he said.
"I wonder?" she echoed. "The reserve is fenced; that must have cost a fortune."

"I suppose if you want to keep the animals you've got, you have to do something," he said.

"There must be at least leopards somewhere, maybe even lions, or the herbivores would overrun the place," she said. "We should keep an eye out for predator signs. So, are you making dinner?"

"I will," he said. "You pour us a glass of wine."

"Hah, we were just talking about lions, do you hear him?" she asked.

"I do," James replied. "And there's another. Do you remember when we tried to be lions in Botswana until those bushmen came along?"

"I do," she said. "That's for after dinner."

"Promises, promises," he teased.

After dinner, they showered, then retired to bed, extinguishing the oil lamps and leaving the place in darkness. They lay listening to the night noises, to the sounds of the skops owl, the distant lions, the hyæna, the nightjars and just faintly the hippo, which meant that in a part of the reserve they had yet to explore, there was water. Making love in the total darkness was a new experience for them. They normally preferred to have the lights on to see each other and take in the sights as well as the touches. After a little groping around to find each other, they managed well enough and savoured this new experience of doing everything by touch and feel. They finally fell asleep listening to a lion who had moved closer and who was calling to others from just outside the cottage, or at least that is what it sounded like.

James was up first the next morning, up with the dawn and the dawn chorus of birds and baboons. He wondered just what it was that they all had to say to each other so early in the morning. He made tea and took some to Katrina, then did a quick walk around the cottage looking to see if anyone had, in fact, been close at night. About ten yards down the road, he found his lion tracks; they just led across the road and were gone into the dry grass beyond. He also saw where a snake had crossed the road, and it looked like a big one. Hopefully, he was long gone about his own business, somewhere else.

"That lion did come close," he told Katrina. "He crossed the road about ten yards from the front door."

"I wonder why there weren't more?" she thought. "Maybe he was going to join with others somewhere. I was thinking about yesterday, I'm glad you got the snip, it makes things so much easier, and I can stay off the pill."

"I'm glad too," he said. "You hear men worry about whether or not they will be able to perform. I haven't noticed any changes, have you?"

"Only one," she said. "You seem to have got randier."

"That's you," he said. "I can't help it, I look at you and my mind wanders."

"Yes, straight into the bedroom," she laughed.

"Not necessarily," he said.

"Well, it's too bloody cold to do it here in the kitchen," she said. "So, if you've finished your tea, we'll go back to bed for a while."

"What shall we do today?" Katrina asked as they sat eating a late breakfast.

"I think take a drive, maybe the other way from where we went yesterday and see if we can find the waterhole where those hippo were," he suggested.

"Good idea," she said. "We'll do that, come back here for a late lunch, then pack up and leave to go home. I'd like to be home before dark if we can."

"Okay, so we'd need to leave here by three, three-thirty at the latest," he said.

"Okay, so why don't we pack up now, take all our stuff with us, pack a lunch and then just go for a drive and leave straight from there?" she suggested.

"I'll start packing," he said. He looked around the cottage and packed up the bedding they had brought with them and the clothes they had discarded the night before. Everything packed, he helped Katrina clean up the kitchen, then he went outside and put away the chairs and the hammock. They did one last check, then locked up the cottage and left. Katrina drove, and they went looking for the waterhole. It was quite a way from the cottage and showed just how far sound travels at night. There was a small herd of hippo, and James wondered where they came from and where they would go when the waterhole dried up. Neither he nor Katrina could see any stream running into the waterhole, so unless it was fed by a spring, it was going to dry up until the rains came. The hippo were not the only ones by the water, there were waterbuck and impala, all drinking and yet keeping a wary eye out for lions. There were also birds by the score, and both Katrina and James wished for Bridget or Will to tell them what they all were. Katrina knew many of them, but there were some that were new to her. They just sat and watched the waterhole, watched the comings and goings of birds and animals, watched the dragonflies dancing over the water, and the fish jumping to either catch insects or evade bigger fish. They ate their lunch, then regretfully left to start wending their way back to Edenvale.

They were home before dark, but not long before. The sun was setting as they pulled into the driveway, which portended darkness in half an hour or so.

"That was lovely," Katrina said as they unpacked their belongings. "We should thank Jan Hofmeyr for letting us use his cottage."

"Which do you like better?" James asked. "The place that Will took us to, or the one by Rooiberg?"

"They're really different," she said. "I like both, but if I had to choose only one, then I'd go for Rooiberg."

"If we go again, should we ask Will and Bridget if they'd like to come with us?" he asked.

"That would be nice, but if we do, then there's no sex in the hammock," she laughed.

"We'll talk to Jan on Wednesday and find out how often he goes and how often we could use it. I wouldn't want to take advantage and be someone who just sponges," James said.

"I doubt that he sees you that way," she said. "He was probably just being nice."

"Are we going to drive to the Cape at Christmas time and visit your folks?" he asked.

"That might be nice," she agreed. "I wonder if Will and Bridget would like to go as well. We should ask them."

"I will," James said. "I'll look to see when we're going to shut down for Christmas, and we can make some plans."

New jobs

James and Katrina each drove into the centre of Johannesburg on Wednesday for the luncheon engagement with Jan Hofmeyr. He was waiting for them and suggested that they walk over to the Carlton and eat there. It was the first time Katrina had been, but for James, it was almost becoming a regular eating place, as he had eaten there with the big wigs from Oak Creek and several major customers.

"Mr Hofmeyr, we want to thank you for letting us use your cottage, it was very nice," Katrina said.

"It's a bit basic," he replied. "We haven't been out much lately, we're getting to the age when we'd like a little more in the way of creature comfort."

"I liked that about it," Katrina said.

"Well, you're welcome to use it any time," he said. "So, Katrina, James told me that you used to be in the transport business."

"My folks had the business until they sold up and moved," she said. "I worked for the buyer until we moved to another mine that was quite a way from any cities."

"Tell me a bit about that business?" Jan asked. Katrina then told about the business, how many people they had, how many trucks, what kinds of things they moved and where.

"Then James told me that you sold industrial minerals. What did you sell?" Jan asked.

"China clay, feldspars, sand for glass, and other minerals, I sold to the paint factory, the toothpaste plant, the pottery and the glassworks," she explained.

"And, before you came here, you were in the Parts Department of J&B," Jan commented.

"I started there in traffic and moved to parts," she said.

"And what did you do in parts?" he asked.

"Apart from fulfilling orders, I looked at what sold for what machines and to whom, and with the help of one of the computer programmers, came up with some analyses that helped us stock the right parts and also pointed us to problems with the designs," she explained.

"And did that help?" he asked.

"It helped in that we stocked different parts out in the depots, parts that moved a lot, with design changes, sometimes the engineers made a change, sometimes the cost of making the change was really high, so they decided against it and we just made sure we had those parts stocked everywhere, we also ran financial analyses on what to carry and how many," she explained. "I was also enrolled at a university in the States and was taking a degree in finance."

"And now?" Jan asked.

"I'm not doing anything outside the home at the moment," she replied.

"I don't know how much James has told you about CMI, but we have a number of companies, all engaged in one way or another with road construction and other contracting like pipe laying, either for water supply or sewers, we also just picked up another company that makes wheelbarrows and hand tools, a lot of which are used in the mines. I need help with finance to look at where we've got money tied up. Would you be interested in coming to work for me in our finance department?" Jan asked.

"That sounds interesting," she said. "There is something that I should tell you: we need to go back to the States every six months to keep our visas there valid, and I'm committed to taking an American on a safari in September."

"*Ag* man, that's no problem," Jan said. "I couldn't pay you for all the time away, so you'd have to take unpaid leave, but I'm sure we could work that out. When's your next trip?"

"Next week, actually," James said. "I've got customer visits, so we'll go with them and spend a week in the States."

"So you'll be back?" Jan asked.

"On the thirty-first," James said. "I want to be back to start some classes for the staff in September."

"So, Katrina, you could start on the 1st of October," Jan suggested.

"What are you offering?" Katrina asked.

"Let's see, analyst, base salary of 1,500 Rand a month, three weeks holiday a year," Jan replied.

"That sounds attractive, working from where?" she asked.

"We've got most of our records here and our computer here," he replied. "So, it would make sense to work from here. So, what do you think?"

"I think I will," she said. "What do I do, just come here on the 1st of October?"

"Well, we could sign you up back at my office today," Jan suggested. "Then I could introduce you around and you could just come back on the 1st and start, how does that sound?"

"That would be fine," she said.

"Good," Jan said. "That's one of my problems solved. Now, I have another business that has nothing to do with manufacturing; it's a travel agency setting people up with safaris here and in Botswana, you wouldn't happen to know anyone who might be interested?"

"I wonder if Bridget might be interested?" Katrina asked James.

"Might be," he said. "My sister-in-law was working for Modderfontein until she had a baby; she left there and might be interested in something new."

"Would you ask her for me?" Jan asked. "I don't have any issues with children, she could work from home, we'd just put in an extra telephone line, most of our clients are from England or Europe, so it's a lot of letters and telephone calls and telexes, we have an office in London that handles airline bookings and collects the money for the safaris, but we need someone locally to handle everything here, local ground transport, hotels, safari camps and lodges."

"I think Bridget may find that interesting," James said. "Why don't I get her to call you?"

"Dankie," Jan said. "Katrina, I forgot to ask, do you speak Afrikaans? Some of the bankers are more comfortable in Afrikaans."

"Ja, ek kan Afrikaans praat," she replied.

"Goed," Jan said. "Have you finished with your lunch? Shall we take coffee at the office and discuss details of the job?"

"That would be fine," she said.

"I'm sorry, but I should go," James said. "Thank you for the lunch, Jan, and thanks again for the use of the cottage, Suikerbossie. I'll see you at home later."

James returned to his office and sat down with Piet to review their itinerary for the next week. They would fly to Milwaukee and meet the customers in Oak Creek. Then they would fly out to Rock Springs in Wyoming and look at a machine that had just been commissioned and that was now busy digging its way through overburden at a coal mine. James had been to the mine before it was even a mine and had been part of the initial sale of the machine to the company. There would also be plant tours and meetings with contracts people to negotiate the potential sale of the machine. For James, it was an important event as it would be the first two large draglines that he would see brought into South Africa and erected, one at a coal mine and one at a diamond mine. It represented a huge sale for J&B Africa, and James felt that it was really important for him to be with the customers as they toured the mine in the States. While he was gone, Leon would be in charge, so James also sat down with Leon and went through what was pending in the way of sales and service. The shovel and drills that Piet had sold earlier in the year were due to arrive on a boat docking in Cape Town shortly. He asked Leon to send one of their service people to make sure they were unloaded properly, then sent on their way by road to the mine site. That would require several low loaders, in fact, quite a few, as all the machines came in pieces and had to be assembled on site. Transport by rail was limited by the loading gauge of South African Railways and a couple of inconvenient bridges and tunnels on the line that ran between Cape Town and the mine site. Once the machines had arrived on site, then the erection engineer would direct assembly and commission of the machines. James had promised himself that he would go out to the mine site when that activity started, but he had a few weeks before that would happen.

Katrina was already home when James arrived.

"So, how was the afternoon?" he asked her.

"Interesting," she said. "I'll start when Bobby's left to go back to the States. I called Bobby and told her that we're coming and I'm going to stay with her while you're busy with your customers, we'll talk about the trip to M'Bali and make sure she has everything she needs."

"Did you have a chance to call Bridget?" he asked.

"I thought you'd do that," she said. "You know Hofmeyr better than I do, and he asked you to call her."

"Let me do that now," he said. "Would you get us a drink?" James called Bridget and told her about their day, and then told her about the possibility of a job in the travel agency business. She was excited about that and said that she would call Hofmeyr in the morning.

"She's going to call?" Katrina asked James when he hung up.

"Tomorrow morning," James said.

"We're leaving on Friday, right?" she asked.

"That's right," he confirmed. "I got Will to take us to the airport. I'm going to leave the car at the office, then Charlize can pick us up when we get back."

"How are you going to get home on Friday?" she asked.

"Charlize will drop me off," he said. "She doesn't live that far from here, so it's easy for her to just make a small detour."

"Thanks for dropping us off, Will," James said as they were deposited at the departures area of the Jan Smuts airport.

"Have fun in the States, oh, we forgot to tell you, Bridget got the job with Rand Travel, she starts next week as soon as they get the new phone line installed," Will said. "She met with Hofmeyr today, and they agreed on what he wants and what he'll pay. It'll help us a lot."

"We'll see you in a week or so," James said. They gathered up their luggage and went in to check in for the flight. James wondered if they would see any of their customers on the flight, but he saw no one that he knew. Piet was taking the flight on Saturday, and James thought it likely that the customers would be on the same flight. The flight was uneventful, which was good, no excessive turbulence, no delays, nothing that interfered at all with the smooth running of the flight. The crew was all new to James, which was not surprising; a daily flight meant that there were many crew members who flew back and forth from Johannesburg to New York, so the chances of seeing those whom they knew were slim.

Roberta met them in Milwaukee and drove them back to her house. James would check into a hotel on Sunday night when the customers arrived.

"So, have you settled in?" Roberta asked them.

"We have, thanks, Bobby," Katrina replied. "I got a job which will keep me busy."

"Will that affect our trip next month?" Roberta asked.

"No, I start on the 1st of October," Katrina told her. "We're still set to go to M'Bali on the 7th."

"So, I'll have a couple of days to get over the jet lag before we go," Roberta commented. "That's good. Here we are, let's see what John is up to." John was wandering the garden, looking at his apple trees and trying to estimate how long it would be before the apples were ready for picking and he could start pressing them to make cider.

"Katrina, James, great to see you, good flight?" he asked.

"Very nice," James said. "Left on time, arrived five minutes early."

"Your customers all arrive on Sunday?" John asked.

"They do," James confirmed. "I should probably hire a car Sunday morning so that I can squire them around for the next few days."

"Well, everything is set for our trip to Rock Springs," John said. "We laid on another Lear, so you can fly out with one, and your man Piet can fly out with the other. I'll be coming with you, as will Dan Wells. Maybe you should go with Dan, and I'll go with Piet."

"We could do that," James agreed.

"So, everything set for Bobby's visit?" John asked.

"We're all set," Katrina confirmed. "We go to the safari place on the 7th and stay for two weeks. M'Bali is right next to Kruger, so has all kinds of animals, we should see a lot. I'm going to drive to Phalaborwa and spend the night there, then early in the morning we can drive down to M'Bali, should take an hour or two to get there."

"Katrina got a job," James told John. "She's going to work for Hofmeyr at CMI in his finance department."

"Well, there's no conflict there," John thought. "Since CMI no longer represents us, what they do is their affair. While we're thinking of them, how are our sales of construction machines going?"

"Well," James replied. "We are thinking of terminating the agreement with have with CMI to rent space for machines. We're finding that having machines scattered around the country is not bringing in the sales we thought it might, so we're going to pull them all back to Jo'burg and set up some parts warehouses instead. We'll put on in each of the four towns where we already have a presence, and we'll add Port Elizabeth and Kimberley."

"Do you know what to stock?" John asked.

"We've got a pretty good idea, and Hans brought a lot of information from the depot in Glasgow," James replied. "Hans is working out very well. Oh, I know I put this in the weekly report, but Kevin, the parts manager, quit. He didn't like the idea of giving classes to all employees, so we've replaced him with Danie Botha."

"You know how to stir things up, James," Roberta laughed.

"I just want to make my life easier," James said. "With a better educated workforce then my life becomes easier."

"It's time for lunch," Roberta announced. "It'll be ready in ten minutes, so go and wash up."

They spent the rest of the day talking about the impending trip to M'Bali and what Roberta might see. Katrina was also called in to pass on the wardrobe that Roberta had selected. While they did that, John showed James his still and pointed out the thermocouples and the heating coils; he was as well set as he could be to do his distilling when the time came. On Sunday morning, John dropped James at the airport, and James hired a car so that he could run at least some of the customers around. Piet would hire another car, so between them, they could manage. When the plane from New York arrived, James was waiting at the gate.

"Piet, howzit?" he said, as Piet deplaned, followed by the rest of the party.

"Good, thanks, James," Piet replied. "You know everyone, don't you?"

"I do," James said. He greeted each of them and went with them to the baggage claim area, and Piet disappeared shortly to hire a car. He was back quickly in time to see his suitcase go around the carousel for the second time. With all bags claimed, James walked them out to the rental car lot, and he took the coal customers, while Piet took the diamond crew. He drove to the hotel, followed by Piet and saw them all checked in, then checked in himself, and they made plans for dinner.

On Monday morning, early, James took his party and drove them to the airport to the fixed-based operator that James & Brown used for their plane. James saw another plane pull up beside theirs, so both were ready to go. John and Dan were already there, so James introduced everyone, and they then split up into the two groups for the planes. They taxied out to the runway and James watched as the first took off, and they followed five minutes afterwards. In the air when they had climbed to their cruise altitude, they could see the other plane ahead of and below them, glinting in the morning sun. The flying time from Milwaukee to Rock Springs was a little under three hours, but the time went quickly as there was much to talk about on the way. Dan plied the customers with questions about their coal mine, and they asked him all kinds of technical and operational questions about the dragline they were going to see. They heard the plane ahead get their instructions for landing and went into a brief holding pattern until they heard that they were on the ground, then they descended and landed.

"James, good to see you again," Keith said as they all walked into the small terminal building. Keith Sanders was the local sales representative who covered Wyoming, Colorado and Montana.

"Nice to see you, Keith," James replied. "Keith, this is George Marshall, he's the project manager for the Drakenstein coal mine, this is Colin

Bennet, he's the engineering manager and Harry Hobbs, he's the mining engineer."
"Nice to meet you guys," Keith said. "Dan, how are you today? I rented another suburban here. Who wants to drive?"
"You've been here before, James, you can drive," Dan said.
"Okay, we'll just round up the others," Keith said. "They all took off for the bathroom. Okay, here they are, sorry guys, didn't get your names."
"Keith Sanders, this is Darryl Hopkins, he's the project manager for the Swartkop diamond mine, Henry Webb, engineering manager and Bill Cranwell, mining engineer, and this is Piet Kruger, he's our mining machine sales manager at J&B Africa," James said.
"Okay, welcome, guys, the mine's not too far from here, maybe about half an hour to drive out there," Keith said. "John, would you and your guys like to come with me, and James can bring Dan and the others?"
"Sounds good," John agreed. Keith led the way to his Suburban and gave James the keys to the other. James waited until his charges had all got into the vehicle, then he took off for the mine. As Keith had said, he had been before so knew where he was going; even so, he let Keith take the lead, it was his territory after all.

At the mine, they were met by Dean Jones, the mine manager.
"Howdy folks," he said. "Come on in, Keith tells me, that some of you guys have a coal mine and some a diamond mine?"
"That's right," James said. "This is George Marshall, he has the coal mine, and this is Darryl Hopkins, he has the diamond mine."
"Well, what I've laid on is for my maintenance folks to talk to your engineers, I'll run George and Darryl around, and I guess that you've also got a couple of mining engineers, they can go with Simon, he's my mining engineer," Dean suggested. "John, Dan, what do you want to do?"
"I think I'll stick with you, Keith; you can come with us," John replied. "Dan, will you take the maintenance crew and James, you can go with the mining engineers? Who do you want Piet to go with?"

"I think it would be useful if Piet went with Dan and the engineers," James replied. "We're going to have to think about maintenance and parts in the future."
"Okay, so this is Roger Evans, he's my mechanical engineer and can talk about erection issues, routine maintenance and parts that may be required. This is Simon Davies, he's my mining engineer and can talk about the operation we have here, production rates and such," Dean said.
They split up and went their separate ways.

"So, how are you, James?" Simon asked as they got into his truck.
"You *ouks* know each other?" Harry asked.
"We were at college together," James explained. "Simon went to Oz, I went to Zambia, now Simon's here and I'm back in Africa at J&B Africa."
"Where'd you go to college?" Bill asked.
"We went to RSM," James replied.
"I'm a Cambourne man myself," Bill said. "Harry's a Wits chap."
"How do you like it here, Simon?" Harry asked.
"It's bloody cold in the winter and we can get snow like I've never seen before, but I like it, the mine's not too much of a challenge, but there are always things that crop up," Simon replied.
"What about the mine, any real issues?" Bill asked.
"No," Simon said. "You can see the dragline over there, it's lived up to our expectations, we're on plan for overburden removal, and we've started shipping coal to the power station."
"Any issues getting it built and running?" Harry asked.
"Not just because James is here, but we had no issues with either erecting it or getting it commissioned," Simon replied. "The local chap they have, Keith, followed the progress and anything that came up, he got onto it right away, and even then we only had a few minor issues that were largely due to the railroad guys losing some bits, how they managed that we'll never know. We saw everything leave Oak Creek, but when we inventoried it all here, there were a couple of bits missing, probably in some scrap yard now."

"What are your availability numbers?" Bill asked.

"We're running ninety per cent mechanical and electrical right now," Simon replied. "I expect that to trend down over the years, but not too much, and we're running at ninety per cent utilisation as well, so we're actually ahead of the cutting plan, because we had factored in lower numbers in our planning."

"What are you going to do when the overburden depth increases?" Harry asked.

"We thought about rehandling with the dragline," Simon replied. "But, James here convinced us to use shovels and trucks to knock down the peaks and leave the dragline working at its optimum depth. Doing that, we saved on first costs by buying a smaller dragline that will work well for the first ten years, then adding the shovels and trucks in year nine. When we ran the DCF numbers, it was a no-brainer."

"I like that," Harry said. "We've got a similar problem. The overburden starts out fairly thin, then increases in time, and then thins out again in the far-out years. We had thought that we'd just do fill the pit operations and rehandle all the overburden out, but I like the idea of only handling it once. I'll have to look more into that. I'm sorry, James, when you suggested that I shot you down, now I need to take another look."

"Time value of money is a big driver," James said. "It takes really low future operating costs to outweigh lower upfront investments."

"What discount rate did you use?" Harry asked.

"We ran everything from five to ten per cent," Simon replied. "We found out that even as low as five per cent, it made sense to push capital spending out and go with the higher operating costs for shovels and trucks. We looked at around the pit conveyor systems, we looked at cross-pit conveyor bridges, but for sheer flexibility and ease of operation, we kept coming back to shovels and trucks, scrapers too, where the ground is soft enough."

"How much blasting do you have to do?" Bill asked.

"We do a fair amount," Simon said. "Again, it comes down to an economic decision: what is the cost of drilling and blasting, and how much more productive is the dragline if we do blast everything. James can give you all the stuff on that. He really studied it in Zambia when he was trying to keep his front-end loaders running. More blasting led to better fragmentation, which led to easier loading and less wear and tear on the loaders. It was an economic balance between drill and blast costs and maintenance and lack of availability costs."

"You still have all that stuff, James?" Bill asked.

"I do," James confirmed. "The conditions are different here because the dragline bucket is so big, but overburden that is blasted is easier to dig than overburden that is in situ and undisturbed, which means that shock loads on the drag and hoist systems are less, which means less probability of failure."

"And I thought you guys at RSM were just glorified shift bosses," Bill laughed. "Does everyone buy the idea of matching shovels and trucks for excess overburden removal?"

"No," James replied. "In some cases, it does make sense to use the dragline to rehandle overburden, and some operators just don't want any trucks running around that are not full of coal; some seem not to be able to count, so the idea is not universally accepted. There are also cases where projects start out with deeper overburden, so they're into the rehandling from the beginning, so there's no time value of money considerations, because all the investment, for the dragline and if they went with shovels as well, would have to be made at year zero. What Simon is doing works because the extra capital costs for the shovels are out in year nine or ten."

"Can we get up on the machine and take a look?" Bill asked.

"Of course," Simon said. He reached for his radio and told the operator that he was going to get on the machine, then he drove closer and parked, and they walked the last bit to a spot where they waited until Simon motioned them to move. They were all up on the machine before it made its next swing, and Simon led them through the machine to the cab where the operator sat. James hung back and let Harry and Bill watch the operations for a while and talk to the operator about his experiences with the machine. They spent about half an hour watching the operation and talking to the operator, asking questions and listening intently to the answers. When they were ready to leave, they thanked the operator, and Simon led them back through the machine to the point where they had got on. At the right moment, they all climbed off, then walked away from the machine quickly. It never ceased to amaze James that this huge machine could dig up a bucket of rock, swing around and dump it and be back to dig more in about a minute, and just go on doing that hour after hour.

“Anything else I can show you?” Simon asked.

“No thanks,” Harry said.

“No, I’m fine,” Bill added.

“Okay, well, let’s go back to the office and see if everyone else is done,” Simon suggested. They drove back, and the others were in fact done.

“There you guys are,” Dean said. “We were about to send out a search party for you.”

“Our fault,” Harry said. “We got talking to the operator, and time just went.”

“Did you learn all that you wanted to?” Dean asked.

“I did,” Harry said. “Thanks for showing us around. It’s been a great help.”

“I’d echo that,” Bill said. “Gave me a good idea of what to expect when we start up.”

“We’ve got some lunch here,” Dean said. “Dig in, and if there’s anything else you’d like to ask, now’s the time.” They did dig in and all got plates then sat around and talked about the mine, the weather and its impact on the operation, the breakdowns, such as there were, the problems with trail cables, the length of time an operator could actually run the machine before fatigue set in and how to manage relief operators, whether or not an oiler was needed to be back in the mechanical works of the machine to just watch and make sure everything ran well.

“Dean, we want to thank you for your hospitality and your kind invitation for us to bring our guests out here,” John said.

"My pleasure," Dean said. "If you guys need anything else, you've got our contact information."
"Thank you, Dean," George said. "If you ever make it to South Africa, call me and we'll arrange a visit for you."
"I'd echo that," Darryl said.
"You know, I've never seen a big diamond mine," Dean said. "I might just have to wangle a trip out there."
"Thanks again, Dean," John said. "We've taken up far too much of your time."
"No problem," Dean said. "See you guys."

"Well, that went well," James commented to Dan as they drove away.
"You *ouks* must be doing things right," Darryl commented. "If things weren't running well, Dean wouldn't have been as accommodating."
"Thanks, Darryl," Dan said. "I hope you got what you wanted."
"I did," Darryl said. "Henry, Bill, you?"
"I did," Henry said. "Roger was really open and answered all my questions."
"James and Simon gave me a lot to think about when it comes to drill and blast," Bill said. "I need to go back and look at our assumptions and the economics of drill and blast versus machine maintenance. They've obviously given it a lot of thought."
"Does it change the project economics?" Darryl asked.
"If it does, it will be for the better; else there's no point," Bill said.
"We'll go over it all when we get back," Darryl said. "So, Dan, what's the plan, factory visit tomorrow?"
"We have a tour set up so that you can see machines, or at least parts of machines, being built," Dan confirmed. "We've also got the erection manager and the parts and service guys set up to talk to you."
"Then, Wednesday, pricing and terms?" Darryl asked.
"We can do that," Dan agreed.
"Good, then we can go home on Thursday, hopefully with a signed contract," Darryl said.
"We're here," James interrupted. "If anyone needs the loo, now would be a good time."

"For the flight back, let's trade," John suggested. "I'll take Darryl and his crew, Dan, you take George and his guys. If we're all ready, we'll load up. Keith, thanks for setting this up."

"No problem," Keith said. "Nice to meet you all, good to see you again, James, have fun down there in South Africa."

"Thanks, Keith," James said. "I'll see you again someday."

"Okay, George, shall we go?" Dan asked. He led the way out to their plane, and they boarded. With the doors closed up, they taxied out to the end of the runway and ran up the engines, then let off the brakes and sped down the runway, taking most of it before they lifted off. One of the pilots had explained to James before that Rock Springs was an issue at times because it could get hot, and it was at well over 6,700 feet, which meant that the density altitude was a serious concern. Still, they were off and in the air and climbed out to colder air quickly enough. As they made their turn to go east, James could see the other plane making its take-off run.

"So, what do you guys fancy to drink?" Dan asked.

"What do you have?" George asked.

"We've got most things," Dan replied. "What's your poison?"

"I'll have a Scotch," George said.

"Beer for me," Colin said.

"Same for me," Harry said.

"James?" Dan asked.

"I'll take a beer," James replied.

"George," Harry said, when he had his beer. "We should take another look at machine sizing and reconsider the shovel truck option for year nine out, Simon told us that that's what they're doing, and he said that the DCF calculations supported that decision."

"Better to do it now than when we have a machine on order," George said. "What does it mean in terms of a dragline?"

"If I have my numbers right, then we could use a 60-yard machine with a 330-foot boom, just like the one in Rock Springs," Harry said. "Then in year nine, we buy a couple of shovels and some trucks and strip off the excess overburden, leaving the dragline to operate at optimum conditions."

"I thought you'd dismissed that idea when James raised it before?" George asked.

"I did," Harry agreed. "But, in hindsight, I was wrong not to investigate the economics better. Simon gave me some rough numbers, and they would work for our mine."

"Maybe tomorrow, instead of the plant tour, you should run the numbers again and give us a better answer," George said.

"I can help you with that," James offered. "I have a program that will run the numbers if we enter the conditions."

"Do that and run it for a series of discount rates," George said. "Dan, another Scotch, if we shift machine sizes, what does it do for parts?"

"The parts types won't change," Dan replied. "And we have a bigger population of 60-yard machines, so more data on usage."

"And price?" George asked.

"Twelve million, give or take, versus fifteen million," Harry replied. "That three million today is huge compared to the cost of shovels and trucks out in year nine."

"Well, firm up the numbers tomorrow," George said. "Dan, any problems dropping down a size?"

"None at all," Dan assured him. Whereas the sale of the smaller machine meant less revenue for James & Brown, it was still a good sale to make. It was also likely that the other mine would use a similar machine, which made parts and service easier as well.

"Pity you didn't think of this sooner, Harry," George said.

"I should have," Harry agreed. "I suppose I was too focused on the conventional solution to mining the deeper overburden, by going with rehandle, I should have considered what James suggested. I'll have good numbers for you by lunch tomorrow."

"Good," George said. "Well, I'm glad we went out and visited the Rock Springs mine, at least we didn't go up in size for the dragline, that would've really fucked up the numbers."

"Colin, anything come up that changes your mind on anything?" George asked.

"No," Colin said. "Roger gave us good information, and much of it was what I expected. If the others go with a 60-yard machine as well, we should talk to them about a common stock of the bigger parts that would take time to get in."
"Good idea, talk to Henry about that and give me some numbers," George said.

They then turned to more mundane matters, the terrain they were flying over, the plane they were flying on and the differences between South Africa and the US. Politics came up, the politics of apartheid, and what it meant to them on a daily basis. James got the impression that of the three, George was the most liberal and Harry the least. George was for abandoning the system immediately and moving rapidly to a one-man one-vote system that included all of the population, whereas Harry felt that that was a process that would be better managed over a twenty-year period, with time for both sides to adjust. All Dan wanted to know was when the current form of government was likely to collapse. All three guessed seven to eight years, by which time the reality of a continued armed struggle by the black population would have brought home to all but the most ardent racists that change was upon them, and that change would have to happen to avoid an all-out civil war. There were enough countries around the world that would supply arms to the dissident black majority, and those weapons could come in easily through Mozambique. The one issue that they were all concerned about was the nationalisation of the gold and diamond mines by a future government. They pointed to the abject failures of the coal mines of England and the copper mines of Zambia as examples of why government ownership did not always mean success. That led to a long discussion about certain members of the ANC and how far left some of them were, to the point of advocating communism. George might have been the most liberal of the three, but he was adamant in his opposition to any form of communist state, pointing out that those countries that still proclaimed to be communist were essentially just dictatorships, with the elite doing very well, and the rest suffering. James was reminded of *Animal Farm*: all animals are created equal, but some animals are more equal than others.

When they landed, the South African contingent was quite merry, and James was thankful that he had had the one beer only he had to drive after all. They waited for the second plane to land, then made plans for the morning. The tour would begin at nine, so James and Piet were asked to have everyone at the office at a quarter to the hour. James and Piet drove their charges back to the hotel and agreed to meet them for dinner in half an hour. That gave James enough time to go to his room and call Katrina, and tell her about the day. Dinner was interesting; it looked like the two projects were going to settle on the same machine, with the same bucket size and boom length, so they started talking about a parts-sharing agreement. To James, this was positive as it increased the odds that they would, in fact, get the orders. After dinner, James called Katrina again, then asked to talk to John. He gave him the tenor of the two companies and suggested that they might have two teams ready to negotiate on Wednesday, perhaps even the afternoon of the next day after the plant tour.

On Tuesday morning, while most of the customers toured the factory and saw machines and sections of machines being built, James sat with Harry, and they went through screeds of numbers. James already had a model for the combination of mining methods, so it was a question of entering the right conditions, building the capital spending plan, estimating operating costs then running the discounted cash flow analyses with varying discount rates. The numbers, even at the lowest discount rate, pointed to the smaller dragline and two shovels and a fleet of twenty trucks to start operating in year nine. They were done by ten, then James called Hank Miller's office and asked if he might have a few minutes. He was told to go right down.

"Well, James, how are things in South Africa?" Hank asked.

"Busy," James replied. "We've moved premises, taken the construction machine line, and have two customers here for draglines and drills."

"Good, how are you doing on bucket wheel excavators?" Hank asked.
"We've made a good deal of progress," James said. "We should have a final report in about a month."
"My sense, for what it's worth, is that we would not be well advised to dive into that business," Hank commented. "It's a bit too specialised and the market is limited and there are already well-established players."
"That's the initial conclusion we've reached," James said. "But, we're still looking at the potential market and whether or not that could be broadened. There seems to us to be two markets, one for excavation, as in the brown coal mines, and one for bulk material reclaiming, like you would get in an iron ore or coal transporting facility. Those machines are less robust than the excavators, but the market may be bigger. There are established suppliers to that market, however, and breaking into it would be a challenge."
"Well, keep me informed," Hank said. "I gather that you may have upset Dan again with talk of a smaller dragline."
"I had discussed an option with the Drakenstein coal people a month or two ago," James said. "They dismissed the idea, then when we were at Rock Springs yesterday, the Rock Springs people told us that that's what they were doing, deferring some capital costs until out years, that made the Drakenstein team rethink their ideas, so I spent a couple of hours this morning with their mining engineer going through numbers."
"Well, do what is right," Hank said. "Dan tends to have tunnel vision and sees only dragline sales; we should recommend to the customer the best solution that we see."
"I will do that," James assured him
"Good, I'll see you in a month or so?" Hank asked.
"Yes, Sir," James replied. "I should get back to the meetings with the customers" James went back upstairs to find that the tour was over and that lunch had been given to the two teams privately, giving them the chance to discuss what they wanted to do next.

"So, what do you think?" John asked James as he joined the company team.

"I think we'll sell the two machines," James replied. "And, we'll stay in touch with the Drakenstein chaps and sell them a couple of shovels in the future."

"I wish I'd have known that they were thinking about that," Dan complained. "This is the second time you've done this."

"I thought that they'd dismissed the notion of a mixed solution long ago," James said. "It was the Rock Springs folks that raised it again when they explained what they were going to do."

"I suppose," Dan grumbled. "George did say that Harry had dropped the idea before and was just looking at one large machine."

"What about drills?" John asked.

"Both of them want two drills," James replied. "The Drakenstein chaps will want to add a third in year nine, at the same time they add shovels. Drakenstein also needs a coal shovel at the same time that they get their dragline."

"They've had time enough for lunch, let's go and see what they want to talk about this afternoon," John said. They went and knocked on the door of the office that the Swartkop team were using and asked them what their plans were for the afternoon.

"We'd like to talk about pricing and terms," Darryl said.

"Okay, give us five minutes and we'll be back," John said. He moved on quickly to the next office and asked the Drakenstein team what they wanted to do.

"We'd like the chance to discuss things a bit," George said.

"Of course," John said. "Just let us know if there's anything we can get you." They returned to the Swartkop team.

"So, would you chaps excuse us for a bit?" Darryl asked. "I'd like to talk to John." James, Piet, Dan, Henry and Bill left and went to find coffee.

"Anything you can tell us?" Dan asked Henry.

"If we can agree on a price, then you chaps have the sale, a 60-yard dragline and two 12-inch blast hole drills," Henry replied. "I have to start thinking about moving all the various pieces from Cape Town to the mine. We can use rail to Bitterfontein, then it's going to be by road to Springbok and then the mine. Then, I've got to get an erection crew and put the thing together. I also have to get a power line strung out to the mine, fix up a water supply, all that stuff."

"You're going to be busy," James commented.

"I am," Henry confirmed. "Roger from Rock Springs gave me a copy of his plan that he used to assemble the machine; it's very detailed, and I can use it."

"I gather that Harry is catching shit for changing the machine size," Bill commented.

"When Simon started to talk about the early capital cost reduction and the DCF returns, I think Harry had a change of heart," James said. "I had suggested it to them some months ago, but he dismissed the idea; now, when we ran a whole set of calculations, he sees where it would benefit them."

"Pays to listen," Bill said. "We don't have that problem; we're not looking at any appreciable change in overburden depth. I don't know why Harry dismissed the idea of a mixed solution; it's such an obvious thing to look at, particularly when you add up the capital costs."

"Is Cape Town the best port for you?" Dan asked, changing the subject.

"It is," Henry confirmed. "The Saldanha Bay port is closer, but it's for bulk loading of iron ore only, no general cargo facilities at all. If the Drakenstein chaps go with your machine, you'll want to ship that into Durban. The Richards Bay port is closer to them, but it's another bulk loading port, but for coal."

"Looks like we have a deal," Bill commented as Darryl and John both came out of the office smiling.

"We're set," Darryl said. "I just need to sign some contracts, then it's over to you, Henry, to get the machines on site and running."

John decided that they would split up for dinner that night. He and Dan took the Swartkop team out, and James and Piet took the others. Over dinner, George wanted to know if Darryl had agreed to buy a machine, something that James could confirm. George then told James that they had had a useful meeting that afternoon and were now firmly settled on the 60-yard machine. He was delighted that he could tell the corporate office that he would be looking for about three million dollars less on initial capital outlay, which would make them very happy. James wondered how Harry was going to weather this, but if Harry had paid more attention earlier, he would not have had to make the about-face. Still, J&B Africa had met its sales goals for the year and more, and a second sale would be very gratifying. George did hint over dinner that he had made his decision and was looking forward to concluding the deal. After dinner, James called Katrina to tell her about his day and to ask what she had done. It seemed that she and Roberta had gone shopping for safari clothes for Roberta and were busy making final arrangements.

The deal with the Drakenstein team was concluded the following morning, with a signing just before lunch. Now all that remained was for the Oak Creek plant to make the machines and get them shipped to Houston, where they would be loaded on a freighter bound for Cape Town and Durban. Business concluded, everyone was keen to get back to South Africa and their projects. Both customer teams left that afternoon and flew to New York to catch the South African Airways plane to Johannesburg the next day. Piet went with them, leaving James to finish up his business with Oak Creek before returning home. James checked out of the hotel and decamped to John and Roberta's house.

"James," Roberta said as he knocked on the door. "Come in, come in, Katrina's just been showing me on the map exactly where we're going."

"Hi, Bobby, thanks for having us," he said. "Is John home yet?"

"Not yet," she said. "Why don't you go and talk to Katrina? She's on the patio, and I'll find us something to drink."

"So, all done?" Katrina asked James.

"All done," he confirmed. "We can go home now."

"Hey, guys," John said as he joined them on the patio. "Good day today, orders for two draglines, four drills and a shovel and the possibility of more shovels in the future, that deserves a toast."

"What are we toasting?" Roberta asked as she joined them, a tray of drinks in hand.

"A good day," John said. "James managed to piss off Dan again, but Hank told Dan to back off and remember that we sold other machines apart from draglines, we sold a bunch of machines and sent away two happy customers, a good day."

"If Dan had read the reports I sent in, he would have seen that I proposed the idea of a smaller machine to Drakenstein before and that they turned it down, so it's nothing new," James said.

"I know," John said. "Hank pointed that out, so he must read the reports you send in, but sometimes we all have short memories."

"Well, the orders today make up for those we lost in the past few years," James said.

"Can't win them all, James," John reminded him. "Anyway, you're all set to take Bobby back with you tomorrow?"

"We are," Katrina confirmed. "We've got the flights set, the booking made at the reserve, and they're expecting us."

M'Bali

"Hello again, Maryke," James said as they boarded the flight from New York. "You remember my wife, Katrina, and this is our friend, Roberta Williams, she's coming out to spend a couple of weeks with us."

"Nice to see you again, Mrs Martin and Mrs Williams, if there is anything I can do to make your flight more comfortable, please let me know," Maryke said.

"You could make it shorter," James joked.

"Sorry, I can't fix that," Maryke said. "But today is not too bad, we should be in forty-five minutes early, according to the flight plan."

"This is nice and airy," Roberta commented, looking around. "I like the Jumbo jets, they seem to have so much more room than the smaller planes, maybe it's the cabin height that makes it feel spacious." They took their seats, and the plane filled up. Finally, the doors were closed and they set off on the long flight to Johannesburg. Dinner was served, naps were taken, and breakfast was served as they flew over South West Africa and Botswana. They did indeed land forty-five minutes early, and unlike Heathrow, where early flights were often consigned to penalty boxes to await a gate, there was a gate immediately available and they went straight in. Charlize was there to meet them outside the customs hall and helped them with their luggage.

"Would you drop me at the office, then take Katrina and Mrs Williams to our house, please?" James asked Charlize.

"Of course," she replied. "Everyone is excited by the news, all those machines to come in."

"It was a good trip," James agreed. "Now we just have to make sure they get erected on site and commissioned, but we've got people in the company who have done that before, so I don't see any real problems."

"Is this your first trip to South Africa, Mrs Williams?" Charlize asked.

"It is," Roberta confirmed. "Katrina's going to take me to a game reserve for two weeks. I'm really looking forward to it."

"Which one?" Charlize asked.

"M'Bali," Katrina replied. "It's in the Timbavati Reserve."

"Here we are," Charlize said. "I'll just run over to your house, and I'll be back."

"Thanks, Charlize, I'll see you later, Lovey," James said. He watched as Charlize sped off to deliver Katrina and Roberta to their house, then went into the office to tackle whatever may have arisen while they were gone.

"James, good to see you back," Leon said.

"Good to be back, Leon," James replied. "Are you well?"

"Well as ever," Leon replied. "Things went well in the States, I gather."

"They did," James confirmed. "Anything new and of concern here?"

"Just one issue," Leon said. "Assault white on black."

"What the hell happened?" James asked.

"It seems that one of our new hires from CMI was working with his helper, Joseph Zuma, and asked for a tool, the helper gave him the wrong one and the *ou* went on a tirade and finished up by hitting the helper. A couple of the other CMI mechanics intervened, then called me."

"So, who is this idiot and where is he now?" James asked.

"Harry Swain, I suspended him and told him to get off the property," Leon said.

"Did the helper need medical attention?" James asked.

"No, but he's got a shiner," Leon said. "I considered calling the cops, but concluded that it was a waste of time; they wouldn't do anything."

"So, what's the next step?" James asked.

"A disciplinary hearing," Leon said. "You get to hear his sad tale and then decide what to do."

"So, if I dismiss him, how many of the other mechanics will leave?" James asked.

"That I don't know," Leon admitted.

"I have to say, my predisposition is to just dismiss the chap; we don't need racial tensions caused by stupidity," James said. "Any history in his personnel file?"

"A couple of warnings in the past," Leon said. "He's had the same helper for four years and this is the third time he's gone off the rails."

"Just great," James said. "Well, we'll call him in tomorrow and hear his story, then I'll institute a program that teaches the helpers what is what in the way of tools, maybe set up a competition where the winner and his mechanic both get a company tool set as a prize, give the mechanics an incentive to teach their helpers instead of just yelling at them. Anything else?"

"I got a sense that the black staff members have us on probation right now to see what we'll do," Leon said. "I wouldn't be surprised if we didn't have a few political activists."

"I think you're right," James said. "What a bloody mess."

"Indeed," Leon agreed.

"Left to you, what would you do?" James asked.

"I'd just dismiss Swain and let the rest make their own decisions," Leon said. "We really don't need people here who have that kind of attitude."

"I'd agree with that," James said. "Well, call Swain and tell him to be here tomorrow at ten, also ask Zuma to be here at the same time."

"I'll do that," Leon promised.

"Who were the witnesses?" James asked.

"Bill Mason and Daniel de Wet," Leon replied.

"I should probably go and find them and hear their stories," James said. "Better I think for me to go there than summon them here. Reminds me of the days on the mine in Zambia when we would have hearings after someone had been brought up on charges. Okay, Leon, I'll go and take a walk around."

James found Bill and Daniel and asked them about the incident. He got essentially the same story from each, not so much the same that it came across as rehearsed, but similar enough to ring true. He then went and found Kagiso Dube.

"Good morning, Kagiso," he said. "Are you well?"

"Good morning, Mr Martin, I am well and you?" Kagiso replied, completing the ritual greetings.

"Well enough," James replied. "Tell me, Kagiso, what do you hear of Swain and Zuma?"

"Ah, that man," Kagiso said. "He has no patience; he expects Zuma to know what he has not been taught. I hear he has done this before."

"What did Swain ask for?" James asked.

"Swain told Zuma to give him a one-inch ring spanner, and Zuma gave him a one-inch open spanner, a mistake I do not understand, as I thought we all knew the difference between a ring and an open spanner, but perhaps Zuma does not, or perhaps he just picked up the wrong one," Kagiso explained.

"So then, Swain went off on his tirade?" James asked.

"Swain then shouted at Zuma and called him a stupid kaffir," Kagiso replied. "Zuma did not like the stupid kaffir and called him an ignorant white man, then Swain hit Zuma, then the other two, Mason and de Wet, stopped it and called Mr Williams."

"Have they, Swain and Zuma, worked together long?" James asked.

"About four years," Kagiso said.

"And this has happened before?" James asked.

"Two times," Kagiso said. "Each time, Swain was warned."

"Thank you," James said. "Stay well."

"Go well," Kagiso replied.

James went back to his office and collected Leon, and they went to lunch to discuss the process for dismissing someone. James was not familiar with South African labour law, so he also called their lawyer and asked him if he had someone on his staff who dealt with labour matters. He did, a Wilson van de Merwe. James asked if Wilson could join them for lunch if they drove into town. That was easily done, so they set the place and set off to meet Wilson. Over lunch, Leon went through his learning of the incident and his actions, then James added what he had learned through his interviews. Wilson advised them on the course of action they should take, the records that should be kept and in what form, and even how to do the dismissal. He asked whether or not Zuma was also going to be discharged, and James said no, Zuma was not at fault; he merely reacted to the insult given by Swain. He then told Wilson what he planned to do to get the helpers better acquainted with the tools, so that the likelihood of similar incidents in the future would be reduced. Wilson asked if they wanted him to come to the meeting, and James and Leon both agreed that it might be prudent. If there were subsequent dismissals, then they would know the process and the documentation required, and having a lawyer present would reduce the likelihood of a Labour Board appeal by Swain, and if there was one, then Wilson could represent the company. It was an expense James could do without, but his reasoning was that if they did the first one well, then there were unlikely to be many more, or at least not many that would be contested. Swain's personnel file, sent over from CMI, contained details of the previous two events and what action was taken, the first time a verbal warning, the second, a written warning, so at least the history was documented. James was surprised that CMI even shared the personnel files; he had thought that the people transferred over would have been regarded as new hires with blank personnel records.

James and Leon returned to the office, and Leon called Swain with instructions to report at ten the following day. He also found Zuma in the workshop and told him to report to James's office at the same time. James then called in Frank Cronje, the service manager and asked him about the incident. Frank had no sympathy for Swain, telling James that he had, on several occasions, made fun of or denigrated the black African workers. Frank described Swain as a passable mechanic who would probably have a difficult time advancing in England, but who survived in South Africa merely because there were shortages of good mechanics. James told Frank that he was going to dismiss Swain, then went on to talk about his idea of a competition where the top helper and his mechanic would win toolboxes if they came out best. How the competition would be staged, he left to Frank, but the basic requirement should be an immediate recognition of all tools, uses and sizes, and that the helper should have an understanding of basic mechanical concepts, so James suggested adding the Bennett Mechanical Aptitude Test. Frank came up with some ideas and suggested that the competition he held in three months to give the mechanics time to coach their helpers. Frank also suggested that the prize for the helpers be a 40-piece mechanics set and for the mechanics a 250-piece set, incentive enough to involve the mechanics. They would need to recruit a new mechanic to replace Swain, and Zuma would be placed with him. Meanwhile, Frank said that he would start coaching Zuma. That led to another question: was there something similar they could do for the parts warehouse men? Frank suggested that James discuss that with Danie Botha.

That night, James related to Katrina all that had happened and asked her how she had dealt with disciplinary issues when her family had the haulage business. That had been simpler; all their drivers had been black Zambians, no whites, so there had not been the racial issues that seemed to plague segments of the South African society. James was sure that his closet ANC supporters would be watching to see what happened with Swain and if the company actually lived up to the stated non-discrimination policy, which included unwelcome remarks and actions. This was something that his executive MBA program had been silent on, merely glossing over the fact that there were people in businesses and pointing to the MBA program that dealt with personnel development. When he had worked for the mines in Zambia, there had been an established disciplinary procedure that led to suspensions and even terminations; some offences, like sleeping underground, had been regarded as particularly heinous. Roberta came out to join them, so James switched away from work issues to their day.

"I took Bobby to see the Voortrekker Monument this afternoon," Katrina said. "We drove up to Pretoria, had some lunch, then visited the monument."

"What did you think?" James asked Roberta.

"It put me in mind of the American expansion west," she replied. "It happened in the same time period with the white settlers clashing with the indigenous peoples, who usually came off worse, like my Lakota ancestors, so I have sympathy for the local peoples."

"And what do you have planned for tomorrow?" James asked.

"We're going to the old Crown Mines and taking the tour," Katrina replied. "Give us both a chance to see what working underground was like."
"That should be fun," James thought. "Wear old clothes, I've no idea how fancy the tunnels will be that you'll be walking through, but we never took out any more than was necessary, so some of our drifts and levels were quite narrow."
"I've got some trousers and a shirt that Bobby can use," Katrina said. "I'm presuming they'll give us a hard hat for the tour."
"Bring me a gold bar as a souvenir," James jokingly suggested.
"Give me the money to buy one," Katrina replied, laughing. "Now, we're going to treat Bobby to a *braai* tonight, so you should go and light your fires and get ready to cook."

At ten the next day, James, Leon and Wilson met in James's office and Swain and Zuma filed in. Poor Zuma, he still had a shiner, but it would get better in time.
"Good morning," James said. "I would like you to tell me in your own words what happened last week."
"Well, I was working on a backhoe and told Zuma to hand me a ring spanner, and he didn't; he gave me an open spanner. I told him that was not what I wanted, and he argued and made to strike me, so I hit back," Swain said.
"I see," James said. "Mr Zuma?"
"He asked for a spanner and I gave him one, but it was not the one he wanted, so he shouted at me, then he hit me," Zuma replied.
"Mr Swain, did you or did you not call Mr Zuma stupid?" James asked.
"Well, he is," Swain said. "Everyone knows what rings and opens are, only someone stupid doesn't."
"So, you are saying that Mr Zuma is stupid?" James asked.
"He is," Swain said.
"Tell me, Mr Swain, how many languages do you speak?" James asked.
"Just English," Swain replied.
"So, no Afrikaans, Zulu, Xhosa, Venda?" James asked.
"No, not time for them local lingos," Swain boasted.

"And, if I told you that someone spoke all of those, would he be stupid?" James asked.

"No," Swain said.

"But, Mr Zuma speaks all of those," James pointed out.

"What's that got to do with anything?" Swain asked. James sighed. Clearly, trying to reason with Swain was a waste of time.

"This is the third occasion where you have struck a fellow worker," James said. "You had a verbal warning, a written warning, and now this is the final note for you. We have no choice but to terminate you now. We cannot have violence in the workplace. Your actions were witnessed, and the witnesses state that Mr Zuma made no attempt to hit you, but that you hit him. Mr Williams and our lawyer, Mr van de Merwe, will see you out and advise you as to your rights of appeal. Good day to you."

"I'll get you, all of you," Swain said. "I'll get Mason and de Wet, I'll get all of you." Leon and Wilson escorted him out, and James heard Wilson cautioning Swain about making threats and possible legal action that could follow.

"So, Mr Zuma, how are you?" James asked.

"I am well," Zuma replied. "But I have no one to work with now."

"We will find a new mechanic," James assured him. "Until we do that, you are still employed here, and it might be a good idea if you became familiar with all the tools in the toolboxes. Mr Cronje has said that he will help you."

"Thank you, Mr Martin," Zuma said. Zuma left, and James sat back and thought about the rest of his day. At lunchtime, he would get all the other mechanics, servicemen and their helpers in and tell them about the competition. The prize for the mechanics was attractive enough that he was confident that most, if not all, would want to take part. He was right. After he explained what he had in mind, there was a buzz of conversation and some predictions as to who would win. Well, they had three months before the examination, so they had work to do. The biggest challenge was going to be the Bennett test; it was not just about memorising items, but about understanding concepts, as one never knew what questions might be asked and how.

That evening, Katrina and Roberta were full of their adventures of the day. They had gone out to the Crown Mines and taken the tour that had taken them underground, not far down, only about 700 feet, but far enough.

"You used to do that every day?" Roberta asked James.

"We went a little further down, but yes, every day," he confirmed.

"But, it's hot and damp," Roberta said.

"It gets hotter as you go deeper," he said. "If you go down to 10,000 feet, then it's really hot, you have to get acclimatised before you can work that far down."

"We didn't get a gold bar," Katrina said. "But we got a little gold, we had a go at gold panning, and each found a little."

"So, not enough for us to retire to the Riviera?" James asked.

"Sorry," she said.

"So, tomorrow you leave for Phalaborwa?" he asked.

"We do," Katrina confirmed. "We'll drive out to Pietersburg, then we'll go east to Tzaneen and on down to Phalaborwa."

"You'll call me when you get there?" he asked.

"Of course," she said. "I won't be able to call you when we go to M'Bali, they probably only have the one phone, and that will be for their office."

"I'll manage," he said. "So, who's cooking tonight, you or me?"

"Actually, Bobby is," Katrina said. "She's been busy since we got home."

"I think you'll find it worth waiting for," Roberta said.

James saw Katrina and Roberta off in the morning and then locked up and went to the office. Leon was waiting to see him.

"James," he said. "Our man Mr Swain is all repentant and was begging for his job back. Apparently, we're the third company that has dismissed him for workplace violence, and the word is out, and he can't find a job."

"That's unfortunate for him," James said. "But, we're not taking him back."

"That's what Wilson and I both told him," Leon said. "Wilson suggested that he join the army, but I think he's going to pack his bags and head for Australia."
"Why Australia?" James asked.
"He kept talking about Goonyella, and it finally dawned on me that he meant the mine there," Leon explained.
"Well, maybe he'll be happy there," James thought. "So, what else do we have to think about?"
"You have your first class after work today," Leon reminded him. "I'll be there, as will quite a few others. Are you ready?"
"Ready," James confirmed. "How many copies of my stuff do I need?"
"I'd bring twenty," Leon suggested.
"That many?" James asked.
"That's the rumour," Leon laughed. "Come and listen to the boss expound on the niceties of mining."

James gave his class, and as far as he could judge, it went well. There were questions, many of which he said would be answered in the next class. That done, he went home and arrived in time to take a call from Katrina in Phalaborwa. Their drive had been uneventful, and they had taken the opportunity to go to the lookout point that the mine had. She told James what she had seen and described trucks, shovels and drills. They were set to drive down to M'Bali the next morning, so they would be incommunicado for the next two weeks, unless there was an emergency. The whole point of going to a bush camp was to shut out the world and focus on the plants, animals and birds. He was going to miss Katrina; they had been separated before, but never for as long as two weeks, so there would be a lot to make up for when she returned.

The next two weeks were a blur; there were no significant issues that arose, there were no more workplace incidents, in fact, relations between all the staff seemed to have improved. A replacement for Swain was found and told upon being taken on about the competition for helpers, and he embraced that notion with enthusiasm and got to work with Zuma. The construction machines that had been out in Cape Town and the other sites were withdrawn to Isando and smaller premises rented with room for parts and an office. James was happy with the parts sales and the service contracts and began to wonder what the next crisis would be. The only thing of note in September was the suspension by the Dutch of their cultural agreement with South Africa. James was hard-pressed to see how that might affect him or the company and decided that it did not, but it did give a sense of how things were turning against the South African government. James went with Piet to the Northern Cape to a new mine to talk about their needs, which would be shovels and drills. They drove out to the mine site, which was not quite as far as the iron ore mine at Sishen, but not that far from it. The Northern Cape is hot and dry, and the further west of Johannesburg they drove, the hotter it seemed to get. This was not the time for suits and ties, but for khaki shirts and trousers and boots. James let Piet do the driving and just sat back and watched the world go by. It was late into the dry season, so any greenery that was left was the scrubby bushes and small trees that dotted the landscape. It looked inhospitable, but James knew from his excursions into the bush with Katrina that it was teeming with life of all kinds; one just had to know where and how to look. He commented to Piet that he would not like to break down out there, traffic was few and far between, and water would have to be searched for. They stayed overnight at a small hotel in Postmasburg and in the morning drove out to the mine site.

At the mine, they were shown to a temporary office, then Tony Webb arrived.

"James," he said. "I didn't know you were with James & Brown."

"Hi Tony, yes, a couple of years now, when my mine in Zambia was mothballed because of the copper price drop, I thought I'd try a new tack, so started in the States as an application engineer and now they sent me here for a couple of years," James replied. "This is Piet Kruger, my mining machines salesman. Piet, Tony and I were in the same class at college."

"So, how are things in the States?" Tony asked.

"Busy," James replied. "Coal is really busy, and new mines are being started up all over the place. We were with Simon a couple of weeks ago; he's the mining engineer on a new coal mine in Wyoming."

"I thought Simon had gone to Oz," Tony said.

"He had," James confirmed. "But the company pulled him out of Oz and sent him to Wyoming."

"I'll bet it can get bloody cold there," Tony said.

"Cold and windy," James confirmed. "So, how are you doing here?"

"Busy," Tony said. "We're going to open up a new limestone operation, mining blocks for construction and stone for crushing. We need new shovels and a drill to go with it."

"What sort of production levels?" James asked.

"About 10 million tonnes per year, from two simultaneous faces," Tony said.

"So, two six cubic yard shovels," James thought. "What size trucks?"

"Fifty-ton trucks," Tony replied. "So load in four or five passes, that would work."

"When do you need them?" James asked.

"Operational, next June, I've got a new crushing and sorting plant coming online then and need the feedstock for it," Tony replied. "Can you do it by then?"

"I'll check on production schedules," James promised. "We've just shipped two similar machines in recently, where are they, Piet?"

"They're being erected now and should be operational within a month," Piet replied.

"Could I take a look?" Simon asked.

"I'll check with the mine," Piet promised.

"So, when can I get price and delivery?" Simon asked.

"Two weeks," James promised. "I'll contact Oak Creek as soon as we get back and have them send me delivery ex-factory dates and shipping time from Houston, or another port, to Cape Town. What size drills are you looking for?"

"I want to go with 6-inch holes, again, I'll need two," Tony replied.

"I'll get you a quote and delivery time," James promised.

"You *ouks* like some lunch?" Tony asked. "There's a new place just opened in Postmasburg that I'd like to try."

"Should we follow you, then we can leave from there?" James suggested.
"Good plan," Tony agreed.

After lunch, James and Piet said their goodbyes to Tony and set off for the drive home. They made it as far as Potchefstroom before giving up for the day. They could have soldiered on and driven to Johannesburg, but it would have put them in late, very late. They finished the journey the next morning, fresh after sleep and breakfast. As they drove, Piet asked James how he rated their chances of getting the order.

"It's going to depend on price and delivery," James replied. "It sounded to me as if delivery might have a higher weighting than just price. He was clear, he wants the machines commissioned and running by June."

"I'll check where our other two six-yard machines are in the erection process," Piet said. "I'll also make arrangements for Tony to go and see them. So, we've met two of your classmates, where are the rest?"

"We scattered when we graduated," James replied. "The chaps that had been sent by their governments went home, back to Malaya, Turkey, Ghana, Zambia, the rest of us got jobs where we could, so Australia, Zambia, South Africa, Canada, Chile, even a couple in the UK."

"I never went to uni," Piet said. "If I signed up, would the company pick up the tuition fees?"

"Yes," James replied. He was not sure if there was a policy that covered further education, but he reasoned that if the company was prepared to pay for his Executive MBA, then they should be prepared to help others better themselves. "What are you thinking of taking?"

"Business," Piet said. "I toyed with the idea of mining, but unless I go to work for one of the mines, business is probably more use to me and to J&B."

"I'll set things up with Leon," James said. "Let us know when you start and what the fees are."

"Thanks," Piet said. "Okay, we're back. I wonder what happened while we were gone?"

"We were only gone two days," James laughed.

Little untoward had happened while they had been gone. Things had gone along nicely under Leon's guidance. James met with Leon to talk about reimbursements for education.

"We've not done that in the past, at least I haven't found anything in the accounts that says we have," Leon said. "We don't have a budget for it."

"I wonder how much we'd be looking at?" James asked.

"I can find out what the fee structure is," Leon suggested.

"We have a training budget. How flexible is that?" James asked.

"I would say pretty flexible," Leon thought. "We could also apply for government assistance; there are programs that fund further education."

"For all races?" James asked.

"That I'd have to check on," Leon said. "It could well be that it's for whites only, but I'll check to see; however, don't expect much, the Bantu Education Act covers a lot and restricts even more."

"How long will this system survive?" James asked.

"A few years yet," Leon said. "My prediction, for what it's worth, is that we'll have free elections in the mid-nineties, that's between us, I'd rather not be labelled as a radical and have the security services after me."

"You're safe with me," James assured him. "Anyway, back to education reimbursement, Piet wants to sign up for an external degree in business. He told me that he'd thought about mining, but unless he wants to work for a mining company, business is more useful."

"I'm sure we can find money from somewhere," Leon said. "And, I'll check on government funding, all the better that he's Afrikaans, the government loves that."

"You know, when Zambia became independent, the number of black Zambians who had degrees numbered only in the hundreds," James said. "There had been no real effort by the colonial government to educate the black population, there was also this stupid notion that blacks were less intelligent than whites. Well, post-colonialism has shown that not to be true, and the University of Zambia is graduating students who will measure up well in the world. The Zambians who were at college the same time as I was had the same success and failure rate as anyone else."

"I suppose each culture wants to cling to its perception of superiority," Leon said. "We all have to be able to look down on someone else."
"I've sometimes wondered about that," James said. "I suppose that's why the Brits have this thing about the French, have to feel superior to those Froggies, what?"
"Right," Leon said. "Here, if you're Afrikaans, you have to look down on someone else; the Rooineks are iffy, so it's the blacks."
"Well, we're not going to change the political situation, but we can get a better-educated workforce that will pay off in the long run," James said.
"I agree with that," Leon said. "So, who's the informer for the security services on our staff?"
"You think we have an informer on our staff?" James asked.
"Almost certainly," Leon said. "I wonder who it is?"
"Your guess is probably better than mine," James said.
"Sam Beyers is my bet," Leon said. "He doesn't feel quite right; he lives better than he should be able to on his salary."
"Maybe his wife works?" James suggested.
"No, she doesn't," Leon said. "They've got money coming in from somewhere."
"He embraced the idea of the mechanic's helper competition," James commented.
"He had to," Leon said. "If he didn't, we'd all ask why, so to maintain cover, he has to support the idea."
"Well, I'll keep an eye on him," James said. That set him to thinking; he knew he had an ANC activist working for him, now he probably had an informer working for him, and he wondered if Beyers knew about Dube and vice versa.
"Is there anything else?" Leon asked.
"I don't think so," James replied. "I just need to send a telex off to Oak Creek, getting price and delivery for two shovels and two drills."
"So, a worthwhile trip?" Leon asked.
"Possibly," James replied. "It looks like the deciding factor will be can we deliver and have the machines ready to run by next June?"
"What's the schedule look like?" Leon asked.
"I haven't seen a recent one," James admitted. "So, I'm not sure where the factory is on deliveries. We'll find out. I need to get this telex off,

and then I should go home to be there when Katrina gets back from the bush."

James sent his telex, then went home and waited. He wandered about the house, walked around the garden, wandered around the house again, wondering where on their journey Katrina and Roberta were. They must have been fairly close because just after six, they pulled into the drive.

"Hi, James," Roberta said as they unloaded the vanette.

"Bobby, did you have a good trip?" he asked.

"The best," she said. "Let's get our stuff inside, and we'll tell you all about it."

"How are you, Lovey?" James asked Katrina as he kissed her and took her bag.

"Glad to be home," she replied. "It was a wonderful trip, we should go out there one day, you and me."

"So, tell all," James said as he handed around cold beers.

"Well, you know we got to Phalaborwa because I called you from there," Katrina started. "The next day we drove out to the camp."

"The first animal we saw was a giraffe," Bobby interjected. "It was just there by the side of the road munching away at a tree."

"We found the turn-off to the reserve and had to check in at their gate; they gave us directions to M'Bali," Katrina went on. "It's really nice, overlooks a dam with water in it, eight tents set up on platforms each covered by a roof, with a loo and a shower downstairs. From our tent, we could look over the dam and see anything that came to it."

"We had cots to sleep on," Roberta added. "They even had electric lights in the tents."

"We had our meals by their *boma*, under a veranda," Katrina said.

"Many other people there?" James asked.

"Four, a party of four from England, very superior Brits, knew every bird and animal, at least they thought so," Katrina replied. "They stayed a week, then they left, and four others came, Swiss, they were nice."

"And you saw animals?" James asked.

"Lots," Roberta said. "Elephants, lions, cheetah, a rhino, kudu, impala and lots more, oh, I almost forgot, buffalo and a leopard."

"So, worth the trip?" James asked.

"Absolutely," Roberta said. "I'm going to find a way to get John out here and take him to M'Bali."

"We should go," Katrina repeated. "It's worth the trip. We *bundu* bashed, we wandered around their tracks, we sat and watched all kinds of animals and birds. Will and Bridget would have loved it."

"I suppose if they go, they couldn't take Francesca, she's too small yet," James thought.

"They do have an age restriction," Katrina confirmed.

"Were the guides good?" James asked.

"Very," Katrina replied. "They gave us a white guide and a black tracker, both were really good. I heard them talking a few times, and they used Fanagalo, so I could understand what they were talking about."

"Did they make any comments about the guests?" James asked.

"A couple of times," she said. "For the most part, they talked about the tracks and signs and what they meant and how recent the tracks were. I suppose they were careful not to say too much about the guests; they had no way of knowing if anyone might understand. Let's face it, if you'd worked in the mines in South Africa, Rhodesia or Zambia, you'd know the language."

"You drove back all the way in one day?" he asked.

"We left early and traded off driving," Katrina replied.

"So, what's the plan tomorrow?" he asked.

"We plan to laze away the day," Katrina said. "Then I thought we'd ask Will and Bridget to come over in the evening."

"Good idea," he agreed. "Nice for Bridget to meet Bobby, and I'm curious to see how the travel business is going for her. Oh, Bobby, you should probably call John and tell him that you're alive, you haven't been eaten by lions or trampled by elephants."

"I was planning to do that," Roberta said. "May I just go and use your phone?"

"Of course," James said.

Will and Bridget came, with Francesca, and it was not long before Bridget and Roberta were deep into chemicals and processes. Roberta was fascinated by the fact that Bridget had been in charge of the chemistry for an explosives factory; it was a far cry from her fibres business. Bridget also talked about her new job, organising transfers, local hotels, camp and lodge bookings and even in a few cases, air travel. It kept her busy and also provided an extra income. Both Will and Bridget wanted to know all about the M'Bali camp, what the game was like, what the accommodations were like and what the meals were like. M'Bali scored highly on all, at least for Roberta and Katrina. The nice thing about it was that, being a private reserve, it did not have the constraints that the national parks like Kruger had to live with, so it was possible to follow up an animal off the roads if necessary, something that would incur a fine in the national parks. James cooked dinner, and it may not have been up to the standard of M'Bali, but it was well received and eaten with gusto. After Will and Bridget had left, and Roberta had gone to bed, James and Katrina bathed together, then in bed, made up for the last two weeks.

"I have some answers on educational reimbursement," Leon told James later in the week. "We can get government assistance for training, but it looks like it's worded such that priority is given to white employees."

"Can we get any reimbursement for the black staff?" James asked.

"A little under the Bantu Education Act, but there are constraints; the whole system is set up to discourage improvement," Leon replied.

"Can we set up our own program?" James asked.

"We can," Leon said. "But we'd have to fund it ourselves. How much leeway has Oak Creek given you?"

"John said carte blanche," James replied. "But I doubt that that means I can go putting in expenses that are new and unusual; I should run this by them and see how they respond."

"We might want to talk to someone at Escom," Leon suggested. "They're going ahead with training programs for black workers, I think, because they see a longer-term shortage of white workers. How that will sit with the government, I'm not sure, but for now, they're doing what they see as best for the company in the long run."

"I'll talk to them and to Oak Creek, I might just tell them that in order for us to have mechanics and other skills in the long term, that we're going to have to develop them ourselves," James thought. "It might just be cheaper for us to recruit a trainer and have him develop classes."

"I like that idea," Leon said. "Perhaps we could raid one of the technical colleges and get one of their instructors."

"We'd have to get one who was not going to object to training blacks as well as whites," James thought. "Let's look at that."

"I'll run an advertisement for an instructor and see what we get," Leon suggested.

"There was another thing we need to discuss," James said. "I've been asked who will replace me when they pull me back to the States."

"Do you have a candidate in mind?" Leon asked.

"I was thinking that you'd do well in the job," James said.

"But, I'm just the accountant," Leon protested.

"You've got a firm grasp of the business," James said. "You understand that we're mostly a parts and service business, but that we do help with sales of machines. If I were to tell Oak Creek that you're my replacement, what do you need to know? What aspects of the business do you not feel comfortable with?"

"I think the machine sales," Leon said. "I gather from Piet that when you were out talking to the limestone people, they gave a number for production, and you immediately knew what size shovel."

"That's just experience," James said. "What I could give you is a card with required production levels and machine sizes. It will vary depending on the shift schedules they work, but you'd get the idea very quickly. Piet also has the TI calculator with everything that you'd need to size a machine programmed in. We could get another one for you and load all the same programs."

"That would be helpful," Leon said. "I might also help if I started to meet the major customers."

"That's a good idea," James agreed. "When I go next to see one, come with me and I'll just introduce you as my long-term replacement."

"What do the others think?" Leon asked.

"They all respect you," James said. "They'd all listen to you. The trick is to get them to do their jobs well, then you wouldn't have to worry about knowing everything, talk to them, listen to them, ask questions, of course, but they probably know what needs to be done."

"Well, if you think I could do the job," Leon said.

"I do," James confirmed. "So, what we should do is work out a plan, so that when I leave in May 1979, you can just take over."

"What about compensation?" Leon asked.

"I'd do a survey of similar companies here and make sure that it was competitive," James said. "I wouldn't want you taking over, then leaving the next month because we didn't pay you adequately. I'm also thinking that when I make my next trip back to Oak Creek, you should come with me."

"That would be really interesting," Leon said. "I'd like to see the factory, I'd like to meet Stuart Palmer, and I'd just like to visit the States, maybe I could add a week onto the trip and take a holiday there as well."

"Good idea," James agreed. "Just remember that the US is big and you won't see it all in a week."

"No," Leon agreed. "I'd like to see the Grand Canyon and Yellowstone."

"You know, I haven't had the chance to see either of those yet," James commented.

Are we in danger?

Roberta went back to the States, and Katrina started work. She drove into Johannesburg daily and acquainted herself with the various aspects of CMI. For the first couple of weeks, there was actually quite a lot to learn as she looked at all the various companies and subsidiaries that made up CMI. James continued with his classes and was happy with the results. He noted that there were impromptu classes popping up as mechanics sat with their helpers and explained tools, their uses and sizes and how that related to things like torque settings. He also saw little demonstrations of basic mechanical principles, preparing the helpers for the Bennett test. Leon went with Piet and James on several sales calls; sadly, only one turned into an order, the others all awarded their purchases to competitors, but, as James pointed out to both Piet and Leon, the probability of them winning all that they bid on was remote, to say the least. For all that, they had had a very successful year and had plenty to do going into 1978. All the machines that had been ordered had to be delivered, erected and commissioned, so the service department was busy and leaned heavily on erection engineers sent out from the States to oversee the process. The construction machine side of the business was actually doing very well. Hans Strydom had embraced the job with enthusiasm and had brought a level of confidence to the sales team that they had not had before. They were shipping six to eight machines a month and had to re-order from Didcot regularly. The rate of shipment was such that they added another two Oshkosh tractors with trailers. Shipments outside the Johannesburg area often took two to three days, mainly because of size limitations that governed when they could run on the roads, so what might take a day in a car could take at least two days with the low loaders.

When Katrina got her first paycheque, she was delighted and celebrated by taking James to dinner.

"What does it feel like to be a wage earner again?" he asked her over dinner.

"*Ag* man, it's only *lekker*," she said. "It's nice to be able to contribute."

"It's getting close to the rains, do you fancy another trip to the bush?" he asked.

"That would be great," she said.

"I'll call Jan in the morning and ask him if it's convenient," James said.

"Should we ask Bridget and Will if they want to come?" she asked.

"Not this time," he said. "I'm not sure how Francesca would manage, or rather, how Bridget would view the lack of amenities."

"She might surprise you," Katrina said.

"She might at that," he agreed.

"So, when?" she asked.

"I was thinking about this weekend, could you take Friday off?" he asked.

"I should think so," she said. "I wouldn't get paid for the time off, but it won't make that much difference, why? What do you have in mind?"

"I was thinking of driving to Thabazimbi on Friday morning and visiting the mine there, then we could go on to the camp afterwards," he explained.

"That sounds fine," she said. "Talk to Jan tomorrow and see what he says. If he's fine with us going, I'll take Friday off. How long will it take to get to Thabazimbi?"

"About three hours," he replied. "So, if we leave at eight, we can be there by lunchtime, visit the mine and be at the camp well before dark."

"Thabazimbi, what's that, an iron mine?" she asked.

"It is," he confirmed. "Everything will be red, I gather they're just taking the top off a mountain of iron ore, one of the storemen told me that Thabazimbi just means iron mountain."

"I'd like to see that," she said. "Eat up, bath and bed are calling!"

James did call Jan and asked about the cottage, and was told that, of course, it was fine with him, and that he would alert the lodge that James and Katrina would be arriving on Friday afternoon. Jan also commented, as an aside, that Katrina was doing a marvellous job. Of that, James had never had any doubt. Katrina might not have gone to a university, but she was probably more capable than many graduates he knew. A degree was not the only measure of intelligence or capacity to learn. Along those lines, Katrina had checked with the Witwatersrand University and discovered that there were courses she could take that would fit well with her chosen field of study, finance. It would be interesting because it would lend an international aspect to the classes she had already taken. It would also help her with her job at CMI. She had already co-opted James a few times to help her understand net present values, internal rates of return and discounted cash flows. He had also helped her with income statements and balance sheets, all useful when looking at potential companies that CMI might acquire. James did not ask for details of CMI, but occasionally Katrina talked about the company and how it was faring. Jan seemed to have cleaned up things a lot, and the company was now prospering and still looking at acquisitions, but now with a great deal more analysis. Jan had no intention of repeating past mistakes and growing so fast that the burden of just paying off the interest on the debt was more than the company could manage.

James and Katrina took her Land Cruiser for the trip to Thabazimbi and the game camp. *Bundu* bashing, or just driving through the bush off the roads, was not possible with the Mercedes that the company provided James. The drive took the three hours that James had said it would, and they arrived just before eleven. James had called and made arrangements to meet with the mine manager, and he passed them on to a young mining engineer to take them on a tour. The mine was really interesting; it was as if they were running along the contours of the hills, cutting them back and removing the iron ore.

"You still use railways," James commented as Koot Strydom, the mining engineer, drove them out into the workings.

"They've been here a while," Koot replied. "We've got a plan to replace the system in time with trucks."

"They're doing the same thing at Bingham Canyon," James commented. "They're looking to increase shovel size as they go deeper and use bigger trucks."

"I'd heard that," Koot said. "Have you been in many mines?"

"I worked in Zambia for Kasalia," James replied. "And since we moved to the States, I've been to iron, copper, coal and phosphate mines."
"And you, Mrs Martin?" Koot asked.
"When we lived in Zambia, I delivered mining equipment to the mines, and when we lived out in the bush, I saw the mine that James ran quite a bit. I only recently made my first trip underground on the Crown tour. In Zambia, we weren't allowed to go underground," Katrina replied. "I did get to see Bingham Canyon from the public viewing spot, and just saw Palabora the same way, and I got to see what would become a new coal mine in Wyoming."
"Well, as you can see, this mine is a little different to Palabora, we're taking the top off the hill, not digging a pit," Koot said. "We're still going through the effects of the lack of financing that we had in 1975, so it's a struggle right now."
"Everything gets taken by Iscor?" James asked.
"It does," Koot said. "They smelt it. They're lucky that they've got the Sishen deposits that they can export through Saldanha Bay. That brings in hard currency so that we can pay for shovels and trucks from the States. Have you seen the handling facilities at Saldanha?"
"No," James replied.
"You should go out there and take a look one day, go and have a look at Richards Bay as well," Koot suggested.
"I think I will," James said. Trips to Saldanha and Richards Bay would fit nicely with his current project for Hank Miller to look into the market for bucket wheel excavators and stacker reclaimers.
"How long have you worked here?" Katrina asked.
"Three years now," Koot replied. "I started here when I got out of Wits."
"Will you stay?" Katrina asked.
"I'd like to go to Sishen," Koot said. "It's a bigger mine and would be a new experience. But for now, it's a challenge; there's always something to learn. Is there anything else I can show you?"
"No, thank you," James replied. "This had been really interesting, I'm glad we came."

"So what do you think of Thabazimbi?" James asked Katrina as they drove to the game reserve.
"It wasn't what I expected," she replied. "I was thinking of something more along the lines of Palabora, a big hole in the ground, not a whole load of cuts along the mountainside. Wonderful views though of the valley below."
"Shall we eat at the cottage or try and find something along the way?" he asked.
"I doubt that there's anything between here and the reserve," she said. "We should just go to the cottage and make our own lunch. So, back there at Thabazimbi, is there any business for you?"
"In time," he replied. "As they shift from trains to trucks, they'll also shift to larger shovels, so I'll have Piet keep an eye on things; he can combine trips with his visits to Sishen."
"Do you miss working in a mine?" she asked.
"Not really," he said. "This is different, I don't regret at all the time I spent in the mines, it was interesting and I enjoyed the job, but this is interesting too, and I enjoy this job. We may just be lucky, but J&B seems to be easier to get ahead in than I think Kasalia would have been; they were much more hidebound by hierarchy and company structures than J&B seems to be. I wonder if really big American companies would be different, would there be layer after layer of management with steps up only after someone dies?"
"What did I hear someone call that, dead man's shoes?" she joked.
"Good way to put it," he agreed. "When I think back to Kasalia, we had a lot of shift bosses and mine captains that were never going to move up, partly because the jobs for managers were fewer and partly because they just weren't capable of anything more."
"Isn't that rather arrogant?" she asked.
"I don't think so," he said. "A lot of them were in their jobs just because they were white, and after Independence, they were moved up from being rock breakers to being shift bosses, so had no real technical skills or education."
"I remember some of the issues you had with the review panel when we were out in Mkushi, and the way the company just shoved new managers onto you and then told you that you hadn't been in the job

long enough to warrant a promotion, didn't matter to them how good a job you were doing, you were just not old enough," she reflected.
"I know, that's why I like J&B, that doesn't seem to matter as much," he said.
"Maybe they just like you," she said.
"Well, why not?" he asked. "I'm a likeable person."
"Not to everyone," she reminded him. "Some are afraid, some are intimidated, but I agree, a few even like you."
"Anyway, enough about me, how's CMI?" he asked.
"It's interesting," she said. "It's a challenge, but I'm managing. We've looked at ten companies already and done all kinds of analysis of their financial statements and dismissed eight of them as unlikely to succeed, no matter what. What is hard is to guess how much the people who are running the places can make them work or drive them into the ground."
"And Hofmeyr?" he said.
"I think he's quite smart," she said. "He's full of ideas and has big plans, but he does listen, and he's like you, he asks a lot of questions."
"Well, it's nice of him to let us use his cottage," James said. "The cynic in me asks sometimes, what does he expect in return, but perhaps that's being unfair?"
"I've wondered that a couple of times," she said. "We'll wait and see. We're just about there. We should check in at the lodge and let them know that we've arrived."

While James unpacked their belongings at the cottage, Katrina got a fire going and made tea. She kept a wary eye on the vervet monkeys that were chattering away in some of the trees that surrounded the cottage. Vervets could be thieves and could raid kitchens, and it seemed that once they got a taste for human foods, they were hard to contain, so the best plan was to try and make sure they never started. James took chairs outside, and they sat and ate lunch, looking out over the bush and watching the odd antelope wander by in the distance. This was truly being back in Africa, blue skies, insects making a racket, monkeys in the trees and antelope on the grasslands.

"Look over there in that candelabra tree," Katrina said, pointing.
"Oh, I see, a snake, what kind?" he asked.
"Spotted bush snake," she said. "Non-venomous."
"Good to know," he said. "I hope it stays there and doesn't come over here."
"Snakes have their place," she said. "Without snakes, we'd be overrun with rats and mice."
"Maybe," he agreed. "But that doesn't say I have to like them."
"True," she agreed. "But this is Africa, and Africa means snakes, didn't you have any in England?"
"Three," he replied. "Grass, smooth and adder, of those only the adder is venomous, but nothing like the venomous we have here, an adder bite may cause swelling, and you may feel dizzy, but fatalities are very rare."
"Did you ever see any?" she asked.
"Twice," he replied. "Both times they were sunning themselves on a railway embankment."
"What preys on them?" she asked.
"I suppose birds of prey, and I've heard of crows, badgers and even smooth snakes," he replied.
"So, everything exists at the expense of something else," she said. "Anyway, look over there."
"What?" he asked.
"Steenbok," she replied, identifying the small antelope that had emerged from the thick bush and was now walking across the clearing in front of the cottage.
"You know, for all the snakes and other issues that are here, I'm glad we were able to return to Africa, even if it's only for a short while," he said.
"So am I," she concurred. "So, when can we take off at Christmas and drive down to the Cape?"
"Well, Christmas is on a Sunday, so we'll close up on the Friday, early, and I thought we could leave around lunchtime, would that be okay?" he asked.
"I'll arrange it," she said. "We'll take the car, not my *bakkie*, maybe we'll stop in Colesberg and then drive on to Calitzdorp on Saturday. I'll call

my folks and tell them that we'll be there about lunchtime. When do you start back in the New Year?"

"On the 2nd, if everyone is sober by then," he said. "So, we should probably drive back on Friday and Saturday and spend New Year's Day at home."

"Sounds like a plan," she said. "Shall we go for a drive and see what we can find?"

"Good idea," he agreed.

By the time they made it back to the cottage, the sun was almost gone, leaving just enough light to find the oil lamps and light them, and to light the stove to cook dinner. James found the woodpile had been replenished, and he wondered by whom; perhaps the lodge had an agreement with the cottage owners that things like wood piles would be kept up at each place.

"We've just got time for a beer and watch the sun go down," Katrina suggested. They each grabbed a beer and went outside and watched as the sun did, in fact, go down. James could never get over how fast the sun set in southern Africa. He was sure that if he took pictures, each frame would show the sun further down.

"It's gone," he said. "We got back just in time."

"I like to watch the sunsets," she said. "But, I think I prefer the sunrise, the dawn of a new day and wondering what it will bring."

"I wonder what tomorrow will bring?" he said.

"Why don't we go west and see what we can find?" she suggested.

"How far north can we go before we hit the fence?" he asked.

"I suppose eight to ten miles," she thought. "We should get into the hills out there, and there could be all sorts hiding."

"Should we take lunch with us?" he asked.

"No, let's leave early and come back for a late breakfast, early lunch, then take a nap and then go out again in the afternoon," she said.

"It's a plan," he agreed. "Now, I'll cook dinner."

Saturday and Sunday morning, they drove slowly around, taking in the sights and sounds and just enjoying the peace of the place. They did actually see two other cars, off in the distance, intent on their own adventure; otherwise, they had a large area of the reserve to themselves. Sunday afternoon, they drove home, refreshed and ready to start the week and whatever challenges it would bring. For James, that started with a machine breakdown and a broken part that they did not usually carry. For it to break suggested something unusual, so James suggested to Frank Cronje that they drive out to the mine to try and learn what they had been doing when the part broke. Before they left, they sent off an urgent order to Oak Creek for a replacement and asked that it be air freighted out to them. That might cost more than ocean freight, but it would get the machine back up and running much quicker. The drive out to the mine took two hours, and along the way, they speculated as to the cause of the failure.

"I think they were using the swing to push an overloaded truck out of soft ground," Frank suggested. "I've seen them do it before; maybe this time they just went a little far."

"Why would the pinion break?" James asked. "I would have thought that the drive would just have tripped out."

"They may have also adjusted the trip settings," Frank suggested. "*Ag* man, these *ouks* are cowboys, they'll do just about anything."

"Who are we going to see?" James asked.

"Koot Lamprecht, he's the mine manager," Frank replied. "He's been there about four years now, and I've heard rumours that the owners are not that happy with him, too many breakdowns. How's your Taal? This *ouk* doesn't speak much English."

"I know enough to know when my wife is mad at me," James said. "So, you should do the talking and I'll follow along as well as I can."

"*Môre,*" Frank said when they went to Lamprecht's office. "*Hoe gaan dit?*"

"Ag, man, die verdomde masjien is gebroke," Koot replied. There followed a conversation in Afrikaans, most of which James understood, and the upshot was that Frank suggested that they go and look at the machine.

Koot passed them on to his maintenance man, a Danie Botha, no relation to the Danie that worked for J&B. They drove out into the pit and climbed aboard the machine. Frank went straight to the electrical cabinets, and to him the evidence was clear: the trips had been adjusted and then reset back to their factory settings. He pointed that out to Danie, who looked at the floor, looked at the ceiling, anywhere but at Frank. They then got off the machine and went as far underneath as they could to look at the broken pinion. Frank told Danie that they had a new one being flown out and that he would be there with a mechanic to help replace it. Danie told them that the mine could do the job, but Frank insisted that they would be there with the part. While this conversation was going on, James wandered around the front and found the shovel operator and, by dint of roundabout discussion, learned that what Frank had suspected was true. They had had an overloaded truck, and it had mired in the soft ground, and rather than try and pull it out with a bulldozer, they had used the shovel to try and sweep it out of the way. The shovels might be stoutly built, but they were not designed for that kind of abuse. The operator complained bitterly that he was always using the shovel to sweep rocks and debris out of the loading zone for the trucks because the bulldozer that was supposed to be there was always off on some other mission. The operator also told James that they would occasionally run into these soft spots and have trouble with the trucks, and he said that he had suggested that they not load them as heavily, but that had been dismissed, and he had been instructed to load the trucks to overflowing. No wonder the loading zone was so littered with rocks. James wondered what their tyre life was like. All those rocks lying around had to damage tyres. He went back and joined Danie and Frank and asked Danie what their tyre life was like. He got his answer. In the past year, expenses on tyres had doubled. James thanked Danie for his time, and they went back to see Koot.

The discussion with Koot was heated, with Koot denying they had done anything unusual with the shovel and Frank, then James, pointing out that the swing mechanism was not designed to be used as a bulldozer. James also pointed out that the amount of loose rock lying around the loading zone was bound to lead to tyre damage. Koot tried to deny that they had had any unusual increase in tyre damage, but the wind was rather taken out of his sails when his accountant burst in unannounced and waved an invoice in front of him. It was for tyres and for twice the amount paid the whole previous year. James and Frank took their leave quietly, leaving Koot and his accountant in a shouting match.

"All happy families there," James commented to Frank as they drove away.

"*Ag* man, I told you, cowboys," Frank said in disgust. "I've never seen a loading zone so littered with rocks. I wonder if they ever clean it up?"

"The shovel operator told me that he was constantly sweeping the area with the dipper and that the bulldozer, which is supposed to be assigned to them, is never around, which is why their tyre bill is so high," James commented. "I wonder why they operate like that. What is it that Koot is afraid of? He can't not know that his operation is a mess?"

"Probably some *ouk* from their head office came out and told them that they were spending too much on dozers," Frank suggested.

"Happened to me once," James said. "I had been on leave and came back to goolies everywhere. It turned out that one of the higher-ups had come out and told my acting to open up the blasting pattern, so we used less primary powder, but spent a fortune on secondary blasting. I had to go to the head office and explain myself. Fortunately, I had numbers, so could show the overall impact of changing the pattern. I was told to go back to my pattern, and the bloke from the head office got a bollocking for interfering. His excuse was that Nchanga used a wider pattern, but Nchanga had 15-yard shovels, and I had 6-yard front-end loaders. You really want to be out there when then change the pinion?"

"I want to get the old one," Frank said. "I want to see how much tooth damage there is and look for signs of old cracks; this didn't just happen."

"Makes sense," James agreed. "How's the mechanics' competition going?"

"Well," Frank said. "It's going to be a close thing. I'm wondering if we shouldn't get a neutral third party to come in and run the test."

"Maybe we could get a prof of mechanical engineering from Wits," James suggested. "I'm also thinking that we have a small tool kit for everyone who participates."

"Good idea," Frank agreed. "I'll call them and see if I can get one of them to help. What day are we thinking of doing it?"

"I was thinking of the Thursday before Christmas, so the 22nd, then I was going to close up early on Friday," James replied. "It may be that Wits will have already finished for the year before then, so what about talking to Escom and getting one of their trainers?"

"I like that," Frank said. "They're doing a lot, so I'd think they'd help, and we're a customer."

When the replacement part arrived, Frank went with one of the other mechanics and helped direct what needed to be done to replace it. That was not as bad as having to replace swing rollers, but it was still quite an operation. The whole job took almost a week, and Frank did come back with the broken part. Leon then sent an invoice for the part, the air freight and the time of the mechanics. James wondered if the company would in any way change how it operated; he doubted it, unless there was a change in the mine management. He did have an opportunity a week later to talk to the consulting engineer for the head office. He had known the man in Zambia and had got on quite well with him. James was asked if he knew about the pinion failure, and James then had the chance to explain what had happened and why the part had failed. That was news to the engineer, so he was quite taken aback at the full story, which was at odds with the reports he had received from the mine.

Frank packaged up the broken part and sent it back to Oak Creek for the engineers there to look at it and determine the failure mode. He had committed to Koot that when he had the report, then he would send a copy to him. James wondered how Koot would react if the report came back confirming their suspicions that the failure was due to undue stress put on the part by improper use. At least they had one worry less; the machine and the part were well out of whatever warranties might be offered for workmanship and materials. James was a little amused to see that the invoice was paid without demur or question, which did surprise him, until he heard from Danie that the consulting engineer had been to the mine, asking all kinds of difficult questions, and that Koot had been reassigned as a lowly assistant on an underground mine in the Northern Cape, in a place renowned for its high temperatures, lack of rain and general unpleasantness. When the report did come back from Oak Creek, James sent a copy to the mine and to the consulting engineer. It confirmed all that Frank had suspected.

October seemed to come and go in the blink of an eye, and November and the rains came. Summer was almost upon them, and it was heating up, politically as well as physically. There were rumours, almost daily, of some event, some protest or dissent against the government. Almost to the end of November, James was surprised when he found a cryptic note on his desk one morning, typed on a blank piece of paper. It warned him to stay away from the Carlton Centre for the next two or three days. He wondered who might have left it, but was reluctant to go out and ask. If he asked, then knowledge would be denied, and if there really was something afoot, then perhaps not everyone would be happy at his being forewarned. He went home that night apprehensive because Katrina worked in an office only a stone's throw from the centre.

"I got an odd note today," he told Katrina when he went home that evening. "It was typewritten and just warned me to stay away from the Carlton Centre for the next couple of days. Should I go to the police?"

"That's a difficult one," she thought. "If you go and they find nothing, then they won't listen to you in the future; if they go and find something, then will you ever get another warning?"

"Can you find a reason to be out of the office for the next couple of days?" he asked.

"As it happens, I've got exams at Wits for the next two days," she said. "So, I won't be near the centre."

"So, what do I do?" he asked.

"I'm not sure," she said.

"This feels a little like Churchill in the war," he said. "When they broke the Enigma codes, how much warning did they give the convoys? If too many convoys were obviously forewarned, then the Germans would have changed the codes, so what was Churchill supposed to do?"

"I can hint to Jan that I heard something about the Carlton Centre and let him warn the police," she suggested.

"That's a good idea," he said. "I don't think anyone here knows that you work for CMI, so if a warning comes from Hofmeyr, it won't be tracked back to us."

"The note didn't say what might happen?" she asked.

"No, just stay away," he said. "That suggests something, maybe an armed raid, maybe a strike, maybe a bomb."

"How many bombings have there been this year?" she asked.

"February, a police station, March a restaurant in Pretoria, and there have been two instances of railway lines being damaged," he replied.

"Do you know who sent you the note?" she asked.

"I've got my suspicions," he replied. "But I think if I went to him and asked, I'd get a blank look and no warnings in the future."

"Why do you think you were warned?" she asked.

"Maybe it goes back to a discussion I had with some of the parts *ouks*, talking about Zambia, maybe it has something to do with our trying to improve the workforce that we have, maybe it's because I fired Swain," he thought. "I'm not sure."

"Are we in any danger?" she asked.

"Probably not directly," he said. "But if we're in the wrong place at the wrong time, then things might not go well for us."

"What do you suppose the main targets are?" she asked.

"I would have thought police stations, parts of the government, the infrastructure, so the railways, the restaurant surprised me, perhaps it's patronised a lot by government officials," he replied.

"Then, why the Carlton Centre?" she asked.

"It probably represents the wealth that is white and the poverty that is black," he suggested. "I'm not sure, but tip Hofmeyr off, would you?"

"I'll do that first thing in the morning," she said. "Before I go off to Braamfontein and Wits. I'll also call Bridget and tell her that we heard something and to avoid the Carlton Centre for the next two days."

Nothing happened at the Carlton Centre the next day, so James wondered if the warning had been a hoax or if the police had investigated and found whatever it was that had been planned. He went to work the next day, still uneasy, but determined not to let the spectre of terrorism completely ruin his day. That spectre became real on Friday when he heard on the news that a device had exploded outside the Comair offices in the Carlton Centre shopping level and a number of people had been injured.

"So, that warning was right," Katrina said when she got home that evening.

"It looks like it," he said. "I don't have many details yet, only that it blew a hole in the concrete floor to a storeroom underneath."

"I'm glad I mentioned it to Jan. I'm not sure if he told anyone, but if he didn't, maybe the next time I pass something on, he'll listen," she said.

"I wonder if there'll be a next time?" he said.

"Unfortunately, I expect there will be, but I hope this isn't going to become like Northern Ireland," she said.

"You're right," he agreed. "I don't fancy living wondering all the time if someone's going to do something. Anyway, how were your exams?"

"I think fine," she said. "I felt happy about each of them."

"When will you know?" he asked.

"I think next month, before the college breaks up for Christmas. Someone has to read through all the papers and mark them; these were not yes or no answers, or just calculations where you can look at the answer, and if it's right, all well and good," she replied.

"You'll be fine," he said, confident in her abilities. "Going back to the Carlton Centre, I think I'd stay clear of any police stations in the future, I'm sure they will be targets."

"Well, there's no problem with that," she said. "I've got no reason to go near any police stations, and I don't pass one on my way to work."

"What shall we do for dinner, eat here or go out?" he asked.

"Let's eat here," she said. "I don't fancy going out tonight."

The next day, James found another note on his desk. This one just said to stay away from police stations. Well, he and Katrina had already decided to do that, so the warning was superfluous. He wondered who was leaving him the notes and sat down to eliminate possibles. Whoever it was had to be either at the offices after he left or before he arrived in the morning. As he typically arrived at about eight and the parts warehouse and workshop opened at seven, that meant it was one of about twenty-six. If he dismissed the white employees as unlikely, that left seventeen. Of those, his most likely was Kagiso Dube. He was not sure why he gravitated to Dube, but he seemed to James to be the one who acted as the spokesman for the black workers. He was obviously intelligent, and James could see him as an active member of the ANC. He decided that making any direct approach would be futile, but perhaps it would not hurt to test the waters a little with more discussion about Zambia and the politics there. James also wondered if he had any informants for the government's internal security apparatus, ready to pass on information about the company and its employees. He doubted whether he would ever learn if that was a reality, so he gave up wondering and decided to just run the company the best way he could, and to make the effort to better train and educate his whole workforce. Better-educated and trained people made life easier, no matter what the objections were within the white community to blacks getting a decent education.

Barely five days after the Carlton Centre bombing, there was another, this time on a train bound for Pretoria. Railways seemed to be part of the targeting for the nascent uprising; there had been a few attacks on various railway lines over the past year. The attack coincided with an election, for whites only, the National Party won. James wondered if the timing of the bomb on the train was deliberate, set to go off while the election was going on. The National Party's win kept the apartheid adherents in power and probably guaranteed more future violence against the system. All this was going on as a backdrop to what was becoming a successful business for J&B Africa. Parts sales for mining machines were up, keeping pace with the population of machines in the country. Construction machine sales were up, and a steady stream of new machines was being ordered from Didcot, with the odd one from the States.

James sat down with his team and asked them what else they could do.
"We could expand our service to small contractors," Hans suggested. "We could equip a couple of *bakkies* with tools and send them out on small jobs to do field repairs."
"How do we get paid?" Leon asked.
"Parts, labour and a call-out fee," Hans suggested. "We may get a few bad debts, but I think most would pay, rather than have word go around that they don't pay and have everyone put them on a cash-only basis."
"What would you suggest, one in Cape Town, one in PE, one in East London, one in Bloem and one in Durban to start with?" James asked.
"I'd start with them and Kimberley and see how it went," Hans agreed. "We've already got parts places there, so we just add the service *ouks* at the same office."
"What kind of *bakkies* were you thinking of?" Frank asked.
"Not sure yet," Hans replied. "I'd want to fix them up with tools and add a compressor, maybe a hoist of some kind."
"Maybe start first with something small like the Isuzu *bakkie,* and if we're successful and make money, move up to the Isuzu Elf and add the compressor and hoist," Leon suggested.
"We could do that," Hans agreed.
"Where will you get mechanics?" James asked.
"I've had a few enquiries," Hans replied. "I'm sure I could find enough mechanics fairly quickly."
"Why wouldn't they just go and work for the contractors?" James asked.
"A lot of contractors don't want to keep service mechanics on their staff, unless they're big enough to keep them busy," Hans explained.
"Leon, can we afford six small Isuzu *bakkies*?" James asked.
"This is a good year to do it," Leon said. "We're still generating high margins by selling off the inventory we picked up from CMI, so if ever there was a time to do it, it would be now."

"Okay," James said. "Hans, go ahead and get us six *bakkies*, and find service mechanics, starting when?"

"I thought in the New Year," Hans said.

"I'll leave it to you," James said. "Now, how are we looking for the mechanics competition?"

"Looking good," Frank said. "The Escom *ouks* like the idea and they'll be here on Wednesday, the day before we hold the test to set things up, and they'll administer the test on Thursday and get the marks for everyone. I like the idea of having someone independent, then there can be no talk of favouritism."

"We have enough tool kits for everyone who signed up?" James asked.

"We do," Leon confirmed. "It surprised me, but two of my accounting clerks signed up."

"What do we do if there's a tie?" James asked.

"I think we put it to Escom to then ask questions of those in the tie and see if we can get a winner," Frank suggested. "All those that I know who signed up are really keen, and they've all been working hard."

"Have we noticed any changes in the workshops?" James asked.

"We have," Frank and Hans both said, and Frank went on to say. "We're seeing less time to work out what's wrong and less time to fix things."

"So, it's been worth doing?" James asked.

"It has," Hans agreed. "I was also thinking of some classes to teach my sales reps and service *ouks* how to use the machines. I know that Cat has some *ouks* who will come from either Peoria or Geneva to teach people how to use their machines."

"I remember that from Zambia," James said. "The chap from Peoria was not as successful as the other they sent out from Geneva; the American had a difficult time understanding the Zambians. I'll check with Didcot and see if they have a trainer they could send us for a week or two. Is there somewhere where we can dig holes?"

"I'll check into that," Piet said. "I may know of a place where we can dig away."

"Has anyone been affected by the recent bombings?" James asked. He got negative nods around the room. "Good, well, stay safe and stay

alert, we don't want any injuries among our staff. How's the new pinion in the shovel, Frank?"
"It's working well, and maybe better than that, they've stopped using the shovel to push trucks out of the way, and they've also stopped overloading the trucks," Frank replied.
"Anything else I should be aware of?" James asked. "No, then thanks, I'll see you all on Monday."

"How was your day?" Katrina asked James when he arrived home.
"Busy," he replied. "And yours?"
"Interesting," she said. "I'm looking into the finances of a possible acquisition for CMI."
"Anything I should be concerned about?" he asked.
"No," she said. "This is stuff that would be used to put in water pipes and sewer lines, all made in Vanderbijlpark. So, I suppose some of your customers might be the contractors that use the stuff, but CMI isn't looking at building digging machines. When's our next trip back to the States?"
"We should go in February," he thought. "That's less than six months since our last trip, and Miller is expecting a report on bucket wheels. Which reminds me, I need to organise trips to Saldanha and Richards Bay."
"We're still set to leave on the Friday before Christmas Eve?" she asked.
"We are," he confirmed. "Did you get us a booking in Colesburg?"
"I did," she confirmed. "I told my folks to expect us by noon on Christmas Eve. What are Will and Bridget doing for Christmas?"
"I'm not sure," he said.
"If they've got nothing planned, then we should ask them if they want to come too," she suggested. "My folks have got room and they'd be happy to have them as well as us. Call them and see if they want to come for dinner, and we can talk about it."
James called, and Bridget said that they would be delighted to have someone else cook for them and would be there in less than half an hour.

"So, James, how's things?" Will asked as they both stood over the *braai* and watched things cooking.

"Not bad," James replied.

"Thanks for the tip about the Carlton Centre," Will said. "Bridget had had a visit planned to talk to Comair, so just as well she didn't go. How did you hear?"

"I found a note on my desk," James replied. "How's Francesca?"

"Growing fast," Will said. "Into everything, I think the first words she ever said were, don't touch."

"How's Bridget's job working out?" James asked.

"Good," Will replied. "She's learned a lot already about the tourist trade and who runs good camps and who doesn't. Might come in handy one day."

"And the paint business?" James asked.

"Busy as ever," Will said. "I've increased security levels; we've got too much in the way of volatile solvents, so any problems I might have could lead to an impressive bang."

"Just don't blow up Albertina," James laughed.

"I wish we'd switch to more water-based paints, but I suppose there's still a strong demand for oil and nitro-cellulose-based paints," Will said.

"Have you two cooked anything yet, or are you just gossiping?" Katrina asked, interrupting their conversation.

"All done," James said.

"Good, let's eat," Katrina said. Dinner was eaten, things were talked about, including the new jobs that Katrina and Bridget had, and then Katrina asked them if they wanted to join them in the Cape at Christmas.

"That would be super," Bridget said. "We haven't seen your folks in a while, and they haven't met Francesca yet. You don't think us bringing Francesca will make your Mum nag you about grandchildren?"

"She may," Katrina said. "But it doesn't matter. We've talked about it a lot, and she understands that I don't really want children."

"Francesca wants to know all about the telex machine," Will said. "She watches Bridget type messages, and I wouldn't be surprised if one day one of the clients got a weird message."

"That could be entertaining or embarrassing," James thought. "Has she tried making phone calls yet?"

"Just once," Bridget said. "She had picked up the phone and was talking into it. I suppose one day she'll work out that you have to dial a number to actually talk to someone."

"Better put some kind of lock on the phone when she works that out," James laughed. "Or you'll have a horrible bill."

"I know," Bridget said. "Still, I think that will be a while yet."

"You're staying the night?" Katrina asked.

"If you don't mind," Bridget said.

"No, man, you should," Katrina said. "You don't need to be out driving the streets."

"In that case, I'll have another beer," Will said. "So, here's to what?"

"A quiet Christmas," Katrina suggested.

"As quiet as a two-year-old will permit," Bridget laughed. "Cheers!"

"So, do you want to drive down with us, or take your own car?" James asked.

"I think we'll take our car," Will said. "I can't get away until later on Friday, so we'd be in Calitzdorp early afternoon on Saturday."

Christmas

James noticed, as December wore on, an increase in the intensity of the classes that were held. He saw quite a few huddles in corners as ideas and concepts were passed on. His own classes that he held on Friday afternoons were still well attended, and he began to think about what his next series of classes should be about. Bombings continued, with the police station in Germiston being hit, so he was very glad that they had made the move from Germiston to Isando. Shortly after the Germiston bombing, there was another at the Benoni railway station, which he was sure would deter some commuters. Hans acquired some Isuzu trucks and sent them to a shop to have them painted in the company colours, brown and green. He was also in the hunt for good service mechanics who could think on their feet and diagnose problems. Two of his shop mechanics had asked for the chance to take the jobs in Kimberley and Durban, so he had to replace them. Katrina got the results of her exams, she passed with flying colours, something that James had been sure of and which she had also expected. She felt that she had done enough in Wisconsin and Wits to earn a degree, but that would depend on whether or not Wits would accept her results from Wisconsin. She put the question to one of the professors, and he directed her to the administrator who dealt with those matters. He waffled, worried and went on about standards and different systems, then asked for the curriculum and the exams that Katrina had already taken. His opinion was that the American high school system left a lot to be desired, but did grudgingly admit that the college system was quite good. He wanted to know what Katrina's high school education had been, and accepted that the matriculation that she got from Rhodesia was as good as one from South Africa. Katrina left his office with a mission: to get all the relevant information from Wisconsin and have it transmitted to South Africa. For that, she enlisted the help of Roberta.

"Bobby, would you do something for me?" she asked.

"Of course, what do you need?" Roberta asked.

"The curriculum for the finance degree I was working on at UW-Milwaukee and the grades I got," Katrina explained.

"So you need the curriculum and your transcript?" Roberta asked.

"I suppose that's what it would be," Katrina said. "The uni here will consider all the work I did at UW and include it towards my degree."

"I'll get that," Roberta promised. "How's things in South Africa? I heard about some bombings. Was that near you?"

"One of them," Katrina replied. "The office I work in is close to the Carlton Centre, John's been there, he'll tell you."

"Well, stay safe, stay away from odd-looking people," Roberta said.

"I will," Katrina promised. "How's John's cider and calvados?"

"Surprisingly good," Roberta said. "His cider is really good and he's been plying all his friends and our neighbours with some. The calvados he's put away to age, but we tried some, and it's got a kick to it, and it tastes good to boot. I think he's trying to find some oak barrels to age the calvados in, he says it will add to the flavour."

"Keep some handy that we can try when we come in February," Katrina said.

"I'll make sure we have some handy," Roberta promised. "I suppose it's hot there?"

"It is high eighties," Katrina said.

"Well, we've got snow on the ground and thirty degrees," Roberta said. "I'm looking forward to skiing this Christmas. What are you and James going to do?"

"We're going to drive down to the Cape and see my folks," Katrina said. "We won't get calvados there, but we will get hanepoot, a kind of port made in South Africa. My dad makes it."

"Don't drink too much," Roberta cautioned.

"I won't," Katrina said. "More than a small glass and I get a headache."

"I'd better get myself organised, I have a client to meet," Roberta said. "I'll call you when I've got what you want."

"Thanks, Bobby, I really appreciate it," Katrina said.

The Wednesday before Christmas, Johannes Botha from Escom came to J&B Africa, and he and Frank set about setting things out for the event the next day. They found tables and chairs enough to accommodate all those who had entered the competition and set them out in one of the workshops. There was also plenty of room for people to observe if they wanted to. James met with Johannes and asked if he had a sense of how things might go.

"I think you will be surprised," Johannes said. "My experience so far is that the people who want to do this take it very seriously. I see that two of your accounting clerks also entered, apart from the repair people and the parts people. What will you do if one of them wins?"

"Then, Leon, my accountant, becomes the proud owner of a fancy tool kit," James replied. "But I have two more for the runners-up."

"In the event of a tie from the written portion of the test, what then?" Johannes asked.

"I was under the impression that you had a plan for that," James said.

"I do, I have a series of more complex questions," Johannes said. "They can all be solved, but it takes some thought; the first to get it done wins."

"And if there is another tie?" James asked.

"Then I have other even more complex questions," Johannes replied. "They do take some thought, but are solvable."

"And if neither manages?" James asked.

"Then you're going to need your three prizes," Johannes laughed.

"So, we're set for ten tomorrow morning, and the written test is what, one hour?" James asked.

"That's right," Johannes said. "Each participant will be given a toolbox, and they must correctly identify everything in the box. Then, follows the Bennett test, the toolboxes are ours, so there may be items in them that not all your people recognise, but they could work out what they are in terms of form and function. They'll get the toolbox and the Bennett test at the same time, so they can decide which to do first."

"We're providing lunch afterwards, will you and your people stay?" James asked.

"We'd be delighted," Johannes said.

"How have you managed to keep the Bantu Education people at bay?" James asked.

"We made it clear that we project running out of skilled people before too long, and like it or not, we needed more, so the only way left open to us was to tap into the black labour pool," Johannes said. "It has led to some testy discussions with the government people, but they like electricity to be delivered to their houses and offices, so grudgingly agreed. Don't be surprised if one doesn't come calling on you to see what you're up to."

"It's a safety issue," James said. "At least that's what I'll tell them. We can't afford to have one of the mechanics handed the wrong tool."

"There are many whites who see this kind of thing as an assault on their privilege," Johannes said. "There are many who see good jobs like those of your mechanics as being the divine right of your white workers."

"I know that," James said. "It was interesting when we lived in Zambia, the presumption was that the black Zambians could be taught to do things by rote, but not to reason. I found that not to be the case, but convincing some of the higher-ups was a challenge. In some ways, Zambia was like here; the government and the big employers had done a poor job of educating the workforce. They did the training they had to do, but neglected the education that went with it. Things were changing, but it's still only 13 years after Independence."

"We've got a lot further to go," Johannes said. "But, small steps, small steps. Until tomorrow?"

"Until tomorrow," James echoed.

"We're all set for our big event tomorrow," James told Katrina that evening over dinner. "Do you want to come and see?"

"I might persuade Jan to come with me and watch," she replied. "If this works for you, then maybe CMI could follow suit."

"The Escom people seem to have a program that's well thought out and that works," he said. "Their man did tell me today that they've had issues with the government, who I don't think like the idea of educating the black workforce."

"I have to admit that when I was growing up, I didn't think the black Zambians could do much, then when I started to work and dealt with the drivers and deliverymen, I realised that they were just as capable as anyone else," Katrina said. "It was a hard thing for me to face, my own deep prejudices."

"I suppose we all have our prejudices of one type or another," James said. "All driven by how we're brought up, learning that long-held beliefs are false is hard."

"Anyway, enough of work," she said. "I heard from Bobby, and she's got all the information I wanted. She's going to send it out to me by courier and then in the New Year I can give it to the Wits *ouks*."

"Hope that goes well," he said.

"So do I," she echoed.

Thursday was essentially a non-working day; the whole place was waiting to see how the competition went and who would be the winner. The Escom team arrived at eight and set things up, a toolbox and papers at each station. Then, at a quarter to ten, all the competitors came in and took seats. The space at the back of the workshop filled up with the rest of the J&B staff, all wanting to see. Charlize came in and had with her Katrina and Jan Hofmeyr, she found seats for them, and then went back to her post at the front desk. She was back soon enough; she had recruited temporary help to watch the door and man the telephones, and just needed to pass on last-minute instructions. At five minutes before ten, Johannes addressed the competitors.

"Ladies and gentlemen, in front of you is a toolbox. When I tell you to begin, open the toolbox and identify everything that it contains. A full description is required; spanner is not adequate, it needs to be ring spanner, 1/2 inch. You will note that these are special tools; they have no sizes on them, you must determine the size where appropriate. When you are done with the toolbox, there is a paper with questions that you should answer. You have one hour to complete the test. Write your names on the front page. Good, you may begin."

The crowd watched as the competitors opened the toolboxes and started taking items out and listing them on the paper provided. James was surprised at how many items there were in the toolboxes, and at the variety of tools and gauges. He watched with fascination as they all had different ways of determining the sizes of the various spanners; some knew just by looking, others had devised ways to let them use feeler gauges and other tools to let them get the sizes. The room was quiet, except for the ringing of steel occasionally when items were put back into the boxes. James could hear muffled remarks at times, as people in the crowd made comments about the tools they saw being taken out of the boxes. James did note three items that were not generally used in their business, but which could be identified with logic and thought. He noted who turned to the Bennett test first and who was the last to finish the toolbox test. The minutes seemed to him to drag, but he was sure that to the test takers they were flying by far too quickly.

"Five minutes," Johannes intoned. That last five minutes dragged on until finally, Johannes said. "Pens down," and his two assistants quickly gathered up the test papers.

"While we wait for the results," Frank said. "We've got coffee and tea here and some things to eat."

James watched as the various test takers gravitated to their sponsors and started talking about what was in the toolbox and what the Bennett questions were. He wondered who had sponsored the two from accounting and saw that it was Hans and Danie. The paper marking took about thirty minutes, then Johannes called for attention.

"Ladies and gentlemen, this is a very close competition; no one scored less than 187 out of a possible 200, but we have three tied for first at this time, so the tie will be resolved with more questions that I will pose. Would Elizabeth Sithole, Samson Baloyi and Joy Nkuna please come forward?"

That caused a stir that Elizabeth Sithole should be one of the finalists. James saw Hans grinning ear to ear as he nudged her forward.

"Thank you," Johannes said. "I have here a further set of questions; the first to get them all correct will win." He passed out papers, face down and then went back to the front and told them to turn their papers over and begin. James noticed frowns all around, then he could see the frowns go as they each understood the questions and set about answering them. The first to put his pen down was Samson, and Johannes quickly went over and took his paper and looked at the answers.

"We have a winner," he declared. "Now for the runner-up."

Next, to put his pen down was Joy, followed in less than a minute by Elizabeth. Johannes picked up their papers and scanned them.

"Joy is the runner-up and Elizabeth gets a most honourable mention," Johannes said.

"Thank you, Johannes," James said. "Samson and Brian, congratulations on a superb job. Please accept these toolboxes as prizes. Joy and Andrew, please come and get yours, and Elizabeth and Hans, amazing job. For everyone else who took part, thank you for doing so, and thanks to the sponsors who gave so much of their time to help. We have toolboxes for each of you. I hope you'll cherish them and use them. We also have lunch that will be arriving shortly."

Charlize had a camera and posed the winners, then gathered all those who had taken part and photographed them as a group. Then she was bombarded with requests for individual photographs by those who had taken part, posing with their new boxes that Frank handed out.

"So, Leon," James said. "Are you going to lose an accounting clerk to the service *ouks*?"

"I don't think so," Leon laughed. "But it shook up a lot of those who took part, who would have thought that Elizabeth was so good?"

"What is she like as an accounting clerk?" James asked.

"Good," Leon said. "I suspect that she'll leave us at some time to join her father's car repair business; he's one of the better-known mechanics in Soweto."

"So, what do you think, Leon? Was this worth it?" James asked.

"Definitely," Leon replied.

"Johannes, any comments?" James asked.

"Elizabeth Sithole was a bit of a surprise," Johannes said. "I think your sponsors did an amazing job preparing everyone."

"Johannes, this is Jan Hofmeyr of CMI. I invited him here today because quite a few of the people who took part used to work for CMI before they relinquished the construction machinery line back to us, and this is my wife, Katrina, she works for Jan as one of his financial analysts," James said.

"Please to meet you," Johannes said.

"If we were to do something like this, would you be prepared to help us?" Jan asked.

"We would," Johannes said. "But you have to know that the Bantu Education *ouks* are not that keen and might raise questions."
"I doubt that they would be," Jan said. "But they don't have to go out and find mechanics, electricians and other tradesmen."
"Are you staying for lunch, Jan?" James asked.
"I will, thank you," Jan replied.

Johannes and his team were then pressed by all the participants for their papers back, to see what items or questions they had got wrong. James saw quite a few go off into corners with their respective sponsors, and he hoped the conversations focused on the positives and not the negatives of the few items they had missed. Privately, he was amazed at the results; he expected a much wider spread of scores and wondered if the wrong answers were random or if there was a pattern to them. He talked to one of Johannes's assistants and got the answer. The wrong answers did not seem to have any pattern; they were scattered all over the place, a few for misidentified items in the toolboxes and a few for some of the Bennett questions. When lunch was brought in, there was some retreating to racial corners, but perhaps not as much as there had been in the past. He was interested to see who separated themselves from the others, both white and black, and made mental lists. For James, it was easy; he had guests to entertain, so he sat with Johannes and his team and with Jan and Katrina.

After everyone had gone back to work and the visitors had left, James took a wander around and found Kagiso Dube in the parts warehouse.
"Mr Dube," James said. "How are you today?"
"Well, Mr Martin," Dube replied. "And you?"
"Well," James replied. The ritual complete, James then asked if Dube had any comments about the morning.
"I was surprised by Elizabeth Sithole," he said.
"I think we all were," James said. "How did you fare?"
"I stupidly missed a couple of things that, as I think about it now, I knew," Dube said. "My own fault, but I'm glad I took part, and all the

comments I hear are good. I think some of the white mechanics were surprised at how well we all did."
"Well, I have to say that I was a little surprised at the effort they put in and the time they took to educate and train," James commented.
"Giving them the chance for a nice prize gave them incentive," Dube said.
"Should I do something else next year?" James asked.
"It would be good," Dube agreed. "But what, I don't know."
"I'll think about it," James said. "On another matter, I am concerned that some of the bombings we have seen lately may affect the people here. I don't want any of our people to be injured."
"I think we will be safe enough," Dube said. "Most of the attacks seem to be against police stations or government places."
"That's true, but attacks on railway stations and trains worry me. I'm not sure how many of our people use the train to get to work," James said.
"I will keep my ear to the ground when I am moving up and down," Dube said.
"Thank you, Mr Dube," James said. "Have you any plans for the holiday?"
"I will go and see my parents," Dube replied. "I will travel to Umtata to see them, and you, Sir?"
"We travel to the Cape to see the parents of my wife," James replied. "Go well on your travels."
"Go well," Dube echoed.

James returned to his office satisfied that if, as he suspected, Dube was an ANC activist, then they might get warnings, probably oblique, about any planned bombing that might affect the company or its people. He then sat down with Leon, Frank, Hans, Danie and Piet to talk about what they might do the next year. He would have liked to just have some form of competition open to all, but wondered how his black staff would fare. Frank suggested an open competition with examples of failed parts that needed diagnoses and suggested solutions. That led to a long discussion about whether or not the black mechanics and parts people had the fundamental knowledge to be able to do that. The answer to that was education, and James put it to the others that the thing to do was to run a series of classes throughout the year that took failures and analysed them. That was a solution that was accepted by all, then they had the basic problem of finding failed parts or systems and doing the analysis to determine what had happened and then building the class around it. That was a lot of work, and James suggested that rather than overload them all with it, perhaps they should recruit and trainer someone who would do that. Leon chimed in that they could afford it, there were government monies available for such programs, and as long as they had white mechanics registered for the classes, the rules were silent on whether or not they could add blacks to the classes as well. The next question was, where to find a trainer; they needed an engineer who could diagnose problems, then put together a class to show what the diagnostics were, and how that pointed to immediate and longer-term solutions. James wondered if there were not some retired engineers from some of the larger companies that might enjoy the challenge, and Frank volunteered to scout around and see what interest there might be. The other option was to go to the universities or technical schools and see if there were assistant professors who fancied the idea of making a little extra money. Piet volunteered to explore that possibility. Then there was the final issue: if the competition was to diagnose a problem, how would they manage that? It would hardly be likely that they could find twenty or so of the same item with the same problem, so they would have to come up with either problems of like complexity or another route altogether. The consensus of the group was to leave that until the new year and then broach it with whoever they picked as the training officer.

"That was interesting," Katrina told James that night over dinner. "I have to say I was surprised that, what was her name, Sithole, did as well as she did?"

"I think that took quite a few by surprise," he said. "Leon told me that her dad has a car repair shop in Soweto, so maybe she got some private coaching as well as what Hans told her."

"So, what will you do next?" she asked.

"I'm thinking of some kind of mechanic's competition for next year," he replied. "But I'll need to find someone who can educate and train and have them create the competition."

"What will Oak Creek say?" she asked.

"Probably not much," he replied. "As long as we're making decent profits and are cash positive, they'll leave us alone; the bigger problem will be the Bantu Education *ouks*, they won't like the idea that we're training blacks as well as whites."

"I got the day off tomorrow," she said. "So, we can leave for the Cape whenever you're ready."

"Lunchtime," he promised. "We're closing at noon, so I'll be home as soon as I can, and then we'll leave."

"If you take my *bakkie* tomorrow, then I'll put petrol in the car and have everything packed, so we can leave as soon as you get here," she suggested.

"I'll do that," he agreed.

James was done by noon the next day. The company had taken on a festive air, and people worked hard to get everything cleared off the to-do lists by eleven, so James let them all go as soon as they finished. He and Charlize were the last to leave, locking the place up tight for the holiday period. James had made arrangements for emergencies with a place that would take telephone calls and then had a roster of who to call on which day. He could almost guarantee that there would be some issue, but he was also confident that his people could take care of it. The roster of people also had his contact telephone number, should they encounter a problem that they were unable to solve. Katrina was ready when he arrived home, and after making a quick stop in the bathroom, he was ready, and they left, Katrina driving and James munching on the packed lunch she had put together. Weaving their way out of Johannesburg was frustrating and took time, more time than either one of them really wanted it to take, but traffic is traffic, and no amount of wishing would make it go away. Once out on the more open road of the N1, they picked up speed and pushed the limits as much as they dared.

The Mercedes ate up the miles, and they passed Vereeniging, Parys, and Kroonstad quickly enough, only to meet heavier traffic in Bloemfontein. Then things opened up again, and they made it to Colesberg by seven in the evening. The hotel in Colesberg was adequate, not the Carlton by any stretch of the imagination, but good enough for an evening meal, bath and bed. Before they retired to bed, James found a petrol station and filled up, so that they could get away in the morning without having to hope that the petrol stations would be open.

They were away at six the following morning, having begged a flask full of coffee and some cake from the kitchen staff. Leaving Colesberg, they had a decision to make: stay on the N1, or take to N9 to Beaufort West and thence the N12 to Oudtshoorn. The N1 route had less in the way of winding mountain roads than the N12, so, in theory, it should be quicker, if less scenic. So, the N1 it was, going south to Middelburg, then Graaf-Reinet, then out into the Karoo with long straight stretches over valley floors and short winding stretches over the lines of hills that divided the valleys. It struck James as odd that the N1 would start in George and not Cape Town, perhaps in time the government would renumber the roads, and have the N1 start in Cape Town and end at Beitbridge on the Rhodesian border, a true one end of the country to the other road. There was little traffic south of Colesberg, so both James and Katrina risked police presence and tore across the valley floors. In one stretch, they actually drove for almost two hours without seeing another car. The Karoo was hot, dry and empty, and James thought more than once that he would not relish the idea of a breakdown. They turned off the main road in apparently the middle of nowhere and turned north towards Oudtshoorn, through which they drove at a sedate pace, taking in the ostrich farms that were scattered along the road and waving to the policemen who were manning a traffic stop. Past Oudtshoorn, it was only a short drive to Calitzdorp and then past there to the Gamka River and the side road that took them to the farm of Katrina's parents.

"Katrina, you're earlier than we expected," Sussana, Katrina's mother, said as they pulled up to the house just before eleven.

"*Ag, man*," Katrina said. "There wasn't much traffic on the road."

"Come in, come in, nice to see you again, James," Sussana said. James was gratified that she spoke English; it saved him the struggle of dredging up the little Afrikaans that he knew. He was sure that when she and Katrina were alone, then it would be all Afrikaans. It had been a couple of years since James and Katrina had been to the farm, but it seemed to James that little had changed, except the grape vines that were now bigger and trailed more.

"Liefling," Koos, Katrina's father, said as he joined them. "Good trip?"

"Good," Katrina replied.

"How's Jo'burg," Sussana asked.

"Busy," Katrina replied.

"Have you been affected by any of the bombings?" Koos asked.

"No, in fact, we were tipped off about the Carlton Centre," Katrina said.

"I think I've got an ANC activist working for me," James explained. "I found a note on my desk one day, telling me to stay away from the Carlton for the next two days."

"So, how's the wine business?" Katrina asked.

"Goed, baie goed," Koos replied. "You can try some later, and, you and James, how are things?"

"Goed, baie goed," Katrina echoed. "James is busy, and I am too now. I like my new job, and it helps with the money, not that we really need it; James gets well paid."

"Did you get any breakfast?" Sussana asked.

"We begged coffee and cake from the hotel kitchen," Katrina said.

"Put your bags in your room and come through," Sussana said. "Lunch will be on the table."

"They seem well enough," James commented to Katrina as they unpacked their bags.

"They do," she agreed. "I think they worry about us in Jo'burg, afraid that we'll get caught up in some bombing. I wonder if there's much going on out here?"

"I wouldn't think so," he said. "No political targets out here, a bomb here wouldn't have the impact it would in Jo'burg or Cape Town. So, what are we going to do for the next couple of days?"

"As little as possible," she laughed. "We might take a drive up the river like we did the first time we came."

"That sounds like fun," he agreed. "Are you unpacked enough to go for lunch? I'm hungry."

"Ja, kom ou maat," she said, slipping out of the door ahead of him. Lunch was actually served outside, which made sense as they were in the middle of summer.

"How were things in the States?" Sussana asked.

"Good," Katrina said. "You know we bought a house, and we kept it when we came here. I was working towards a degree in finance when we came here, and I'll probably just finish it at Wits. We've made some nice friends, you should come and visit when we go back."

"You're only here for two years?" Koos asked.

"That's what they asked me to do," James confirmed. "The *ou* that was here wanted to leave, and as soon as I came out, he gave up the job and left me to my own devices. One of my jobs while I'm here is to see if there's someone to replace me."

"And, is there?" Koos asked.

"The accountant we have, he'll do a great job," James replied. "I'm working with him to give him a better understanding of the mining industry; he already had a pretty good idea about the markets for our construction machines."

"And tell us about CMI, Liefling," Koos said.

"CMI used to represent J&B in Africa," Katrina explained. "They got into financial difficulties, and the machinery business was taken back by J&B. Since then, they've fixed their financial problems and have started expanding again, and I do financial analysis for them."

"Do they pay well?" Sussana asked.

"I get 1,500 Rand a month," Katrina replied. "I may get more when I've got my degree."

"Not bad," Koos said. "And you, James?"
"Compared to salaries here, I get a lot," James replied. "I get paid in dollars, some of which is remitted here and some stays in the States. We also get a housing allowance, which covers the rent."
"When do you think Will and Bridget will be here?" Koos asked.
"Will said early afternoon," James replied. "A lot may depend on how often they stop for Francesca."
"She must be two now, yes?" Sussana asked.
"Two and into everything," James confirmed. "Hope all your family heirlooms are well out of the way."
"I'll make sure," Sussana said.

Will and Bridget arrived just after two; they had stopped overnight in Bloemfontein, so had had further to drive that day than James and Katrina. Sussana took charge and showed them their room, and also one for Francesca. Bridget was a little concerned that Francesca might be uncertain about sleeping in a strange room, but when she saw how close she would be to her parents, she was happy enough. Sussana then made sure that they had lunch.
"So, Will, how's the paint business?" Koos asked.
"Busy," Will replied. "But at least we're not putting anyone on the dole."
"I got a new job as well," Bridget said. "The same *ou* who heads up CMI that Katrina works for, also has a travel business, and I'm doing that from home. My biggest challenge is to make sure that Francesca doesn't call someone or send a telex to someone."
"So, Francesca, what would you like to do?" Sussana asked.
"Mommy told me that you have a farm, I'd like to see," Francesca replied.
"We can do that," Koos said. "If you've finished eating, we can take a walk and see what we have here."
Koos led the way, with Will, Bridget, James and Francesca following. Katrina stayed behind to talk to her mother, and James heard a blizzard of Afrikaans as the two got together in the kitchen. They wandered through the vineyards, looking at vines laden with grapes.

"We'll start picking next month," Koos said. "Then we'll press and start on the fermentation."

"How do you measure harvests?" Bridget asked.

"In tons per acre, or if you're in metric, tonnes per hectare," Koos replied. "We get about 6 tons per acre, and we've got 25 acres planted, so 150 tons, that would give us a little over 100,000 bottles, but we divert some to make grape spirits that we use to fortify the wine."

"So, a little more than we could drink," James laughed. "Who do you sell to?"

"Most goes to Pick n Pay," Koos said. "But I also sell some to a few of the restaurants in Oudtshoorn, and I give some away to people I like."

"So, you have your own distillery?" Bridget asked, ever the chemical engineer, she was intrigued to see how it all worked.

"*Ja,* over there," Koos replied, pointing to one of the buildings.

"Does the government interfere a lot?" Bridget asked.

"*Ag man*, they do, they do," Koos said. "The Customs and Excise Act of 1964 covers a lot, and they want to charge excise tax on all the spirits we produce, so they come and inspect. They also have this weird rule that a pot still can't be less than 610 litres in size. Why 610 litres, who knows? Making the wine is the easy bit, making the spirits to fortify it is becoming so much trouble that I'm going to shut the stills down and buy the spirits. If I do that, I'll have more hanepoot to sell."

"Are the grapes good to eat?" Bridget asked.

"Baie goed," Koos said. He pulled out a pocket knife and picked a bunch of grapes off one of the vines, and offered them around. He was right, they were very nice to eat, even Francesca tried them and announced that she liked them. Koos took them then to the press room, then the barn where the fermentation took place, then the ageing room and finally the bottling line. It was quite an enterprise.

"How many bottles do you have on hand from last year?" James asked.

"I've got fifty cases left," Koos replied. "So, 600 bottles, and I've got a few cases from earlier years, including one case from the first pressing we ever did. Maybe we should try a bottle of that on Christmas Day and see how it's aged."

"That sounds like a plan," Will said.

"Just don't drink too much," Bridget cautioned him. "The last time you and Koos got together, you had a hell of a hangover."

"I know, I know," Will said. "That was before Francesca."

"Look, a snake," Francesca interrupted them. They looked where she was pointing and saw a puff adder sunning itself on a small wall outside the bottling shed.

"We'll just give him plenty of room," Bridget said to Francesca. "We'll leave him alone, and he won't bother us. That's a puff adder, not a nice snake, easy to tread on because they don't move out of the way."

"What do they eat?" Francesca asked.

"Rats, mice, lizards, small birds," Bridget replied. "They wait for them to come along and then grab them."

"So, we should go that way?" Francesca said, pointing back the way they had come.

"It would be better," Bridget agreed. They all retraced their steps and went back through the bottling shed, then back to the house for morning coffee. James noted that Koos left them for a while and assumed that he had gone to move the snake elsewhere. He probably did not want it taking up residence in or around the bottling shed.

After afternoon coffee, Katrina borrowed her father's old Land Rover, and she and James took a drive up the Gamka River. They had done this before, driving as far as they could, then walking up the river to see what they could find.

"It's so nice to be back in Africa," she said as they followed the river north. "This is what I miss the most, the bush, the quiet, the animals and birds."

"I remember when we first came up here," James said. "We saw kudu and klipspringer, then dassies and baboons. Look over there, dassies and up there, kudu. Last time we came up here, it rained. Will it rain today?"

"I checked the weather forecast for Beaufort West, and there's nothing today; it's clear enough here, so I don't think we'll get any rain," she replied. "It's hot though, isn't it?"

"It is," he agreed, and watched as she stripped off all her clothes and stood head back, arms up, embracing the sunlight.

"That's so nice," she said. "Nice to feel the sun on me, nice not to have to worry about anyone peeking."

"I wonder what the baboons think?" he said, following her example and ridding himself of clothes. She was right, the sun did feel good, but he knew he would have to be careful, or he would burn. Their cavorting in the sun led to embracing, which led to lovemaking on the tussocky grass.

"We have an audience," Katrina told James, nodding her head in the direction of a colony of meerkats that were watching. "This is not the most comfortable grass. Sit up so that I can sit on your lap and not get poked in the back by all this scrub."

"Do you remember when we went to the Tsau Hill in Botswana?" he asked.

"Yes, I remember them, a whole colony of meerkats just watching," she said. "Well, they got their money's worth that day."

"Did you enjoy your walk?" Sussana asked them when they got back to the farm.

"We did," Katrina said, surreptitiously picking bits of grass and twigs from her hair.

"It looks like it," Sussana laughed. "I should have warned you, we're getting more people in the *kloof*, scientists looking at the fynbos and other visitors hiking through, but probably not on Christmas Eve."

"Well, the *bobbejane* would have told us if anyone was coming," Katrina said.

"They would," Sussana agreed. "They've been agitated lately. I think a new leopard has moved in. Will and Bridget took a quick run into town, so I've got Francesca. Would you look to her for a few minutes for me?"

"Of course," Katrina said. Watching Francesca could be exhausting; like all two-year-olds, she had an insatiable curiosity and was into everything, so much of the time was spent just making sure that her explorations of the world did not lead to injury or fright. She had already learned that snakes were to be avoided, so that was one riskless.

"Auntie Katrina, can we go and play by the river?" Francesca asked.

"Of course," Katrina replied. She took Francesca's hand and they walked to the river.

"There's not much water," Francesca said.

"No," Katrina said. "A long way up the river, there is a dam and most of the water is kept there, so that we don't get too many floods down here when it does rain."

"Look, there are *bobbejane* over there," Francesca said, pointing to a troop of baboons that were looking for things to eat by the water. Katrina smiled at this. Francesca was going to grow up using Afrikaans words scattered into her English.

"What do you think they're eating?" Katrina asked.

"I don't know," Francesca said. "Roots of some of the plants?"

"It looks like it," Katrina concurred. "Look, they've seen something."

"Oh, look," Francesca said. "What, what, oh, I see, that eagle up there."

"He's probably looking to see if there's a small one he can take," Katrina said. "Everything has to eat, so the eagle eats, but this one usually eats *dassies*, hares, meerkats, maybe even small antelope."

"What kind is he?" Francesca asked.

"A Verreaux's eagle," Katrina replied. "He's a big one, one of the biggest that we have."

"How does he fly without flapping his wings?" Francesca asked.

"He does flap his wings sometimes," Katrina said. "But most of the time, he just glides through the air. As the day gets warm, the air heats up, and then it goes up, he sits on the air that's going up and just glides around looking at what's down here."

"Is that why he has such big wings?" Francesca asked.

"It is," Katrina confirmed. "If you watch him really closely, you can see he moves the feathers at the end of his wings just a little, and he can go this way or that."

"It must be so much fun to just be able to glide around without having to flap all the time," Francesca thought. "Look, Mummy and Daddy are back from the town, shall we go and make them tea?"

"So, how was your expedition with Francesca?" Bridget asked as she sipped the tea that Katrina had made to Francesca's order.
"We got into a simple explanation of thermals as we watched a Verreaux," Katrina replied. "He looked over the troop of *bobbejane* that were down by the river, then went off up the river looking for *dassies*."
"He was big," Francesca added. "So big I wonder that he could fly."
"Birds come in all shapes and sizes," Bridget said.
"Why do they have to eat the *dassies*?" Francesca asked.
"Because if they didn't, there would be too many *dassies* and they would eat too many of the plants they eat," Bridget replied. "If the snakes didn't eat the rats and mice, we'd have too many of them; everything works together."
"Like we eat chickens?" Francesca asked.
"Like we eat chickens," Bridget confirmed.
"So, what are we having for Christmas dinner?" Francesca asked.
"Roast chicken with other things," Bridget replied.

Christmas Day was celebrated outside in the sunshine, with presents, then a buffet lunch that did include roast chicken, among all manner of other good things to eat. As the only child there, Francesca got the biggest haul of presents, but Bridget had asked that everyone not go overboard and spoil her too much. For James and Katrina, it was a chance to be lazy and do nothing for the day, except wash the dishes when things were finally cleared away.
"It's good to be back in Africa," Katrina said again, as she handed dishes to James to dry.
"It is," he agreed. "Do you think we should stay?"
"Not really," she said. "I like Zambia better than South Africa, but I'm not sure what we'd do in Zambia, except the mines, and they're going to have problems here. I think my folks are safe enough here, away from the big cities and towns, but I'd rather we keep seeing what we can do in the States. It seems to me that there's all kinds of opportunities there for us."

“You’re right,” he agreed. “I would like to come back sometime to visit one of the Zambia parks, maybe Kafue next time.”
“That would be fun,” she said. “Kafue’s bigger than Luangwa, and we’d have to pick where we’d want to go, but I like the idea. While we’re here, though, we should go to Kruger, it’s almost as big as Kafue, and it does have more camps and places to stay, and judging by what I saw at M’Bali, there’s plenty to see.”
“What are you two talking about?” Sussana asked.
“Oh, a visit to Kruger, whether we should stay here or go back to the States,” Katrina replied.
“Go back to the States,” Sussana said. “Your Pops and I went to Kitwe because there were opportunities; you need to do the same in the States. You can always come back here when you’ve made enough to do whatever you like without having to worry about working or not. We run the winery because it keeps us busy and we enjoy it, but financially, we don’t have to. Talking about that, your Pops is about to open a bottle of our first vintage, bring glasses, would you?”

Toasts were made and judgment was passed. The hanepoot had aged well and tasted very much like more. Francesca took a nap, and peace reigned, at least for a while. The valley was quiet, the only noises were the river, the insects, birds and the occasional bark of a baboon or call of an antelope.
“I like it here,” Bridget said. “It’s quiet, but it’s not too far from the town.”
“We like it,” Sussana said. “I’m glad we moved here. It might be more of a challenge when we get older, but for now, it suits us.”
“No ANC bombers to worry about here,” Koos added. “We’re too small, too far away from anything important, so no newspaper headlines here. Make sure you all stay safe in Jo’burg, I read about a few bombings of police stations and the railways.”
“I may have a source to warn us of anything,” James said. “Before the Carlton Centre bomb, I found a note on my desk telling me to stay away from there for two days.”
“Do you know who left it?” Koos asked.

"I have my suspicions," James replied. "But I'm not going to ask too much in case I lose the source. I did pass the warning on to Will and Bridget."
"Just as well you did," Bridget said. "I had an appointment with Comair that day, sad that that was the last day for them at that location, they were moving offices the next day."
"Do you have anything like that in Oak Creek?" Koos asked.
"No, all quiet there," James said. "The biggest problems we have are snow and ice in the winter."
"So, who would like tea and who would like coffee?" Sussana asked. "I'm going to put out some snacks just now."

Boxing Day was a lazy day, as were the next couple of days, then James and Katrina thought they should start back for Johannesburg. Will and Bridget said that they would drive with them, so they made a booking at a hotel in Bloemfontein as a stop on the way. The drive back was uneventful as far as the Lootsberg Pass, then a puncture stalled things for a few minutes. James went back and helped Will change his tyre.
"I'll bet this place could be bloody cold in the winter," James commented to Will.
"I've been over here in July," Will said. "Place was covered in snow, and it was bloody cold, howling gale and snow blowing, not a good place to have a puncture in the winter."
"It's pretty wild up here," James agreed, looking around. Behind them, he could see the valley stretching out to the south and the next line of hills and in front a short rise to the summit of the pass, and on either side the line of hills that made up the Lootsberg, and nowhere could he see any towns or evidence of people.
"Okay, all done," Will said. "You ready?"
"Kom ons ry," James said.

Visits

The New Year was celebrated, and work restarted. For James, there was a little catching up to do, but not as much as he had expected. The crew that had covered the holiday period had done a good job of shipping out parts and even responding to three service calls. Next for James was to arrange for visits to the bulk handling ports of Richards Bay and Saldanha, but before that, there was a message to call upon Consolidated African Mining Company, or CAMCO for short, the parent company of Kasalia Consolidated Copper Mines, the company James had worked for in Zambia. He made an appointment, took Piet with him, and they drove into the centre of Johannesburg to the offices of CAMCO. They waited a few minutes, then were shown to an office.

"James," the CAMCO man said. "So good to see you again."

"Hello George, this is Piet Kruger, our mining machine sales manager. Piet, this is George Armstrong, he was the chief engineer for Kasalia Consolidated Copper Mines in Zambia, where I worked, and now George?" James asked.

"Consulting Engineer for CAMCO," George said. "I told you before we shut your mine down, James, that this was a likely spot for me, so here I am. Piet, James did a bang-up job for us in Zambia, even when we dumped a real wanker on him as a mine manager. So, James, this is quite a switch from Mkushi?"

"When we left Zambia, I had an interview set up with the James & Brown people," James explained. "They took me on and I started there as an application engineer, travelling the country and looking at mines and recommending equipment types and sizes," James explained. "The company needed someone out here in a hurry, and they asked me if we wanted to come out."

"Well, I'm glad they did," George said. "I know if you're in charge and I need something, it'll get done."

"So, what can we do for you, George?" James asked.

"We're looking to start up a new coal mine in the Middelburg area," George replied. "The initial look at it suggests a dragline, but I'd like that confirmed, and I'd like the chance to see some machines in action and visit the factory."

"I'm sure we can arrange that," James said. "What's your timetable for the mine?"

"Run of mine coal production two years from now," George replied. "So, I know it's important to get on the order book soon, or the delivery dates will be out there."

"You're right about that," James confirmed. "All of us, BE, Marion, Page, Ransomes and us are all booked out in the short term, business is booming, but who knows for how long. If we set up some visits in the States, who else would you be bringing?"

"Johannes van Deventer, our mining engineer and Keith Adams, our contract man," George replied. "We've got some other visits planned as well, so could we do February 6th to the 9th for site and factory visits?"

"I'm sure we could arrange that," James promised. "I'll be there, as will Piet; he'll be here probably long after I'm gone."

"Why, are you leaving already?" George asked.

"No, but the company indicated that they wanted me back in the States at some time," James replied. "So, do you have geological information on the deposit?"

"Let's get Johannes in," George suggested. He made a quick telephone call, and in about two minutes, Johannes arrived.

"Johannes, this is James Martin and Piet Kruger from J&B. I knew James in Zambia, where he pulled off an amazing job of getting a mine up and running from scratch," George said, making the introductions. "Johannes, do you have the sections and data of the deposit?"

"Ja," Johannes said. "You can see it's pretty straightforward, dipping slightly to the east, so overburden depth increases over time, but there are some *kopjies* along the way, we're looking for a million tons a year."

"So, a J&B 260, 60-yard bucket on 360-foot of boom, then for the *kopjies* add a shovel or some front-end loaders and trucks and knock down the peaks to give the dragline a more uniform cutting depth, saves on the upfront investment," James suggested. "For the coal, a 15-yard shovel and a fleet of trucks, you'll also need a couple of drills."

"We'd come to that same conclusion," Johannes said. "I've got a mate who works for Drakenstein, and he said they're doing essentially the same thing."

"How many other J&B 260s are there, or will there be in country?" George asked.

"So far, eight," James replied.

"So, there is some commonality of parts?" George asked.

"There is," James confirmed. "We carry most smaller spares, but some of the bigger items are a little too much for us to carry as they don't move that frequently."

"So what made you switch from mining?" Johannes asked.

"Kasalia shut down our mine when the copper price dropped, and the job I was offered set me back quite a bit," James said. "I knew the J&B local *ouk* and he set me up with an interview."

"We weren't the most enlightened," George said. "Fortunately, here, our open pit mines are as important as our underground mines, so you won't have to worry about promotions like James did."

"You've seen some mines in the States?" Johannes asked.

"A lot," James confirmed. "I've been in iron mines in Minnesota, coal mines in Arizona and Wyoming and quite a few other states. What comes closest to here is Wyoming, a little colder, but the geology is similar, the production rates are similar, so a good mine to look at."

"I'm looking forward to it," Johannes said.

"I'm looking forward to seeing how they maintain all their kit," George said. "And I'd like to see how these machines are built."

"Are you free for lunch?" James asked.

"We can be," George said. "Let's pick up Keith on the way, and you can get to know him before we go to the States."

"Well, what do you think?" James asked Piet as they drove back to Isando after lunch.

"George seems to like you," Piet said. "He'll give us a fair shot."

"I got on well with him," James said. "I think he had sympathy for me after they brought in a new manager over me at the Mkushi mine, and I basically had to teach him the job."

"It turns out that I know a few people that Johannes also knows," Piet said. "I'm pretty sure we met sometime in the past. Keith is all worried about terms and conditions."

"That's his job," James said. "I'll talk to Oak Creek and have them send us out a proposal for the machines, and I'll get them to set up a trip to Rock Springs. You should make yourself travel plans to be in Oak Creek when George and his folks arrive, stay in touch with Johannes and see if you can get their whole itinerary. It would be interesting to see where else they're going."

"And which other factories they're going to see?" Piet asked.

"That too," James agreed.

"I'm going to see Johannes this weekend," Piet said. "We're both going to a *braai* for a mate, someone we both know but through different routes."

"When I first went to some mines in the States with the local sales reps, what struck me was the personal relationships between them and the mine folks. At a couple of meetings, we seemed to talk more about hunting than mining machines," James reflected.

"I wonder how much corruption there is in this business?" Piet asked.

"I'm sure there's some, particularly in those countries where the laws can be bent more," James said. "We had a meeting with a lawyer in Oak Creek before I came out here, and it was all about that. It was funny, the first thing the lawyer said at the meeting was, don't write anything down in this meeting, don't make any notes. It was all about a new law, the Foreign Corrupt Practices Act. I think a lot of it came out of the Lockheed Tristar scandal and their other sales of Starfighters over the years."

"What was that?" Piet asked.

"Well, Lockheed sold a lot of Starfighters and L-1011 Tristar jets, and there were questions about payments allegedly made to officials to guarantee the sales," James replied. "It all came out in the end, so now we have a new law, but going hunting or fishing with a customer doesn't quite fall into the same category as slipping a government man a couple of million dollars to make sure the decision goes the right way."

"So, you're going to take a trip to Richards Bay?" Piet asked.

"Yes, George gave me a good contact there, and I can take a look at how they stack and reclaim," James said.

"I know an *ou* at Saldanha," Piet said. "If you need a contact there."

"That would be good," James said. "I need to take a look at that place as well as Richards Bay."

"I'll call him. When do you want to go?" Piet asked.

"What about next week, Thursday or Friday?" Jame asked.

"I'll call him," Piet promised.

To prepare for his meeting with Hank Miller, James took an afternoon and sat down and made notes about bucket wheel excavators. He listed the places they were used, brown coal mines in Germany, Australia, India, Czechoslovakia, bauxite mines in Guyana and Surinam, manganese mines in the USSR, some coal mines in the US, tar sands in Canada and a few odd applications, like the copper mine in Zambia, some dam building and even a three machines that had been used in the diamond operations of South West Africa. Then he listed the manufacturers, heavily dominated by the Germans for the large machines, with a few others that built much smaller, more mobile machines. That done, he sat back and thought about the potential markets, obviously new lignite and brown coal mines, possible new bauxite mines in South America, hard coal mines in so many countries, including the US and other possibles. Apart from the mining uses, there was also the bulk material handling market, the kind of machines he was going to see at Richards Bay and Saldanha, but he suspected those would be much less robust than the mining machines, and would also be rail-mounted, so make moving them along piles of iron ore or coal easy. As he saw it, one of the big issues was that a bucket wheel was still not really stand-alone; for the most part, they were also tied to extensive conveyor systems that carried material away to a separate stacker. For J&B to enter the market, it would not only mean competing in an already established field, but either adding significant capability in conveying, or partnering with someone who could bring that skill. The more he thought about it, and the more he played with numbers, the less attractive the proposition became. There were probably better things for the company to invest in than the bucket wheel market. He took all his notes, packaged them up and sent them off to Bill Evans in Oak Creek.

"How long will it take you to get to Richards Bay?" Katrina asked James.

"I'll take a South African flight first thing in the morning to Durban and drive up and be back tomorrow night," he replied. "I'm going to meet George's contact in Richards Bay."

"I'll drop you off in the morning," she promised. "And, I'll pick you up tomorrow night. What about Saldanha?"

"I'll fly into Cape Town and drive up," he replied. "Piet has set things up for me there. I'll be back the same day on the last flight from Cape Town."

"It's a pity the company doesn't have its own plane," she thought. "Then you could fly straight into Richards Bay, what about Saldanha?"

"Piet told me that there was a strip north of the bay, but not usable now. There's an air force base not too far away, but I doubt whether they'd let you land there, so it's Cape Town and drive," he replied.

"Either way, either from Durban or Cape Town, drive safely, watch out for *skelms*," she cautioned.

"I will," he promised.

"It's warm enough today that we'll eat outside in the courtyard," she suggested. "If you'll get us something to drink and a blanket to sit on, I'll bring out some plates of food."

Katrina dropped James at the airport early the next morning, and he caught his flight to Durban. It was still fairly early in Durban, but there was still rush hour traffic, and the airport was on the wrong side of Durban for Richards Bay, so it took James longer than he would have liked to clear the city. Once away from Durban, the risk was traffic police who seemed to be out in force looking for speeders; still, for all that, he was in Richards Bay by ten-thirty. He met his contact there, a Brian Small, who gave him a comprehensive tour of the port load-out facility and explained the stackers and reclaimers. James had been right, the machines were less robust than the excavators he had seen, and it was all conveyors, miles and miles of conveyors, conveyors that took the coal from the dump position where the train wagons were emptied, out to the stackers, and then another whole series of conveyors that took the coal from the reclaimers to the ships. Brian complained bitterly about maintenance issues with the conveyors, but did say that they were learning and had improved the availability of the system quite a bit. James thought about it and cast his mind back to his copper mining days and the few conveyors they had had then, and what problems they could be, so sympathised with Brian for his miles of conveyors. Brian apologised but said that he had another meeting to go to and wished James a safe journey back. It was a little after one-thirty, so James found himself a late lunch in Richards Bay, then started back for Durban. He managed to hit the outskirts of Durban early enough that the afternoon rush hour had not started in earnest and made it through the town to the airport with the minimum of delay. He was in time to catch an earlier flight back to Johannesburg, so he called Katrina with the new time, then scurried off to get the plane.

"I'm glad you're back early," Katrina said when she picked James up at the kerb outside arrivals. "Where shall we go for dinner?"

"What about that Greek place in Edenvale?" James suggested.

"Good, then you can tell me all about your trip," she said as she sped out of the airport. It did not take long to get to Edenvale and the restaurant. They were seated immediately and asked for a Castle each while they decided what to eat.

"So, tell me about Richards Bay," Katrina said.

"Miles of conveyors, piles of coal, everything is grey from the coal dust," he said. "Trains come in and run over a special unloading point, then the coal is conveyed out to a stacker where it sits in a big, long pile until a ship comes in. Then this bucket wheel reclaimer digs away at the pile, and the coal goes by conveyor to a special machine that dumps it into the ship."

"Amazing when you think of Africa, you, or at least I, think of bush, animals and open space, and yet you're talking about something that could be anywhere," she pondered. "I suppose my view of Africa is coloured by my childhood, when to me Africa was Zambia and that was Kitwe and its surrounds, much of which was bush. Even as I grew up, it changed, the pontoon went, replaced by a bridge, the town grew, the animals drifted away, there were more people, more traffic, more of everything that is human and less of the animal world."

"I suppose that happens everywhere," he thought. "I imagine that even where I grew up, if you went back far enough into the dim and distant past, it would have been open spaces, actually, probably not open, more likely to have been forests with wolves and other animals, then people pressure changed all that."

"I suppose I'm hanging on to my romantic view of Africa," she said. "I like the bush, but there will be encroachment of people as time goes by, and the bush will be cleared for farms and houses."

"When we were given the chance to come back to Africa, I think I was thinking more along the lines of Zambia," he commented. "South Africa is an industrial nation, but it has huge problems with disparities of opportunity, education, income and wealth. I don't know that I would want to stay here for the rest of my life."

"I agree," she said. "My folks only have to worry about the next thirty or forty years, if they live to an old age, but even in that time, imagine what could change."

"Anyway, we have the luxury of being able to go somewhere else," he said. "So, shall we eat, then think about a trip into the bush at some time?"

"I like the idea of a bush trip, do you remember the trips we took in Zambia where we gave the ladies something to gossip about?" she asked.

"When we went to the Lukanga Swamp and were messing about on the grass," he laughed. "Just as well they hadn't come by five minutes earlier."

"I think they were there long enough," Katrina said. "I heard them making comments about you and your abilities. So, talking of that, I think we need to eat up and go and roll around on the grass in our courtyard, it's warm enough."

"I like that idea," he said. "I wonder what it is about making love outdoors that's so good?"
"It connects us with nature and our more primitive selves," she thought.
"Well, let's go and be primitive," he laughed.

The visit to Saldanha Bay was almost a repeat of the visit to Richards Bay; the only real difference was that everything was red, not grey. James flew into Cape Town and drove north to Saldanha and met his contact, Koot, and had a tour and was in time to see the actual unloading of a train of iron ore that had come from Sishen. Koot took him out along the conveyors that took the ore out to the piles and dumped it, then they found a reclaimer that was busy digging away at another pile and sending the ore to a ship. Koot had the same complaints that Brian had had: maintenance issues on the miles of conveyors. The stackers and reclaimers had their issues, too, but by far and away, it was the conveyors and particularly transfer stations where things went wrong. Koot also treated James to lunch at the company refectory, basic food, but good. Koot wanted to know what Piet was doing, and James was able to sing Piet's praises a little. On his drive back to Cape Town, James was torn between thinking about what he had seen and speculating about what he might see if he stopped at Grotto Bay. He presumed from the name that there must be some kind of cave system there, whether sea caves or inland caves; he did not know, but his guess was sea caves, and he would have been disappointed to learn that there were no grottoes or other caves; it was just a name. In Cape Town, he had to wait a while for the next flight to Johannesburg, unable to get an earlier flight, so he was back at his appointed time.

"Good trip?" Katrina asked when she picked him up at the kerb.
"Good," he said. "Similar to Richards Bay, but red, everything is red, and the iron ore is more abrasive than coal dust, so things break down more easily. I just need to write up all my notes for Richards Bay and Saldanha and send them off to Bill."
"What else did you see?" she asked.

"The drive down the coast back to Cape Town was pretty, lots of seabirds in the sky and fynbos everywhere," he replied.
"Maybe we should explore South Africa a little more while we're here," she suggested. "I'd hate to go back to the States having only seen Jo'burg and Calitzdorp."
"What about Messina next weekend?" he suggested. "Start at the north and work our way south."
"Let's," she agreed. *"Ons sal 'n plan maak."*
"Did you have dinner already?" he asked.
"I did, are you hungry? I thought you'd get something in Cape Town or on the plane," she asked.
"I'm fine," he said. "I just was worried that you'd wait and I'd already eaten."
"No, man, it's fine," she said. "So, when are we leaving for Oak Creek?"
"One week tomorrow, the 3rd," he said. "Did you talk to Hofmeyr yet?"
"I told him we were going, but didn't give him an exact date yet," she said. "I've got all my projects done, so was waiting for the next one."
"Have you heard from Wits yet?" he asked.
"I'm supposed to hear tomorrow," she said. "I've got an appointment with the admin *ou* at ten."
"What's your guess?" he asked.
"I don't know," she admitted. "I'll just have to wait and see. Okay, we're home, fancy a drink before bath and bed?"

James was sitting in his office the next day, going through financial reports with Leon, when he got a call from Katrina.
"They agreed," she said. "The Wits *ouks* agreed that my courses could transfer, so I'm done except for one final exam."
"That's great," he said. "I'll treat you to dinner later."
"Must go," she said. "I've got to get back to work."
"Good news?" Leon asked.
"Katrina's been taking classes at Wits for a finance degree; she had done a lot in Milwaukee and wondered if what she'd done there would be

accepted and counted by Wits. Apparently, they've agreed," James explained.

"Well, good for her," Leon said,

"I think she's done really well," James said. "She's got one more exam and then she's done. So, this item of the P&L, is that all it costs us?"

"Were you expecting more?" Leon asked.

"I was," James confirmed. "I was sure that the bill would be higher."

"It might have been, but we negotiated things well, which reminds me, we've been told that our application for funds to cover advanced training classes has been approved, and we've also got an *ou* from the Technical College who will do after-hours diagnostic sessions for mechanics. He didn't have a problem with us having our black staff there as well. We do have some *ou* from the Department of Education wanting to see us on Monday to talk about our grant and what we can and cannot do with it," Leon said.

"We'd better be careful what we say to him," James thought. "Are any of our mechanics likely to shop us if we add the blacks to the classes?"

"I don't think so, but you never know," Leon said. "We can always say that the black helpers are just watching to see if they can help their mechanics in the future."

"It's a shame, isn't it, how government policies make you look to find ways to circumvent the rules," James commented. "So, is your Miss Sithole going to take these diagnostic classes?"

"She hasn't said yet," Leon said. "I think she will, but we'll see."

"When do we start?" James asked.

"Wednesday," Leon said. "You should be able to start things before you go off to the States. What are our chances on this order?"

"I think that will depend on delivery rather more than price," James replied. "I got the impression talking to George Armstrong that that was going to be one of the main factors, if not the main factor, so we'll see if Oak Creek can work any magic with the production schedule. Oh, can you get away next week to make a trip to the States to meet with the accounting and finance types?"

"I'm sure I can," Leon said. "I'll make arrangements to be in Oak Creek when you are, but my plan to visit the Grand Canyon may have to wait a little."

"So, tell me about your meeting with the Wits admin," James said that evening as they sat over dinner at a rather nice restaurant in Houghton.

"He was actually quite nice," Katrina replied. "He had been through all the documents that Bobby had sent out for us, and he'd actually called them and talked to Prof Lesnewski, who gave me a glowing review, by all accounts. So, the upshot is that all the classes and grades transferred, so one more exam on macroeconomics and I'm done."

"When is that?" he asked.

"March 2nd," she replied. "I have already submitted my final paper on my financing project, and the initial comments I've got were very good, so don't expect any problems there."

"Will going to Oak Creek mess things up for you?" he asked.

"No, Prof Williams has given me all the material that he's going to cover in the next three weeks, then it's just revision and then the exam," she said. "I can read some of it on the plane and also while I'm in the States."

"What does Hofmeyr say?" James asked.

"He seems happy enough," she said. "I just finished three projects, and one we'll move forward on to acquire another manufacturer. The other two just wouldn't work, so we dropped them."

"Are you going to stay with Bobby while we're there?" he asked.

"I am," she confirmed. "I talked to her last week, and it's all set. Anyway, enough of that, I feel like celebrating, take me home and make mad passionate love to me."

"I'm ready," he said. "Let me just pay, and we can go."

James and Katrina took their trip to Messina and beyond to the Limpopo, which James had crossed before when he first went to Zambia in 1969. It did look grey-green and greasy, but not great, more like a muddy sand river than one with water. Their trip had taken them across the Tropic of Capricorn and into the land of baobab trees. It was quite different to the Cape and Johannesburg, arid with scrub bush and scattered habitations. The official from the Department of Education had come and looked over the syllabus for their diagnostic training and had approved, not even asking who would be in the class, assuming, James thought, that only whites would have the intelligence to take the classes. The classes themselves started on the 1st with Bryn Jones as the instructor. He made no mention of the fact that almost half his class was black or that it included Elizabeth Sithole. He merely set out what he was going to cover and what he expected of the students. James learned that Bryn had emigrated to South Africa just after World War II and had worked for the railways, then had been taken on by the Technical College, where he was one of the senior instructors. He had a wry sense of humour and, in less guarded moments, decried what he saw as the shortsighted attitudes of the white government.

"South African Airways flight SA205 for New York is departing from gate 2; all departing passengers should be on board," the announcement said, and was then repeated in Afrikaans.

"We should get aboard," Katrina said to James. They handed their boarding cards to the agent at the gate and were waved on through.

"Mr and Mrs Martin, so nice to see you again," a stewardess said as she came up to them while they were stowing their carry-on bags.

"Hello, Maryke," Katrina said. "Nice to see you again."

"It's been a few months since I last saw you," Maryke said.

"We're flying over about once a quarter unless James has business," Katrina explained.

"Well, I hope you'll enjoy the flight," Maryke said. "Is there anything I can get for you now?"

"No, thank you," Katrina said. The door closed, and the cabin crew did their final checks, then went through the safety briefings, how to don a life jacket, where the emergency oxygen masks would drop from, how to buckle and unbuckle seat belts, and what to do in case they had to leave the plane through the emergency exits. James and Katrina both paid attention to the briefing; flying was safe, safer than driving, but accidents did happen once in a while. The plane taxied out and took off, bound for Sal Island, the mid-Atlantic rock where they took on more fuel to battle the headwinds into New York. Katrina managed to read some of her material while James dozed. She put it all away for dinner and then left it away while she tried to grab some sleep. They stopped at Sal Island, got fuel, then left quickly enough on the final leg to New York. New York was cold, barely in the teens, with a high of only 21 predicted. Milwaukee was just as cold, with a high of 20 and an overnight low of 0. James and Katrina were thankful that they had remembered to bring hats and gloves as well as coats.

"Good flight over?" Roberta asked when they arrived at her house.

"Nice flight," Katrina said. "But, it's *baie* cold here."

"It's winter," Roberta said. "I've put you upstairs on the right. Come down when you're ready for coffee."

"Thanks, Bobby," Katrina said. James carried their bags upstairs, and then they went down to the kitchen for coffee.

"James, Katrina, so good to see you," John said as he joined them "You'll need something in that coffee, try some of my calvados." He poured a little in each cup, then Roberta added coffee and milk. James took a sip and had to admit it tasted really good.

"So, the cider and the calvados turned out well?" James asked.

"Really well," John said. "You can try both before you go back."

"Did the information from U of W help?" Roberta asked.

"It did," Katrina said. "Wits accepted it and transferred all the credits, so now I have one final and I'm done."

"Well, good for you," Roberta said. "And, James, what boats have you rocked lately?"

"We ran a competition for mechanics helpers and anyone else who was interested," James replied. "It included a section of identifying all the items in a toolbox, then it also had the Bennett Mechanical Aptitude Test. I think the surprise to everyone was that Elizabeth Sithole, one of our accounting clerks, was in the top three. We've now started a series of classes for diagnostics, to help our service people when they go into the field. We've opened those classes to anyone, so it's possible that the office for Bantu Education might whine at some time."

"Just don't get thrown in jail," John said. "If you get fined for educating people, we'll pay, but try not to push things too far."

"I won't," James promised. "I'm not allowed by law to employ my black workers as skilled mechanics; those jobs are reserved for whites, but I can have a skilled helper, it's a fine line, I'll push it as far as I can, but I won't cross it, I've no desire to get arrested and probably deported."

"What about all the bombings?" Roberta asked.

"I think I've got a source in the company who will warn us of anything that will directly affect us," James said. "We were warned off the Carlton Centre when that bomb was set off."

'So, James, what about these CAMCO guys?" John asked.

"They're looking for a J&B 260 dragline, plus drills and shovels; the driver will be delivery on the dragline," James replied.

"Well, we'll do what we can," John said.

James met Piet and Leon at the airport, and they checked into a hotel, then went back to the airport and met the team from CAMCO. Piet told James that they had made the rounds of the dragline manufacturers and that they were last on the docket. That might be good or bad, James was never quite sure. Over dinner that night, George told them what he wanted to see, particularly, and it was as James expected, a machine in operation and a discussion with maintenance people to see how easy the machine was to maintain, what was likely to fail and when, and how easy or difficult it was to fix things that failed. The visit to Rock Springs would answer those questions. The program for the next couple of days was set: meet at the offices the next day and tour the factory, then make the trip to Rock Springs, then reconvene at the offices and discuss the proposal for the machines.

While the factory tour was underway, Leon closeted himself with Stuart Palmer, the chief financial Officer of the company and James and Bill Evans met with Hank Miller and went through their findings on the market for bucket wheel excavators.

"So, essentially what you're saying is that it'll cost us more to get into this business than we'll see out of it?" Hank asked.

"Yes," James confirmed. "There are established competitors who have all the engineering at hand for the excavator and the conveyor systems. Those competitors include Krupp, O&K, Buckau Wolfe and a few other smaller companies. If we were to do anything, the cost of entry would be less with small, more mobile machines like those made by Mechanical Excavators, Anderson Mavor and Barber Greene."

"So, better spend our money elsewhere?" Hank asked.

"I don't see the returns," James said. "The principal markets are brown coal, lignite and bauxite, and the German companies have established positions in those markets. Breaking in would cost us, and there is not enough demand to recover the development costs."

"And the bulk material handling?" Hank asked.

"Conveyors by the mile and lots of transfer points and less robust excavators," James replied. "There are more people in that business, apart from the Germans, there are US companies like McDowell Wellman and Dravo."

"Bill, anything from a manufacturing point of view?" Hank asked.

"The basic machine we could build easily enough, but most of the conveyor equipment and transfer point equipment we'd probably just buy," Bill replied.

"So, you agree with James that this is not for us?" Hank asked.

"I do," Bill said. "If we were to look at that market, we'd be better off buying someone in it, and the excavation side of it is large German companies that we could never afford to buy, and the bulk material handling is another set of players. If we were to buy anything, I'd look at underground mining equipment, someone like Joy."

"We could look at them," Hank agreed. "We could also diversify and look at an industry not is not driven by mining, but not just now, now we've got our hands full just fulfilling orders. Thank you for the report. Will you write it up completely for me, so that we have it on file?"

"I'll take care of that," James said.

"Who is your customer today?" Hank asked James.

"CAMCO, Consolidated African Mining Company, the parent of the company I used to work for in Zambia," James replied. "They're looking for a 60-yard dragline and a couple of drills, and a shovel. Tomorrow we're taking them out to Rock Springs to see the machine there."

"Well, keep me informed," Hank said. "Thanks, now if you'll excuse me, I have other matters to attend to."

"How was the plant tour?" James asked George that evening.
"Good," George said. "It's good to see large bits of kit being made, often makes me wonder if I shouldn't have done that rather than gone into mining."
"Mining is probably more secure," Keith said. "I like the idea of a twenty-year supply contract, you know where you stand, no casting about looking for new business all the time."
"Well, James can tell you that not all mining is that secure," George said. "We closed down the mine he ran when the price of copper dropped."
"That's because the copper was being sold on the commodities exchange," Keith said. "If you'd had a long-term contract for copper, the mine wouldn't have had to close."
"Not necessarily," George said. "The contract would have only been worth anything if the customer could sell his product; if the market for his product collapsed, then they would have cancelled and we would have fought it out in the courts, but the mine would still have been closed."
"Perhaps," Keith said.
"So, James, how long's the trip tomorrow?" George asked.
"A little under three hours," James replied. "We'll do a wheels up at seven in the morning, if that's okay with you, that'll put us into Rock Springs at about nine their time. We'll drive out to the mine, then come back and be back here by seven in the evening."
"And who's coming with us?" George asked.
"Myself, Piet and Dan Wells, you met Dan today, he's the product manager for draglines," James replied.
"So, Leon, I gather you're the financial person for J&B Africa," George said. "How are you doing?"
"We're managing," Leon replied, unwilling to boast about their success lest it give George ammunition to ask for a price reduction.

"Leon has a firm grasp of our business and a firm hand on the money," James said. "We all look to him for help."

"Well, just keep whatever it is you're doing," George said. "I get good reports about J&B Africa."

The trip the next day was almost a repeat of trips that James had made in the past with other customers, the only difference being that this time it was a lot colder, approaching zero degrees Fahrenheit. George told James that he had got what he wanted and had learned a lot as well. He has been impressed with the mine and the people there and was wondering if CAMCO should not look to acquire the company. That was something that James could not advise him on. Johannes had had his plans for the mine confirmed, so he was happy, even Keith seemed happy. The next day, it was all about prices and deliveries, and the discussions dragged on all day. Obviously, there was not going to be a quick decision on this project, as George told them that they would be doing their final review in South Africa and would let them know. James was not sure whether or not this was a good or bad omen, and George was giving nothing away. George and his team left late that afternoon to fly to New York to get the plane the next day back to South Africa, so James and Piet were at a loose end. Piet told James that he had been asked out to dinner by Tom Nelson and Jim Edwards, two of the people from the office in Oak Creek. Leon had gone to dinner with Stuart and Roy Kahl, the treasurer. That left James free to go and have dinner with Katrina, Roberta and John, so he checked out of his hotel and drove to the house.

"All done?" Katrina asked him.

"All done," he confirmed. "We'll get their decision sometime next week."

"I'm looking forward to going home where it's warmer," she said.

"This isn't so bad," Roberta chimed in. "It could be colder."

"It's cold enough," Katrina said. "Oh, James, I checked on our house today, and everything is fine there. The property management company is doing a good job of looking after the house, so no frozen pipes, nothing wrong."

"That's good," James said. "John, before we go back, could we try some of your calvados?"
"Of course," John said. "Pity, you can't take a bottle back with you. Here, try a little."
"It's good," James said as he sipped from the glass he had been offered. "It's got a kick to it as well."
"I'm pleased with it," John said. "Now I need to find people to get it to before I make another batch next year."
"Could you set aside a few bottles for us?" Katrina asked.
"Of course," John said. "Anyway, here's to us!"

"That was a nice trip," Katrina commented to James when they were on the plane the next day, headed for Johannesburg.
"Short," he said. "Whether or not it was productive, we'll have to wait and see."
"How was your meeting with Hank Miller?" she asked.
"Good, I think," he said. "Hank's got something in mind, but it's not bucket wheels."
"Roberta showed me some of her new fabrics," Katrina said. "She even gave me a new swimsuit, all very clingy, supposed to make you go faster in the water."
"How was their winter ski trip?" he asked.
"She told me that they had had a wonderful time," Katrina said. "Bobby's designing new fabrics for the ski business now."
"She does some amazing things," James said. "I sometimes wish I were a little smarter."
"You're smart," Katrina assured him. "You might not have the academic knowledge that others have, but you can hold your own."
"Thank you, but you're biased," he said.
"Maybe," she admitted. "Anyway, for our next weekend trip, where to, more to the north, or where?"
"I was wondering what it looks like around the Blouberg," he said.
"We could drive out there and see," she said. "I'm wondering if we shouldn't get some camping gear, we may be going to places where there are no hotels."

"Good idea," he said.
"Excuse me, Mr and Mrs Martin, could I set up for your dinner?" a stewardess asked.
"Of course," Katrina said.

James met with Leon as soon as he got back to ask about his visit.
"It went better than I expected," Leon said. "Stuart is easy to talk to and we got on well, he's probably going to come out here later in the year."
"Any accounting issues that we need to address?" James asked.
"Nothing that we need to change, I went over some tax items with them, just to let them know what was happening here," Leon replied. "Stuart did take me to meet Hank Miller, and he introduced me as your replacement."
"That's good," James said. "It reinforced what I've been saying. Who else did you see?"
"I saw John Williams, Tom Brooks, Tom Sanders and Fred Johnson," Leon replied. "They all seemed very helpful."
"I think they are," James said. They were interrupted by Charlize, who came in to say that George Armstrong was on the telephone. James took the call and was asked to go and meet George in his office that morning. James drove into the centre of Johannesburg, parked and walked to George's office.
"James, thanks for coming," George said. "There's no easy way to say this, but we're awarding the contract for the dragline to someone else."
"I see, well, thank you for telling me," James said. "What was the issue?"
"Delivery," George said. "We just couldn't live with the delivery promises that you made. We got a better schedule elsewhere, now we just have to see if they can make it. We are going to give you the drills and the shovel; you should be able to make the delivery dates on them."
"Would it bother you if they came early?" James asked.
"Not a bit," George said. "I'm sorry about this, James. I was impressed with the *ouks* at Rock Springs and how well things were going there, but we're up against a deadline and we have to be in operation to make the first shipload. The stuff is already sold, Keith and his contracts, he

forgot that contracts are two-sided, and the customer has some penalties for late shipment. They have a vessel scheduled into Richards Bay already and would stick us with demurrage charges if we can't get it loaded by the contract date."

"That was one thing that I forgot to ask at Richards Bay: how do they know whose coal is whose?" James asked.

"It's done by stacker and location," George said. "Where did you slip off to when we had our plant tour?"

"I had a meeting with the CEO," James replied. "I've been working on a project for him and had to make a report. Now I've got to finish writing it up for the file."

"I heard whispers about some classes you're holding for diagnostics," George said. "I know Bryn and was amused to hear that you've even got a woman in the class."

"She's very bright," James said. "Her dad runs a car repair business in Soweto, and I'm sure I'm going to lose her one day. She's an accounting clerk and by all accounts a pretty good mechanic."

"Any pushback from the white mechanics?" George asked.

"There was a parts manager who would have no part in training our black staff, but he quit. My only concern now is someone singing to the government about us educating the black staff we have," James said.

"You know, we're going to have to work something out ourselves," George said. "We just can't get enough qualified white mechanics, and the government doesn't help with restricting skilled jobs to whites only."

"We talked to Escom and found out what they were doing," James said. "In fact, we even had the Escom people judge a competition for us."

"I heard a little about that," George said. "Let me buy you lunch, and you can tell me about it."

Over lunch, James shared with George the reason he had started the competition and how he had structured it, with the greater incentive going to the white mechanics to get them to participate in the training of the black helpers, and how he had seen huddled conflabs going on over tools, parts and pieces and systems. His overall assessment was that it was worth every penny he had spent on the toolboxes as prizes and for the participants. He also told George about the other classes they were holding, mining methods, basic accounting, computing, and other subjects and how everyone in the company was involved. George was intrigued and wondered what they could do as a company. He knew that historically the mining companies, particularly the gold mining companies, had used huge black labour forces as mainly manual labour, with some semi-skilled jobs, but they were all facing the same problem, a lack of skilled white labour, so they all had to do something, but they were all up against the government. James ran a small enough company that he could probably get away with a lot, but the big gold mines were part and parcel of the basic economy and garnered government scrutiny and attention, whether they liked it or not.

The Blouberg

"Are you ready?" James asked Katrina as he packed the last of their things into her Land Cruiser.

"Coming," she said. "How far do we want to go tonight?"

"I thought we'd stop in Pietersburg," he said. "We should be there between seven and eight tonight, hopefully in time for a late dinner."

"Good, *kom ons ry*," she said. James drove, and they threaded their way through the side streets until they got onto the main road north. Traffic was quite heavy until they got north of Pretoria, then it thinned out a lot, and they were able to make better time. They arrived in Pietersburg at seven-thirty and found a hotel that had rooms and where the dining room was still open.

"So, tomorrow, which road do we take?" Katrina asked over dinner.

"The one towards Dendron," James replied. "Then at Dendron, we take a side road that takes us to Bochum and then into the Blouberg."

"It's dry up here, isn't it?" she said.

"It is," he said. "But there's a lot of farming, so there must be water."

"It can't be too far from the Blouberg to Botswana," she thought. "But, this weekend is not about Botswana."

"Where next?" he asked.

"Pilgrim's Rest," she suggested. "It'll be a little different to this."

"I wonder why Pilgrim's Rest?" he mused.

"We should ask when we go there," she said. "Now, bath and bed?"

They were out on the road early the next morning, headed towards Dendron, so named for all the indigenous trees in the area. When they turned off towards Bochum, they saw a man with a suitcase walking along the road. James pulled up next to him, and Katrina asked if he was going far.

"Far enough," he replied.

"Would you like a lift?" Katrina asked.

“Thank you, at least as far as Bochum,” he said. He put his suitcase in the back of the Land Cruiser and climbed in. Bochum was only about twenty minutes away, and they pulled up there.

“Are you going on?” the man asked.

“We’re going to De Villiersdale,” Katrina replied.

“I am the new school teacher there,” he said. “Would it be inconvenient to take me there?”

“No,” Katrina said. “We will be happy to take you.”

As they drove into De Villiersdale, they were struck by the fact that it was hardly a town, more like a collection of houses scattered here and there, all dominated by the mountains behind and the odd peaks that seemed to erupt from the surrounding country. The man tapped on the window at the back of the cab, and they pulled over.

“May I offer you tea?” he asked.

“Thank you,” Katrina replied.

“If you would just drive and park over by that building,” he said, pointing to what looked like a school. James did as asked, and they got out and stretched their legs.

“I am Charles Buys,” the man said, introducing himself.

“Nice to meet you,” Katrina said. “I am Katrina Martin, and this is James Martin.”

“You are not from Johannesburg,” Charles commented, which James thought was an interesting statement, as the number plate on their Land Cruiser clearly identified it as coming from Johannesburg.

“No, I am from Zambia,” Katrina said. “But we live in Johannesburg now.”

“Please sit,” Charles said. “While I make tea, tell me how was it in Zambia?”

“Since Independence in 1964, there have been many changes,” Katrina said. “Socially, economically and politically, the ruling UNIP party under President Kaunda recently banned the ANC and UPP parties. Economically, the copper mines are still seeing some problems after the price drop a couple of years ago, and socially, whites and blacks are learning to live with one another.”

"Tell me about the schools there," Charles said.

"In the towns, there are primary and secondary schools, but away from the towns, there are some primary schools, but the challenge is to get teachers. The Northern Rhodesia administration didn't do much to educate the black Zambians, so the country is trying to catch up," Katrina said.

"And you, Madam, where were you educated?" Charles asked.

"Primary school in Kitwe, then secondary school in Bulawayo," Katrina replied. "Since then, university in Milwaukee in the States, and lately Wits."

"And you, Mr Martin?" Charles asked.

"Primary and secondary school and then university in England," James replied. "And university again in Milwaukee."

"But if you have been at the university in Milwaukee, why are you here?" Charles asked.

"I have a job here," James said. "I work for an American company, and they sent me here."

"Ah, tea is ready, milk and sugar?" Charles asked.

"Just milk for both of us," Katrina replied. "And you, Sir, where did you go to school?"

"In Messina, then Fort Hare," Charles replied. "The local mission school paid for my education at Fort Hare."

"Many famous leaders went to Fort Hare," Katrina explained to James. "Including Kaunda, Nyerere and Khama, not to mention prominent South Africans."

"Many of whom now are in prison," Charles said, a little sadly.

"Does the government pay for the school here?" Katrina asked.

"No, the mission pays," Charles replied. "But the government wants to control what we teach and in what language. English is not encouraged; Afrikaans is promoted. So, what brings you to the Blouberg?"

"We know that we're only in South Africa for a short time," Katrina said. "So, we decided to try and see as much of the country as we can while we're here. We started at the north at Beitbridge and are working our way south."

"And do you have family still in Zambia?" Charles asked.

"No, my folks sold their business and retired to Calitzdorp, where they now grow grapes," Katrina replied. "I have cousins that I have met only rarely, most living in the Cape, and one in South West, and you?"
"My parents live in Messina, my father works for the railways," Charles replied.
"Will South Africa change its government at any time?" James asked.
"Now that is a difficult question," Charles said. "It would be logical that the majority of the people could vote for their government, but that would mean that some would have to yield their privilege, and they will do that very reluctantly."
"I see difficult times ahead," James said.
"I do too," Charles agreed. "But for now, I must concentrate on giving the children here the best education that I can and that the government will permit."
"We wish you well," Katrina said. "Thank you for the tea."
"Where will you go now?" Charles asked.
"We thought that we'd explore the Blouberg a little," Katrina said.
"In that case, follow that track there; it will take you up into the berg and let you see the plants and animals that are unique to here," Charles suggested.
"Thank you," Katrina said. "Before we go, is there anything that we might bring to the school?"
"Stationery of any type would be appreciated," Charles replied. "Pencils, pens, rulers, exercise books, anything of that nature."
"We'll see what we can do," Katrina promised. "How many children do you have here?"
"We cater to all here, so about 150 in total," Charles replied.
"We'll send something, stay well, Mr Buys," Katrina said.
"Go well, Mrs Martin," Charles replied.

"Buys seems like an odd name for an African," James commented to Katrina as they drove away.
"There was, is, a whole tribe of Buys people that lived in around the Soutpansberg," Katrina explained. "The story goes that one Coenraad

Buys had a harem of native women, and from them, a whole community grew up. So, up here, the Buys name is not uncommon."

"Is this Fort Hare really famous?" James asked.

"It is," she said. "I think it was founded in 1916 by white missionaries and operated basically as a black university until the 50s, then the government stepped in and brought it under the Bantu Education mob and discouraged teaching in English and probably all kinds of other things too."

"Where is it?" James asked.

"It's in the Cape, in what they now call Ciskei," she replied. "Look out, a whole herd of buffalo, we'd better keep our eyes and minds on where we're going."

"This track hasn't been used by much," James said as he looked ahead. The track was rutted, had grass growing in the centre and even in some places in the ruts. There were no tyre treads visible, just the ruts where wheels had been; there were no footprints of people, just animal tracks, like those of the buffalo. They climbed steadily but slowly for about an hour, crawling ever up until they came to a plateau, out of which jutted more crags and peaks.

"Why don't we stop here?" Katrina suggested. "Look, there's a stream over there and a pool."

"It's pretty wild, isn't it?" James commented.

"It is," she agreed. "I haven't seen any cattle or goats, so the villagers don't come up here often. Look, over there, a ratel."

"I've never seen one before," James said, watching fascinated as the ratel scurried about looking for its next meal. "What do they eat?"

"Pretty much anything," she said. "From beetles to rodents to snakes. They're potent little animals, almost fearless; they'll take on almost anything if they're threatened."

"So, if I put up the tent and make a fire, will you get some water?" he asked.

"Is there something we can do for Charles Buys and his school?" Katrina asked when they were eating dinner.

"I'm sure we can come up with something," James said. "I was thinking of just buying a load of stationery, then sending one of our drivers up with it."
"I'm sure he'd appreciate that," she said. "Do any of your drivers come from this part of the Transvaal?"
"I'd have to ask," he said. "I really don't know where they all come from, only where they live now."
"How much stationery can you fit in a *bakkie*?" she asked.
"I would think a lot," he said. "Ssh, look over there."
"A wild cat," she said. "That's a first for me."
"This place has all kinds of things," he said. "Are we safe here from hyæna?"
"We can sleep in the back of the *bakkie* if you prefer," she suggested.
"That's not a bad idea," he agreed. "I'll put the pads we had to sleep on in the back, and the sleeping bags. Will we need the tent, will it rain?"
"I doubt it," she said. "The skies are clear, no clouds anywhere, we can chance it."
"Let me damp down the fire and make sure that there's nothing around that can catch," he said. "Then, we can go to bed."

"James, wake up," Katrina said early the next morning as she poked him in the ribs. "Look, sable, a whole herd of them."
"Pretty, aren't they?" he said as he watched them walk by and disappear behind one of the peaks that jutted up.
"Get the fire going, will you, and I'll make breakfast," she said. James hunted around and found dead branches and twigs and got his fire going again, then Katrina made coffee and breakfast, and they sat and watched the world go by, the birds overhead and the occasional animal they saw. It was a world away from the traffic and noise of the city, but they both knew that in time, there would be people invading the space as they pushed the animals into smaller and smaller habitats.
"When do we need to leave?" James asked.
"Before lunch," Katrina said. "It'll take us an hour to get back down to the road."

"Look, zebra," James said, pointing to a gap in the hills. The zebra filed through, looked at them, then hurried off away from them.

"So, we've seen buffalo, sable, zebra, a cat and a ratel," Katrina said. "Bridget would have loved it here; there are so many birds."

"If you've finished with the fire, then I'll make sure it's out and bury the ashes," James said. Katrina was done, so he got water from the pool and made sure that there were no live embers, then he dug a fairly deep hole and buried the ashes. Their paper products he put into the back of their Land Cruiser, hyæna were renowned for scenting things and would dig up paper plates and scatter them about.

"Are we ready?" Katrina asked.

"We're ready," James said, taking a last look around and making sure that they had left nothing, no tins, no paper, no plastic, just ruts in the ground where they had driven and parked for the night. The drive back to Johannesburg was uneventful, and they were back before dark and looking forward to a soak in the bath. Bush showers with a bucket were fine, but there was nothing like a soak. James cooked dinner while Katrina looked on and offered comments, and sipped her wine. After dinner, they did have their soak in the bath, but then things progressed and bed called.

"Nice weekend?" Leon asked James when he went into the office.

"Great, we drove up to the Blouberg, it's pretty wild there," James replied. "We saw a good-sized herd of buffalo, and we saw a wild cat, first one I've ever seen. So, Leon, where's the best place to buy pens and pencils?"

"We've got plenty," Leon said.

"Not for us," James said. "I was going to donate some to a small school up there."

"Go to the wholesaler we use," Leon said. "SA Paper Products, use our account, buy what you need, then reimburse the company."

"I'll do that," James said. "Okay, anything going on that I should be aware of?"

"The bombing last month, clashes with police, but nothing that affects us," Leon said. "Parts sales are doing well, service is doing really well, and we're seeing some benefit from our classes already. It was a pity about the dragline for CAMCO, but I suppose we can't win them all."

"Do you hear anything about Bryn's classes?" James asked.

"By all accounts, they're going well," Leon said. "Elizabeth told me that she's already learned a lot."

"The next trip I make to Oak Creek, you should come with me again," James said. "You should meet all the product managers this time, and some of the manufacturing folk."

"I'd like that," Leon said. "Maybe when it's a little warmer, this last trip was a shocker, I didn't know it could be so cold."

"You wouldn't have liked it in Wyoming, where we took the CAMCO *ouks*," James said. "Even colder than it was in Oak Creek."

"Just tell me when and I'll have my bags packed," Leon said.

James borrowed Katrina's Land Cruiser and went to SA Paper Products. Their warehouse was like an Aladdin's Cave of stationery items. He went with the manager and picked out pencils, plain and coloured, pencil sharpeners, ink pens and large bottles of ink and little ceramic ink wells, biros by the boxful, exercise books, pencil boxes, rulers, paint brushes and paints and pads of paper to paint on, blackboard chalk, school bags, compasses, large compasses to use on the blackboard, a globe and wall maps of the world, Africa and South Africa, and a few other items that the manager recommended. James charged it all to the company account, then had all the boxes loaded into his truck. It was actually quite a load. At the office, he unloaded it all and stacked it in his office, then went to see Danie about borrowing a driver and a truck to deliver it. Danie had a truck going to Louis Trichardt, so it would not be much of a detour to go west to the Blouberg, deliver the stationery, then come back. Danie arranged for the stationery boxes to be loaded along with the parts, then supervised the tying down of the load. It would not pay to have anything fall off. James gave the driver his card and told him to give it to Charles Buys at the school. The driver was set to leave at five the next morning so that he could make the trip in one day. That done, James went and paid the reckoning to Leon.

"I sent off a load of stationery to Charles Buys," James told Katrina that evening. "Everything from pens and pencils to paper and paint. It should be delivered tomorrow. We've got a delivery going to Louis Trichardt, so the driver is going to make a short detour on the way back and drop it off for us."

"That's *lekker*," she said. "I'm glad we can do something. I didn't see too many desks at the school. I wonder if they even have any?"

"We should find out and maybe get some made locally," he suggested. "I wonder who makes school desks?"

"I'm sure we can find out, but how big was the schoolroom we saw? Does Charles have to teach all 150 himself in that one room, or were there more rooms?" she wondered.

"Perhaps we should go back and take another look," he said.

"Okay, so we'll delay Pilgrim's Rest for a couple of weeks and take a trip back to De Villiersdale," she said. "I wonder if we make anything like school desks. CMI has all kinds of products. I'll take a look."

"It's interesting," he said. "When I was in primary and grammar school, I never gave any thought about where all the stuff came from, it was just there."

"Why would you?" she asked. "That was what school governors and the local authority or the mines did."

"Tell me more about Fort Hare?" he asked.

"I told you all I know," she said. "I just knew that Kaunda had gone there as well as the others, and I heard that many of the South African ANC leaders had gone there."

"The *Boerjies* probably see it as a hotbed of revolution," he thought. "I'm surprised it's still open."

"So am I," she agreed. "I wonder if they welcome visitors?"

"We could drive down one weekend and find out," he suggested.

"I'll put it on the list," she laughed.

"You are back, thank you so much for the supplies," Charles said when James and Katrina finally tracked him down in the village. They had arrived just after nine on Saturday morning and had asked some children they saw where the teacher lived. The directions had been spotty, but by dint of asking two more, they finally got the right place.

“We’re happy to provide them,” Katrina said. “Tell me, Mr Buys, how many classrooms do you have and how many desks?”

“Four classrooms and no desks,” Charles replied. “I have three other teachers working with me, and we have about forty children each.”

“Does the school have toilets?” James asked.

“We have a primitive pit system,” Charles replied. “Would you like to see the school?”

“If it’s not too much trouble,” Katrina said. Charles went with them to the school, and they saw that the building that they had been to before was the office, such as it was. Behind there were four separate buildings, each about 60 feet long and 30 feet wide, with openings for windows, but no glass. The classrooms had concrete floors with some mats scattered around for the children to sit on.

“You can see,” Charles said. “It’s fairly basic.”

“I wonder what it would take to build an ablution block?” James mused. “If there were such a block, who would maintain it?”

“Ah, there again is the rub,” Charles said. “Neither the mission nor the government provides money for maintenance.”

“Would the parents volunteer?” James asked.

“I think they would,” Charles said. “We would have to put it to the headman, but if he agreed, then it could be done.”

“So, desks, how many per classroom, say eight rows by four, thirty-two desks, two children per desk, and four classrooms, and four teachers' desks, and two ablution blocks, boys and girls, ten stalls each, plus washbasins, if we could get water, how does that sound?” James asked.

“That’s a huge project,” Charles said.

“Is there water here?” James asked.

“If you drill for it,” Charles said. “But who can afford a well?”

“Do you suppose that the Mission could come up with the funds for a header tank and a windmill and pump, if the well were drilled?” James asked.

“I can ask,” Charles said.

"J&B makes well drills," James said. "And from time to time we have to teach people how to use them, so we could drill a well, if you could get a liner and a windmill and a pump."

"May I offer you lunch?" Charles said.

"We brought enough for three," Katrina said. "Would you like to share ours?"

"Thank you," Charles said. They ate lunch, and Charles sketched out possible plans for ablution blocks. He based them on layouts at the school he had gone to as a child. He gave James the plan and made a few other notes as well.

"Does the Mission have basic plans for schools and facilities?" James asked.

"I believe they have some," Charles said. "I clearly have a lot to ask them. Tell me, why would you do this?"

"We've both had opportunity," Katrina said. "And that opportunity was rooted in education, so the chance to help others is something to be taken. You happen to be the first primary school teacher we have met, so why not work with you?"

"Where do your employees live?" Charles asked.

"Most of our black staff live to the south of the airport, but a few live out in Soweto, the white staff are scattered about with no particular concentration," James replied.

"So, it would be difficult to tie your business to one community in the Jo'burg area?" Charles asked.

"Probably," James agreed. "We certainly couldn't afford to fund half a dozen schools; we simply don't have the resources for that, we're not a very big company."

"Whatever your reasons, I cannot thank you enough for all the things you've already given us," Charles said. "I was quite surprised when your driver arrived with a whole *bakkie* full of stuff, it was like Christmas."

"We will do what we can," James said. "We should probably leave soon to start back. Before we go, do you have a postal address for the school?"

"We do," Charles said. "Here it is, everything is sent to us through the Mission in Messina."

"Thank you," James said.

"Thank you again," Charles said. "Go well."
"Stay well," James replied.

They did not go straight back to Johannesburg, but spent the night at the Mountain Inn, a hotel perched in the hills above Louis Trichardt, looking down over the town and the flatter lands beyond. Sundowners were served on a terrace with the full view of the town below and with other views along the Soutpansberg range.

"Can we really do all that for the school?" Katrina asked James.

"I can get a well drilled as a teaching project," he thought. "The well liner, pump and header tank, we'd have to see who funds that. I have an idea, a friend of Dad's belongs to a Rotary Club in Bourne End, they do projects like this, if I could get them interested, then I'm sure there's a club in Louis Trichardt that they could partner with."

"That's a good idea," she agreed. "What will you do, write to your dad?"

"That would be best," he said. "I'll give him the basics of the project along with the name of the school and the contact information for the school, then they can proceed from there, if they're interested. I'm guessing the idea of a building project will appeal to the civil engineer in Dad. I should ask Will how big header tanks need to be and what kind of pumps and all that sort of stuff."

"I'm sure he pumps a lot of paint around in his factory," she said. "This is exciting. Perhaps we can do something for the school."

"Are you ready to eat?" he asked.

"Ready when you are," she said.

James called Will, and they talked about the De Villiersdale school and what might be done there. Will knew where they could get a windmill and a submersible pump and a header tank, and a frame to stand it on. So, if they did nothing else, they could get water to the school. He also told James that their father had joined the Rotary Club that his friend belonged to and would probably welcome the challenge of the school ablution block. James was a little chagrined that he had missed that piece of information, that his father had joined a club, but perhaps he just had not read the latest letter carefully enough. With a windmill and the rest of the items necessary for a water supply available, James turned to Hans and asked him if they had anything scheduled for training people to use the well drills that they sold. Hans told him that they had sold a well drill to a company from Alldays and that they were looking for some training. James asked Hans if he would ask the company if they would consider drilling a well as a teaching project. The project would fall under the umbrella of the grant they had received to train white skilled labour, in this case, well drillers. There were no constraints in the grant language that restricted where the training would be done, only that it was for whites only. Hans promised to talk to the company and wanted to know where the well would be drilled. James told him that it would be in De Villiersdale and would supply a school.

"I found a place that makes school desks," Katrina told James that evening. "It's in Centurion. Jan Hofmeyr knows the *ou* that owns the place, and he even offered to buy them and donate them to the school if we can ship them there; he did offer to drop them off at your yard."

"I'm sure we could get them all loaded onto a low loader; it will be volume-driven, not weight, but I'm sure they'd all fit," he said. "Did Jan give any indication when we might get the desks?"

"He said he'd let me know," she said.

"I should write to Dad and ask him about an ablution block. Did you know he'd joined a Rotary Club?" James asked.

"I think they mentioned that in the last letter we got from Cores End," she replied.

"I wonder how I missed that?" James said.

"Because you skimmed it through without reading it properly," she said.

"Are you ready for your final exam in March?" he asked.

"I am," she said. "I have a little revision to do, but I've been essentially doing every day what the exam will cover, so feel confident."

"You'll do fine," he said.

"I haven't asked in a while, but how's your business doing?" she asked.

"Well, you know we didn't get the CAMCO dragline, but we did get the shovel and the drills, which makes quite a few machines since we've been here, but only three this year. The construction machine line is doing well; we have to keep ordering new machines from Didcot. Parts is going well, and our service business is expanding, the classes are paying off," he replied. "I think Oak Creek is happy with the results."

"They should be," she said. "You've given them all kinds of new business and grown the whole place quite a bit. How's Leon doing?"

"He'll be fine," James said. "By the time we go back to the States, Leon will be able to just take over without any hiccups."

"What do the others think about that?" she asked.

"I think they're happy to have someone handle all the admin stuff that comes with running the company," he replied. "They don't want to deal with the financial reporting, the personnel issues, the tax filings, all the stuff that has to get done."

"If Leon takes over, will he need another accountant?" she asked.

"I think so," James replied. "There'll be just a bit much for Leon to do it all."

James spent the next week or so focused solely on J&B Africa business, selling machines, selling parts and conducting more classes on mining methods and machine selection. When was it best to use a shovel, when was it best to use a front-end loader, a backhoe or another piece of equipment? Decisions are driven by digging conditions, expected lifetime of the deposit, available utilities, truck sizes, rock types, fragmentation, and all the various factors that went into making the right choice. Hans conducted a parallel series of classes on machine selection for construction projects, from digging basements for buildings to digging trenches for pipes. It was all an effort to have a better-educated workforce that could all answer possible questions from potential customers. James also finished writing his report on the market for bucket wheel excavators and sent it off to Oak Creek to Bill Evans for his review and comments before giving it to Hank Miller.

At the end of February, James sat down with Bryn and asked him how the classes were going.

"Well," Bryn told him. "They all want to learn and all want to succeed."
"Anyone who stands out?" James asked.
"Sam Beyers," Bryn said. "He has a knack for looking and listening and quickly isolating the problem, as does your Elizabeth Sithole, but I can't include her in the reports I have to submit to the college. They pass those reports on to the government, and we don't want them to come down on us."
"Indeed, we don't," James agreed. "If I were to hold a competition for diagnosis of problems, how would we do that?"
"The best way would be to have a number of the same machines into which we would introduce faults, then the participants would have to identify those faults and fix them," Bryn said. "But, you probably don't have enough of the same type of machine here at any one time, so we may have to come up with something else."
"What if we had two or three machines, all with problems that we sent each team to in turn to diagnose?" James suggested.
"We'd have to keep the teams separate and not let them see what the others were looking at, but we could arrange that," Bryn said.
"We've got plenty of time," James said. "I was thinking of doing it the week before Christmas."
"Let me think about it," Bryn said. "Are you thinking of teams of two?"
"We would normally send out a team of two: a mechanic and a helper," James confirmed.
"So, perhaps the first thing to do is tell everyone that and have them form teams that would then work together the rest of the year," Bryn suggested.
"We'll do that," James agreed. "What does the Technical College do for practicals?"
"We have some equipment, but everyone knows it, and last year's students tell this year's what the issues are, so it's a challenge," Bryn said.
"What if we were to find some machines that are essentially in the scrap heap?" James asked.
"We don't want them too far gone," Bryn said. "We still have to be able to start them up and run them, even if they don't perform as well as they should."
"I'll see what we can find," James said.

"We also have some bench work," Bryn said. "We'll get pumps and alternators that aren't running properly and ask the students why not."
"I'm sure we could find some of them," James said.
"If you can find them, a water pump, a hydraulic pump, an alternator and a generator," Bryn suggested.

James then met with Frank and Hans to talk about a new service. He knew that Caterpillar had a program for the analysis of lubricating oils in their machines. It was essentially an early detection system for failure; various metals would start to show up as different parts wore or got close to failing. James wanted to know what it would cost them to set up their own system and how much he could charge the customers for the service.
"What are we looking to detect?" Frank asked.
"I would think various metals like iron, chromium, copper, zinc," James said. "And I would think we'd need to check for turbidity to see if there's just a lot of particle matter in the oils, also check for viscosity."
"Can we buy equipment for that?" Frank asked.
"I'm sure we can. The question is, how much is it?" James said.
"I'll look into it," Frank promised. "I know the service manager next door at Barlows, so I'll ask him what they use."
"How many of our customers would use a service?" James asked.
"I think the bigger ones might," Hans replied. "But the smaller ones with only one or two machines, it would depend on how much we would charge."
"So, if we were to do it, we'd need some kind of analysis capability, either a machine or a basic chemistry lab, that would mean space, and a technician," James thought. "I wonder if we'd get enough buyers to even make it worth our while?"
"How do we get the samples?" Frank asked.
"Good point, are they sent through the post office? Would we have to collect them, or would the customers drop them off at one of our locations? How long is an acceptable time to wait for results? How do we interpret results? Let's say we see an increase in chromium in the oil, what does that mean?" James mused.

"Looks like we need some investigation," Frank said.

"I wonder if Bryn and the Technical College have any ideas?" James thought. "The Cat program originated in the States, and they probably did all kinds of research before they launched it. Did Didcot have anything like this?"

"No," Hans said. "Maybe we should put it to them and let them do some research."

"I'll do that," James said. "In my next monthly report to Oak Creek, I'll mention it and ask if they or Didcot have done anything, stir them up a bit. On a simple note, are our drain plugs in the engine and gearbox sumps magnetic, will they pick up iron filings?"

"No, but they probably could be," Frank said. "I'll look around for plugs that are magnetic, and we can offer them as an alternate."

"I'll stick that in my monthly report too," James said.

Leon came to see James to talk about a new upgrade for the IBM computer they leased. The computer had seemed like an expensive luxury when they had first installed it, but now they had their parts inventory on it, service schedules, machine sales and populations, accounting, personnel records, in fact, everything pertaining to the business. Leon wanted an upgrade to back up everything they had so that they did not lose it all if the machine died. Leon had taken the precaution of printing everything out each week and keeping the latest printout, so, at the worst, all they had to do was reconstruct one week, but he still wanted some other backup in case of problems. James and Leon talked about the changes and the costs and concluded that they could afford it, so called IBM and authorised the changes. The other thing that Leon wanted was a big paper shredder; hanging on to earlier printouts of the company records was redundant, but he did not want to just discard the unwanted paper; there was too much to be learned from it, so he wanted the shred it all. He had found a machine made by a German company, EBA Maschinenfabrik, that would essentially give them confetti, and he had found a buyer for the confetti, a pet shop that was looking for some bedding material. The price was not that high, but it would pay for the shredder in under a year. James liked that idea, getting paid for a waste product and not having to pay to have it hauled away. Leon had already found a big chipping machine that would grind up the pallets and crates that parts came in on, and he had found a buyer for the chips, a landscaper. All they had needed to do was have someone pull all the nails out of the pallets and crates before they chipped them. Getting someone to do that was simple enough; they just took on another low-skilled labourer who was given the task of pulling apart the pallets, then bagging up the chips. Looking at the chipper, Leon had been concerned that there could be a risk to the man running it, so he and Hans had devised a short conveyor feed so that the operator never got closer than ten feet from the business end of the chipper. The chips only paid for part of the man's wages, so they looked around for what else he could do that would cover his costs. The answer was in the scrap metals that they generated. Repairs almost always resulted in some parts being scrapped, so they had a scrap bin, into which all went, and it was sold to a dealer in town. So, they probably had the first employee in South Africa dedicated to reducing waste. Leon had also looked into what they could do with the waste oils they got from regular servicing and from repairs. Leon had found a market for that, too, a place that used waste oil to burn and generate steam. They would come and collect the oil, but would only pay a nominal amount for it. That did not matter to James or Leon; the oil was taken off their site, and they did not have to pay to have it hauled away. James was impressed; Leon had come up with all kinds of ideas to reduce operating expenses, and that showed on the income statements.

Katrina took her final exam at Wits, and, no surprise to James, did very well. That qualified her for her bachelor's degree in finance. The award ceremony for the degree was to be held at the end of March, so all she had to do was wait. Jan Hofmeyr was as good as his word and gave her a pay increase.

"So, Katrina Martin, BSc," James kidded her over dinner. "How does it feel, any different than before?"

"No," she said. "Only that now when we talk to some of the aunties in the States and they talk about their degrees from Madison or elsewhere,

I can trot out my degree from Wits, then have to spend the next few minutes explaining what Wits is and why they're a reputable university."

"I'm proud of you," he said. "You worked hard."

"It wasn't that hard," she said. "Having you to test ideas on helped, and the last few months working for Jan helped a lot too, because I was using much of the classwork in real life."

"So, could you take over our finances and investments?" he asked.

"Why not?" she thought. "I wouldn't do anything big without talking to you, but I can manage the day-to-day stuff."

"We don't have much in the way of investments yet," James said. "But, I'm hoping that we can do something."

"I'll look at income and expenses and see where we stand," she said. "I presume that for investments we'd be looking at the States, not here?"

"We could look here," James said. "But it would be short-term for us, we're not going to stay here in the long term, so better to invest where we plan to live."

"I'll start looking around at what we could do," she said. "While we're on the subject, we need to think about life insurance. If we both have policies with the other as beneficiary, then if something happens to one of us, the other has something to fall back on."

"I haven't given it much thought, but I get a pension from J&B; it vests when I've worked for them for five years, so a couple of years yet," he said.

"What happens if we leave before that?" she asked.

"Then it doesn't vest," James said. "Then I'd start again with whoever I moved to."

"So, our own investments are probably a good idea," she commented.

"I think so," he agreed. "The first thing to look at this year will be the stock option that I have. On the anniversary of the option, so next month, we have a decision to make: sell the 1,000 shares that I will be due, or wait and see if they go up more. J&B is currently trading at $29.00, so $3,500 or thereabouts, less tax."

"I'll take a look at the company and trends and see if I can guess whether or not now is a good time to exercise," she said. "When must you exercise by?"

"Ten years from the date of award," he said.

"So, 1987," she said. "I wonder where we'll be then?"

"I wonder," he echoed. "I never thought about stock options before we joined J&B, and even when Tony mentioned them, I thought I'd have to wait forever to be on the program."

"If you do exercise, what do we do with the money?" she asked.

"I don't know," he said. "Maybe set up an account with someone and put it in the stock market, but spread around a bit, not just in J&B."

"I'll look into it," she said.

Pilgrim's Rest

A low loader pulled into the J&B Africa yard with a load of crates on it.
"Where do you want them?" the driver asked Frank, who was the one who happened to be in the yard at the time.
"Who's it for?" Frank asked.
"Says here, deliver to James Martin," the driver said.
"Let me get a crane and we'll put them over there," Frank said. The driver shifted his low loader and moved it to the place that Frank indicated. Then Frank got one of the cranes they had in the yard and used it to unload the crates. That done, he said goodbye to the driver and went to see James.
"There's a load of crates arrived with your name on it," he told James.
"Great, it arrived," James said. "It's a windmill that I'm going to donate it to a school up near the Blouberg, so they can get water."
"Ah, is that the place that we're going to drill the well?" Frank asked.
"That's it," James confirmed. "We should also see a water tank at some time and some school desks."
"Where'd the windmill come from?" Frank asked.
"No idea," James said."My brother knew of one and said he'd get it for me, where it actually came from, I've no idea. Same is true for the water tank, he told me he'd get one for me, but didn't say where from."
"Just as long as some farmer doesn't come looking for his windmill," Frank joked. "It looks like it's brand new, never even been unpacked from the shipping crates."
"God forbid someone comes looking for their new windmill," James agreed.
"When are you going to take it all up to the Blouberg?" Frank asked.
"As soon as it's all here," James said. "My wife has a heavy goods licence and she's driven the Oshkosh a lot, so I was thinking I'd borrow one of ours for the weekend and run it all up there."
"If you need any help, just yell," Frank said. "Why the school in the Blouberg?"
"We met the teacher there, and it's sad what they have to work with," James replied. "I'd adopt a school here, but I've no idea how many are

represented by all the workers we have. If we adopt one in Soweto, do we piss off someone who comes from Tembisa?"

"Good point," Frank agreed. "Plus, the rural schools tend to get less than the township schools, which is really sad because the township schools get little enough. We're shooting ourselves in the foot; the more we suppress and deny, the more young kids drift to the extremists and in time, the more problems we have."

"Better not let the government hear you say that," James commented.

"I'm careful," Frank said. "I used to think that the Afs weren't that bright, but after we ran our competition, I've had to rethink a lot of things; they're just like the whites, some bright, some not so bright."

"Anyway, how are sales of service?" James asked.

"Up a lot from last year, even if you allow for the CMI business that came here," Frank said. "We're getting known now as someone who can actually offer service."

"Do you need anything?" James asked.

"We should take a look at bigger *bakkies* that we can put more on," Frank suggested. "Improve and upgrade the hoist on the back, too."

"Any ideas?" James asked.

"I'm digging around," Frank said.

"I should go and see Leon and ask about our insurance coverage for our low loaders," James said.

"James, what's up?" Leon asked as James stopped by his office.

"I was wondering what our insurance coverage is for our low loaders?" James asked.

"*Ag* man, it's probably too broad," Leon said.

"If I were to borrow one for a weekend, would it be covered?" James asked.

"Who'd drive it?" Leon asked.

"My wife had a heavy goods licence," James said. "When her folks ran their transport business in Zambia, they had Oshkosh low loaders, and she drove them a lot."

"But, she's not an employee," Leon said. "I wonder how we can work around that. What are you going to do with it?"

"Deliver a windmill and a tank to a school in the Blouberg," James replied.

"Your wife works for CMI, doesn't she? Do they have a policy that covers their employees?" Leon asked.

"I'll find out," James said.

"We could always take out a rider for the period you'd be using it," Leon thought. "Would you pay for that?"

"If it's less than paying one of our own drivers for the weekend, yes," James said.

"I'll check," Leon promised. "You'd pay for the diesel?"

"Of course," James said.

"How far is it?" Leon asked.

"About 270 miles each way," James replied. "We could do it in a day, there and back, if we left here early in the morning."

"Do you need any help?" Leon asked.

"Not now," James said. "We might need some in the future if my father can get a project together to build an ablution block for the school."

"Let me know what you'd need," Leon said. They were interrupted by Charlize, who came in to tell them that a lorry load of school desks had arrived. James excused himself from Leon and went out to help with the unloading. Now all he needed was the water tank, and his load would be complete.

The tank arrived two days later, and it joined the other items in the corner of their yard. On Friday, James asked for one of the low loaders to be parked where he could easily load everything onto it, and Frank came out and helped him, using a crane to pick up the windmill crates and the tank and load them onto the trailer. With those two items on the trailer, they then added the desks, packing them on the gooseneck of the trailer. Frank supervised the tying down of the load and announced himself satisfied. That done, James took the keys to the Oshkosh and went home.

"We're ready to go tomorrow," he told Katrina. "I've got everything on the trailer, and we've got full tanks of diesel. I thought we'd go to Isando early in the morning and leave as soon as we can. We can leave my car there."

"I hope I haven't forgotten how to drive the Oshkosh," she said.

"I'm sure you haven't," he said.

"How far is it?" she asked.

"About 270 miles," he said.

"So, five hours there," she thought.

"I would think so," he said. "The load's not heavy, just bulky. I have a map and have the route picked out. I'll navigate while you drive."

"Where can we stop for coffee?" she asked.

"I was thinking of Potgietersrus," he said. "We'll turn off the N1 there and go up towards Woudkop."

"I wonder if Will and Bridget fancy a run out into the Blouberg?" she said.

"I'll call them and see," James suggested. Bridget told him that they would be delighted to make the trip. She said that they would pick them up at their house at six the next morning, so that they would not have to leave their car in the yard for the day.

Will and Bridget were at their gate a few minutes before six, and it only took a few more minutes to motor over to Isando. James talked to the security guards who were there and had them open up the gates, then he gave the Oshkosh keys to Katrina. She looked over the load, checked all the tie-down straps, then climbed up into the cab and started up. With the hiss of released air brakes, she drove out the gate and waited long enough for Will to follow, and for James to make sure that the security guards locked up behind them, then they were off.

"This is fun," she told James. "I told Will to go on ahead and to meet us at the first Caltex petrol station in Potgietersrus."

"I hope you asked them to get us some coffee?" James said.

"Bridget said they would," Katrina assured him. When they did pull into Potgietersrus, they saw Will, Bridget and Francesca standing by the side of the road, waiting for them. Katrina pulled over and parked, and climbed down from the cab. She asked Bridget if the Caltex station had a loo, and was assured that they did, a clean one at that. While she was gone, James asked Bridget if she'd like to ride with Katrina.

"That would be lovely," Bridget said. "And Francesca, too?"

"There's plenty of room in the cab," James told her.

"What are you two plotting?" Katrina asked when she rejoined them.

"I asked Bridget if she and Francesca would like to ride with you," James said. "I can go with Will and lead, just follow us."

"Fine," Katrina said. "Just don't go too fast. Francesca, would you like to come with me in the big lorry?"

"Yes, please, Auntie Katrina," Francesca said. Katrina picked her up and hoisted her into the cab, while Bridget climbed up on the passenger side with Francesca's car seat, which she placed in the middle between her and Katrina. James went with Will, and they took off for the next leg of the journey. This leg had twists and turns and quite a few left here, right here, instructions at various crossroads.

"Where did the windmill come from?" James asked Will.

"I heard of a company that had ordered six, but only ever installed five. That one has been sitting in crates for four years. I bought it from them for the price of moving it from their site. Apparently, it had sat there long enough that it was getting embarrassing, so they just wanted it out of the way."

"And the tank?" James asked.

"That was one of ours that we had that has been officially scrapped. We replaced it with a bigger one," Will explained. "We were going to send it to a scrap yard, so I just had them drop it off with you instead."

"What was in the tank?" James asked.

"Just water," Will replied. "We never stored any chemicals in it, so there's no need to wash it out or worry about contamination."

They pulled into De Villiersdale and attracted a crowd of children. Very soon after that, Charles arrived, notified of the arrival of the low loader by several children. The crowd of onlookers grew as people gathered to see what had arrived.

"Mr Buys," James said. "We have your school desks for you and a windmill, and a tank. Could we get some help to unload?"

"Of course," Charles said. He detailed off a dozen men who were in the crowd, and as soon as Katrina had loosened all the tie downs, the desks were unloaded and carried off to the school classrooms. While this was going on, Katrina handed her camera to Bridget and asked her if she would take pictures of all the activities. With all the desks gone, James wondered how they were going to unload the crates and the tank, but Katrina had already worked that out. She unhitched the trailer and let it collapse, then she positioned the tractor in front of it and used one of the winches on the back to pull the crates and the tank off the trailer.

"Where do you want the well to be drilled?" James asked Charles.

"Here, I think," Charles said, marking a spot with his heel.

"Let's mark that, so that when the drill arrives, they'll know where to start," James suggested. "Do you have tools to assemble the windmill?"

"I doubt it," Charles said.

"Here is a basic tool kit that has spanners, screwdrivers, hammers and such," James said. "It should be enough to assemble the windmill, I think I saw the instructions in that box. How will you raise the tank above the ground?"

"We'll build a foundation for it and raise it as we go," Charles said. "Three of the men in the village have done this before. The Mission has a plumber that they will send out to connect the well to the tank and to give us a tap from the tank that we can draw water from."

"Oh, I almost forgot," James said. "I see that that crate is marked as the pump and rods, with 250 feet of rod. If the well doesn't strike water by then, let me know and I'll see if I can find more rods and riser pipe for you."

"I'm sure the Mission can manage that," Charles said. "This is so good, how can we thank you?"

"By giving the children the best education that you can," Katrina said. "How are your stationery supplies?"

"We have enough for this school year," Charles replied. "Will you stay for lunch?"

"I'm sorry, we have to get the truck back to the yard today, so we should set off back," Katrina said.

"Well, again, thank you, go well," Charles said.

"Stay well," she replied.

For the drive back, they switched around again, and Will rode with Katrina as far as Potgietersrus, then they switched again, and James went with Katrina for the final leg. Before they made it back to the yard in Isando, they stopped at a petrol station and filled the tanks, in all 110 gallons. The fuel economy of the Oshkosh was not that good.

"I'm hungry," Katrina said as they left the J&B Africa yard. "Can we stop somewhere for a meal?"

"We can," Will said. "Is it hard work driving that behemoth?"

"Not really, but I haven't driven one so far in quite a while, so I think I'll sleep tonight and probably have stiff legs in the morning," Katrina replied.

"Greek or Italian?" Will asked.

"Italian, I think," Katrina said.

"Okay, I know just the place," Will said. "So, Francesca, how do you like Auntie Katrina's big lorry?"

"It was fun," Francesca said. "I liked being up where you could look down on all the other cars. It's noisy and a bit smelly, but I liked it. Can we stay at your house tonight, Auntie Katrina?"

"Of course, you can," Katrina replied. "Did you bring your pyjamas with you?"

"Yes, Mommy put them in my bag," Francesca confirmed.

"Well, we'll have dinner, then we can go home and you can play in the courtyard until bedtime," Katrina suggested.

"Any problems this weekend?" Leon asked James on Monday morning.

"None, but those things drink diesel," James said.

"I suppose that's to be expected," Leon said. "They've got huge engines."

"Nice big Caterpillars," James said. "So, anything of note today?"

"Not yet," Leon said. They were interrupted by Hans, who came in quite excited.

"We've been asked for a quote on eight backhoes," he said. "Kruger Construction out of Cape Town just landed a big contract to put in a whole new sewer system, and they want some machines."

"So, how many do we have on hand, and when could we get more?" James asked.

"We've got six here and six more on the water; they should be in Cape Town by the end of the week," Hans replied.

"What if we offer them all six that are on the water, plus two from here," James suggested. "In lieu of delivery charges, we just deliver them straight to Kruger."

"Do we give them a volume discount?" Hans asked.

"Might be a good idea," Leon said. "How much?"

"What about 2.5%, plus we'll put a serviceman at their disposal for six months?" James suggested.

"Why don't I start at 1% and three months and then work up from there?" Hans said.

"Sounds good," James said. "What would that do for us, Leon?"

"Well, each machine is $52,425 CIF Cape Town for us, and we mark it up 15%," Leon replied. "So a 2.5% discount would net us $6,356 each, or $50,848 in total, say R43,730, then we'd have to throw in the serviceman and his helper, so that would cost us R27,000 for six months, including all overheads, so we'd make on the deal but not as much as we'd like."

"Okay, Hans, start at 1% and three months and see what they do," James suggested. "How long is the sewer contract supposed to last?"

"The town planners apparently have said that they want it all done in a year," Hans replied.

"Will the *ouks* next door quote?" James asked.

"*Ja*," Hans said. "Their base price is higher than ours, so we may have an advantage; it depends how far they're prepared to come down."

"Their overheads have to be higher than ours, but we shouldn't delude ourselves into thinking they won't be competitive," James commented.

"We won't," Hans said. "I'm going to fly down to Cape Town tomorrow and talk to them."

"Good idea, don't just send them a letter, take one by all means, but hand deliver it," James said.

"Any other good news?" Leon asked Hans.

"Maybe," Hans said. "The CAMCO *ouks* want four cranes, two rough terrain and two heavy-duty crawler cranes, they don't want them for six months, so if we get the order, we'll have plenty of time to get them from the States, oh, and Richsand in Natal is looking for a couple of small draglines, both 3-yard machines with about 70-foot booms. I'll get a price out to them before I go to Cape Town tomorrow."

"When will we know about any of these prospects?" James asked.

"I got the quote off to CAMCO on Friday, and I'm seeing them on Friday of this week. I'll have a better idea then of their timing, I'll see if I can get a date out of Kruger this week as well, and Richsand wants to move quickly, so this week as well, possibly," Hans replied.

"Well, good luck in Cape Town, do I need to come with you and wave the flag?" James asked.

"No, I don't think so," Hans said. "If I think so after I've seen them, then I'll call."

"Okay, Hans," James said.

"We could be busy," Leon said after Hans had gone.

"We could," James agreed. "You know, I'll have been here a year already next month, it's hard sometimes to grasp how fast time goes by."

"Do you think they'll still pull you back in another year?" Leon asked.

"I do," James said. "Will you be able to come with me when I make my next trip to Oak Creek in May?"

"I'm planning on it," Leon said. "I'll leave Estelle in charge."

"Good idea, different subject, Katrina's going to get her degree from Wits later this month, what does Wits expect in the way of dress code for relatives and friends?"

"Suits and ties for men, some kind of dressy dress for women," Leon replied.

"Dressy dress?" James asked.

"No ultra mini skirts, nothing that smacks of sixties hippy generation," Leon explained. "Wits and South Africa in general are still conservative when it comes to the establishment, and Wits is part of that."

"So, I'd better wear a suit and tie, and I presume for Katrina, they'll tell her what they expect?" James asked.

"They'll have a whole protocol," Leon said.

"Thanks for the help, Leon," James said.

James returned to his office and started to write his latest report to Oak Creek. Mining activity had slowed a little, but construction machine enquiries were up. Parts sales were still good, service was more than paying for itself, so all in all, things were going quite well. Bombings had even slowed down; they had had one in Port Elizabeth outside the Bantu Affairs office, with one death. James was sure that there would be more, but took solace in the fact that most were aimed at government offices and police stations. He just hoped that he would have no occasion to visit any government offices. He finished his draft, then went for a wander around. The service bays were all occupied, and it looked like his technicians were busily sorting things out. In the parts warehouse, he found Danie Botha and Kagiso Dube going over a list of parts and checking it against a collection of parts sitting on a pallet waiting to be boxed up. Outside, he found Christian Zulu, their recycle man, busy chipping old pallets and crates.

"Christian," James said. "How are things?"

"Very good, Mr Martin," Christian replied. "I have all the paper done and will have this finished soon. Tell me, Sir, what do we do with our old tyres?"

"They go to a dump," James replied.

"Could I have them?" Christian asked.

"We don't get too many here," James said. "Most of our machines are on tracks, but if we do get some, then they're off our loader backhoes, so like a tractor tyre, how would you move them?"

"I have a cousin with a *bakkie*," Christian said. "We can take two tractor tyres in it."

"You can have them," James said. "But make sure that they are scrap tyres and cannot be retreaded."

"I will, Sir," Christian said.

"Very good, Christian," James said. "There are many bags of chips here. When does the company come to collect them?"

"They should be here this afternoon," Christian said.

"I wonder where we can get old bags from so we don't have to buy new," James said.

"I think we could get them from the chicken farm that is near Benoni," Christian said. "They throw away many bags of this size. My cousin, who has the *bakkie*, works there, and he told me that they throw away ten bags a day."

"How many do we use in a week?" James asked.

"About fifty," Christian said.

"So, would the chicken farm let your cousin have the bags?" James asked.

"I will ask," Christian said. "Is it all right if I have nothing else to do to wash the *bakkies* that we have?"

"Check with Frank Cronje," James said, but privately he thought that Frank would be happy to have their service trucks and low loaders washed. "Stay well, Christian."

"Go well, Sir," Christian replied.

"I have a recycling chap at work who keeps coming up with ideas," James told Katrina that evening. "Now he wants the old tractor tyres that we take off our loader backhoes. What would he do with them?"

"They use them to make raised beds for gardens," she said. "Then the side walls that they cut off get made into sandals, and I've seen some half-buried in children's playgrounds."

"So, only limited by imagination?" he said.

"Right," she agreed. "For gardens, they won't rot like wood, or get eaten by termites, so they're a great way to make a small kitchen garden for yourself."

"When I look back at our days in Kitwe and Mkushi, everything was thrown away, no re-use at all," he thought.

"I suppose we were lucky not to have to worry about where the next Kwacha was coming from, but if you lived in the compounds, then anything you could do to stretch the Kwacha, you did, so if you ever drove around the compounds you saw all kinds of things, houses made of tyres, houses made of old corrugated iron, you would have been amazed by the ingenuity," she said.

"I'm learning," he said. "So, are we on for Pilgrim's Rest this weekend?"

"Yes," she said. "If we leave Friday after work, we can get as far as Belfast comfortably."
"Is there somewhere to stay there?" he asked.
"I'll talk to Bridget, I'm sure we can find somewhere," she said. "If not, we can stop in Middelburg."

Hans called from Cape Town with good news; not only had he secured the contract for the eight backhoes, he had done so with only a 2% discount and three months of a service technician thrown in. That made James and Leon happy. James immediately wired Didcot with the news and a fresh order for another six backhoes to replace those on the water that had been sold. The CAMCO order was split; they got the two crawler cranes, but the rough terrain cranes went to a competitor. James sent off an order to Didcot for the two cranes and was told that they would be in Cape Town on May 1st, which was well within the delivery time that CAMCO had asked for. Hans came back to Isando, then scurried off to Richards Bay to talk to the Richsand people. Two more machines would be a very nice addition to their order book. Frank had done some digging, and the best deal he could find was a job lot of Isuzu Elf trucks. They were cheaper than the equivalent British or American vehicles and were available. There was also the option of Mercedes; they had introduced the T1 pickup the year before and were keen to establish a market presence, so they were flexible on the pricing. What James wanted to know was how many hours of service time they would have to sell to cover the increased costs of the larger trucks, plus the hoists and compressors they were going to add. Frank said that he would have an analysis shortly, and James suspected that he would be closeted with Leon for a while.

By Friday afternoon, James was ready for a break. It had been a busy week, and the following week promised to be as busy. He went home a little early and had time to change his clothes before he and Katrina set off to explore the Eastern Transvaal, more particularly, Pilgrim's Rest. They drove out of Edenvale and took the road to Bronkhorstspruit, where they picked up the N4 that took them east, past Witbank and Middelburg to Belfast. Bridget had found them a small hotel in Belfast that catered to people making the trek to the Kruger National Park for the weekend. It only had ten rooms and was by no means full; in fact, as far as Katrina could tell, there were only four other guests.

"So, busy week?" Katrina asked James over dinner.

"Very," he said. "What about you?"

"I've got a new project," she said. "Looking at a foundry that makes mundane things like manhole covers."

"Maybe mundane, but there's a lot of them," he thought.

"There are," she said. "Just walk down a street in town one day and count them."

"Does the company do drain covers as well as manhole covers?" he asked.

"Yes, drains, manholes, any type of cast iron cover," she said.

"So, what do we know about Pilgrim's Rest?" he asked.

"I finally tracked down a story about the name," she said. "The story I heard was that there was this prospector by the name of William Trafford in the days of the first gold rush of 1873, around Lydenburg, who had had enough one day and he was supposed to have sat down and said, *This pilgrim has come to rest,* or *Now at last the pilgrim is at rest,* depending on which version you buy."

"Was he the first prospector?" James asked.

"No, apparently it was an Alec 'Wheelbarrow' Patterson, I gather, so named because he pushed all his belongings around in a wheelbarrow," she replied.

"Is gold still mined there?" James asked.

"Hofmeyr told me that the Beta Mine closed in 1972; it was the last operational mine," she replied. "I found a paper for you from the South African IMM, and it deals with the history of the mines. It's got maps, diagrams, the works."

"Leon told me that it's a pretty place," James said.

"Well, we'll find out tomorrow," she said. "For now, bath and bed are calling; it's been a long day."

The drive to Pilgrim's Rest took them into hills, hills covered with trees, hills that could have been in Scotland, hills that caused the road to snake around to avoid steep gradients. The town, when they got there, was divided into downtown and uptown, divided by altitude, where uptown was literally above downtown. Their hotel for the night was the Royal Hotel, an establishment that had been there in one form or another for years. They were able to check in early, so dropped their bags then went exploring. Unlike Johannesburg, Pilgrim's Rest could almost be described as quaint. Buildings scattered the hillsides, most with red roofs; there were no skyscrapers, no motorways and for all, it was an old gold mining area, no yellow dumps similar to those that dotted the landscape around Johannesburg. As there was plenty of the day left, they decided to take a drive through the Blyde River Canyon, starting at a place with a very exotic-sounding name, God's Window.

"Wow," James said when they got out of their car and walked to the edge.

"That's the lowveld down there," Katrina said, as they looked over the escarpment that dropped some 2,500 feet below them. "Over there is Kruger and the M'Bali camp."

"It's very different to Beitbridge and the Limpopo," he said. "No wonder it's called God's Window, you can see for miles and what a view?"

"It's a bit like the Muchinga escarpment," she thought. "Looking down towards Luangwa."

"It really is spectacular," he said. "I wonder what the rest of the Blyde River Canyon actually looks like?"

"Let's find out," she said. They drove further north, along the canyon, and the views were just as spectacular as the ones from God's Window.

"It's amazing what water can do," James commented as they looked down at the river below and the huge canyon that had been carved out over time. "I think we should get back to the *bakkie*, it's going to rain."

"It's really coming down," she said, as they sat and looked through the windscreen at the rain bouncing off the bonnet."Reminds me of rainstorms in Zambia."

"I remember my first one," he said. "I had to pull over and stop because I couldn't see beyond the end of the bonnet."

"I wonder if this will be a short, quick storm, or if it's set in for the day?" she said.

"Let's wait for half an hour, and if it's still raining, make our way back to the hotel," he suggested.

The rain continued and continued with no sign of letting up, so they went back to the hotel and had lunch sitting by a window and watching the rain. Katrina had a guidebook of South Africa and quoted from it, telling James that rain was most in the summer months and that the dry time was mid-winter, June and July. Dessert was being served when the rain stopped and the sun came back out, causing steam to rise from the tarmac.

"What shall we do this afternoon?" James asked Katrina.

"I think take a drive the other way to Sabie, then come back through Lydenburg," she suggested. "According to this book, there's the Bridal Veil Falls just outside Sabie, hard to imagine a 230-foot waterfall, when at De Villiersdale they've got to drill for water."

"I read some of that paper on the gold mines," he said. "It was clustered around Pilgrim's Rest and Sabie, with little mines all over the place, oddly many of them with names from the Greek Alphabet, so I suppose the Beta mine is not as strange as I thought it was."

"Well, *ou man, kom ons ry*," she said. They left and drove towards Graskop, then turned off and headed south to Sabie, through miles and miles of forests, all planted by the look of it as the trees grew in rows and columns, all very regimented.

"I read in the paper on the gold mines that there was a row about the Transvaal Gold Mining Estates planting trees, something they had done to support the mining industry since 1910," James commented. "I wonder who runs these forests now?"

"I'm not sure," she said. "Do you have machines that would run out here in the forests?"

"We have sold some backhoes with long booms and grabs on the ends for handling logs," he replied. "But none lately."

"It looks like there'll be plenty to do for years to come," she said. "I've never seen so many big trees."

"By the look of it, some pine and some eucalyptus," he said. "I suppose trees get used for mining, telephone poles, fence posts, building lumber, and paper and cardboard products. At least with trees, you won't exhaust the resource, not like a gold mine where eventually you run out of gold to dig up."

"It's so different to the Northern Cape and to the western part of the Transvaal, isn't it?" she said. "Here it's wet, wooded and hilly; there it's arid, scrubby with some hills as well."

"I suppose that means that most of the time the wind comes in from the Indian Ocean, the air rises here because of the escarpment, the rain falls, and then the dryer air continues on over to the west," he said.

"Sounds reasonable," she said. "Where now?"

"The falls," he said. "Then back to the hotel through Lydenburg, looking at the map, basically circling Mount Anderson."

"Turn here," Katrina said as they drove into Sabie. The side road took them past buildings, then they took another side road that went past fields, then forest plantations, until they came to a small car park. From there, they would have to walk, but it was not far, just over half a mile through native, natural forest.

"It is impressive," James said as they walked into the clearing at the base of the falls.

"I wonder if the water's cold?" Katrina said.

"Are you going in?" he asked.

"Not hot enough," she said. "If this were a really hot day, I'd think about it, but not today, I think."

"I wonder what all those kids from De Villiersdale would make of this?" he said.

"Probably wouldn't believe it was real, so much water just cascading down," she said. "I thought the Kundalila Falls were tall, but this must be twice as high."

"Vic Falls is taller," James said, looking up and gauging the height.

"Yes, but Vic Falls is huge on a big river; this river looks quite small," she said. "As I recall, it runs through Kruger eventually."

"When we get some holiday, should we take a trip to Kruger?" he asked.

"I think so," she said. "M'Bali was great, but Kruger is huge and I'd like to see as much of it as we can."

"Are we ready to start making our way back to the hotel?" he asked.

"Let's," she agreed. They walked back to the car park, then drove back into Sabie, then found the road to Lydenburg, which took them through the Long Tom Pass, so named from artillery pieces used in an engagement in the Anglo-Boer War of 1899. Driving through the pass, they had amazing views of the rolling hills, down to Lydenburg and beyond. They passed through Lydenburg quickly enough, then struck north to pick up the road back to Pilgrim's Rest. More green and brown hills with scattered farms and only occasional traffic.

The Royal Hotel was welcoming when they arrived back. What was doubly welcome was a drink in the bar before dinner. The hotel was filling up with tourists like them, people on their way to Kruger who had stopped along the way to see an old gold mine, and people headed for hikes in and around the Blyde River Canyon. Conversation picked up, and the bar got quite noisy, noisy enough that they were glad to leave and go and have dinner.

"Say, are you folks from around here?" their neighbour at dinner asked.

"We live in Johannesburg," James replied.

"Is all the country like this?" their neighbour asked.

"No, much of it is arid with very little rain," James replied. "So, quite different."

"And the Kruger Park?"

"It's lowveld bush," Katrina said. "Miles of bushy scrub and taller trees where there is water."

"They got animals there?"

"I'm sure you'll see lots," Katrina said. "Kruger has a huge variety of animals and birds."

"We're visiting from Florida, and we can't get over how hilly it is. I'm Elmer, and this is Doris. We're from Fort Lauderdale."

"Nice to meet you," Katrina said. "I'm Katrina, and this is James. As I said, we live in Johannesburg."

"Excuse me for asking, but what do you do there?" Doris asked.

"I work for a manufacturing company and James runs the South African branch of an American company," Katrina replied.

"Oh, which one?" Elmer asked.

"James & Brown," James replied. "They're from Milwaukee and make mining and construction machines."

"I know J&B," Elmer said. "We've got a contracting business that digs sewer lines and such. Have you been to the States?"

"We lived in Wisconsin for a couple of years before we were moved here," James replied.

"Is business good here?" Elmer asked.

"The coal mining business is growing," James replied. "Construction is starting to pick up after a slump a couple of years ago."

"Have you ever been on safari?" Doris asked.

"When we lived in Zambia, we spent quite a lot of time in the bush," Katrina replied.

"Zambia, which one's that?" Elmer asked.

"Two countries north of here, over the Limpopo and the Zambezi, it used to be Northern Rhodesia," Katrina replied.

"What were you doing there?" Doris asked.

"My family had a transport business for heavy machinery, and James worked for one of the copper mines," Katrina replied.

"So, you know all about Africa?" Elmer asked.

"I wouldn't say that," Katrina said. "We know Zambia quite well, and we're exploring South Africa. I went to school in Rhodesia, but the rest of Africa, that is vast, we've not been to."

"I know that you can just about fit the 48 states into the Sahara, so I guess Africa is pretty big," Elmer said.

"How long are you here for?" Katrina asked.

"We've got a week in Kruger, then we go to Cape Town and do a wine tour," Doris said. "That'll be for about another week, then we're going to see the Victoria Falls, before we go home."

"That's quite a trip," Katrina said.

"We flew over on South African, they did a bang-up job, but what's with the two languages?" Elmer asked.

"South Africa has two official languages, English and Afrikaans, which is why on the plane you see SAA and SAL, South African Airways and

Suid-Afrikaanse Lugdiens," Katrina replied. "Plus, there's Zulu, Xhosa, Tswana, Venda, Ndebele, Tsonga and some more minor ones. Most people here speak at least two."

"Do you speak this Afrikaans?" Doris asked.

"I do," Katrina confirmed.

"I thought so, I heard you earlier talking to the waitress," Doris said.

"Does anyone here speak Spanish?" Elmer asked.

"There are probably those that you would expect, but you're more likely to find Portuguese speakers," Katrina said. "The other side of Kruger is Mozambique, which was a Portuguese colony."

"Have you ever been there?" Doris asked.

"When I was younger, we would sometimes take our holidays in Beira," Katrina replied.

"We don't see many blacks here," Doris whispered, looking around to see if anyone was in earshot.

"The government policies control and influence all kinds of things," Katrina replied. "It is unlikely that you'd see black guests here."

"Is that a good thing or a bad thing?" Doris asked.

"It depends on who you ask," Katrina replied. "There are those who don't want any disruption to the status quo, and there are others who see the current form of government as untenable. Change will come, the question is when?"

"Do you have black employees, James?" Elmer asked.

"We do," James replied. "We currently have twenty-one on the books, it's complicated by government rules that reserve certain jobs for whites only. Ford, GM and Chrysler have upset things a bit because they grew so fast that there were no whites for some jobs, so they hired blacks."

"Rather you than me," Elmer said. "I've got issues enough employing Cubans and Puerto Ricans."

"If you'll excuse us, we need to make an early start in the morning," Katrina said.

"Sure, nice to talk to you," Doris said.

"Enjoy your trip," Katrina said.

"I had no desire to get into a long political discussion about Apartheid," Katrina said when they were back in their room.

"What shall we do tomorrow?" James asked.

"I think drive home, but go on the side roads, so we see more of this part of the Transvaal," she suggested. "You know, one of the nice things about this hotel is that we've got a huge bath, plenty big enough for two."

"So, should I go and run a bath?" he asked.

"Yes," she said. "What time should we leave tomorrow?"

"When do they start breakfast?" he asked.

"Seven," she said.

"So, let's have an early breakfast and then start homeward," he said. "Okay, bath's ready."

"I remember the first bath we had together," she said, as she lolled in the bath, legs draped over James's.

"I remember," he said. "We'd been out to a pool in the bush and were enjoying ourselves, but left because Greg and Shirley Young turned up. We went back to your folks' house."

"Oh, I remember, the *regte verkrampt rooinek*," she said. "Didn't he get clobbered on the head?"

"He did," James confirmed. "He was in hospital for a while, his wife did a runner, I'm not sure where Greg ended up."

"Well, he and his *vrou* interrupted us in the bush, but no one will hear," she said. "The only thing is that a bath is not as big as a pool, so we can't do too much, move this way a bit, so that I can sit in your lap."

They made love, then again in bed later on, then just for good measure early the next morning before breakfast.

"That was a nice way to start the day," she said as they tucked into bacon, eggs, boerwors, toast and coffee.

"It was," he agreed. "We've got this afternoon free as well if we drive straight home."

"Curb your randiness," she said. "We're going to explore the Transvaal, and we can get back together tonight."

Trains

The University of the Witwatersrand, Wits, held its graduation ceremony in the Great Hall, an impressive-looking building with columns and a very classical look about it. Inside it was arranged like a theatre with tiers of seats ascending to the rear, giving everyone a good view of the stage and the proceedings. Katrina invited James, Will and Bridget to the proceedings. Francesca was taken to a sitter, a lady she really liked, so she was happy to be left. There was a fair amount of pomp and circumstance about the ceremony, which was to be expected. Doctorates were awarded first, then Master's, then Bachelors. Wits had been struggling because it had protested against the government's Act of 1959 that imposed apartheid rules. The university had seen its share of protests, arrests, deportations and anything else the government could think of to bring it to heel. But on the day of Katrina's ceremony, there were no protests or arrests, just happy graduates and even happier parents and friends.

"So, Katrina, congratulations," Bridget said as they gathered afterwards for photographs.

"Thanks, Bridg," Katrina said. "It wasn't as hard as I thought it could be, but I had help, and what I'm doing at CMI helped."

"You never went to your graduation, did you, James?" Will said.

"No, I'd left the country by then. Why they held the ceremony in October escaped me; I'd have thought it would have been in July at the latest," James said. "I got my certificate in the mail, then left for Zambia."

"We did go to the ceremony in Milwaukee when James got his MBA," Katrina said. "That was like this one, lots of pomp and circumstance."

"So, what's next for you?" Will asked.

"Nothing planned," Katrina said. "I'm just happy to have my BSc. I'm glad it's all done. Can you believe I had to wear skirts to classes? They've got weird dress rules."

"Lucky you didn't go to Oxford," Bridget said. "There they had all kinds of rules, still do, and for graduation, even more rules, and if you don't conform, then no degree."

"No man, genuine?" Katrina asked.
"Genuine," Bridget confirmed. "So, to celebrate, can we buy you lunch?"

A week or so after Katrina's graduation, James received a visit from an official of the Department of Education.
"Môre meneer?" he said. *"My naam is Piet Cronje. Ek kom van die Departement van Bantoe-onderwys."*
"Good morning, Mr Cronje, what may I do for you?" James replied.
"You have classes that are being given by Bryn Jones of the Technical College. Who are those classes for?" Cronje asked, switching to English.
"They are principally for my service mechanics, but anyone else who wants to learn can go and see if they can understand," James replied.
"I have heard that there are some of the Bantu who attend?" Cronje asked.
"As the classes are held in the company lunch room, I can hardly stop them from listening," James replied.
"You need to be careful that you don't contravene the Bantu Education Act of 1953," Cronje warned.
"But none of my employees is a student; they're all well past the six years of education provided them," James said. "I am merely trying to improve our ability to meet the needs of our customers."
"What about this competition you held?" Cronje asked.
"Would you want your helper to give you the right tool or the wrong one when you asked for it?" James asked.
"Don't get clever with me, Mr Martin, we can always send you packing," Cronje threatened.
"You could," James agreed. "You could always send packing the people from Ford and GM, but I don't think you would want to do that."
"Well, I'm watching you," Cronje said.
"Would you like to attend a class? I believe the next one is diagnosing issues with hydraulic pumps," James asked.
"I don't need to see any of your classes; we've got our eye on Jones as well," Cronje said.
"I understand," James said.

"Do you, do you really understand that if you give the Bantu an education beyond his ability to understand, then all you're doing is creating expectations that he can't meet?" Cronje said.
"I see," James said. "That's an interesting way to look at things. I had not thought of it that way."
"Not many people do, they don't understand that your Bantu worker is happiest when he does not have to think, but just does the manual labour he is best suited to," Cronje elaborated. "Why teach him subjects like mathematics when he's never going to be asked to use it?"
"Well, I will certainly bear that in mind," James said.
"Good, I hope I do not hear any more stories of educating blacks," Cronje said.

After Cronje had gone, James called his staff together and told them what he had been told by Cronje.
"Who blabbed?" Frank asked.
"I've no idea," James said. "And Cronje gave no indication."
"We should let Bryn know," Leon said.
"I imagine he already knows," Danie said.
"So, the squealer, white or black?" Frank asked.
"We may never know, but I would be interested to know if there has been any antipathy to having the black helpers in the classes," James said. "In a way, it's sad, Cronje has a point in a weird way, by law we are not supposed to give mechanics' jobs to our black workers, so do they understand that as much as we'd like to help them, there is a limit to what we can do?"
"I'll talk to some of the helpers," Frank said. "I think they understand that you can only go so far."
"Unfortunately, we're not big like Ford, so they can boss us around without much in the way of political repercussions," Leon said.
"That's true," James agreed. "If they shut us down completely, they lose 60 jobs and the taxes that go with them, shut down Ford and it's thousands."

"I still want to know who went to those bastards," Danie said. "I'll ask around discreetly and I'll let my *ouks* know that we're being looked at by the Bantu Education arseholes."

"Maybe it was Kevin," Hans suggested. "He didn't like the idea of the competition."

"Maybe it was. Where did he go?" James asked.

"Last I heard, he was working for a foundry in Vanderbijlpark," Frank said. "From what I heard, not doing too well there either."

"I should talk to the Escom folks and see what kinds of problems they had with the Bantu Education people," James said. "Thanks, guys, let's carry on with what we're doing, but let's keep our ears and eyes open for anyone who baulks at the idea of better training the black staff."

"You know, it could well be Kevin," Leon said. "Cronje didn't mention Elizabeth Sithole, did he?"

"No," James confirmed. "You're right, Leon, if it had been a more recent complaint, then I would have thought that the idea that we trained Elizabeth would have sent him off into apoplexy, bad enough we're training Bantu workers, but Bantu women, that would have probably given him a heart attack."

"Just as well you took down that photo that was on your wall," Danie said.

"He was probably also anti because I didn't talk to him in Afrikaans," James said.

"You're not required to," Leon said. "The requirement is for them to be fluent, or at least passable in both languages."

"We'll check it out," Danie said.

"While we're on the subject of pissing off the government," Hans said. "We're ready to ship the well drill for that outfit in Alldays. Where are we going to drill the test hole again?"

"A small place called De Villiersdale, in the Blouberg," James replied. "I have a map with the route marked. Here you are."

"I'm ready with the trainer," Franks said. "Just let me know when it leaves the yard. I suppose the well site is marked?"

"It is," James confirmed. "I've no idea how far down the water table is."

"Up in that part of the country, it's not too far down," Danie said. "Anything from 50 to 250 feet."

"So, no 1,000-foot wells?" Frank asked.
"Not that I know of," Danie said.
"Just let me know how many feet and how many hours," Leon said. "We've got a grant that covers the cost, we just have to file a report."

"I had a visit from a government bureaucrat today," James told Katrina later. "He said that he'd heard we were educating the blacks, and that might contravene the Bantu Education Act, even told me to watch my step, or they'd kick us out."
"Stupid system," she said. "All it's going to do is develop a generation of disaffected youth, all looking for some way to get back at the government, so they're going to swell the ranks of the ANC."
"No one ever said that the Nationalists were long-term thinkers," he said. "All they want to do is preserve the status quo, jobs for the whites, the blacks off into the Bantustans."
"Well, we've got what, another year, then Oak Creek promised to move us back?" she asked.
"They did, and I'll hold them to it," he said. "When we go next, I'm taking Leon again so that he can meet the rest of the managers and they see that he's quite capable of running the place."
"So, where shall we go this weekend?" she asked. "It's Easter, so anywhere is going to be busy. But it's a long weekend, Good Friday and Easter Monday."
"Why don't we drive out to Kimberley? It's not a big tourist draw like Kruger or the Blyde River Canyon, so we can probably find a place to stay," he suggested.
"I had been thinking of the Drakensberg, but you're right, I imagine everything there has been booked up for weeks if not months," she said.
"Why don't we try that in April on the weekend of April 8th? The Thursday is Van Riebeck's Day, so if we take Friday off, we can have a long weekend then too," he suggested.
"I'll call Bridget and see if she can get us in there somewhere," Katrina said.
"So, we'll leave early Friday morning and drive to Kimberley?" he asked.
"Let's do that," she agreed. "Take the car, no *bundu* bashing this trip."

"How far is it to Kimberley?" she asked.
"Just about 300 miles," he said. "So, an easy drive for the day. We can come home on Easter Monday."

"When we go to Oak Creek in May, we should set up a brokerage account with someone," she said. "Then, when and if we can exercise on your stock options, we'll have somewhere to put the money."
"Have you been tracking the J&B price?" he asked.
"It's up to $30.50 as of yesterday, so $5 over your option price," she said. "Let's hope it stays there and doesn't drop back down. We have to gamble on $5,000 less tax now, or hope that next year, when your next 1,000 shares vest, that the price is higher than $30.50."
"I suppose the trick is to follow the market in general and see what types of stocks are trading up or down, then see how J&B fits in," he said. "This is all new to me."
"No wonder John and Bobby kept such a close eye on the market prices," she said. "I'll bet that John has a lot of options, and he could stand to make quite a lot of money."
"I understand now what John said once, he said accumulation of wealth wouldn't come from a salary, but from other forms of remuneration," James said.
"Well, I hope they continue with this stock option bit, it could set us up nicely," she said.
"Providing the company does well and the market thinks it's doing well," he cautioned.
"True," she agreed. "But enough of filthy lucre, time for dinner."
"Instead of driving, why don't we take the train down to Kimberley this weekend?" he suggested, as they ate dinner later.
"That's a great idea," she said. "I'll get us a couple of bookings."

The train ride to Kimberley was very pleasant. They got a taxi to the railway station and watched the train arrive from Pretoria. The train departed Johannesburg at 10.30 am on the dot and set out for Potchefstroom and points south. The nice thing about the train was that they could have lunch as they went. Lunch was served before they reached Potchefstroom, and it was a nice leisurely affair, with multiple courses and wine. The journey was slower than it would have been in the car, but it was relaxing, with no traffic issues to worry about, no police speed traps and no need to concentrate on the road ahead; the drivers of the locomotives were doing that for them. After lunch, they repaired to their compartment and sat and watched the world go by. Much of the land was fairly flat; this was not the dramatic mountain climbing that the train did coming out of Cape Town, this was the more mundane veldt with farmlands and occasional towns. In places, they actually ran quite close to the road they would have been on had they driven. Potchefstroom came and went, as did Klerksdorp, as did Bloemhof, then they came to Warrenton and a railway junction. From Warrenton, a line ran north to Vryburg, then Mafeking, all famous names from the Boer War of 1899. Not too far past Warrenton was Kimberley, and they left the train there and found a taxi to their hotel in time for dinner.

The Big Hole called the next morning, and they walked the short distance from their hotel to a lookout point where they could see down inside the hole.

"Hard to imagine that this was once a hive of activity," James said.

"Do they still mine diamonds here?" she asked.

"Not under here, but around here," he replied. "My guess is also that if you were to scrounge carefully through the old waste piles, you'd still find diamonds there."

"It's amazing to think that that hole was dug by people, not machines, but people," she said. "Did I see something in the hotel about a museum?"

"You did," he confirmed. "Shall we go and take a look?"

It was not just a museum; it was a whole village that made up the museum complex. It was fascinating, showing the history of the discoveries, then the mining methods, then the personal stories of well-known men like Rhodes and Barnato, but also of lesser-known fortune hunters who came from far and wide in search of riches, some of whom actually attained riches, but many did not, losing what little they had in the turmoil that was the diamond fields.

"It's interesting that *Oom* Jan had diamonds before all this digging," she said, referring to her ancestor, Jan Englebrecht, who had trekked into what was then Bechuanaland looking for ivory, but who instead lived with the Kalahari San people until murderous circumstances took the band away from him, leaving only his son. On their trek back to the Cape, they had gathered diamonds in Bechuanaland and made their fortune.

"Must run in the family," James joked. "As I recall, your father took his money south with him in the form of emeralds."

"Ja, slim kêrel," she said. "I wondered for a long time how he had managed it, but I suppose the use of the Kazangula Ferry should have tipped me off."

"I saw some art galleries advertised as well," James said. "Shall we take a look at one of them?"

"Yes, I'd like to see this Duggan-Cronin Gallery," she said.

"Let's get lunch first, then we'll do that," he suggested. They found lunch at a small café and then went to find the gallery. It was a solid-looking red brick building, rather ornate in construction, and it housed photographs that Duggan-Cronin had taken from when he first went to Kimberley in 1897.

"Are you folks visiting from overseas?" a museum docent asked as they wandered through the exhibit halls.

"No, just Jo'burg," James replied. "We decided to take a weekend out to Kimberley."

"But, surely, you're not from Jo'burg?" the docent asked.

"No," James admitted. "I'm from the UK and my wife is from South Africa, from the Cape."

"Oh, where in the Cape?" the docent asked.

"Oudtshoorn, then Zambia," Katrina replied. "My folks moved to Zambia when I was less than a year old."

"Oudtshoorn, I'm from there. What is your family name?" the docent asked.

"Englebrecht, Katrina Englebrecht," Katrina replied.

"I'm also an Englebrecht, Anna Englebrecht, my father was Piet, grandfather was Nicolaas, then Koos, then Jan, who went on a trek to Botswana," Anna said.

"So, you must be my second cousin," Katrina said. "My father was Koot, then Daniel, Koos and Jan. I have *Oom* Jan's journal from the trip."

"You do?" Anna asked. "Would it be possible to get a copy of it one day?"

"I'll make a copy of it when we go back to Jo'burg," Katrina promised.

"So, like me, do you keep the San part of our heritage hidden?" Anna asked.

"We really don't have to worry too much about it in the States," Katrina said. "And, here, I'm just someone with a British passport who is here on a visa, so no worries. I think I met your dad in 1974, we were on our way to the States, and we stopped at my folks' place in Calitzdorp, and there was a family gathering."

"Oh, I remember Dad saying something about that," Anna said. "I couldn't go, I was in Pretoria at the time finishing my doctorate on the history of the San. *Oom* Jan's journal would have been really helpful then."

"It would have been," Katrina agreed.

"I wonder how much of my thesis would be challenged by a first-hand account of someone like *Oom* Jan?" Anna said.

"Well, you have your doctorate, and I doubt that they'd take it away from you on the basis of one man's account," Katrina said.

"Are you busy for dinner?" Anna asked.

"No, we just came for the weekend, to see the Big Hole," Katrina said.

"You must let me treat you to dinner," Anna said. "Do you remember much of what *Oom* Jan wrote?"

"Some," Katrina said. "We did make a trip to Botswana to recover a box compass that he had buried; we found it along with spare lead for bullets. The lead we let the Botswana *ouks* take, but the compass we kept."

"Let me just tell George that I'm leaving and we can go," Anna said.

Anna took them to a small restaurant hidden away in an old building that looked as if it could have been from the very early days of Kimberley as a city.

“Now tell me, what did your folks do in Zambia?” Anna asked.

“We had a transportation business,” Katrina replied. “We moved heavy machinery and equipment for the mines.”

“My folks have a farm not too far from Oudtshoorn,” Anna said. “My brother runs it now. I really didn’t have any interest in farming. Where did you go to school?”

“I went to Bulawayo, then I started a degree at the University of Wisconsin, Milwaukee, and just finished it at Wits,” Katrina replied.

“I went to Oudtshoorn, then Cape Town uni, then did my doctorate in Pretoria,” Anna said. “What were you doing in Wisconsin?”

“I work for an American company,” James said. “They sent us out here to run the sub in Jo’burg.”

“What else do you remember from *Oom* Jan’s journal?” Anna asked.

“They spent a lot of time around the Tsodilo Hills in Botswana,” Katrina replied. “But they seemed to have a fairly wide range. He talks about going to Vic Falls, and north into either Angola or Zambia.”

“I know from stories my dad told me that his ivory hunting didn’t go well,” Anna said. “But Dad didn’t have too many details.”

“The journal covers the early part of his trek almost daily,” Katrina said. “Then his entries become more spotty, almost as if he only wrote if he felt there was something important to note. He did make a few notes about encounters with Portuguese slave traders, which was what killed the band, a pitched battle between them. *Oom* Jan finished it off when he went after what was left of the slave trader’s gang.”

“It sounds almost like a film,” Anna said.

“It probably would make a great Hollywood epic,” Katrina said. “It’s got adventure, sex, Africa, what else would it need? The only thing that I think Hollywood would change would be the ending, Motshaba would survive as would Katrina, and the whole family would trek south, not just *Oom* Jan and Koos.”

“I didn’t know there was a Katrina,” Anna said.

"She was the older of the two children," Katrina explained. "She and Motshaba were killed in the battle with the slave traders. Koos had been off with *Oom* Jan, and they came late to the place, when it was pretty much over."

"It must have been a really frightening but interesting time," Anna said.

"What do you do now, apart from the gallery?" Katrina asked.

"I teach history at the university in Cape Town, but I like to come here to spend time at the gallery," Anna replied. "I take the train up from Cape Town, and I can sleep on the train both ways."

"Well, if you ever make it as far north as Jo'burg, do come and see us," Katrina said, extending the invitation.

"Thank you, and, if you come to Cape Town, this is where you can find me," Anna said, giving them her card, with her home address written on the back. "When do you go back to Jo'burg?"

"Monday morning," Katrina replied.

"Ah, yes, that's an early start," Anna said.

"It is," Katrina laughed. "Who knew that there were two 5.50s in a day?"

"Do you know anything about the cousin you have in South West?" Anna asked.

"No, only that she exists," Katrina replied.

"Do you have plans for tomorrow?" Anna asked.

"Nothing definite," Katrina said.

"Let me be your tour guide," Anna suggested. "If you don't mind the walk, I can give you a guided tour of Kimberley."

"That would be nice," Katrina said. "Thank you, we're staying at the Savoy."

"I'll pick you up at nine, will that work?" Anna asked.

"That would be fine," Katrina agreed.

"This is bloody early in the morning," James commented to Katrina as they boarded the train at a quarter to six on Monday morning.

"It is," she agreed. "Let's find our compartment and get some tea, then think about breakfast."

"I like your cousin, Anna," he said.

"She is nice," Katrina agreed. "Terrific tour guide as well, I'm glad we took up her offer."
"Well, we can't say we haven't seen Kimberley now," he laughed. "We've traipsed all over Kimberley."
There was a tap at the door, and a steward was there with coffee, well, coffee served as well as tea, so they accepted the proffered coffee and looked out into the early morning as the sun was starting to show. The train left on time and headed off north towards Bloemhof. It did not seem long before they heard the chimes for breakfast, so wandered down the train to the dining car.
"What do you fancy?" James asked Katrina.
"I think the grapefruit, then liver and onions, I'll skip the kippers," she said. "Then scrambled eggs with mushrooms, boerwors, bacon and toast, and you?"
"The same, I think," he said. "Kippers just don't appeal this morning. We're stopping."
"This must be Bloemhof," she said.
"What's the next stop?" he asked.
"Klerksdorp," she said. "Here's breakfast, eat up, we won't get to eat again until lunchtime."

The train pulled into Johannesburg, right on time at 2.00 pm, and they quickly found a taxi to take them home.
"I think I overate on the train," Katrina said to James as they unpacked their bags.
"So did I," he said. "Maybe only something very light for dinner."
"I enjoyed the trip," she said. "Maybe we should think about a trip to Durban at some time, taking the train, I mean."
"Let's pick another long weekend," he suggested. "I heard on the train today that they're going to be cutting back on the Drakensberg train in June, so we should go before that."
"I suppose the era of fancy express trains is over, the 727s of SAA have killed that market between the big cities the way that the 747 killed the mail boats between Cape Town and Southampton," she said. "We

should take the opportunity while we can to experience as much as we can."

"You know, I saw that they have wagons on the back of the train to take cars. What if we take the train down on a Friday night and drive home on Sunday, then we can see Durban without using up one of our long weekends?" he suggested.

"That's a good idea," she agreed. "I'll make arrangements for the weekend after next."

"So, this weekend, should I talk to Elizabeth Sithole about Soweto?" he asked.

"We should," she said. "We need to understand how bad the divide is between white and black."

Elizabeth Sithole said that she would be happy to show them some of Soweto. Soweto, quite simply southwestern township, one of the sprawling areas where the black population was permitted to live under the Apartheid regime. She suggested taking the train to Orlando, and she would meet them there.

"Are we being too mistrustful?" James asked Katrina as they got ready to visit Soweto.

"Better safe than sorry," she said. "Take the house key and twenty Rand each for the train fare and perhaps lunch. I've never been to one of the South African townships, so I've no idea what things might be like. It wasn't that long ago that there was violence in the streets there, so we should be careful."

"I asked Will if he'd drop us at the station," James said. "I said we'd drive to their house and leave our car there, so is there anything else we need?"

"Just a hat," she suggested. "You don't want to get sunburnt."

"So, shall we go?" James asked.

"Howzit, James, Katrina, so today off for a big adventure to the townships?" Will said when they arrived at his house.

"We should see how most of the people live," James said.

"True, just watch yourselves," Will said.

"We will," Katrina assured him. "And one of James's bookkeepers is going to look after us."
"I'll drop you at the Jo'burg main station," Will said. "And I'll pick you up there at three this afternoon."
"Thanks, Will," Katrina said. "You're sure you don't want to come with us?"
"I've got errands to run," he said.

The train to Orlando was busy, but not crowded as it would be on a weekday with everyone going to work. It was a typical electric commuter train, with seats, but also room to stand. James and Katrina got some odd looks, but just smiled and nodded. Elizabeth was there on the Orlando platform to meet them.
"Mr Martin, no problems?" she asked.
"No, none," James assured her. "Elizabeth, this is my wife, Katrina."
"Nice to meet you, Madame," Elizabeth said. "Come, I have a car."
"Thank you for showing us around," Katrina said. "We had townships in Zambia, but I don't think anything as big as this."
"How was Zambia?" Elizabeth asked.
"It was changing," Katrina said. "After Independence, a lot of the rules began to change, but it takes time. The government was working to fix housing problems, but that takes money, and they could only tax the people and the companies so far. The mines had provided some housing, but there was a drift in from the rural areas, so there were the mine townships and on the fringes of them, shanty towns."
"We have similar issues here," Elizabeth said. "We will see normal brick houses, then shanty towns, with the shanties built of anything people can find."
"Your family has a garage, I understand," James said.
"We do," she confirmed. "My father is one of the better mechanics, and he keeps heaps of junk going, I think sometimes with bad words and prayers. Here is the car, Mrs Martin. Would you prefer the front or the back?"
"James can sit in the back," Katrina said. "He doesn't mind."

The car was an older Morris Minor, but looked in wonderful condition. Elizabeth drove them into the township, going first to the garage that her family had.

"Would you like some tea?" she asked.

"Thank you, that would be nice," Katrina replied. Elizabeth pulled the car into one of the bays that made up the garage, and they saw a hive of activity. There were cars of all shapes, sizes and conditions, some of which looked as if they would never run, and some of which looked as if they had just been driven off the salesroom floor. They got out of the car and followed Elizabeth to a covered porch on the side of the garage.

"This is my father," Elizabeth said. "This is Mr Martin from J&B Africa, and his wife, Katrina, my father, Isaac Sithole, my mother, Rachel and my two brothers, Abel and Moses."

"Welcome to our garage," Isaac said.

"I'm making tea," Elizabeth said. "Who else would like some?" Hands went up, and she and her mother disappeared into the back part of the garage.

"Elizabeth told us that you had been in Zambia," Isaac said.

"Yes," James replied. "I worked for one of the mines, and Katrina's family had a transport business."

"Oh, transporting what?" Isaac asked.

"Mining machinery and other heavy equipment," Katrina replied. "My folks sold the business and retired, and I went to live with James on a more remote mine."

"I see you have all kinds of cars here," James said.

"The people do the best they can," Isaac said. "Not many can afford a car, so we take old, scrapped cars, and try and build ones that will run at least. It took us five years to find all the parts for the Morris Minor, but now it is like new. We like to toolbox that Elizabeth won in your competition, we're very proud of her for that."

"Does the government create problems for you?" Katrina asked.

"They make it difficult to license cars that we rebuild," Isaac replied. "So, in many cases, people just don't bother."

"Of all the people that live around here, how many can afford a car?" James asked.

"Not many," Isaac said. "Perhaps one in three or four hundred, perhaps less, but with so many people, even if it's only one in a thousand, that is still 1,000 cars. But it's not just owning a car, there is the driving licence to get, then there is always the question of insurance, then there is the police, if you're black and driving a car, you must be a criminal, the police are here often looking for stolen cars that they assume we are breaking up."

"I would have thought that they would know that if you were breaking up cars, it would not be done here for all to see," James said.

"Not all the police are that clever," Isaac said.

"I see you have pits under the cars; you cannot get hoists?" James asked.

"We probably could," Isaac replied. "But what we cannot get is reliable power. We have electricity, but it will come and go in the day, so all our tools are hand tools, and we work from pits."

"We had a visit from the Department of Education the other day, warning us about who we might be teaching things," James said. "How did you learn about cars?"

"I started many years ago just taking them apart," Isaac said. "I found an old Hillman Minx that had been abandoned. It did not run, so I pushed it home, then started to take it apart. I took it all apart, the engine and everything, then started to put it back together. It took me quite a few years to find all the parts. I think I must have taken eight others apart to get everything I needed, but in the end, I did, and it ran. I sold it to an Indian doctor, and he still uses it today."

"Are you planning to steal Elizabeth away from us?" James asked.

"No, you're safe," Isaac laughed. "Some months it is her salary that keeps us afloat, not all our customers pay as quickly as I would like."

Elizabeth served tea, and then Isaac said that he would take James and Katrina on a quick trip around Soweto, but this time with James in the front and Katrina in the back. They were shown the lines of houses that made up the developed part of the township, then the slums and shanty towns that had grown up on any vacant land. Isaac was obviously well known, because everywhere he stopped, people said hello to him, and a few even talked about business. James was depressed by what he saw, but also amazed at the sheer ingenuity of people. They made do with whatever they could find. Three times they saw police vehicles patrolling the streets, all given a wide berth by the people. Since the riots of 1976, which did not really end until October of 1977, the police had stepped up patrols and made their presence known. They were stopped once by an aggressive policeman who demanded to see Isaac's identity card and driving licence. He looked at James and Katrina and asked them if they were reporters. Katrina answered in a blizzard of Afrikaans that James could only partly follow. Satisfied that they were not there to write unflattering stories about South Africa, he just waved them on.

"They are here a lot," Isaac said. "There are often problems with them; we hate them, but there isn't a lot we can do about them. But crime has gone down a little since they increased their patrols. Now we focus our efforts on avoiding them and frustrating them."

"Not a job I would want," James said.

"No," Isaac agreed. "I think there is a certain type of person who is a policeman here. How were they in Zambia?"

"I knew a police inspector quite well, and he was very professional," James replied. "But I'm sure that there were some that were not so good."

"You should not come here on your own," Isaac warned them. "It would not be safe for you, feelings are still running high after the ruling on teaching in Afrikaans and not English. We are in time for lunch. I hope you like chicken."

"You survived then?" Will asked when he collected James and Katrina from the railway station.

"I wouldn't want to go there alone," James said. "I'm not surprised that there are problems; Soweto makes our compounds in Zambia look small and welcoming."

"Well, if you look at the history of the townships, the government has made no real effort to provide housing for the thousands of black workers," Will said. "The mines house some, but what about all the manual labour that is employed by the railways, the shops and offices?"

"I suppose we had the same problem in Zambia," James admitted. "The mines provided housing for our employees, but everyone else had to fend for themselves; there were no council estates like in England, and who can afford to buy?"

"It's a problem," Will agreed. "Anyway, are you eating with us tonight?"

"That would be super, thanks," James said.

"How was Soweto?" Bridget asked.

"Interesting, frightening, depressing," Katrina said. "You can see that there will be problems in the long term, maybe not so long either."

"Anyway, what's you're next outing?" Bridget asked.

"We thought we'd take the train to Durban and drive back," Katrina replied. "We can put the car on the back of the Drakensberg Express."

"That sounds like fun," Bridget said. "Maybe we'll come with you."

"Do," Katrina said. "I thought we'd take the train down on Friday night, stay somewhere in Durban on the Saturday night, then drive home on Sunday."

"Do you want me to make arrangements?" Bridget offered.

"Would you?" Katrina replied. "Thanks, Bridg."

"One hundred and eighty-one feet," Frank said to James on Monday morning. "One hundred and eighty-one feet, and we hit good water at De Villiersdale. There was water at ninety feet, but it wasn't very good, so we kept going."

"And the drill worked well, no problems?" James asked.

"No, man, it was fine," Frank assured him. "We got the hole lined and left the villagers busy installing the pump and the rods. You know, they already had the header tank up on a platform, those *ouks* worked hard."

"Is the customer happy?" James asked.

"Happy," Frank assured him. "We got their operators well-trained, and they're set to go now. Charles Buys fed us with so much food we could hardly walk."

"Did you have much of an audience?" James asked.

"Seemed like hundreds of kids," Frank said. "Few adults as well. We slept in the school, and they fed us outside."

"Thank you, Frank," James said. "I really appreciate the time you put in."

"No, man, it was fine," Frank assured him again. "I just need to go and give Leon the numbers."

James went for a wander around to see how things were. Piet had some possible interest in a blast hole drill, and Hans had enquiries about a couple more backhoes, two more crawler cranes and another well drill. The parts department was busy, fulfilling orders left over from the week before, and there were five machines in the service bays, all being worked on. When things went smoothly, James often wondered when something would arise that would disrupt things. In Zambia, there had been new managers imposed on him, and issues with the various freedom fighter groups that were camped near the mine. He hoped that in Isando it did not mean bombings or other episodes that would affect his people; some of the bombings had been aimed at the railways, and most of the black workers came in by train, so that was always a concern. James also revised his view on who had sent him the warning note about the bombing at the Carlton Centre; he now leaned more towards Elizabeth Sithole. There had been a few things during their visit to Soweto over the weekend that made him think that Elizabeth could well be an ANC organiser. She would have access to a typewriter and access to the offices more easily than Kagiso Dube to send him the note, but that did not remove the chance that Kagiso was also an ANC activist.

The week passed quickly enough, and on Friday, James left a little early to get home so that he and Katrina could be at the station in time to have the car loaded onto the train. The train left at ten to six in the evening, so they were asked to be there with their car at five. They dropped the car off with the railways people, then went back and consulted the reservations board to find their compartment. James noted that Will and Bridget had the compartment adjacent to them, and that the carriage was forward of the restaurant car. They had just stowed their luggage when Will, Bridget and Francesca arrived. This was to be a new experience for Francesca, not only the train ride, but also sleeping on the train.

"Bridget, Francesca, howzit?" Katrina said.

"Oh, you're already here, Auntie Katrina," Francesca said. "Which is your house?"

"This one, next to yours," Katrina said, showing Francesca their compartment.

"There's not many people on the train," Bridget commented. "I only counted 35 on the reservations board."

"Why take the train when you can fly there in just over an hour?" Will asked.

"I wonder how long before the express trains like this die out?" James pondered.

"I like the colour of the train," Francesca said. Indeed, it was a pretty lime green colour, quite different from the regular maroon and yellow. The carriages were also emblazoned with 'drakensberg', picked out in black script. "When do we get there?" she asked.

"Tomorrow morning," Bridget replied. "We'll sleep on the train, after we've had dinner."

"Where will we sleep?" Francesca asked, looking at the seats.

"You'll see, after dinner, these seats will become beds," Bridget explained.

"Where will you sleep?" Francesca asked.

"Well, there can be four beds here, two on this side, top and bottom, and two on that side," Bridget explained.

"Did you hear that?" Will asked.

"What was that noise?" Francesca asked.

"That's the signal for us to go," Will said. "See, look, you can see that we're on our way."

Dinner was served at seven and was a sumptuous affair, with a multitude of courses. Bridget picked out things that she knew Francesca would eat and made sure that she did not embarrass them by either dropping anything on the floor, or worse, throwing it, not that that had happened in a while, but one never knew with toddlers.

"It's a shame the trains don't have a nursery service like the mail boats used to," James said. "Then you could have someone watch Francesca and have dinner without having to worry."

"There's probably no real demand for that," Will said. "The train rides are just not long enough, one night only, not twelve like the boats."

"How do you like the train, Francesca?" Katrina asked.

"It's nice," she replied. "There's more room than in the car."

"That's true," Katrina agreed. "It's a pity that it's not daytime, then we would see what's out there."

"Will we ride home on the train too?" Francesca asked.

"No, Uncle James is driving us in his car," Bridget said. "The car is on the train too, on a wagon at the back. Are you ready for bed, Francesca?"

"I'd like to see the beds," she replied.

"Stay with Katrina and James a bit, Will and come when you're ready. I'll just get Francesca bathed and ready for bed."

"She's growing up fast," James said to Will, after Bridget and Francesca had left.

"She is," Will agreed.

"She's lucky to be getting all these experiences," Katrina said. "Trips to the bush, train rides, the trip in the Oshkosh, I wonder how much she will remember when she's older. I don't remember much at all from when I was that age."

"I should go and help Bridget," Will said. "See you two for breakfast?"

"We'll be here," James replied.

"I wonder how soundproof the walls are?" James said to Katrina when they were back in their compartment.

"You think we'll shock Will and Bridget?" she laughed.

"Not really," he said. "But they'll probably have to curtail any thoughts they may have had with Francesca there."

"They'll survive," she said. "Which bed shall we use?"

"This one," he said.

There was a knock at their door at six-thirty the next morning, and a steward was there with tea and coffee. They both took tea and then repaired to the dining car for breakfast. The others were already there, plying Francesca with bacon, eggs, boerwors and toast.

"Sleep well?" James asked.

"We did," Bridget replied.

"How do you like sleeping on the train, Francesca?" Katrina asked.

"It's nice," she replied. "When do we get to Durban?"

"At a quarter to nine," James replied. "Then, we'll have to wait a few minutes while they unload the car, and then we can go and explore Durban."

"Can we see the sea?" Francesca asked.

"Of course," James replied. "We're going to stay at the Edward Hotel, which is right on the beach."

"What is the sea like?" Francesca asked.

"Big," James said. "We're going to see the Indian Ocean, it goes between here and India, which is a long way."

"Is it bigger than Lake Kariba?" Francesca asked.

"Much, much bigger," James replied. "You cannot see the other side."

"Are there fish in the sea?" Francesca asked.

"Lots," James replied. "Fishes, whales, turtles, all kinds of things."

"What's a whale?" Francesca asked.

"James, you're digging yourself in deeper and deeper," Bridget laughed. "I'll show you a picture of a whale, Francesca. But now, we should go back to our compartment and pack our things, we're almost there."

"I thought you were going to have to get into a long discussion about whaling," Katrina said to James as they watched the wagons with the cars on being shunted down past them to the loading and unloading ramp.

"I wondered that," he admitted. "Do they still go for whales here?"

"I read somewhere that they stopped in 1975," she said. "I suppose the markets for whale products were shrinking, and there was a lot of international pressure to stop whaling."

"Is that our car?" Francesca asked as she and her family joined them.

"It is," James replied. They watched as the tarpaulins were removed, the cars unshackled from the wagons and then driven off. They collected theirs, loaded the luggage and set off for the Edward Hotel and the sea.

"Maybe one day we should try the new Blue Train," Katrina suggested.

"Good idea," James agreed. "They told me on the train that this was the old one, the one that we went on; from what they said, we must have been on one of the last trips before they brought in the new carriages."

"So, definitely another train trip to plan," she said.

Anniversary

"How was the trip to Durban?" Leon asked James when he returned to work.

"Short," James replied. "Train down on Friday night, a visit to the beach with my niece, then drive back on Sunday. How was your weekend?"

"Not bad," Leon said. "Went to a cricket match, first time in ages."

"Hey, you *ouks*," Piet said, interrupting them. "Have you heard the news?"

"What?" James asked.

"Kenhardt Copper had a massive slide that took out part of the footwall ramp and a drill with it," Piet explained.

"Were there any injuries?" James asked.

"The drill operator and his helper were killed," Piet replied.

"Was the drill one of ours?" James asked.

"No, but they'll need to replace the one they lost, even if they can dig it out and repair it; it'll take time, and they'll need something, in the interim, at least," Piet said.

"Let's see what the Oak Creek schedule has," James suggested. He looked at the latest schedule that they had, and it looked as if six months was going to be the earliest that they could get a machine from the factory, add to that another month to ship and another couple of weeks to get it to the site and erected.

"That doesn't look very helpful," Leon commented.

"Doesn't, does it?" James agreed. "I wonder if Oak Creek would switch things around a bit if we asked them for an immediate delivery?"

"We can only ask," Leon said.

"Maybe you and I should take a trip out there, Piet, and take a look and see what we could do," James suggested.

"I checked, it's about 560 miles. If we traded off driving, we could be there in a day," Piet said.

"Let's do that," James said. "Why don't we leave tomorrow at five, then we can be there early in the afternoon, maybe even see the pit before it's dark?"

"I'll call the mine and tell them that we'll be there tomorrow," Piet said.
"Okay, as soon as they're in, I'll call Oak Creek and see if we can offer anything to the mine. What size holes were they drilling?" James asked.
"Nine inch," Piet said.
"Okay, make sure petrol tanks are full, and I'll be here at five in the morning," James said. "I should call George Armstrong at CAMCO and see what he knows."

James called George, and George answered the telephone himself.
"James, how are you?" George asked.
"I'm well, George, thanks. I gather you had an accident at Kenhardt," James said.
"We did," George confirmed. "I've been telling the mining *ouks* that they need to look at slope stability, but that costs too much, so now two poor bastards pay the price for that. It wasn't one of your drills that we lost, was it?"
"No," James confirmed. "I'm going out there tomorrow to take a look."
"I'll probably see you there," George said. "We're flying out this afternoon to the company strip. I'm going with Harry Boshoff, he's our consulting mining engineer, he's the one in the hot seat right now."
"Whose decision was it on the slope stability?" James asked.
"You didn't hear this from me, but Harry blocked all talk about making the footwall angle less, and blocked all studies around slope stability," George said. "Kept telling us that the footwall was stable enough. If we'd lowered the angle, then we'd have to take out a lot of overburden, and that would have changed the economics of the mine, and as you know, copper prices haven't been the best for a couple of years. Now, we're going to have to do it, just to rebuild the ramp, at least in the area of the slide."
"How long will that take?" James asked.
"A few months," George said. "Harry says we can do it in a month, stupid bastard forgets that all the shovels and most of the trucks are below the slide, so we can't get them out until we build a new ramp."
"Can you put down another ramp somewhere else?" James asked.

"Physically, yes, practically, what with?" George said. "We'll have to bring some equipment in, no matter what. When could we get a drill and a shovel from you?"
"If I go by the schedule I have, then seven months on site ready to run," James replied. "But I'm going to contact Oak Creek as soon as they're there and see if they can juggle anything. Your coal mine machines are in the schedule now. Do you want to switch them?"
"I'll check. Whatever you can do to speed up delivery of anything would be good," George said. "Harry's running around like a bloody chicken with its head cut off, probably worrying about some widow suing him."
"I would have thought that after Chuquicamata, then people would have been more open to discussions about slope stability," James said.
"You'd think," George agreed. "Sorry, James, have to go, big meeting with the *bwanas* to talk about a recovery plan. I'll see you out there tomorrow."

James called Oak Creek with the news of the accident and was able to assure them that it was not one of their drills, so they would not be named in any lawsuits that might arise from the deaths. That settled, he asked about machine deliveries and if any juggling could be done. The answer was tentative yes, but they would need to confirm as soon as possible the sizes of the machines. As to switching the coal mine machines to the copper mine, all that they would need to do would be to change the dipper on the shovel. Satisfied that he had done all he could for the moment, James went for a wander around the place.
"James, you're not going to believe this, but I found a buyer for a couple of the parts that we thought we'd never sell," Danie said. "Some *ouks* in Angola have a really old machine, and they've been looking around the world for some parts. Now, all I have to work out is how to get them to the mine site."
"My guess is by sea to Lobito, then inland," James suggested. "Let the mine work out how to move them from Lobito, we'll just organise the ocean freight from Cape Town. How are they going to pay us?"

"Letter of credit drawn on a bank in London, so we get pounds, not escudos or the new kwanza," Danie said.

"Where're they going?' James asked. "The diamond mines?"

"That's right," Danie said. "The iron ore mine is shut down because of the civil war; don't look for that to open up again any time soon."

"If the parts are going to the diamond mines, scratch Lobito and send them to Luanda; it'll be much easier to get them inland from there," James suggested.

"We can't fly them in?" Danie asked.

"Where to, I suppose we could fly them to London, then Lisbon and then Luanda," James thought. "Check with the forwarding company that Didcot uses and see if they can do something."

"I'll do that," Danie said.

"Anything else?" James asked.

"Not really, parts are shipping, no problems there, but I do need to jack up Didcot and Oak Creek to get our orders here quicker than they have been doing," Danie complained.

"If you need help, let me know. How is Christian working out?" James asked.

"*Ag* man, he just does whatever we ask, he's building the crates now to ship parts in, so we're reusing some of the pallet wood and crates from Didcot and Oak Creek, so our wood chips are less, we got him an electric saw and a bench, we tell him what size crate we want, and he just knocks it up," Piet replied.

"Good to hear that he's earning his keep," James said. "Now, I should go and see how Frank is going."

"*Howzit*, James?" Frank said when James found him looking over a new Isuzu Elf truck.

"*Howzit*, Frank?" James replied. "These look nice enough."

"*Ja*, I have the hoist fitted to this one and the compressor. I think it will work well," Frank said. "I talked the Isuzu *ouks* into taking our old *bakkies* in trade, so the rest will come next week. I tried the compressor in a few places before I settled on there, and I like the hoist here at the back. Now, we just have to sell enough service to pay for them."

"I'm sure you'll do the best you can," James said. "Where is everyone?"
"Can you believe all out on paid jobs?" Frank replied. "I hope this keeps up for a few months, then we'll have these paid off. I heard that there was an accident at Kenhardt."
"A slope failure that took out part of the ramp and a drill, unfortunately, the drill operator and his helper were killed," James said. "I'm going out there with Piet tomorrow to take a look. They've got to make some decisions now as to how to proceed."
"Can the machine be repaired?" Frank asked.
"No idea," James said. "Piet said they'd have to dig it out first, then see. I suppose they must have already dug out enough to get the two operators out."
"Bad day for those *ouks*," Frank commented.
"Bad," James agreed.

James told Katrina about the accident that evening. She had heard the basics on the news, but had no details, only that two men had died.
"I'm going to drive out there with Piet tomorrow," James told her. "We should be back the day after."
"How is it that you never had anything like this at Mkushi?" she asked.
"Well, first of all, the deposit was very different, and secondly, we kept our slope angles reasonable, mainly because we weren't too deep," he explained.
"Did the two men who died have any families?" she asked.
"I don't know, I'll find out tomorrow," he said.
"Shame," she said. "If they do, I'm sorry for them. What time are you leaving tomorrow?"
"We thought we'd leave at five, that'll put us in Kenhardt about three, we can look over the mine, maybe talk to the mine manager about new machines and start back that evening, or stay in Kenhardt and leave early the next morning to come home," he replied.
"Drive safely," she said.
"I will," he promised. "Did Will or Bridget say anything about the trip to Durban?"

"Only that Francesca liked the train, was impressed with the sea, that the walls in the train compartments are not as soundproof as one would like, but that Francesca was fast asleep, so no questions to answer," she replied.

"Drive safely," Katrina cautioned James again when he left the house just before five the next morning. There was little traffic on the road, so he was at the Isando depot in time to see Piet pull up. James opened the gates and parked his car inside, then closed up and left with Piet.

"I got a little more information," Piet said. "They were tramming the drill down the ramp, and it got caught in the slide, so the drill is buried under a pile of rock, but they did manage to dig out enough to get the two *ouks* out, but they both had been suffocated."

"Was this an electric drill or diesel?" James asked.

"Diesel, so no trail cable crew," Piet replied.

"What about all the others that were in the pit at the time?" James asked.

"They had to walk out, at least as far as the top side of the slide," Piet said. "That must have been hairy, walking across the slide. How did they know it wouldn't go again?"

"Where do you want to stop for lunch?" James asked.

"Kimberley's as good a place as any," Piet said.

"I went to a place there recently and it was good," James said. "Hidden away a little, but worth it. What do you want to do, drive for two hours, then trade off?"

"*Ja*, good idea," Piet agreed.

They arrived at the mine at two-thirty, and James saw George talking to a couple of people.

"James, this is Andrew McKenzie, he's the mine manager here. Andrew, this reprobate used to work for us in Zambia, did a hell of a job at our Mkushi open pit until we closed it down," George said, making the introduction.

"I remember you," McKenzie said. "You're the poor bastard that Becket accused of swanning around in your Land Rover, not one of the macho men who worked underground."

"I remember that," James said. "Sorry to have to meet you again like this. I was fortunate never to have anything like this. This is Piet Kruger, he's my machine sales *ouk.* We were wondering if there's any way we could help in getting new machines for you?"

"We're going to have to start small," Andrew said. "We can get our hands on front-end loaders, fifty-ton trucks and percussion drills easily enough. As we go deeper and have take more out, we'll need bigger stuff. What's the earliest you could have something here?"

"Seven weeks," James replied. "We could have a ten-yard machine on the water by next week, four weeks on the ocean, then a couple of days to bring it up here from Cape Town, then a week to assemble."

"Whose did you steal for that?" George asked.

"A US customer," James replied. "But Oak Creek can shuffle things around and make good on their delivery schedules."

"What about a drill?" Andrew asked.

"Same," James replied.

"That's worth thinking about," Andrew said. "When do you need to know?"

"For those two machines, Monday at the latest," James said. "After that, we'd have to look again at the schedules."

"Okay," Andrew said. "We'll talk about it. Do you want to see the slide?"

"If we may," James said. All four got into a Land Rover that was there and drove to the hanging wall side of the pit, where they could look across and see the slide.

"You can see there where it broke away," Andrew said, pointing. "There's a bedding plane that it sheared along, and a whole lot came down and took the ramp and the drill with it."

"I'm sorry to hear that two of your people died," James said. "Do they have families?"

"Both do," Andrew said. "The personnel folks from Jo'burg are with them now. George, if James can get us machines that quickly, can you get them put together and running in a week?"

"I can," George promised.

"Looking at the slide, it looks as if you'll have to push that part of the footwall quite far back to accommodate a ramp," James said.

"We are," Andrew confirmed. "We've looked at another spot further down that end of the pit, but the issue is the same; we'd have to push back the footwall side of the pit quite a way to get the ramp in."

"I know you're dying to ask, James, so I'll do it for you," George said. "If we look at the end of the pit, we can see the bedding planes and the dip. Wouldn't that have been a clue that this might happen?"

"In hindsight, yes," Andrew said. "I took over a year ago and had the same thought and asked to lessen the slope angle, but head office said no, so here we are."

"Will you be able to recover the drill?" James asked.

"We will," Andrew said. "We're going to have to clear much of the bottom end of the slide, because it impacts the sump. We don't get much rain here, but we get enough, so I'll need the sump before the next rains. George says that he'll sort out the drill and get it running again, we'll see just how much damage there was."

"So, Andrew, what was this about James swanning around in his Land Rover?" George asked.

"You didn't hear about that?" Andrews asked, surprised. "It was a review panel, and James was next up, and Phillip Becket as good as told him that he'd topped out, then Henry Moore waded in and told James we needed real men who worked underground, not pansies that drove around in their Land Rovers. There was a big fight in the room after James had gone."

"As I recall, Beckett was always a bit of a wanker," George said. "Come to think of it, so was Moore."

"Well, I had some of the same ideas, but since I took over here, I've learned that while I may have a Land Rover to drive around in, there are always problems that have to be solved, like that slide over there," Andrew said. "So, James, you have my sympathies and apologies for that meeting back in Kitwe. You don't miss the mining business?"

"Sometimes," James admitted. "But the job I have now is challenging, and it has its issues too."

"I can imagine," Andrew said. "Are you *ouks* driving back tonight, or are you staying over?"

"We hadn't decided," James replied.

"Stay over and join George and me for dinner," Andrew suggested. "Piet, you won't be bored if we talk too much about Zambia?"

"No, man, it'll be fine," Piet replied.

Dinner was interesting. James noted that there was another table, and according to George, it was Harry Boshoff and three others from the CAMCO head office in Johannesburg. They came over and said hello, but left almost immediately.

"Harry's star is waning a bit," George commented. "A big fuck up like this can rather mess up your life, and Harry's on record as stopping any moves to change the slope of the footwall."

"So, James, after we shut down Mkushi, what did you do?" Andrew asked.

"I knew George Murphy, the J&B Africa rep, so he arranged an interview for me in the States," James replied. "They took me on as an application engineer, so I travelled the country looking at mines and projects and recommending machines."

"When did you come out here?" Andrew asked.

"About a year ago," James replied. "They'd put me through an executive MBA program by then, and they had a mentor program with the top brass, mine was, is, Hank Miller, the CEO."

"So they do a better job of management development than CAMCO?" Andrew asked.

"This is new for J&B," James said. "So, whether or not it's better than CAMCO, I can't say."

"So, Piet, how did you get into this?" Andrew asked.

"I was in the Northern Rhodesian Army until Independence, then I came south and worked for a couple of companies selling construction machines until I joined J&B Africa, then when George retired, James gave me the shot at this job," Piet replied.

"So, what, you were based in Ndola?" Andrew asked.

"I was," Piet confirmed. "We seemed to spend most of our time along the Congo border. I was in the Selous Scouts, back then it was an armoured car unit with Ferrets."

"James, I'll call you in a day or two about machines. I'll need to talk to Harry Boshoff and the other *ouks* in Jo'burg about getting the money," Andrew said. "Up to me, I'd give you the order now, but they won't let me spend that much money without about a hundred signatures from all over the place."

"Will we get an order?" Piet asked James as they drove home the next day.

"No idea," James admitted. "There's politics at work there in CAMCO, Boshoff wants to save skin, he's probably trying to push to make the reconstruction of the ramp not a big issue, so my guess is that he'll try and make do with front-end loaders and small trucks."

"So, the Barlows *ouks* may do well?" Piet asked.

"If they've got any inventory that they can ship," James said.

"What would you do?" Piet asked.

"I'd contract out the work until I could return to work. I'd order a new drill now, but skip the shovel," James replied. "I think one of the issues Boshoff will face is signature authority; he probably has up to half a million, over that probably needs board approval, and I'm sure he wants to keep this as far away from the board that he can."

"Is McKenzie at fault?" Piet asked.

"If he's on record as saying that he wanted to knock back the slope, then he's probably covered, but he's the manager in charge, so legally he's the responsible manager," James replied.

"So, wait and see?" Piet asked.

"Wait and see," James confirmed.

"How was Kenhardt?" Katrina asked James when he returned home.

"Sad," James said. "Two men dead, and big delays in getting the mine back into production."

"Will it mean more business for you?" she asked.

"I really don't know," he said. "I think the best we'll do is a drill. Oh, I met a chap there who had been on the review panel back in Kitwe when they told me that I'd topped out and that it was pansies in Land Rovers that worked in the open pit."

"I remember that day," she said. "I remember thinking what a bunch of bastards. So, the *ou* you met today, was he the one?"

"No, he was the one who told the others to have a heart. I'd pulled them out of a jam, now they were saying too bad," James replied. "He admitted to having some of the same thoughts about swanning around in Land Rovers until he took over Kenhardt a year ago; now he sees things differently," James replied. "Kenhardt is a big mine, much bigger than Mkushi, so it's a big job."

"I'm glad when you were running the mine in Mkushi, you never had anything like that," she said.

"So am I," he agreed. "So, our anniversary is coming up soon. What shall we do?"

"Well, when are you due your holidays this year?" she asked.

"Early in April," he replied. "I'll get two weeks off, plus the weekends at each end, so 16 days in all."

"So, why don't we take a week and drive through Kruger, then the next week just wander around Natal?" she suggested.

"Okay," he said. "Shall I set up the reservations in Kruger?" he asked.

"Let's ask Bridget to do that for us," Katrina suggested.

"I'll call her with dates as soon as I've got them," he said. "What will you do, take unpaid holiday?"

"I'll talk to Hofmeyr and do that," she said.

George Armstrong called after three days with news.

"Sorry, James, no orders for you," he said.

"No problem, George, what are they going to do?" James asked.

"We've taken on a contractor and are using his equipment and as much of ours as we can, given the size difference. We're moving a drill from Stilfontein, we're winding down that operation," George explained. "Thanks for the offer to help, but Boshoff thinks he's got it sorted."

"How long before the new ramp is in and the slide cleared?" James asked.

"Two to three months," George replied. "A lot depends on what we find as we dig down. It looks like we may have contributed to the problem; we've been dumping water into the ground, and it looks like it seeped into the bedding planes."

"That probably didn't help," James commiserated. "How's the coal mine project?"

"So far, so good," George replied. "Infrastructure is going in, the railway siding is in, we're just waiting for the main equipment to arrive, but you know that's not imminent."

"Our machines for you should ship the week after next," James said.

"Good, that'll put them here in plenty of time; we might actually start with the shovel and start stripping before the dragline gets here," George thought. "Let me know the vessel name when you ship."

"I'll do that," James promised.

James sent off a telex to Oak Creek, telling them that there would be no orders forthcoming from the Kenhardt accident. He had not been that confident that they might place an order, so he was not too disappointed. He told Piet the news, and Piet told him a little more about what he had heard. Boshoff had been given three months to get back in production, even though he did not actually run the mine. McKenzie was still in charge of the mine, and all Boshoff could do was advise. Piet said that the word on the street was that Boshoff was likely to retire very soon and emigrate to Spain. Apparently, this was the third incident in the past five years that had Boshoff's fingerprints on it, so his star, far from waning, was probably dead. Piet then went on to talk about a new mine in Lesotho and another in Botswana, both for diamonds. The Lesotho property would, in all likelihood, be small equipment, but it was worth a visit. Botswana was going to be a larger operation, and Piet had a visit already arranged. The iron ore mine in Swaziland was being shut down, so no need to go there. There were opportunities in South West Africa, but there were risks with the war of independence from South Africa in progress. There were some small opportunities in Rhodesia, but the biggest problem there was getting paid in hard currency, plus the fact that the bush war was still very active. Zambia was looking up as copper prices were recovery rapidly from their decline a couple of years earlier, so Zambia had hard currency to spend and was in the market for some machines. Piet said that he would make the circuitous trip via Malawi to get there and would visit the major mines to find out what interest there really was.

James and Katrina learned of their trip itinerary when Will, Bridget and Francesca came to see them.

'You start at the Pafuri gate, which is right at the top of the park," Bridget said. "Then work your way down to the south end of the park, then a quick trip through Swaziland to Natal and St. Lucia. Then, Umfolozi and start working your way home, via the Drakensberg."

"It seems so little of the country," Katrina said.

"It's a big country," Bridget said. "You can do the west and the dry places another time."

"Are you going to see lots of wild animals?" Francesca asked.

"If we look for them," Katrina replied. "They're there, whether or not we see them is up to us."

"Will you go to Durban?" Francesca asked.

"I don't think so," Katrina replied. "We'll probably just take little roads and see some of the countryside."

"When can we go, Mommy?" Francesca asked.

"When we take our next holiday, we'll take a trip through Kruger," Will promised. "You can ride in the car and see the animals."

"Can we go for a walk there?" Francesca asked.

"No, they have rules there, and even we aren't allowed to get out of our cars and go for a walk," Will replied.

"One day, though?" Francesca asked.

"When you're this big, we can go to a place where we can walk," Will promised, holding his hand above her head.

"But we walk when we go to *Oom* Hansie's place," Francesca protested.

"That's because it belongs to him and he can make the rules," Will explained.

"Would you like some dinner?" Katrina suggested rescuing Will.
"Yes, please, Auntie Katrina," Francesca said.
"Would you like to help me make it?" Katrina asked.

"So, how are things, Bridget?" James asked as Katrina and Francesca disappeared into the kitchen to create.
"Busy," she said. "I'm learning a lot. When and if Will and I make the decision to go and run a safari camp in Botswana, I'll have all the transfer stuff organised and know who to turn to for what."
"It's looking more promising," Will said. "We have a plan now, and all we're doing now is putting aside enough money to start us up and keep us going for a year or two."
"What do you have to do?" James asked.
"You have to start with the government, naturally," Will said. "You have to give them a plan of what you want to do and where, then when you get approved, you've got to set everything up, find clients and then see how it works."
"Well, when you get set up, let us know and we'll come as paying customers," James promised.
"Thanks," Will said.
"Are you all ready for dinner?" Katrina called.
"We are," Bridget replied.
"Come and get it," Katrina said.
"What do we have?" James asked.
"*Husse met varkore*," Katrina replied.
"Is that what this is called?" Francesca asked.
"Your Auntie Katrina is making a joke," Bridget explained. "This is chicken à la King."

James and Katrina left on their great trek, driving first to Louis Trichardt and staying the night at the Mountain Inn. Then it was north, almost to Messina, but before they got that far, turning east to enter the Kruger National Park at the Pafuri Gate.

"I wonder what the story is behind this Crooks' Corner?" James said to Katrina as they drove in the park and meandered their way east.
"According to the guide, it's the corner of the park that basically meets Mozambique and Rhodesia, so the story was if you sat on the beacon at Crooks' Corner, then whoever came to get you, you could always slip into someone else's territory, so it became a haven for ivory poachers, smugglers, gun runners, any kind of villain on the run," she explained.
"There's a lot of nyala here," James commented.
"Pretty, aren't they?" she said. "Where next?"
"We wander down to the camp at Punda Milia," he said.
"What does the guide say about Punda Milia?" she said, flipping the pages. "Ah, here it is, originally Punda Maria, renamed Punda Milia because zebras were the first animals that the first ranger here saw."
"I haven't seen any zebra yet, have you?" James asked.
"Not one," she said. "Buffalo, nyala, impala and ground hornbills, but no zebra. It's quiet here, not many tourists."
"Probably because it's a fair drive to get here," he thought.

"I liked Punda Milia," Katrina said as they wended their way south the next day. "Look, hartebeest and wildebeest, and over there elephants."
"All kinds here," he said. "I haven't seen many other cars."
"Just those two this morning going up to the Pafuri area," she said. "Look, there's a side road, let's take that."
"Looks like we're following something down the road," he said. "Do you know what it is?"
"Stop a minute and let me look at the tracks," she suggested. He stopped, and she opened her door and leaned out, peering at the tracks in the dusty road. "Eland, not too far ahead of us."
"There he is," James said, pointing ahead of them. The eland turned off the road and disappeared into the bush, so that when they drew up to where he had left the road, they could not see him, but were rewarded instead with two warthogs who darted across the road on a mission to be somewhere. They continued on until they came to the camp at Shingwedzi, where they stopped the night. The next day was the day of their wedding anniversary, so they made it special, spending the night at

the Olifants Camp, probably the camp with the most spectacular views. Views over bushy plains, views over the winding watercourses of the Olifants and Letaba Rivers and off in the distance, faint mountains.

"It's pretty here," Katrina said as they watched the afternoon sun drop in the sky. "I suppose this will always be Africa to me, the bush, the animals, the amazing sunsets, the thunderstorms and the feeling of wide open spaces."

"I can understand that," he said. "But we can't forget all the people that live here, a lot of whom are struggling with their lives."

"I know," she said. "I think back to Zambia and all those that I knew, I wonder what they're all doing now?"

"All the people that were at our wedding in Kitwe, I wonder where they're all now?" he said.

"I wonder?" she echoed. "It's easy to lose track of people, and writing was never one of the things I did well, so few if any letters from me, I suppose it's no wonder that we lose track of people."

"What's the eighth-anniversary gift?" he asked.

"Bronze or pottery," she said.

"Well, I got it right," he said. "Wait, I'll be right back."

"What's this?" she asked.

"Happy anniversary," he said. She unwrapped her package, and it was a bronze rose.

"Where did you get this?" she asked. "It's lovely."

"One of the mechanics at J&B does sculpture in his spare time, and I had him make one for me," James explained.

"I'm sorry, I don't have anything for you," she said.

"There's no need," he assured her. "Just us here together is a gift enough."

"We should have some kind of celebratory dinner," she said. "Wine and all, and then I can show you how much our marriage means to me."

After a magical evening and night, they motored on south, staying at the Satara and Pretoriuskop camps, before leaving the park at Crocodile Bridge. From there, it was a quick hop to Komatipoort and the border with Mozambique. But their route did not lie east into Mozambique, but south to Swaziland, which they traversed that day, stopping the night back in South Africa at Cape Vidal in the Saint Lucia Reserve, after doing some necessary shopping in St. Lucia for groceries.

"This Indian Ocean doesn't look as inviting as it did in Durban," James commented.

"I think that's just the wind that's picked up," she said. "I like this little wooden cabin, just keep an eye on those monkeys so they don't try and sneak in and steal our dinner."

"Did you see the size of those kudu when we came in?" he asked.

"Huge," she said. "I wonder why it is they seem to like to jump out in front of your car. If we had a fishing rod, we could probably catch dinner; there're plenty of *ouks* along the beach with lines out."

"I've never fished in the ocean," he said.

"No, I haven't either," she said. "All mine has been on the rivers of Zambia and Lake Kariba."

"Why don't I get the *braai* going?" he suggested. "There's firewood outside."

"If you'll do that, I'll get the rest," she said.

"So, what tomorrow?" he asked as they sat later eating steaks and watching the antics of the monkeys who were trying to work out how to invade the kitchen and steal food.

"Hluhluwe and Umfolozi," she replied. "We should get to see rhino there, they've been protecting them there since the sixties. We need to take our own food, but we do have a place to stay, and apparently, the staff there will cook for us."

"Amazing when you think about it," he said. "But much of Natal has been caught up in wars and battles, either between the Zulus and many of the other peoples, or between Boers and the Zulu, or the Brits and the Zulu or the Brits and the Boers."

"Did you see Zulu?" she asked.

"I did," he said. "How far away from here is Rorke's Drift?"

"I'd guess about 150 miles," she said. "But the roads are windy and up and down, looking at the map, there's no quick, direct route."

"So, a stop between Hluhluwe and Ladismith?" he suggested.

"We could do that," she agreed.

The Umfolozi delivered on rhinoceros sightings, in fact, so many of them that they became almost commonplace. Then it was on to points west and Rorke's Drift.

"Eerie place, isn't it?" James said as he and Katrina wandered around the buildings that were there.

"I think it's the same with all battlefields," she said. "There's an aura about these places."

"Did your ancestors fight against the Zulu?" he asked.

"Not that I've heard," she said. "*Oom* Jan went north to the Kalahari. I don't know about the others."

"What about in the Boer War?" he asked.

"*Oom* Koos, the son of *Oom* Jan, helped George Wheelwright, a Brit officer on a spying mission," she replied. "He was supposed to infiltrate the Smuts commando in the western part of the Cape and let French and Haig know where it was going."

"Did they succeed?" he asked.

"Infiltrating, yes, but they couldn't communicate in time where Smuts was going, and in the end peace was negotiated and *Oom* Koos went back to being a farmer and *Oom* George went back to England," she replied.

"What was the relationship?" James asked.

"*Oom* Jan had a sister, Anna, who married a British banker, George Wheelwright. George was their son, so cousins," she said.

"Did either of them keep any journals?" he asked.

"I understand that *Oom* George did, but what happened to it, I've no idea," she said.

"So, you're ancestors were spies," he joked.

"Only the one that I know of," she said. "Did any of your family serve in the army?"

"Dad was in the engineers in the War; both my grandfathers were in France in the First World War, before that, I don't know," he said. "As far as I know, no one came to Africa for the Boer War or the Zulu wars."

"It's sad sometimes how little we know about our families," she said.

"It is," he agreed. "Your family has been in Africa, how long?"

"Since 1652," she said. "At least that's the first date we have of the first Englebrecht in South Africa."
"So only a few years after the Mayflower landed in the US," he said.
"That's right," she said.
"So, you're as much an African as a lot of people are Americans," he commented.
"Most people in the States and Europe don't look at it that way," she said. "They forget that some of us have been here three hundred years."
"It's odd, when we talk about Africans, we mean black Africans, but when we talk about Americans, we mean white Americans descended from immigrants, not the native peoples that were there first," he said.
"Enough philosophy for today, shall we drive on to Ladismith?" she suggested.

From Ladismith, it was a fairly short journey to the Royal Natal National Park in the Drakensberg. The place was spectacular, a huge amphitheatre of mountains that could be seen from the park lodge.
"Pretty dramatic," James said as they stood outside their cottage, beer in hand, looking out at the mountains.
"Amazing, isn't it?" Katrina said. "And the other side of that is Lesotho, which must be a hilly place."
"I wonder how Lesotho managed to stay independent and not get run over by the Boers or the British?" he pondered.
"Probably didn't have anything anyone wanted," she said. "Too hilly for easy farming, no gold, no diamonds."
"Maybe not then, but now they have diamonds, good ones too," he said. "I read somewhere that they have a really high proportion of large stones, so worth a bit."
"Have you sold any machines there?" she asked.
"Not yet," he said. "We're looking at it to see if there might be an opportunity for us."
"It's interesting, we've seen a lot more green on this trip than when we went to see my folks," she said.
"My guess is that the prevailing winds come off the Indian Ocean, the mountains here and in the Transvaal, push the air up, it rains, and then

the other side towards the Free State and the Cape is much dryer," he suggested.

"That makes sense," she thought. "Well, at least we've seen a bit of South Africa, what's left?"

"The Garden Route from East London to Cape Town, the Northern Cape, most of the Free State," he said.

"So, plenty to see yet," she said.

One year on

"Leon, are you ready for our trip to Oak Creek?" James asked in early May.

"Ready," Leon said. "At least it shouldn't be too cold."

"Shouldn't be," James confirmed. "But they have had late spring snows in the past, so you never know."

"They should be happy to see us," Leon commented. "We had a good 1977 and so far 1978 looks as if it'll be as good."

"I'm sure all they'll want to really talk about is the potential markets for large mining machines and, to a lesser extent, construction machines," James said.

"Who are you going to leave in charge?" Leon asked.

"Hans," James replied. "He's run a depot before in Scotland, so he's got a feel for the whole operation. If anything comes up that he's not sure of, he can telex or call us in Oak Creek."

"I saw that the SADF just attacked Cassinga," Leon said.

"I suppose it's against *ouks* there looking to move into South West," James said. "No wonder the iron ore mine there is shut down, it's right in the middle of a war zone."

"Have you any idea how much iron ore is there?" Leon asked.

"I've seen all kinds of numbers," James replied. "The number that sticks in my mind is about a billion tons of 30% iron."

"The iron ore that was mined, how was it shipped?" Leon asked.

"There's a railway spur from Cassinga to near Dongo and that line goes to the coast at Moçâmedes, actually to Saco, a port just north of there, but I think if anyone wanted to open up the iron ore mines again, the first thing they'd have to do is fix the port facilities there and the railway line," James replied.

"How do you know all this stuff?" Leon asked.

"I was interested in what country had what natural resources when I was at college," James replied. "So, I spent a fair amount of time in the library going through all kinds of odd things. Economic geology was something that just struck a chord with me. Krupp started up the Cassinga mine in the sixties, and they probably provided all the stacker and reclaimer equipment that's at Saco, now, it's anyone's guess as to who might restart mining, when and if it's peaceful enough to do so."

"So, no business there for us?" Leon said.

"Not for some time," James agreed. "I should go and take a wander around."

James did go for a wander and stopped and talked to Elizabeth Sithole, then Piet to talk about sales prospects for new mining machines, then Danie to see where parts sales for both mining and construction machines stood, Hans to talk about construction machine sales, and finally Frank to check on the service business. There were some issues; there always were. It seemed one could not run a business without issues, but none were so dire as to really affect the company. Most of the issues had to do with late receipts of parts from Oak Creek or Didcot. Late receipts meant that they had delays in fulfilling parts orders or completing a service project, but they had discovered that if they told their customers what was happening, they could usually mollify them and avoid too much ill will. Satisfied that there was nothing that needed his attention, James went back to talk to Piet about his recent trip to Zambia and, more likely, new mining prospects. They went through the various industries and talked about coal, iron, manganese, copper, diamonds, phosphate and then the industrial minerals like sand, gravel and limestone. Gold was a really big export for South Africa, but gold for them meant nothing in terms of potential business; all the big gold mines were deep underground mines, mines going down thousands of feet into the earth, some as deep as 10,000 feet. James had worked underground, but never that deep; all he could think of was how hot it must be down there. He did wonder about alluvial gold deposits, the kind that were found in parts of Alaska, New Zealand and the Klondike. Those deposits had been worked with large floating dredges, but he saw no market for them in South Africa; but perhaps there might be some possibility in Sierra Leone, but that was far, far out of his territory. There were dredges in some of the rivers in the Congo, but they were after diamonds, and James had no idea if they were even still operating. The Congo, Zaire, under Mobutu, was a chancy place to run a business.

At lunchtime, James drove into Johannesburg for his monthly meeting with Jan Hofmeyr.

"James, howzit?" Jan said as he joined James at the Carlton Centre.

"Good, Jan, and you?" James asked.

"Busy, I've been busy consolidating the companies we bought last year, and so far things are going well," Jan said. "Katrina told me a little about your recent trip. Where next?"

"Probably the Garden Route," James said. "But we'll need a few days for that, can't just drop down to East London, motor to Cape Town and come back up here in a couple of days, it would be a week at least."

"You're off to the States in a couple of days, any changes there?" Jan asked.

"Not for another year," James replied. "I'm busy now making sure that I can pass on enough to Leon so that he can take over when we leave a year from now."

"What will they have you doing when you go back?" Jan asked.

"I've no idea," James said. "I'm rather hoping they may give me some clue next week."

"You'd never think about staying here longer term?" Jan asked.

"I don't think so," James said. "I've got no roots here, and apart from her folks, Katrina doesn't either; her real roots are in Zambia. We think we can make a nice life for ourselves in the States."

"Well, if you ever change your mind and don't want to stay with J&B, give me a call," Jan said.

"Thank you," James said. "So, what's next for you?"

"You know we bought the foundry that does manhole covers and such, well, now we're looking at telephone and light poles, wood, concrete, steel," Jan said. "As the government makes some effort to electrify the townships, they're going to need poles, so I'm looking at a forest concern and a yard that fabricates the poles."

"Who makes the insulators?" James asked.

"Good point," Jan said. "I need to look into that too, they're glass or ceramic, so will need firing, that might be a good business."
"How long does it take trees to grow tall enough to make a telephone pole?" James asked.
"Ten to fifteen years," Jan said. "Poles need to be at least 40 feet long, straight and free from all kinds of things, so it's a long-term business, but one which once you get it going will be here for a while."
"When do you use wood versus steel, versus concrete for poles?" James asked.
"Wooden poles are easier to use than steel or concrete," Jan said. "It's easier to fix the cross arms and the climbing arms; they do better in salt air, and overall, they're actually cheaper. They last a long time too, sixty to seventy years, but there's a shorter-term replacement market from high winds and car accidents."
"We saw a lot of forests over by Pilgrim's Rest," James said.
"That part of the country and down on into Natal is where most of the tall trees for poles are grown," Jan said. "You probably went right by the forest that I'm looking at."
"Why are most of the high-voltage poles steel?" James asked.
"As you go up a pole, the voltages go up," Jan explained. "So, the bottom lines are telephone, then lower voltage, then higher voltage. For really high voltage transmission lines, you want to get them high off the ground so people don't come near them, so you need a tall steel pylon."
"Well, I hope it works for you," James said.
"It will, it will," Jan said confidently.

"I gather you're going to be looking at forests," James said to Katrina that evening.
"So I learned today," she said. "We went right by the place when we were over by Pilgrim's Rest. There's a forest there, and there's also the mill to clean the poles up and treat them to stop rotting."
"Does our trip mess up your work?" he asked.
"No, I can have all the basic financial analysis done before we leave," she said. "Then it's up to Hofmeyr."

"It looks like he's setting up an empire of basic commodities that are unlikely to go away," James said. "But a lot of it is driven by local, state and national government spending and policies."

"That's true," she agreed. "But they're the kind of things that they really need, whether they like it or not. Anyway, are we set for our next trip to Oak Creek?"

"We are," James confirmed. "Leon and I have everything they want to see, and I sat down with Piet today and went through all the possible machine enquiries that come up over the rest of the year."

"At least it will be warmer this trip," she said.

"Should be," he agreed. "But take a coat and hat in case they get a late spring snow."

"Anything more from the Bantu Education *ouks*?" she asked.

"Nothing," he replied. "They've probably found someone else to annoy. Oh, there was a letter from Dad, his Rotary club has been in touch with one in Louis Trichardt, and they've come up with a project to build an ablution block at the school at De Villiersdale, they're raising the money now, and should start work next February."

"I'm sure Charles Buys will be happy about that," she said. "I wonder where you buy sinks and things that are small enough?"

"I'm sure the *ouks* from Louis Trichardt will know," he said. "Dad also said that he's going to come out here with a couple of others to help with the building."

"Does that mean we'll have your Mom while he's up there?" she asked.

"No, my guess is that she'll stay with Will and Bridget and spend time with Francesca," he replied.

"Is it unkind of me to say, good?" she asked.

"No, I was thinking the same thing," he laughed.

When James and Katrina flew to New York, it was with a crew that was all new to them, but they did do a good job, and the flight was as pleasant as one of sixteen hours could be. From New York to Milwaukee seemed almost like a commuter hop in comparison. They hired a car and James had Katrina drop him at the office while she went on to the house of Roberta and John Williams.

"James, good to see you," John said. "When's Leon arriving?"

"He should be here tomorrow," James replied.

"So, how's things?" John asked.

"Not bad," James replied. "Not much in the way of new machine sales likely in the next six months, but parts and service are doing well."

"I liked the number from last year," John said.

"Don't expect similar numbers this year," James cautioned. "Last year we had a lot of sales of construction machines that we took back from CMI at a discount, and when we sold for list, we had high margins."

"I know," John said. "But people forget, and memories are short, so remind us once in a while."

"How's business?" James asked.

"The biggest challenge right now is just building machines and working through the backlog," John replied. "It makes selling new machines more difficult as deliveries are out there."

"We found that out with CAMCO," James said.

"Yes, shame about that, but we can't win them all," John said. "Any more from the government down there?"

"No, after they told us to be careful, we haven't heard from them," James replied. "It's possible they may visit again after we have our competition later this year."

"How's that going?" John asked.

"Well," James replied. "We've seen an improvement in the time it takes to diagnose problems in the field."

"So, it's worthwhile?" John asked.

"I think so," James said. "I have an appointment with Hank Miller in a few minutes; I should probably tell Lou where I am."

"Mr Miller will see you now," Lou told James.

"James, come in, coffee?" Hank asked.

"Yes, please," James replied.

"Lou, would you mind?" Hank asked. She was back very shortly with coffee for both of them.

"So, it's been a year," Hank said. "Things are going well?"

"They are," James said. "There's a good team there now, parts and service numbers are good, and we're selling construction machines, and we've bid on all the new mining projects that have come up. As you know, some we won, some we didn't."
"Well, the numbers for last year looked good," Hank said.
"That was driven in large part by the sales of machines that we'd taken back from CMI at a discount," James reminded him.
"Right," Hank said. "So, don't look for such good numbers this year?"
"They'll be good, but not as good as last year," James said. "We've grown parts and service, so we're doing better than I projected, but we won't have the benefit of discounted machines to sell."
"I understand," Hank said. "And cash?"
"We're not looking for cash from here," James assured him. "The issue we may have is repatriating cash from there."
"Yes, we're looking into that," Hank said. "So James, here's what I'd like you to look at next: look at off-highway truck builders, who they are, what share of the market they have, and are any of them possible targets for us to buy. That might be a bit of a challenge from South Africa, but I'm sure you'll find a way. No hurry, but the next time you come over, I'd like to see preliminary findings."
"I'll do that," James replied.
"The next thing is, what do you do when you come back in a year? Oh, by the way, are you still thinking of Leon Schumann as your replacement?" Hank asked.
"I am," James confirmed. "I'm giving him a crash course in mines and mining, and he already has a fairly wide knowledge of the construction industry."
"Good, I'd like to meet him while he's here," Hank said. "Now, back to you, we're thinking of setting up a corporate development team to look at the company and where we might diversify. When we set it up, I'd like you to be part of it."
"Thank you," James said.
"Don't thank me just yet," Hank laughed. "It may all lead to dead ends and nothing of consequence, but we have to try."
"Who else would be on the team?" James asked.

"I haven't finally decided yet," Hank said. "I'm still mulling over who has the kind of diversified background and expertise that I'd like to see, and am trying to put together a team that won't be hide-bound by past experience."

"I understand," James said.

"I think you might at that," Hank said. "So, tomorrow when your man Schumann gets here, bring him down to see me, let's say at eleven-thirty, then we can get come lunch."

"So, James, I gather that Hank wants you to look at trucks now," John said when he and James drove to John's house after work.

"That's what he said," James confirmed. "It seems to me that trucks fall somewhere between our mining and construction machines. On the one hand, there are the Cat, Terex, Euclid, Foden and Aveling Barford trucks, essentially sold through a dealer network, and then there's the Unit Rig, Dart, WABCO and other trucks that are pretty much direct sales. So, where do we want to be?"

"I think that's what Hank wants opinions on," John said.

"Has he engaged any outside consultants?" James asked.

"He has, but I think he wants another view and he trusts you to tell him what you think, not what you think he wants to hear," John said. "That's often the problem with consultants, they listen very carefully and pick up hints as to where you're leaning, and then they construct the report to affirm what they think you think or believe."

"Is it that bad?" James asked.

"Probably not in reality," John admitted. "But I think there's a tendency there to play back what they hear. Sometimes people do retain outside consultants to confirm what they think they know, and for the most part, consultants are usually skilled listeners who can pick up those signals and nuances. So, let's find out what Bobby and Katrina did today."

"James, nice to see you again," Roberta said as he and John arrived at the house.

"Nice to see you, Bobby. Did you and Katrina have fun today?" James asked.

"We went to the property manager and then to your house. Everything is in good shape, no frozen pipes this winter, no ice dams," Roberta replied.

"They've even tidied up the garden a little," Katrina added.

"I gather you've been stirring things up in South Africa," Roberta said. "Educating and training the black work force, naughty naughty."

"We have to be careful," James admitted. "But what we're doing is paying off in the parts and service areas."

"So, tell us a little about Leon Schumann," Roberta asked.

"He's our accountant, he's quite capable of running the business, he's good with customers and the others all respect him," James said.

"Schumann, is he related to the composer?" Roberta asked.

"He's never mentioned it, but somehow I doubt it," James replied. "But you never know."

"How's your new job, Katrina?" Roberta asked.

"It's interesting," Katrina replied. "CMI keeps looking at companies that we might buy, most of them we dismiss as not suitable or just not worth it, but some we like and some we've acquired."

"And now you have your finance degree," Roberta said. "I'm glad that worked out for you."

"John, the first lot of shares under the stock option program has vested. Should I exercise now or wait?" James asked.

"I'd wait," John replied. "My crystal ball says that the stock will slowly climb over the next year, then after we work through the current backlog of orders, the bloom will go off the company and the price will drop back a little in about two years. I plan to exercise what I can probably this time next year."

"Talking of that, do we put people from Didcot or the other subs on the stock option program?" James asked.

"We haven't yet," John said. "It hasn't been that common yet in the UK, Australia or South Africa, and there's been a big debate about whether or not we should include the top managers at each location, the crux of the arguments being what contributions by the subs materially change the results of the parent."

"But surely the MD of Didcot contributes?" James asked.
"I like to think that I did, and that Richard does, but so far we've sent someone from here, what we'd do if we promoted someone from there, I'm not sure, it's probably something we need to discuss," John replied.
"There you go again, James," Roberta said. "Stirring things up."
"I didn't intend to; it just struck me that if we put Leon in charge next year, it would be appropriate if we made him part of the management in the true sense," James said.
"We'll look at it, but we'd have to understand the local laws and tax systems," John said. "It may be that granting an option to Leon creates a tax problem for him immediately, not at the exercise point like it is here, so we should get the laws of the UK, Australia and South Africa to see what the implications are. It may be that it's just not practical, in which case we should probably just go with a simple bonus scheme based on sales, or profitability, something like net income before taxes for J&B Africa."
"How far down in the organisation should that go?" James asked.
"We need to talk about that," John agreed. "Why don't we sit down with Ray Pierce in the next day or so and talk about it?"
"Thanks," James said.
"So, enough business for the day," Roberta said. "What do we have to drink?"

"Howzit, Leon?" James asked when he picked Leon up at the airport the next day.
"Fine, James," Leon replied. "Ready for these *ouks*."
"Good, our first meeting is with John Williams and Fred Johnson, they want to talk about our projections for the year and what we see coming in the next year to eighteen months," James said. "Then Hank Miller wants to meet us for lunch, and then we'll meet with Stuart Palmer to talk about financial projections for this year."
"Sounds like a busy day," Leon said. "I'm glad I slept on the plane coming over. There's my bag."
"Okay, *kom ons ry*," James said. He drove them to the office, and they met with John and Fred and went through all the possible mining

projects in South Africa and the surrounding countries, then talked about the market for construction machines and what the drivers were and what they saw as likely sales volumes. At eleven-twenty-five, James excused himself and Leon and told John and Fred that Hank Miller was waiting for them. John came with them, as the VP International, he had a stake in this, so wanted to be part of the discussions.

"Hank, this is Leon Schumann," James said, making the introduction.

"Nice to meet you, Leon," Hank said. "James tells me good things about you. Where did you get your accounting degree?"

"The University of Cape Town, and then I did articles with Ernst & Ernst. Then I worked for a local company that sold construction machines, until I hired on with J&B Africa," Leon replied.

"How are things in South Africa?" Hank asked.

"With J&B Africa, we're on a solid footing," Leon said. "In South Africa as a whole, there is unrest, which is to be expected, and in time, we'll see a change in government, but my guess is that won't be until the early nineties."

"Will that change the markets?" Hank asked.

"There'll be some uncertainty," Leon said. "But the government will need hard currency, so it will need exports of gold, diamonds, iron and coal, so the mines will continue, and a new government will want to expand infrastructure services to more people, so there are likely to be municipal contracts for water, sewer and electricity projects. The big question for them will be how to pay for it all."

"What about parts and service?" Hank asked.

"We've stepped up our sales of parts," Leon said. "We're doing a better job of stocking the fast-moving parts and have added teeth and buckets, which, as wear items, the mines go through quickly. The teeth and buckets we source locally, and because we have a distribution network, we can do a better job than the foundries that make the parts. Service is doing better since we took on the Construction Machines line and added service engineers. That part of the business is paying for itself nicely. Parts and machine sales are essentially pass-through, with us just taking a small margin."

"Should we contract out portions of the mining machines to be made locally?" Hank asked.

"That's an issue of splitting hard currency versus Rands," Leon said. "If part of the machines could be made locally, then that activity would be paid for in Rands and provide local employment, always politically attractive, but the question is who has the welding technology and the machining capability to do the job right. To find that we'd need someone from here to make a tour of our local fabricators and give us an assessment."

"I'll get Bill Evans to come down and look the companies over," Hank thought. "James knows Evans; they've worked together on a number of assignments. How is your accounting staff?"

"They're good," Leon said. "They manage very well while I'm gone and we've got two chartered accountants on the books apart from me, so we're well covered, in fact, compared to many companies we have more than is usual."

"How do you get on with the customers?" Hank asked.

"I've been going with James and Piet Kruger to meet many of them, and it's been interesting and instructive," Leon replied. "When it comes to buying large machines, they all like financial analyses, so we try and show them how the machines will benefit them. Piet gives them the application pitch and the mechanicals and electrics, and I talk about contracts, payments and return on investment."

"Good, now, let's get something to eat," Hanks said.

"Well, that went better than I expected," Leon said to James that evening as they sat over a beer at the hotel where Leon was staying.

"Hank Miller is more approachable than most people think," James said. "He's seen as a dour accountant who has no feel for people or markets, but I haven't found that. He does like you to tell him the truth, even if it's not what everyone wants to hear. As he told me once, it's hard to plan for the future if people are feeding you what they think you want to hear, not what the reality is. Better to know the truth, no matter how ugly it may be, because then you can work out what to do and not go further into the mire."

"I'm thinking that it might make my job easier in the future if I get a little better understanding of how the machines actually work," Leon said. "I need something simple that explains the electric drives and how they work."

"I'm sure we can find something," James assured him. "Tomorrow, I've got you set up with Bill Evans, he can go through the machines for you and talk about the parts and the mechanicals. I'll check tomorrow and get one of the electrical engineers lined up for the afternoon."

"Thanks," Leon said. "I've got meetings the day after tomorrow with Stuart Palmer and Roy Kahl to talk about repatriating earnings; you should join us."

"Thanks, Leon, I will," James said.

"Long day?" Katrina asked him when he went back to John and Roberta's house.

"Long day," he confirmed. "Tomorrow, more meetings and again the day after, then we're done and can go home. What did you do today?"

"Bobby and I tried on ski clothes," she said. "Bobby has come up with a new fabric that stretches and conforms, but also keeps the wind out and yet still breathes, so you don't fry."

"I'm amazed at what she can do," he said.

"So am I," she echoed. "I feel like a country bumpkin sometimes, but then she asks me something about the bush and Zambia and I realise that I know stuff she can only imagine."

"James, have you eaten?" Roberta asked as she joined them.

"I have, thank you, Bobby," he replied.

"Let me get you a nightcap then," she suggested.

"Thank you," he replied. She disappeared for a minute or so and came back with four glasses and a bottle of brandy.

"John will be here soon, he's just finishing bottling some calvados," she said.

While Leon was busy with Bill Evans, James sat down with John and Ray Pierce to talk about incentive schemes for the J&B Africa staff.

"Do you have anything in mind?" Ray asked James.

"I had been thinking of a sales bonus," James said. "But that only looks at top-line growth, I think it might be better if we went for net profit before tax, whether that should be a number or a percentage, I'm not sure."

"I think we'd prefer a number," Ray said. "So, let's say your gross sales are 5,000,000 Rand for the year, your net before tax should be 500,000 Rand, more or less?"

"Our plan for this year is for a gross of 5,500,000 Rand, with net before tax of 550,000," James said. "So, what if we set a target of 5,000,000 Rand? If they attain 120% of the target, the five managers each get 5,000 Rand, then if they only attain 80% of the target, they get zero, and all between is a simple sliding scale?"

"So, if you hit 110% of your target, which would be 550,000, they each get 3,750 Rand, but if they only make 80% of your target, they get zero?" Ray asked.

"That's about it," James agreed. "We pay out 18,750 of the extra 100,000 we earn, so the company nets an additional 31,250."

"On the flip side of that, if you only make 90% of your target, which would be 450,000, you'd want us to pay out 6,500, reducing the net before tax to 443,500," Ray pointed out.

"I appreciate that," James said. "But if we pay out nothing for not hitting the target, then human nature is such that targets will get set low, so that the probability of meeting, or beating them is high."

"What percentage of their annual is 5,000?" John asked.

"About 25%," James replied.

"What if you use a more exponential scale?" John asked.

"I could do that," James agreed. "But I think it should be simple enough that they can understand easily."

"What if you have a banner year, like last year, and you actually make 600,000 before bonuses and taxes? Is the bonus capped at 5,000?" Ray asked.

"What if we just say that for every dollar over the target times 120%, then they get an additional 10 cents?" James suggested.

"So, we get fifty cents on the dollar for everything over 120% of target, and your management team gets fifty cents?" Ray asked.

"That's a suggestion," James said.

"That's a lot," Ray said.

"But if we can achieve that, then we will be doing very well," James said. "The difficult part is going to be setting targets that are real and achievable, but not too low."

"That's an understatement," John said. "So who sets the targets?"

"It has to be a local management decision, with veto power from here," James said. "If the team here thinks the targets are too low, then there needs to be a dialogue to come to an agreement."

"Okay, we'll work on that," Ray said. "We'll need to look at Australia and Didcot and come up with something that is equitable around the world."

"Thanks," James said. "I should go and find Leon, we've more meetings to go to."

"Are we all set to go home?" Katrina asked James later that week.

"All set," he agreed. "I've never been in so many meetings, meetings with accountants, product managers, parts people, lawyers, even the *bwana mkubwa* himself."

"I suppose that's to be expected," she said. "They don't see you that often. Anyway, I'm ready to go home; we've imposed on Bobby long enough. I did check out some things for Hofmeyr with local foundries and forges. Let's go down and have dinner, then we can pack."

"Ready to go home?" Roberta asked them as they joined her in the kitchen.

"We are," Katrina replied. "We've imposed on you long enough; it's time we were out of your hair."

"You're no bother," Roberta assured her.

"Maybe," Katrina said. "But we must disrupt your life, so it's time we went home."

"I've persuaded John to take vacation in September, could you set up a trip for the two of us to M'Bali, where you and I went?" Roberta asked.

"Of course," Katrina said. "Just give me your dates and I'll set it all up for you. Just M'Bali, or do you want to see somewhere else as well?"

"What if we do a week at M'Bali and then a week in the Cape touring wineries?" Roberta suggested.

"We can set that up," Katrin assured her. "Just give me flight dates and I'll fix everything."
"Arriving on September 10th, leaving on the 24th, I'm looking forward to going back to Africa," Roberta said. "Mainly to drag John away from the office, and I know that at M'Bali there'll be no phone calls."
"We can always send a runner out for you," James joked.
"Don't even joke about it," Roberta said. "He might just take you up on that."
"Where is he?" Katrina asked.
"He's having dinner with the board," Roberta said. "Big board meeting tomorrow, so they're softening them up now."
"That explains all the activity in the last couple of days," James said. "When we met with Stuart, he wanted numbers, projections for the year and what next year might look like."
"So, as John's dining out, why don't we go out and grab something?" Roberta suggested. "Would Italian suit?"
"That would be fine," Katrina agreed. "Then we can come back and pack and be off tomorrow morning for New York."

"Mr and Mrs Martin, how nice to see you again," Maryke said as she showed them to their seats on the South African flight to Johannesburg.
"Nice to see you again, Maryke," Katrina replied. "Is the flight full today?"
"Not quite," Maryke said. "But close, we've only got two empty seats forward and ten aft. We're expecting an on-time arrival into Jan Smuts, if we can get away on time. Have you been here on business?"
"James has," Katrina replied. "I just came along for the ride."
"Well, enjoy the flight," Maryke said. She left and went about the business of settling everyone and making sure that all was secure for the takeoff, and then they were off on their way back to Africa.
"What will you do for Bobby?" James asked.
"I'll talk to Bridget," Katrina replied. "I'm sure that between us we can come up with a nice trip, maybe send them down to Cape Town on the Blue Train, so they can see part of the country."

"We were going to take a Blue Train ride down to Cape Town, when's the next long weekend?" he asked.

"Republic Day, the end of this month," she replied. "But that's not really a long weekend, it's on Wednesday this year, let's see the next long weekend would be in September, the first Monday is Settlers' Day."

"So, not for a while," he said. "Well, it'll come soon enough; let's plan for that."

"Excuse me," Maryke said. "May I set things up for dinner?"

"Of course," Katrina replied.

They arrived in Johannesburg ten minutes early, and immigration was quick enough; then there was a wait for luggage. After what seemed an eternity, it finally showed up, and they were able to join the throng, now swelled by arriving flights from Europe, and clear customs. Charlize was waiting for them, and she dropped Katrina and the luggage off first before taking James back to the office.

"Hans, how are things?" James asked.

"Good enough, James," Hans replied. "No issues while you were away, no new prospects for mining machines, but a few for construction."

"No issues, I like to hear that," James said.

"How was Oak Creek?" Hans asked.

"Meetings and more meetings," James said. "I don't think Leon had a chance to just sit down and relax for a minute."

"When's he due back?" Hans asked.

"Monday," James replied. "He took a quick trip to Arizona to see the Grand Canyon."

"*Ja*, he said that he wanted to do that," Hans recalled. "Have you been there?"

"Not yet," James replied. "The closest I got was a coal mine to the south of the Colorado River and east of the canyon."

"I heard that CMI was buying a foundry that makes bucket teeth," Hans said. "You know Hofmeyr, don't you?"

"I do," James confirmed. "I meet with him once a month, I'll talk to him about teeth and buckets and see if we can't come to some agreement. Any sense of how the new service *bakkies* are working?"

"Frank likes them," Hans said. "He's got hoists mounted now that let us pick things up, the compressors help with tools and tyres, *ja*, they're working well."

"Have we had any more bombings?" James asked.

"Not that I've heard of," Hans replied. "I get the feeling that we've got a few ANC people here."

"I'm sure we do," James said. "I think if we treat the people fairly and provide whatever opportunities we can, then they'll not make trouble here."

"That *ou* from the Bantu Education was here again," Hans said. "We had no classes that day, so he just came, offered us help with relocating our black *ouks* to the homelands if we'd hire more whites, even those with no training or experience, and then left."

"I'm surprised that the government is still pushing that," James said. "But I suppose it fits with their policies, but it's not going to work in the longer term, there just aren't enough skilled whites, and I'm not about to go out and take on some *oukie op die plaas,* just because he's white."

"I agree with you on that," Hans said. "I told the Bantu Education *ou* that we couldn't afford to take on more whites."

"We need to be careful," James said. "We've come to their attention, and that's never good. We need them to go and bother someone else."

"That may happen," Hans said. "While he was here, there was a delivery of parts, and he noticed that the driver wasn't white, so he went off to see the haulage company."

"Great, so now we'll probably see rates go up if he makes them take on whites as drivers," James commented.

"It's always something," Hans commiserated.

"It is," James agreed. "Thanks, Hans."

"Will and Bridget are coming over," Katrina told James when he arrived home that evening. "They want to hear all about our trip to Oak Creek. I already told them that all you had was meetings, but I think they just want someone to talk to who isn't two, almost three."

"I can understand that," James laughed.

"They're here," Katrina said when she heard their car at the gate. She pressed the button that opened it and went out to meet them. "Come on in, James is busy with the *braai*, Francesca, how are you?"

"*Baie goed*," Francesca replied. "When you were in America, did you see any Indians?"

"We didn't," Katrina replied. "But there are some in Wisconsin where we went, the Chippewa and the Oneida, but they're mainly to the north of the state."

"Do they live in tepees and ride horses?" Francesca asked.

"No, I think they live in houses and drive cars today," Katrina said.

"Oh," Francesca said. "When are we going on our next trip to the bush?"

"Perhaps this weekend?" Katrina suggested, looking to Bridget.

"We can do that," Bridget agreed.

"Would you like to try the place that Hofmeyr has?" Katrina suggested.

"That would make a change," Bridget agreed. "Shall I ask him or will you?"

"I'll do that," Katrina promised. "I have a project for you for September, John and Roberta Williams from J&B, a week in M'Bali and a week in the Cape touring wineries, I've got the dates."

"I'll fix it all up," Bridget promised. "Self-guided tour in the Cape, or with a guide?"

"I'll ask," Katrina said. "And I'll put you in contact with Bobby, and you can work things out with her."

"So, Francesca, shall we go and supervise your uncle James?" Will suggested. "We can tell him all about the new Land Rover we bought."

They used Will's new Land Rover to go to Rooiberg. It was similar to the one James had taken to Zambia when he had first gone there in 1969, but a later version. They set out on Friday evening and drove as far as Warmbaths and spent the night there, driving to Rooiberg in the morning. The gate guard was expecting them, so they checked in at the lodge, got the keys and then went further into the reserve to the cottage.

"This is nice," Bridget said. "Makes you feel like you've gone back to Africa, with the thatched roof, the candelabra trees and the bush all around."
"It does, doesn't it," Katrina agreed. "James, will you get the stove going to heat some water?"
"Right," James said. "Francesca, are you going to help me carry wood?"
"Of course, Uncle James," she replied. Will took them to the woodshed, and first James made sure that there were no snakes lurking in the pile, then he and Will took an armful each of the logs, and James gave some smaller pieces to Francesca.
"Shall we have a light lunch, then go for a drive?" Katrina suggested.
"Good idea," Bridget agreed. "Look at those monkeys, no wonder there are bars on the windows, you'd need to keep them out."
"Someone must have fed them in the past," Katrina said. "They've learned that people mean food, so now when people show up, so do they."
"What can we see here?" Will asked.
"Buffalo, kudu, sable, most of the other antelope, lions, leopards, jackals, birds by the score," Katrina replied.
"What do we do for light here after dark?" Bridget asked.
"Oil lamps," Katrina said. "Those over there, there's a tin of oil for them in the woodshed."
"So, no generator?" Bridget asked.
"No, no generator, it's quiet in the evenings, you can hear everything for miles," Katrina said.
"How nice," Bridget commented. "I wonder how Will's folks would do if we brought them here when they come to do their project?"
"Probably just fine," Katrina said. "When they came to see us in Zambia, we took them on a trip, and we camped out for a couple of nights, and they did fine."
"Are we set for lunch?" James asked.
"If you set the table," Katrina said.

After lunch, they took their drive and meandered around the reserve, stopping and just listening to the birds and animals.

"This would be better for a safari if there were no roof," Will said. "Maybe I should look into a Land Rover with no roof or doors, then when we set up our safari business, the clients will get a better view."

"Oh, so it's a when now, not an if and when?" James asked.

"We have a plan," Will said. "We've laid out what we need to do and when and how much we think it will cost us, so we're just working now to build up the funds to where they need to be."

"In Botswana?" James asked.

"We've decided, definitely Botswana," Will confirmed. "We'll let you know when we get set up."

"We'll come and we'll even pay," James promised. "So, what's that bird over there?"

"That is a white-throated robin-chat," Will said.

"Complicated name," James said.

"True, what about that one, the southern pied-babbler?" Will asked. "Then over there, the ground hornbill."

"What's the one we can hear?" James asked.

"Monotonous lark," Bridget said. "It seems to have one song that it just sings over and over again, no variation, but if you listen carefully, you can also hear a melodious lark; they're tough because they mimic other birds."

"Mom, I need to go," Francesca interrupted them.

"Will, can you stop?" Bridget asked. He did, and they both got out of the Land Rover and looked around. "Down here, behind the Land Rover," Bridget said to Francesca.

"Thank you," Francesca said when they got back into the Land Rover. "I was bursting."

"Shall we head back and get a beer before dinner?" Will suggested.

"Good plan," James approved. They wended their way back and were back in plenty of time to light lamps and get the *braai* going before the sun went down.

"Wisconsin must be a bit like England," Katrina said. "Long summer evenings, not like here."

"How far north is it?" Will asked.

"Forty-two, forty-three degrees," James replied. "Not as far north as London, but enough to get the longer summer days."

“So, what’s next for you?” Will asked James as they tended to the *braai*.

“I have a project to look at off-highway trucks,” James replied. “And when we go back, they’re talking about a mergers and acquisitions group to look at new opportunities.”

“Sounds interesting,” Will said. “Will you be able to come back to Africa?”

“I’m sure that we will,” James said. “Katrina’s heart is here, so without doubt we will come back to Africa.”

www.ingramcontent.com/pod-product-compliance
Lightning Source LLC
LaVergne TN
LVHW010052110826
845155LV00028B/300

* 9 7 8 1 9 4 0 0 1 2 5 8 2 *